SCREAM CRUISE

A MOTOR CITY THRILLER

D1715875

JIM DeLOREY

SCREAM CRUISE

A Motor City Thriller

Jim DeLorey

Published by Adams Road Enterprises, LLC, Birmingham, MI 48009

ISBN: 978-0-9800461-2-0

Acknowledgment of Trademark

"Woodward Dream Cruise" is a registered trademark of Woodward Dream Cruise, Inc., a 501(c)3 Non-Profit Organization.

Disclaimers

This novel takes place in a fictional representation of the metropolitan Detroit area. Liberties have been taken in portraying municipalities, institutions and local geography. There may also be inadvertent errors. All characters and events are totally fictitious and any resemblance to actual incidents or to actual persons, living or dead, is entirely coincidental. Close cover before striking. Void where prohibited by law.

Dedication

To the honest, hard-working people
of Metro Detroit and Southeast Michigan

Table of Contents

Definitions

mass murder: (noun) the savage and excessive killing of many people; (synonyms) slaughter, massacre, carnage, butchery.

Witzelsucht: [vit´sel-zookt] (Ger.) (noun) a mental condition marked by excessive facetiousness and inappropriate or pointless humor; a condition characteristic of frontal lobe lesions.

~ Dictionary entries

Prologue   Coffin In the Sky
Saturday, August 20 - 12:00 Noon

WE WERE a mile high over the Dream Cruise when the engine died.

Instantly we began plummeting toward the vast crowd below. Three horrified men, trapped inside a shrapnel-riddled helicopter. A three-quarter-ton metal-and-fiberglass coffin that would soon go smashing into the massive horde of cars and people beneath us like a giant hunk of streaking lead.

The copter's passenger doors were still open and the wind immediately began ripping through them like the shriek of a hundred crazed banshees as we hurtled earthward. Up in the cockpit the pilot, Goolsby, was frantically flipping switches, but to no effect. Strapped into the seat beside me La Borgia, the mafia porn king, was spewing out a violent stream of Italian curses, his sheet-white face contorted with panic. He was gesticulating wildly, waving his Glock around and looking as if he might at any moment begin pulling the trigger out of sheer, raging terror.

Heart hammering, my stomach in my throat, I glanced out the window beside me. Thousands of colorful cars and hundreds of thousands of milling spectators were rushing up at us with scrotum-tightening speed. The sea of humanity alongside the broad boulevard began parting as people ran for their lives. YES! I wanted to howl down at them. RUN! GET AWAY WHILE YOU CAN!

As we plunged toward what seemed like certain death, I became conscious of the Springfield .45 clenched in my own quivering hand. For an instant I considered putting it to my temple in order to escape the death-crash.

But then a rush of images began flashing in front of my terrorstruck eyes. As if I were looking at them through some kind of crazy, high-speed kaleidoscope, the events of the past twelve days swirled before me. I saw a series of powerful explosions and their horrific aftermaths. I saw rows and rows of body bags containing the corpses of innocent men, women, and children. I saw the stunned faces of shell-shocked survivors. I saw the shredded bodies of fellow FBI agents. I saw the world's ugliest cat. I saw the ghostly features of my long-dead sister.

1

When the image of the woman I loved rushed toward me, I did my best to hang onto it. An excruciating pang of regret lanced through me at the realization I'd never see or hold the beautiful doctor again. Never have the chance to finally win her and feel our two bodies consummate our love.

Then her gorgeous face was swept away by the onrush of more split-second images. I saw passenger-filled cars exploding, one after another. I saw mangled and mutilated SWAT cops, shrieking in misery. I saw a downtown intersection turned into a hellish inferno.

I was flashing back all the way to the very beginning now. To when the gut-wrenching terror that had hung over the Motor City for the past dozen days first came creeping out of the shadows. To the night when those two unsuspecting hot rodders came face-to-face with a deranged, murderous fiend.

To that muggy summer night on Woodward Avenue when the parade of horrors began...

Chapter 1   Chuck And Buck
Monday, August 8 - 11:05 p.m.

THE TIGERS have just finished dropping the opener to a three-game series with the Twins when Chuck Kowalski and Buck Godwin bang out through the doors of Vinnie's Woodward Bar & Grille. As they lurch out from the entrance awning's shadows, Buck raises his hands into the air and shakes them at the pale moon overhead.

"Free at last, free at last!" he calls out. "Good Lawd Almighty, we be free at last!"

"Glory hallelujah, bro'!" Chuck adds.

In tandem the giggling pair weave toward the bar's dimly-lit parking lot. Both have the same stocky, athletes-gone-to-seed build and are in almost identical getups: tasseled dress loafers with no socks, Dockers shorts, and polo shirts that billow out over their fiftyish male bellies. Outside of the bar's A/C, the humid night air wraps itself around them like warm, sticky cellophane.

"Damn!" Chuck says. "Feels like Okee-frigging-fenokee out here."

"Careful you don't step on the alligators, dude-o," Buck says, stumbling a bit as he awkwardly extracts a small cigar tin from the pocket of his shorts.

While he waits for Buck to fire up his peach rum cigarillo, Chuck turns around, hawks, and spits back toward the bar's door. "Up yours, Vinnie," he says, fingering it for good measure.

No one at the bar had actually asked them to leave. But the looks from the waitresses and other patrons had gotten progressively more hostile, and for the past half-hour the bartender had shunned them as if they were radioactive.

"Jeez-o-pete," Chuck grouses as they resume looping across the lot. "What a boring, dead-ass dump that was!"

"Buncha frigging zombies in there, you ask me. Last time I'll ever drink at that mausoleum," Buck says.

"And what's with those frigging tiny TVs, anyways?" Chuck says. "I could barely see the damn game. Not that it was worth watching."

"Man, I don't know. Shoulda brought our damn binoculars," Buck says.

Chuck snickers. "Only reason I didn't drag you out of there were the hooters on that one blonde."

"Which?"

"That waitress. One looked like she was polock or bohunk."

"The one with the big schnozzola?"

"Bitch had a nose? Jeez-is! I never even noticed!"

"Man, that ho' had a honker on her stuck out further than her rack. Nostrils big enough to put your dick in."

"Hey - *yours*, maybe!"

The two boomers cackle as they approach Buck's canary yellow '32 Ford coupe. Neither notices the three eyes watching them from a black Dodge Ram pickup parked several slots away.

"Hey, what do you say we go back in there and offer to pay the bimbo for a nostril-job?" Buck says. "Bitch could do both of us at once. Maybe give us a two-for-one discount."

"Shit, she should pay us. Better for her sinuses than Dristan, I'll bet."

"Think about it, Chuck-o," says Buck, holding his fist up to his nose. "Her honking away like a Canada goose. All that nice warm snot running down your pecker."

"Buckie, you perv, you are one sick puppy. You know that?"

"Thanks, man. I try."

The pair climb into the deuce coupe and buckle their seatbelts over their pot bellies. Buck hits the ignition on the exposed, chrome-laden Chevy 350. The fuel-injected, four hundred twenty-five horsepower engine gives a short, explosive cough and rumbles to life. Buck then punches the forged aluminum gas pedal a few times, sending guttural, whining roars and loud, hammering pops from its shiny lake pipes through the surrounding neighborhood.

Beside him Chuck chortles. "Wake up, grandmaw!" he says.

"What a couple of assholes," the man in the pickup mutters to the wall-eyed pit bull squatting on the passenger seat. The yellow dog is short and deep-chested, with a huge head and small, pointy ears. His phlegmy snarl sounds like agreement as his one good eye shifts from the booming yellow car to the big, muscular man beside him.

Behind the wraparound shades he wears, the man's blue eyes are shiny with anticipation. On the console between him and the dog lie a specially-modified universal TV remote and a forty-caliber Glock with a six-inch-long cylindrical silencer attached to its barrel.

The sunglassed man grins as he and the dog watch the two men in the deuce coupe back out of the parking slot. He flicks on his lights, slips the truck into gear, and pulls out after them.

"Get ready, Bub," he says. "The show's about to begin."

For a few moments the deuce coupe sits grumbling in the bar's exit drive. Earlier that evening there'd been plenty of fellow hot rodders out on Woodward, but traffic is sparse now. Buck flicks his cigarillo out the open window and eases the coupe into a northbound lane. After checking his mirrors and the blinking fuzz-buster on his dash, he gives the gas pedal a quick stomp.

"Yee-HAH!" Chuck says as the oversized rear tires break traction and screech out several seconds' worth of smoky, high-pitched rubber squeal. The tires give another short shriek when Buck slams the skull-knobbed Hurst shifter into second gear. Backing off on the gas then, he cuts over three more lanes and makes the turnaround to go south.

Though the hot rod's rapid movements have made him realize just how woozy-headed he is, Chuck isn't at all worried by the fact that Buck is no doubt equally trashed. They've been doing their weekly Boys Night Out for over a dozen years, while their wives - Rhonda and Gail - stay home and play cards together. He knows that, thanks to all the practice he's had, Buck is a bona fide expert at impaired driving.

After a couple more turns the pair are heading east on 11 Mile Road, back toward their homes in Eastpointe. Their meaty forearms rest on the sills of the coupe's open windows. The hot rod has no A/C and the breeze feels good as they cruise through the sticky summer night.

"Man, how about that lame-o dude in the goat you smoked earlier?" Chuck says.

Buck gives a happy snicker. "You mean Moby Dickhead?" he says.

On their way across town that evening, they'd come up alongside a candy apple red '71 GTO driven by some overweight boomer in a Tigers cap. After some mutual goading and checking for cops, the two drivers dropped down to twenty miles an hour and then punched it in tandem. Buck's little deuce coupe ate the poor goat alive.

"Might've been half a race if that guy wasn't such a lard ball," Buck says, chuckling as he recalls his triumph. "Fat bastard looked like he weighed about three hundred pounds, easy."

"That's a lot of frigging ballast," Chuck agrees.

Traffic is light on 11 Mile. It isn't long before they've passed through the city of Royal Oak and are into Warren, where the traffic is even thinner. Buck checks his mirrors and once again spots the bluish headlights that have been following them since they left the bar.

"Man, is that dude tailing us or what?" he says with a frown.

"Who'zat?" Chuck says.

"Some douchebag in a pickup. Pulled out of that shithole bar right after we did. Swear he's been dogging us ever since. "

Chuck cranes his head around and peers out through the coupe's oval rear window. About a hundred yard back is a big, black Dodge Ram pickup.

"I dunno, Buck-o," he says, turning back around. "I think maybe you're getting a bit paranoid in your old age. Why the hell would anybody be tailing us?"

"Damned if I know. Maybe it's some schmuck unmarked cop."

"In a pickup truck? That'd be a first," Chuck says.

As the two vehicles enter a stretch of 11 Mile lined by empty fields and dark, abandoned factories, the man in the pickup does a quick check for traffic before and behind them. He glances at the yellow dog.

"Clear both ways, Bub," he says. "Perfect."

The pit bull has picked up on the man's excitement. He's leaning forward now as he squats on the passenger seat, his muscular body rippling with tension. His good eye is focused on the yellow car ahead. The bad one is twitching around in excited semi-circles.

In the man's right hand is the modified TV remote. He's already keyed in the trigger code. Did it back in the parking lot, right after he'd crawled out from under the hot rod and just before the two boomer jerk-offs he'd spotted in the bar came outside. With his thumb over the Play button, he lifts and aims the remote, at a spot just below the hot rod's license plate.

"Get ready to see some serious fireworks, boy," he says, nostrils flaring.

Beside him the dog chuffs eagerly.

"Say your prayers, asswipes," the man says, one eye closed as he sights, his voice a husky whisper.

But just as he's about to press the button, a better idea occurs to him.

He sets the remote down on the passenger seat. Glancing over at the dog, he sees the questioning look in Beelzebub's googly eyes.

"Don't worry, boy," he says, pressing down on the gas. "We're just gonna have ourselves a little fun with the two twinks before we waste them."

Soon they're pulling up alongside the yellow coupe, on its passenger side. The man's lips curl into a tight grin.

"You're gonna love this, Bub," he says, reaching for the Glock.

Forearm still resting on the coupe's open window ledge, Chuck stares over at the big black pickup now cruising beside them. Tipping his head, he looks up and watches the smoked glass window slide down. He sees the guy behind the wheel is wearing wraparound shades.

"Guess Captain Douchebag up there thinks we got midnight sun around here," he says.

The sunglassed guy is staring back down at him, a nasty grin on his face. For a moment Chuck considers fingering him, but decides against it. For one thing, Mr. Shades looks pretty big. But even more unsettling is that creepy-crazy look on his face. It clearly suggests a dude you'd not want to mess with.

He turns to Buck. "What do you figure's up with this lame-o? Think he wants to race you?"

"Hope so," Buck chortles. "I'd love to smoke his sorry MoPar behind."

Grinning, Chuck rotates his head back toward the truck. He doesn't spot the black cylinder resting on its window ledge until it's too late.

"What the-?" he begins to say, just before there's the tiniest of muzzle flashes and a *thoop* that sounds like an air gun being discharged.

"Hey, goddammit!" Buck says, jerking the wheel as something hot buzzes under his nose and what feels like the insides of a stuffed burrito smacks into the right side of his head.

But his outrage instantly evaporates when he turns, sees the gaping hole in his buddy's skull, and realizes that the gloopy mess sliding down from his ear to his shoulder are bloody chunks of Chuck's blown-out brain.

"HOLY SHIT!" he yells, instinctively slamming on the brakes. The deuce coupe fishtails wildly as its wheels lock and it slides to a shrieking halt.

The big black pickup follows suit, nose dipping and outsize tires squealing until it comes to rest a few car-lengths past the hot rod. The truck's rear wheels then began screeching and smoking as it reverses and heads back toward the yellow coupe.

Having neglected to clutch during his panic stop, the big chromed engine has stalled out. Bug-eyed, Buck frantically cranks the dead 350 as he watches the truck come closer and closer. The crazy bastard driver is leaning his sunglassed face out the window, looking back at him with an evil leer.

The instant the engine catches, Buck pops the clutch and stomps down on the gas pedal. Immediately the steering wheel rips itself out of his sweaty hands as his tires break traction and the coupe begins veering wildly from side to side. With each swerve his buddy's body goes slamming up against him and then back against the passenger door.

"GET OFFA ME, DAMMIT!" Buck yells, elbowing Chuck-o's lurching corpse aside as he fights the whipsawing wheel. Icy rivulets of sweat are pouring down from his forehead, neck, and underarms, and his heart is racing faster than his Toro mower at full throttle.

Finally, with a superhuman effort, he manages to regain control of the fishtailing hot rod. Tires still smoking, he streaks past the pickup, the coupe's chromed tailpipes emitting a frantic, whining roar.

Chuck's lifeless body has meanwhile come to rest pressed up against him. Glancing to his left, he sees the blank eyes and open mouth. He also sees that the huge hole in his buddy's head is oozing an unsightly stew of blood, skull fragments, and gray matter onto the shoulder of his polo shirt. "JEEZ-IS!" he blurts, roughly shouldering the corpse to the other side of the car, its slack weight reminding him of an oversize sack of top soil or yard manure.

His bloodshot, fear-distended eyes flick to the rearview mirror. The pickup is barreling after him, but is rapidly diminishing. Its speed is no match for his little deuce coupe.

Then it hits him. He's going to get away!

"SCREW YOU, YOU SONOFABITCH!" Buck screams up at the mirror, an hysterical feeling of elation suffusing him as he shoots up 11 Mile, away from the crazy dickhead. "YOU'LL NEVER CATCH ME NOW!"

The man in the speeding Ram pickup snickers as he watches the yellow hot rod pull away from him.

Beside him the pit bull gives out a frustrated growl.

"Don't you worry, Bub," the man says. "I'm just letting that poor, dumb sucker think he's home free."

When there are fifty yards between them, he aims the TV remote at the speeding hot rod.

He waits until the deuce coupe is a hundred yards off before he says "Nighty-night, asshole," and presses his thumb-tip down on the PLAY button.

KA-WHOOM!!!

The road before them becomes day-bright as the hot rod disappears inside a great ball of fire. The fireball then rises up into the night on a stem of red-orange flame.

Bringing the pickup to a halt, the sunglassed man drinks in the sight of the huge, hellish blossoming and the flaming, canary-yellow wreckage beneath it. "Damn!" he whispers breathlessly as an ecstatic spasm ripples through his pumped-up torso. Beside him the wall-eyed pit bull stares in fascination, tongue lolling excitedly from his open, snaggle-toothed jaws.

The man is sorely tempted to pull up to the wreckage. How he'd love to savor the acrid odors from the smoldering debris and absorb the delicious, radiant waves of departing life energy from the two asswipes.

But there's a problem. They've completely passed through the old, vacant industrial area and are now on the fringes of a residential neighborhood. For sure some local citizens have already jumped up out of their beds, scared shitless. They'll be running outside to see what the hell THAT was about. From out on their porches they'll see the smoke rising off of 11 Mile, curling up toward the hazy summer moon. It's a done deal someone's dialing nine-one-one at this very moment, if they haven't already.

"Prudence, boy," the man says to the dog. "That's the ticket."

"It's like my old buddy VanBoort used to say, back in Sudan," he says, whipping the wheel to hang a U-turn.

"'We slaughter, then we run away. And live to slaughter another day.'"

The man is careful to maintain the speed limit as he heads the pickup west. In the distance before and behind them he can hear approaching sirens. They've barely gone a mile when a Warren police cruiser makes a screeching turn onto 11 Mile, a couple of blocks ahead of them. Multicolored lights from its overhead flashers strobe across their faces as the cop car shoots toward them. The man tenses, reaching for the Glock with his free hand. But the pair of grim, blue-shirted men in the front seats of the police cruiser don't even glance their way when it roars past.

He watches the speeding black-and-white rapidly recede in his rearview mirror. Releasing his grip on the pistol, a snide grin crosses his face as he pictures the cops inside.

"Look at those clueless pigs go, Bub," he says, with a contemptuous shake of his head.

"They've got no idea the party's just beginning."

Chapter 2   My Dead Sister Pays A Visit

Tuesday, August 9 - 3:30 a.m.

I WAS deep asleep when my dead sister materialized in my bedroom. Just walked right through the wall like it wasn't there. It was no big surprise to see her. Ofelia talks to me regularly, and sometimes visits me in dreams.

You just keep resting, McCoy, she said. *Won't be here but a minute.*

Even lying there in bed with my eyes closed, I could see her clear as day. Hasn't aged at all in the twenty-five years since she was murdered. Holding a stack of schoolbooks in the crook of her arm and wearing that same outfit she had on the last time I saw her alive. White blouse under a sky-blue cardigan sweater. Red and black plaid skirt. White knee sox and black penny loafers.

She set her books down on the dresser and stood at the foot of my bed. There was a look of concern on her pretty brown face.

There's something real nasty coming, McCoy, she said. *That's what I came to warn you about. This one's going to be a doozy.*

When I didn't answer, she put her hands on her hips and frowned down at me.

You hear me, little brother? You be sure and watch your back, you understand?

Big sisters. Bossy as ever, even in death.

I hear you, Ofelia, I mumbled. *Now how about you just let me get some sleep?*

You'd best watch out, little man, she said. *That's all I'm saying.*

I chuckled into my pillow. *Little man.* I was a twelve-year-old runt when she died. Now I'm six foot six, two hundred twenty pounds.

She turned around then and picked her school books up off the dresser. She was starting to fade out through the wall again when I called to her.

Wait a second, Ofelia, I said, feeling my sleeping body twitch on the bed. *Tell me more. What do I need to watch out for?*

But she was already gone. Back to wherever she is now.

When I woke up an hour or so later I crawled out of bed and headed for the bathroom. I felt groggy and out of sorts. The dream of my dead sister's warning was still floating in my mind, hovering there like a patch of low morning fog. After splashing some water on my face, I went down the dark hallway to the kitchen and started the coffeemaker. It was just starting to hiss and sploosh when I heard a grotesque moaning growl behind me. I turned around and saw a familiar pair of evil yellow eyes staring up at me from the doorway, down near the floor.

"You still here, you homely mother?" I said.

The Thing is a small, furry creature that lives with me. Three years back - at the end of a particularly gruesome serial murder case - I'd found out my wife was cheating on me. When we divorced, Vonessa got the house in Farmington Hills and I bought the small condo in Southfield where I live now. Shortly after I moved in, the homeliest mammal I'd ever seen showed up one afternoon at my back door. I made the mistake of inviting it in and feeding it, and ever since the ugly sucker refuses to leave.

I'm pretty sure the Thing is a cat, but I wouldn't necessarily bet money on it. Fact is, he looks more like some kind of genetic experiment gone terribly wrong. As if some cellular biologist had maybe got blind drunk and accidentally crossed a rat and a wolverine. One thing's for sure: if he *is* a cat, he's got to be just about the ugliest, surliest feline that ever lived.

His nasty eyes flashed at me in the dark kitchen as he gave another one of his snarls - this time a creepy wet hissing sound, like something from an Alien movie.

I turned to the cupboard. "Suppose I better feed you before you chaw off my damn foot," I said.

I put his outsize metal bowl up on the counter and emptied a couple of big cans of Alpo dog food into it. Then I set the bowl down on the floor and hastily got out of his way.

By that point my coffee was ready. I poured a cup and got out of there. I don't like listening to the Thing eat. Sounds too much like carcasses being fed into a wood chipper.

I sipped at my coffee as I went down the dark hall. It was depressing to realize that my most intimate companion in the whole wide world was that vile little critter back in the kitchen, who was about as warm and affectionate as a mosquito. In the years since my divorce from Vonessa I'd dated a few women, slept with a couple of them, and had a sex-crazy affair with one who was married. But there was no one in my life now, and I was growing increasingly sure there never again would be.

In the living room I picked up the remote and switched on the TV. There was a news report on about a hot rod exploding in Warren. According to police on the scene, body parts found suggested two dead, presumably the driver and a passenger. The newscast video showed several smoldering black heaps of twisted metal and a couple of badly scorched and mangled chrome wheels with fragments of tire hanging off them. Police were theorizing the rodders may have been using nitromethane or some sort of exotic racing fuel that had inexplicably detonated.

As I stared at the scene of the disaster, sweat broke out on my brow and my heart started beating lickety-split. I'd done a tour of duty in Iraq when my reserve unit got called up back in 2005. I was in a bomb disposal squad and in the year I was there disarmed about fifty IEDs. By the last few weeks of my tour I was a nervous wreck, absolutely convinced that the next crude but lethal device I touched was the one that was going to blow me to kingdom come.

Taking my coffee with me, I headed back to the bathroom to shave and get ready for my morning commute. I'm an FBI agent and I work out of their field office in downtown Detroit. As I was razoring off my beard that morning I thanked God - not for the first time - that I'd come back from my Iraq tour with life and limb intact, and that my days of dealing with bombs were over.

Little did I know how premature my thanks would soon prove to be.

Chapter 3   Darth Vader

Tuesday, August 9 - 10:20 a.m.

A FEW hours after Ofelia's dream visit I was in my cubicle, up on the twenty-sixth floor of the McNamara Federal Building, when Eric Dawson - the agent in charge of the Detroit Bureau office - called Wilson and me into his glass-walled office.

"I assume you both heard about the hot rod that blew up in Warren last night?" Eric asked as we sat down in front of his desk. "Killed the two guys from Eastpointe who were in it?"

"Sure," Wilson said. "It's been all over the news. Online report I read this morning had pictures of the car beforehand. A sweet little yellow deuce coupe."

"Last I heard the Warren police were speculating it was some kind of freak accident," I said. "That the owner was maybe running nitromethane as fuel."

Dawson shook his head. "Hasn't been made public yet, McCoy, but the forensics people from the state police lab in Sterling Heights are already discounting that theory," he said. "They're saying it was a bomb somebody attached to the car's undercarriage."

"A bomb?" I said. A flutter of nausea went through my belly.

"And there's more," Dawson said. "The medical examiners' autopsies showed one of the victims was apparently shot in the head prior to the explosion."

Wilson and I did double takes.

"They're sure?" I said. "From the video I saw of the aftermath, the bodies of those two guys must've been awfully messed up."

"I'll say," Wilson agreed. "Like a bunch of charcoal briquettes somebody tossed out on the road."

"They're sure," Dawson said. "They recovered a forty caliber slug from the debris."

"Damn," I said. "Who the heck *were* these two guys?"

"Upright citizens, as far as the police have been able to determine," Dawson went on. "Both were in their early fifties and lived in Eastpointe, not far from each other. One was a plant foreman at a shop in Clinton Township, the other was a department manager at the Lowe's on Van Dyke. No evidence of enemies, gambling debts, or suspect political connections. Appears to have been completely random."

I frowned. "Random killings aren't so rare. Random car bombings are."

"So the Warren police want to bring the Bureau in on it?" Wilson said. "They're thinking there might be some kind of terrorist connection?"

"Nobody's assuming anything," Dawson said. "But they're asking us to check into it to be sure."

"Who are our contacts?" I asked.

"It's all right here," Dawson said, picking a slim manila folder up off his desk and handing it to me. "Reports and contact info for the Warren Police's lead detective on the case and the tech from the Sterling Heights lab who did the initial analysis on the debris. With their summaries of what's known so far.

"Bottom line is," he went on, "I want you two to check the whole incident out and determine if it's something that falls under the Bureau's purview."

"Hey, Mojo here's an expert on perv view," Wilson deadpanned.

I ignored him. "How much time do we have to make the determination?" I asked Dawson.

"I want you to shoot for end of day," he said.

"Whoa," I said, taken aback. "End of day? So you're saying drop everything for this?"

"That's what I'm saying. This thing may just be a weird one-off. But I've got a bad feeling about it. I want to know if we need to jump in with both feet or just put it to rest and let local law enforcement handle it."

At that we got up and left Dawson's office. Wilson and I went to our cubes and got ready to hit the road.

I wasn't inclined to disagree with Eric, whose instincts are generally pretty solid. I'd had my own bad feeling myself about the hot rod explosion ever since seeing that video report, right after my sister's dream warning.

But the fact that I was now heading into a bomb investigation was not doing any wonders for my stomach.

Fifteen minutes later Wilson and I were on I-75 in my government Chevy, on our way up to Sterling Heights. He was going through the file Dawson had given us, reading the highlights aloud to me as I drove.

"I just don't get the motive," I wondered aloud when he finished. "Why shoot and bomb a pair of middle-aged hot rodders?"

"Maybe the perp was jealous," Wilson said. "Poor schmuck drives some gas-sipping abomination like a Fiat or SmartCar. Hates anyone who's got some real wheels under him."

"Hates them enough to shoot and bomb them?" I said. "He'd have to be a real wacko."

"And there's a shortage of them out there?" he said.

"Point taken," I said.

"On the other hand, maybe he's Dream Cruise hater," he went on. "It's coming up in a week or so. There are poor, sick souls out there who absolutely despise it, you know."

The annual Dream Cruise is a big deal in Detroit. Held the third weekend in August, it typically draws over a million people to watch the forty thousand or so hot rods, muscle cars, sports cars, and restored vintage autos that show up to cruise the northern stretches of Woodward Avenue. I knew from living in Detroit for the past eight years that, amid the general enthusiasm for the event, there's also a good deal of griping from some quarters about the noise, the fumes, and the obnoxious traffic snarls.

"Still sounds pretty farfetched to me," I said. "Kill off a couple of guys just because they're driving a hot rod? And use a bomb to do it?"

"Hey, maybe bomb-making's the perp's hobby. Picks up his pointers on the Internet."

I scowled, creeped out by the thought. In the course of doing terrorism investigations, I've come across an unnerving number of websites dishing out detailed instructions on how to make bombs, poison gases, and other weapons of mass destruction. The scum-suckers behind them almost always savvy enough to successfully hide their identities under layers of Internet anonymity.

Our plan was to meet up with Dr. Mitchell Kwazniak, the lead forensic tech on the investigation, at the state police lab in Sterling Heights. Since it wasn't too far out of our way, though, we decided to head by and visit the spot where the hot rodders were killed first.

The place wasn't hard to find. The Warren police still had that section of 11 Mile Road blocked off with barriers and crime scene tape, and were re-routing traffic around it. It was a stretch of road lined mostly with abandoned factories and warehouses that had big *For Lease* signs out in front. It's a common sight around Greater Detroit, the economy of which has been badly hollowed out by the precipitous decline in the domestic auto industry, especially since the crash of 2008.

Just outside the perimeter a small shrine of flowers, plastic crucifixes, teddy bears, and shiny balloons had already accumulated - mementos apparently left by sympathetic neighbors. That was another characteristic sight around Detroit, where for all the hardships they've undergone, folks still manage to care about tragedies befalling people they don't even know.

We got out of the car, went under the crime scene tape and, after showing our FBI IDs, went toward the explosion site - an area of scorched concrete around forty feet across, with a ten-foot-wide crater in the center of it. By this point most of the remains of the destroyed car and the two victims had already been hauled away to the forensic lab and medical examiner's office, and only a handful of cops and junior forensic techs were left at the site. The techs were squatting down close to the road and the surrounding grass, picking up micro-fragments and putting them into ziplock bags.

As we approached the crater I noticed my heartbeat speeding up and I began to feel a little out of breath. When we got to the edge of the blackened pit, my mind suddenly transported me back in time...

It was a blistering-hot day in the dusty boonies of Al-Anbar Province. It was October thirty-first, 2005 - Halloween. I was in my bulky bomb disposal suit, hobbling stiffly past a smoking crater. Alongside the crater a smoldering Humvee was lying on its side. In spite of its air filtering unit, the smells of burning diesel fuel and human flesh inside my helmet were overpowering. Up ahead in the road the grunts had marked off another IED like the one that had taken out the Humvee. It was my job to disarm the bomb and I was scared shitless. Three days before I'd seen Manny Borges, my best bud in the unit, die after an IED he was disarming went off. The crazy thing was that it wasn't the blast that killed him. His bomb suit was relatively intact. He'd died because his heart stopped. He was all of twenty-seven. As I approached the marked-off IED, I kept hearing Manny's taunting voice inside my helmet, as if his ghost were on the commlink. *Trick or treat, Johnson!* he kept saying. *Trick or treat!*

"Hey, Mojo," I heard beside me. "What's up with you?"

The flashback evaporated when I turned and saw Wilson frowning at me. I realized I was teetering on the edge of the crater, sweating bullets, my stomach churning like a washing machine.

I turned on my heel and strode away from the spot. Wilson followed. I didn't feel like explaining the flashback to him.

"Told you a million times to stop calling me Mojo," I said, feeling better the further away I got from that crater.

"Right," he said.

After leaving the site, we headed up Mound Road to 19 Mile and turned east. We took another turn onto Merrill Road and soon arrived at the Sterling Heights crime lab. It's one of several the Michigan State Police operates around the state.

Mitchell Kwazniak, PhD, the senior forensics specialist on the case, turned out to be a congenial, roly-poly guy in his late forties. We met in his small office, which was covered with sci-fi posters and paraphernalia. You could see he was a big fan of Comic-Con and Trekkie fests.

"Extremely disturbing case," he said, rubbing his plump, pink hands together as we sat down.

"Why's that, Dr. Kwazniak?" I asked.

"Call me Mitch, please."

"Not Darth?" Wilson said, eyeing the black outfit suspended from a coat stand behind the forensics tech.

Kwazniak chortled. "I-am-Vader-only-at-con-ven-tions," he intoned, in a surprisingly credible James Earl Jones baritone.

"Seriously," he went on, "what troubles me is that the forensic evidence indicates this bomb wasn't some klutzy, amateur affair. It was the work of someone who knows how to build compact, sophisticated devices and who's got access to commercial or military-grade plastic explosives."

"Excellent," Wilson said. "That's great news."

"Wait a minute," I said. "You're saying he's using plastics?"

"Correct," he said.

I felt a bilious surge in my stomach. Plastics and conventional explosives like TNT are two different ball games. It's believed the bomb that blew up the Lockerbie plane was a chunk of plastics inside a handheld tape recorder.

"How come that's not in your report?" I asked.

"Because I haven't got a definitive spectrographic analysis back yet from your lazy FBI lab colleagues in Washington. I'm just telling you because I'm ninety-nine percent sure it's going to come back as plastics. Either Semtex or C-4."

"Okay," I said, "let's say you're right. Why use them on some innocent, apparently randomly-chosen victims?"

"Sorry," Kwazniak said, shaking his head. "Can't help you there. All I know is that, explosives-wise, whoever put together the device that blew up that hot rod has got some serious bomb-making chops."

Wilson and I exchanged glances. "Holy snake snot," he said.

The feeling of unease in my gut worsened. What Kwazniak just told us meant we weren't dealing with some rank amateur. I knew from my bomb squad experience in Iraq that the more skillful the bomber was, the more devious and deadly their devices would be.

A short time later we got up to leave. "Thanks, doc," Wilson said as we headed for Kwazniak's door. "You've really made our day."

The forensic tech raised a plump hand and gave us an apple-cheeked grin.

"May the Force be with you," he said.

After leaving the crime lab, we headed down to the Warren police department and met with Detective Jack Todd, the lead on the bombing case. Nothing new came out of the interview. He'd already done a good job of background-checking the dead Eastpointers, but was continuing to dig to see if there was anything that would make either of the two men targets of someone's wrath. When Wilson and I got up to leave, he promised he'd let us know if any new info broke.

On our way back downtown, I already knew what my recommendation to Dawson would be - that the Bureau bring the case under our purview. The why of it was still miles beyond me. But something was going on here. Something very strange and very scary.

It was more than just the flutters in my stomach. Every cell in my being was telling me this wasn't the last we'd heard from our hot rod bombers.

Chapter 4   Deadly Intruders   ⌣

Saturday, August 13 - 11:55 p.m.

IMAM ALI Mohammed Al-Rafi is in his study - a book-lined room on the second floor of his west side Detroit home - when he hears the noises downstairs.

His grizzled gray head jerks up from the treatise he's reading. Brows knit, he blinks a couple of times, his eyes magnified into huge dark orbs by his wire-rim spectacles. The first noise had sounded like shifting furniture; the second like the growl of some extremely unpleasant animal.

A flutter of unease goes through him. Did he lock up before coming upstairs? He thinks back to earlier that evening, after he'd cooked and eaten his usual modest dinner of lamb and vegetables. He can distinctly remember latching the dead-bolts on the front and side doors before climbing the steps to his study.

An age-mottled hand goes to his gray beard and nervously tugs at it. Who could possibly be in the house at this hour?

In addition to the open treatise, the desk before him is covered with neatly stacked piles of his books, journals and papers - most in Arabic, a handful in English or French. Atop the bookshelves encircling him are several pewter-framed photos of a smiling, plain-faced woman - his beloved wife, Buhjah, dead two years ago of uterine cancer. Next to his desk the computer his nephew Ibrahim built for him hums on its metal stand. He glances at the monitor. The swirling shapes of its screensaver now look oddly eerie and ominous.

Tilting his head toward the open door of the study, he strains to listen. But the house appears to be silent now. After a couple more minutes his sloping shoulders lift in a shrug.

"Getting old," he mutters in Arabic, resettling his glasses on his slender, hooked nose. "Hearing things that aren't there."

He adjusts the green glass shade of his desk lamp, leans back over the treatise and resumes reading. Three minutes pass before he hears it - a familiar squeak of weight on old wood.

Someone coming up the stairs?

An icy fingertip seems to caress his vertebrae, raising the hairs on his arms and the back of his neck. Hastily, he pushes himself up out his desk

,air. Despite the chill running up his spine, the sight of the smiling portrait of Buhjah near the doorway makes his cheeks go hot as he passes it by, embarrassed at the fear curdling in his belly.

Stepping out into the hall, he anxiously looks both ways. But the balcony and landing at the top of the stairs are empty. Did he mishear? Was it just the old house settling?

He takes a dozen stealthy steps to the right, which brings him to the top of the staircase. He grips the railing, more to stop his hand from trembling than for support. Tipping his torso forward, he squints down into the darkness. At the base of the stairs is the foyer. To the left is the living room, and to the right the portal to the dining room. But the front door is windowless and all the first-floor shades and blinds are drawn. It's as black as a tomb down there.

"Who is in my house?" he calls down into the gloom. "Answer me!"

There's no answer. But he could swear he can hear the sound of breathing. A strangely moist and husky breath.

Imam Al-Rafi is now certain an intruder has somehow gotten into his home. Another shiver runs up his back, which is somewhat curved by age and scoliosis. His knees feel strangely weak and it's a struggle to keep them from quaking.

"Ibrahim! . . . Sayeed!" he calls out, though he knows quite well neither his nephew nor his assistant at the mosque have keys to his house.

He wipes his forehead with the back of his hand, and it comes away dripping with sweat.

He wonders who the prowlers in his home could be. Burglars, most likely. Ignorant thugs who foolishly imagine there'll be money or valuables in the house of a respected imam.

Would the sound of an angry, authoritative voice frighten them away?

"Ibrahim!" he snaps out sternly, trying to make his tremulous voice sound harsh and commanding.

A shudder goes through him when the answer comes: the same menacing animal sound he'd heard earlier. But louder and clearer this time. The dark, ugly snarl of some terrible beast. He tries to imagine what kind of awful creature could make such a repugnant sound, but soon stops himself. It's too frightening.

Allah protect me! he prays as images of unholy demons flash through his mind.

He's still staring down into the darkness when he senses it - a presence directly behind him!

With a gasp, instinctively throwing up his arms to shield himself, he swings around. Just in time to catch sight of a blurry form disappearing into his study. He blinks. Or was it an illusion? he thinks. Just a floater in my eye?

But a moment later the lights in the study go out.

He whimpers, plunged into total darkness now. Instinctively, he staggers backwards. Feeling his heels rock on the top step, he lurches forward again, realizing he's almost gone tumbling down the stairs. Toward that hideous beast down there - whatever it is!

"What do you want?" he says into the darkness, almost gagging on the words as he forces them out of his fear-parched throat.

"Take it! Take whatever you want from me!" he says.

He thinks he hears a soft, nasty laugh then. But there's no other reply.

"Anything you want! Anything! Just leave me in peace!" he calls into the blackness. A spasm of self-loathing goes through him as he feels a warm trickle begin running down one of his thighs.

HELP! he wants to scream. But knows that this late at night, with the house closed up the way it is, there's little chance his neighbors will hear him.

He has no cell - only the wall phone down in the kitchen. Can he reach it? Call that nine-one-one emergency number for help?

No! He has to get out of the house - now! Has to try to get past that beast below! While there's still time!

He takes a couple of shuffling steps backward, feeling for the top stair. His groping hand finds the knobby wood bulb at the top of the staircase and then the handrail. Slowly, clasping the rail with both hands, he takes the first step down. Followed by a second. But the third gives out a loud, dry-wood squeak.

Another long, low, terrifying snarl comes from the dark foyer below him.

He steels himself to take another step. Again there's a soft squeak.

This time the bestial growl that comes up to him is even deeper and more guttural. And the menacing sound has drawn closer. Now it's at the very foot of the stairwell.

He's trapped.

He stands frozen, trembling from the top of his balding head to his sandaled feet. The trickle going down his thigh has turned into a humiliating stream, rolling down his calf and wetting his ankle. The stink of it rank and salty in his quivering nostrils.

Helpless, knowing it's the wrong thing to do, but unable to stop himself, he begins backing up the stairs.

Down there is some kind of awful beast. Up here at least the other being is, he senses, human.

A burglar, he thinks. But a man, at least. Perhaps I can reason with him!

He's just backed up to the top step when he hears a faint hissing from the landing behind him.

A horrible sharp pain cuts into his throat, strangling off the shocked scream that tries to burst out of him. Gagging, he's roughly pulled down and back onto his scrawny behind. A powerful knee presses painfully into his spine, so huge and hard it feels as if it could be the knee of a bronze statue.

The wire sinks deeper into the flesh of his throat. His pale old scholar's hands scrabble, like the fluttering wings of some oversize, panicky moth, at the band of searing pain around his neck.

WHO ARE YOU? he tries to cry out, arthritic fingers clawing futilely at the constricting wire. *WHY ARE YOU DOING THIS?*

But the only sound the burning ring around his neck permits him are the grotesque gurgling croaks he's making.

The assassin then gives a vicious tug on the wire. Something deep up inside Al-Rafi's sinuses seems to rupture, and a medicinal-tasting spurt of blood goes sluicing down into his throat. The increased pressure inside his head is now making it feel like his brain is about to pop out of his skull.

He sees his deceased wife's face shimmering before him. *BUHJAH!* he cries out in his mind as she looks back at him, a look of pained confusion on her features. Then her image drops away, replaced by the hundred golden asterisks of light that begin to flash wildly before his bulging eyes.

He senses himself being dragged out of this life and hurled toward the next. *ALLAHU AKBAR!* he screams inside his exploding head, though it comes out as no more than a faint, incoherent retching. *ALLAHU AKBAR! GOD IS GREAT!*

He's still screaming it when something like a bloody-black bubble bursts inside his skull and he drops like a tossed stone into the vast, dark pool of eternity.

Thirty seconds later the killer is standing over Al-Rafi's body. He wears camouflage cargo pants, a dark, long-sleeve polo and black cross trainers. He's beaming the mini-flashlight that's strapped to his left arm down at the dead imam's face. The features are purple and bloated, the glassy, sightless eyes bulging wide with shock and horror as they stare back up him. With a faint smile he watches the corpse's limbs flutter and twitch. He's always found post-mortem spasms kind of comical.

The husky man's breathing is slow and deep, his heartbeat only mildly elevated. The homemade garrote he's just used hangs at his side. His pumped-up arm muscles, still taut from the killing, tingle deliciously. A shudder of pleasure ripples through him as he feels the energy-release from the dead man pass into him.

He closes his eyes and, with a blissful smile, lets the man's escaping life energy seep into his being. Feels it course through his nervous system, a pulsing black current that's almost like low-voltage electricity. He savors it as it hums up through his limbs and spine, lifting every hairlet on his body. With an ecstatic shiver he lets the energy coil its way up through his chakras and flood the universe of his mind with its unholy, squirming shadows.

Two minutes pass as he stands there shuddering, taking his fill of the imam's departing life force. When he's absorbed enough of it to satisfy him, he opens his eyes. They are a crystal-clear blue and shine with cold, fiercely-focused purpose.

He checks the black titanium special ops watch on his left wrist. Five hours left before daybreak. Time to get to work. By his calculations the Detroit Police SWAT team will show up in from forty-two to forty-six hours from now. He has lots to do to prepare the surprises he has in store for them.

Guided by the flashlight's discreet beam, he squats down near the body's feet, facing away from the torso. He reaches back for the old man's ankles.

25

Rising, he twists the body around and drags it toward the stairwell. Grinning to himself, he starts downstairs, listening to the soft thumps of the dead imam's head as it bounces down the wooden steps behind him.

"Hi-ho, hi-ho," he sings softly. "It's off to work we go."

In the dim glow of the flashlight he sees Beelzebub waiting for him, squatting in the foyer near the foot of the stairs. The wall-eyed pit bull follows him as he drags the body through the dining room and then down a short hallway that leads to the side-door landing. There, after hefting the imam's corpse over a shoulder, he stoops and picks up the toolbox he'd left after picking the side door lock.

The dog trails him down into the basement, where there's an old wooden workbench standing against one wall. After dumping the body on the dusty linoleum floor, the man clears away the tools, paint cans, and hardware that clutter the top of the workbench. He then hefts the imam's corpse onto it, face up.

He goes to the laundry area, grabs a heap of soiled bedding from a hamper, and begins stuffing it into the narrow, cobwebbed window openings at the top of the basement's walls. When they are all blocked off, he switches on every light he can find. Standing in the bright light, he then strips off his clothes.

When he's completely nude, he goes to the toolbox, kneels, and takes out a hacksaw. After crossing over to the workbench where the imam's body lies stretched out, he glances over his shoulder at the yellow dog.

The pit bull is squatting nearby, good eye staring up him with intense interest, bad eye floating languidly in its socket. His long, grayish-pink tongue sways good-naturedly as it hangs from his grinning jaws.

"Better stand clear, Bub," the man says, giving the dog a sly wink as he lines up the hacksaw over the dead imam's Adam's apple.

"This could get a bit messy..."

Chapter 5   The Thing And I

Sunday, August 14 - 3:30 p.m.

DESPITE MY apprehensions, the week passed with no further bombings - hot rod or otherwise. After a couple more days of fruitless digging, Wilson and I went back to our regular case load. The only update was when Mitch Kwazniak from the Sterling Heights crime lab called us to confirm that the explosive used was, indeed, a plastic - Semtex, to be precise. No motives had emerged as yet for the killings of the Eastpointe hot rodders. It appeared the two guys just happened to be in the wrong place at the wrong time.

I'd planned on working half the day Saturday, but ended up putting in a full one. When Sunday rolled around, I decided to stay home and take it easy. After a lazy morning of reading, in the afternoon I fell asleep on my living room couch, watching the Tigers game on TV. Not sure how long I was asleep before the dream started...

I was in jeans and a t-shirt, walking barefoot through a vast landscape of rotting garbage, holding my nose against the god-awful smell. The place reminded me of a landfill I'd once visited on a serial murder case, except that that one had included plenty of metal, stone, plastic, and paper trash. This one seemed to be made up entirely of decomposing biomass. For as far as the eye could see, there were heaps of rotting fruits and vegetables, mixed in with clumps of decaying, fly-covered carcasses - animal, fish, and avian. Much of the meat was in rib-lined slabs that looked like the discards from a slaughterhouse, but an equal amount resembled plain old crushed and mangled road kill.

The sun was beating down hard and the air was a miasma of sticky foulness. Much of the mess had decomposed into a semi-liquid state, which made traipsing through the muck as difficult as it was nauseating. My bare feet made obscenely-horrible sucking sounds each time I yanked one of them out of the slimy, viscous soup to take another step. With growing desperation I searched around for some kind of exit, but the disgusting sea of garbage seemed to stretch to the horizon in every direction.

Horrific as it was to look at, the worst part of being there was the horrendous stench. Even though I was holding my nose and had covered my mouth with my hand, I was still gagging from the putrid reek. Steamy clouds of sickly-colored greenish fumes were wafting up out of the heaps of decay like half-rotten ghosts. Every now and then a revolting burble of sulfurous gas would belch up out of the sickening morass. The fetid smell kept getting worse and worse, to the point where I could no longer hold back my retching. I began to gag uncontrollably and was just about to hurl my cookies out onto the revolting landscape when my eyes flicked open.

A gargoyle-ugly face was inches away from my own. It had evil yellow eyeballs and its breath smelled like week-old corpses simmering in a stew of rotten eggs. When I screamed in horror, the dreadful face shot away. A set of hot, ripping pains simultaneously erupted on my chest and belly.

Groaning at the stinging hurt, I rolled off the couch and stood up to get my bearings. In a flash I realized what had happened. The Thing must've climbed up onto my chest. Had probably been standing there for a while, his stagnant feline breath inspiring the repulsive dream. No doubt the creepy little sucker had gotten impatient for me to perform what to him is my sole purpose for existing. Namely, to feed him.

"Damn you, you freak," I said, lifting my t-shirt to inspect the bloody scratches his claws left when he'd leaped off my chest.

The foul-breathed little mutant was sitting on his haunches at the portal that leads out of the living room. He was staring at me expectantly, looking not at all repentant. If anything, the creepy mother appeared pleased with himself for having so effectively roused me out of my nap.

"Alright, you overgrown cockroach," I told him as I left the living room, "I'll feed you. Pretty sure I've got some rat poison up in one of the cupboards."

When I started going down the hall, he raced past me and went straight to the kitchen, as if showing me where I needed to go.

"I'm going to lace that meal of yours with a nice, big dose of strychnine," I told him, reaching up into a cabinet for a couple of his dog food cans. "Then I'll sit there laughing when you keel over and go meet your maker. I'm talking Dr. Frankenstein, of course. Bet he's down in hell waiting for you right now."

After I'd fed the voracious little mugwump, I went back out to the living room and sat down on the couch. With the ball game over, I picked up the remote and started flipping through channels.

There was a show on one of the local stations about the upcoming Dream Cruise. The video clips showed a fantastic, miles-long mélange of autos - the vast majority of them Detroit iron - rumbling down the steamy lanes of Woodward Avenue. The clips brought back to me one of the striking things I'd noticed about the Cruises I've attended, which is the insane variety of vehicles that show up.

Being from Chicago myself, it's a trip to see how many folks around here own and drive custom or restored cars. Automobile culture is strong everywhere in America, but nowhere is it stronger than in Detroit, where for generations the auto and supporting industries built not just cars but decent, middle-class lives for millions of people. As soon as the weather turns nice in the spring, folks all around the metro area begin taking their babies out for spins in the evenings and on weekends - wild, customized hot rods, muscle cars from the 1960s, '70s, and '80s, and restored classics - some of them, like the early Ford Model T, over a hundred years old.

In August, however, in the weeks and days leading up to the Dream Cruise, is when you really see them out in force. There'd been a slew of them out on the local highways when I'd come home from work the previous evening.

As I watched a clip of a pearlescent purple, chopped-top Model A smoke its oversized rear tires, my mind went back to the dead Eastpointe hot rodders and the gunshot and bomb that had killed them. I'd felt dead certain that something along the same lines was going to happen again, right on the heels of it. But I'd been wrong. The week had passed and there'd been no more bombs, no more hapless victims. It now appeared to have been a one-off. Just another blip of the crazy, random violence that besets modern-day America.

But if I really believed that, why was a sense of unease periodically fluttering around in my gut? Like the one I was having just then?

Probably just being paranoid, I told myself.

It's coming soon, my dead sister said. *I can feel it.*

The quiver in my belly turned into something like a clenched fist. *What's coming?* I said.

You don't want to know, she said.

Wrong, Ofelia, I said, annoyed by her coyness. *I do want to know. So how about a hint?*

I can't see everything, she said. *But it looks like-*

Like what?

A bloodbath, she said.

Her voice went silent then and I couldn't coax anything more out of her. I sat back on the couch, a chill running up my spine. Ofelia's warnings and predictions could be maddeningly obscure and were by no means always reliable. But the fact was, sometimes they were right on.

For about the ten-thousandth time my mind flashed back to her gruesome, untimely death, twenty-five years before.

We were kids in Chicago. I was in seventh grade and she was a senior in high school. One spring morning, after we'd separated to go to our different school bus stops, I noticed a man on the street staring at her. I'd never seen a look of such hungry, stalking evil on a face before, and it scared me right down into my bones.

That night I had a bad dream about the man sneaking up on my sister and hurting her in some obscure but terrible way. I warned Ofelia about it the next morning, but naturally she just made fun of me and told me not to worry none.

Two days later she went missing on her way home from school. It was three more days before a couple of detectives let me lead them to the place I'd seen in my dream. A storage shed out back behind Elijah's, a neighborhood market and liquor store. The kind of place Detroit folks call a party store.

I suppose it was because they didn't take me very seriously that the detectives let me be there when they opened the door to the shed. Because behind it lay the body of my teenage sister - raped and murdered, her body horribly mutilated.

"Holy shit!" one of them gasped, just before he clapped a hand over my eyes - a few seconds too late.

Though I don't talk about it much, I've never made it a secret that what I saw in that storage shed is what led me into my law enforcement career. Not that I made a decision about it at the time. Fact is, if the police had caught the son of a bitch who killed my sister, maybe I'd have seen things differently. But they didn't. Despite my description and the facial composite

I helped them create, the killer never even got identified, much less caught and prosecuted. The freaking monster got away scot-free.

Several years later I began to periodically hear Ofelia's disembodied voice, giving me hints, warnings, advice, or predictions. Sometimes about things going on in my life, but more often about cases I was working. It creeped me out at first - thought I was maybe going crazy. But over time I got used to it. A handful of times she's told me things that've helped me break some big cases. But there have also been plenty of times when they've been so out in left field they've done nothing but leave me scratching my head in bewilderment.

The TV came back into focus then, and I watched a clip of the massive crowd of people that gather along Woodward during the Dream Cruise. Thousands of people in sunglasses and summer clothing, milling around the custom cars on display and smiling or mugging for the video camera.

Ofelia had been wrong in her predictions before, and I hoped like hell this would be another instance. But even after I turned up the volume on the TV, I kept hearing what she'd said was coming, the words echoing in my head as my stomach once again quivered.

A bloodbath...

Chapter 6   A Piece Of Cake

Monday, August 15 - 4:55 a.m.

IT'S STILL dark out when he pulls the red '95 Chevy Beretta up to the trash-lined curb. He cuts the rumbling engine and turns to the yellow dog.

"Okay, Bub," he says. "You stand guard while I'm gone. Understand, boy? *Stay*. And *kill*."

The pit bull, squatting on the passenger seat, gives him a low growl of affirmation. His right eye gleams back at the man with diabolical intensity, while his left floats aimlessly. Both eyes have huge black irises and beady red pupils.

Out of the car, the man glances east and sees the first glow of dawn sneaking up over the horizon. At the Beretta's rear, he opens the trunk and removes a heavy-duty orange plastic toolbox. He then heads down the block, without bothering to lock the doors. Although the bus yard is on the edge of a crummy, rundown residential neighborhood, no one's likely to mess with a car that's got a red-eyed, demented-looking pit bull inside. No one in their right mind, at least.

He strides past several abandoned houses. A couple are burnt-out shells with caved-in roofs. Their blackened chimneys remind him of scorched middle fingers flipping off the starry sky.

When he rounds the corner the bus yard - two blocks long and surrounded by a twelve-foot-tall chain link fence - comes into view. He walks slowly toward the entrance gate, trying to look sleepy and bored. It's an effort, given that the tool box he's carrying contains a fifteen-pound, kiloton-force bomb and he's as geeked-up as some meth-head about to score a pound of crystal.

Near the gate a security camera peers down at him from a tall metal pole. He glances up at the hooded gray videocam. But only with his eyes. He doesn't want to give it a direct shot at his face.

With his chin down, it'll mostly pick up the curly black wig and fake beard, mustache, and eyebrows he's wearing. Beneath them, sunless tanning lotion has darkened his face to a dusky brown. He's used the same artificial tan on his hands. The three-inch lifts in his steel-toed work boots give him some extra height, and his navy blue mechanic's uniform has realistic oil stains on the shirt front and trouser knees. The oversized work shirt helps hide his pumped-up body-builder's chest and arms.

Later, when they review the security cam's video and interview witnesses, the facial disguise will jump right out at them. But his actual features will be maddeningly obscure.

Infiltrating the bus yard has been pathetically easy. Over the past week he's done two dry runs, the tool box filled with a set of greasy old wrenches. Each time the same heavyset, middle-aged guard with mutton-chop whiskers has been in the main gate's security booth. The man has one of those digital mini-TVs in the booth with him. He barely looks up from its flickering screen when visitors go in or out. Today the guard doesn't even bother to glance at his fake name badge, with the name "Nabil Harari" below the transit authority logo.

After passing through the gate, he heads for the oversized repair garage. His nose wrinkles as he sniffs in the scent of the bus yard. Built back in the '50s, it smells like a sixty-year accumulation of grease, dust, crumbling asphalt, rusty metal, and diesel fumes. The stench of Detroit, he thinks, hawking and spitting onto the yard's oily, hard-packed dirt.

There's another video camera looking down from a corner of the garage's roof and he again keeps his face lowered as he enters the broad open door. The handful of mechanics inside are standing near the partially-disassembled bus engines they're working on, drinking coffee and idly bullshitting with one another. They give him no more than mildly curious glances when he walks past them, twenty yards away, toolbox in hand.

He continues on through the garage and out into the huge open parking lot area where the city's transit buses are lined up. There are thirty of them, all gassed up with diesel fuel and ready for their daily runs. The buses are arrayed in three long lines. He moves between them so he'll be less visible as he paces down the rows, searching for his target bus. Each of them is numbered, in ten-inch-high letters, at its upper rear. His eyes flick back and forth until he finds the one he's looking for: 0911.

He grins, recalling the afternoon three weeks ago when he'd spotted it. He was downtown on a reconnaissance mission, cruising the stretch of Woodward between the Fisher Freeway and Jefferson Avenue in his Escalade. He'd laughed out loud when he saw the bus number. It was perfect. The investigators would have to be total frigging idiots not to make a connection to the World Trade Center attack.

He walks up to the bus's rear and sets his tool box down on the pavement. After undoing the two chrome steel latches that hold the engine cover in place, he swings it up and braces it open. On the right side of the engine compartment there's a flat, rectangular space that's unobstructed by any parts or wiring. He pulls a red mechanic's rag out of a pocket and wipes the area clean of dirt and grime. Then he kneels down and opens the orange toolbox. In the upper tray are his silencer-equipped, forty-caliber Glock and a pair of latex cleaning gloves.

After pulling on the gloves, he sets the tray aside and lifts out the bomb. It's in a metal casing and is not much bigger than a shoebox. Bent over, he holds it up to the area he'd wiped. As the casing draws near to the metal, he feels the powerful neodymium-iron-boron magnets bolted to its exterior snap the device into place. He throws and locks the black switch on the side that arms it. He then closes and re-latches the engine cover, picks up his toolbox, and walks away.

As he's emerging from between the bus rows he spots a heavyset black guy ambling his way. The man is uniformed, has something in his hand, and is looking directly at him.

His eyes widen from the sudden adrenaline rush. For an instant he's on the verge of dropping the toolbox and yanking out the Glock.

But then the man stops, yawns, and turns toward the buses. He realizes the black guy's outfit is a transit authority uniform and the thing in his hand is just a clipboard. He must be doing some sort of pre-run check-off.

He continues on his way, his pattering heartbeat slowing as he moves away from the bus rows.

On his way out, he's again mindful of not gazing up at the security cams. At the main gate the guard with the oversize sideburns is giggling at the vintage Road Runner cartoon he's watching. The man gives him no more than a glance and an absent wave as he passes the booth. He nods back, avoiding a direct look at the cretin. When he rounds the corner to the street where the Beretta's parked, he checks his watch.

He's gotten in and out in nine minutes flat.

Back at the Beretta, he returns the toolbox to the trunk. When he climbs inside, Beelzebub gives him a gravelly growl of greeting.

"Piece of cake," he says to the dog, with a contemptuous chuckle. "Those jerk-offs let me walk right in there again."

There's a chrome plastic Islamic crescent moon and star device dangling from the car's rearview mirror. It sways and rotates when he starts the engine and pulls away.

He heads toward the freeway. The sun's upper edge is now over the horizon and it's beginning to bathe the rundown neighborhood in peach-colored light. Gripping the steering wheel, he arches his back and flexes his heavily-muscled neck and shoulders, letting the tension flow out of them.

"That's it for this one, Bub," he says. "All I've gotta do now is be downtown today at 5 p.m. Program the remote, hit the button, and *whammo* - dead Detroiters up the wazoo."

The squatting dog looks over at him and licks his chops approvingly.

"With any luck," he goes on. "Fifty to a hundred people will get whacked. Probably the same number will get burned or mutilated, but I don't even count them. Want to know why?"

The dog looks at him expectantly, tongue hanging out of the side of his grinning muzzle.

"Raw body count, Bub," he says with a wink. "To get serious media attention, you've got to produce lots of corpses for them. And that's exactly what I'm gonna do."

For the past five years he's spoken to other human beings only when absolutely necessary. Maybe that's why he finds himself blabbing to Beelzebub all the time. He knows it's a bit crazy. But the way he figures it, after the horrific thing that got done to him that night in Fallujah, he's got a right to be crazy. As crazy as he effing wants to be.

When they reach the Edsel Ford freeway, he turns down the trash-strewn entrance ramp and merges into the light, early-morning traffic. From the Ford he'll exit onto I-96, and from there get onto the Southfield expressway. In twenty minutes or so they'll be home. Or, to be more precise, back at the suburban house he's turned into a combination bomb factory and defense compound. There he'll change outfits and vehicles before heading out to plant his next device. On a certain school bus in Northville.

He glances over at the pit bull. Like all dogs, Bub enjoys riding in cars. He's gazing around at the traffic with his good eye, his bum one periodically flicking into sync but then futilely floating away again.

There are times when Bub gets a certain cunning, devilish look on his ugly mug. One that makes him wonder if that damn dog doesn't know a lot more than he lets on. But the rest of the time he looks and acts like any old dumbshit canine.

"One thing's for sure, bad boy," he says. "After five o'clock today, it'll be a whole new ball game. Frigging local media will be jizzing all over themselves, cranking up the terror with all kinds of bulletins and special reports. And with that many dead, the national networks will for sure pick up the story.

"Know what else? After they finish shitting bricks, you can count on the Feds putting together a big-ass task force. Hopefully one that includes my old buddy. My all-time favorite FBI agent in the whole wide stinking world. Want to guess who that is, Bub?"

He glances over at the yellow dog's erratically-weaving eye.

"McCoy Johnson, that's who," he says through clenched teeth, his eyes icy with hatred. "Special Agent McCoy Scumbag Sonofabitch Johnson."

The pit bull, seeming to recognize the loathsome name, gives out a menacing, lip-lifting snarl that bares most of his long, snaggly teeth.

"It's going to be payback time," he says. "I'm going to make that big, black bastard wish he was never born, Bub. Just you frigging wait."

His nostrils flare as he pictures Johnson lying blank-eyed under a pile of rubble. Brains oozing out of his caved-in skull, his guts spilled out like a crushed fly's.

The happy thought leads to another. Very soon he's going to be rich. Big time rich. Rich enough to buy anything and anyone he wants, for the rest of his frigging life.

He's still smiling when, a few minutes later, he veers off onto the Southfield Freeway.

Day by day this week the violence he's orchestrated will claim more and more lives. Come Saturday - Dream Cruise day - the carnage will peak in a deadly crescendo. He'll unleash The Big One and there'll be so many bodies lining Woodward Avenue it'll take them a frigging week to count them all.

"I tell you what, Bub," he says. "It's gonna be like a 'Goodbye Detroit Symphony.' Composed and conducted by yours ⌣.

"Or maybe," he says with a laugh, "I should call it the 'Hey, Detroit! - Kiss Your Sorry Ass Goodbye Symphony.' What do you think, boy? Which one do you like better?"

As he weaves around some lame-ass who's doing the Southfield's idiotic fifty-five mile-an-hour speed limit, he glances at the crescent moon and star device dangling from the Beretta's rearview mirror.

"*Allahu Akbar,*" he says with a mocking sneer.

He sees the pit bull looking at him. "That's raghead for 'God is great,'" he explains.

The look on his face darkens. Under the mechanic's uniform, a tingle of the bottomless rage that drives him runs up and down his hard-muscled body. "Yeah," he says. "That son of a bitch is great, alright."

"But you want to know what's even greater, Bub?" he goes on, his eyes sheening over with madness as he stares at the road ahead.

"Mass frigging murder."

Chapter 7   Mayhem At Campus Martius

Monday, August 15 - 5:00 p.m.

I WAS packing up my briefcase at the McNamara Building, just about to leave work for the day, when I heard the explosion.

It came from the direction of Woodward Avenue: a deep, ominous *whump*, followed by a long, menacing grumble. Powerful enough to rattle the window alongside my cubicle.

I froze in my seat. It was the sound of serious ordnance - a sound I hadn't heard since leaving Iraq five years before. I felt my stomach tighten as I flashed back to some of the horrors I'd witnessed there.

Get a grip, I told myself. This is downtown Detroit. Maybe a gas main exploded.

"Holy rhino farts, Mojo - what'd you have for lunch?" Wilson asked from the next cubicle.

I stood up and stepped out of my cube just as Dawson came out of his glass-walled office, his forehead creased.

"What the hell was that just now?" he said.

"Sounded like a big blast - close by," I said.

"I keep telling Mojo here he needs to lay off those bean burritos," Wilson said, stepping out of his cube.

"Can the jokes, Wilson," Eric snapped. "Nardella! Rasheed!" he called out. "Check the local news stations on your computers. See if there are any bulletins."

A group of us hurried over to the east-facing windows and looked down from our twenty-sixth floor vantage. Howling sirens were already audible from the streets below. I spotted a plume of black smoke billowing our way from the direction of Woodward. "Check it out," I said, pointing.

"Anything on the news?" Eric called back to Norm Rasheed and Angie Nardella.

"Big blast over on Woodward, according to Freep dot com," Angie said. "Possible gas main explosion. They're getting tweets and calls from eyewitnesses."

"Took out a city bus and a bunch of surrounding cars," Norm said. "Clickondetroit dot com is saying there looks to be a lot of victims. Police, fire, and MichCon emergency units are en route."

"I'm going to head over there and see what's going down," I said. "I've got a bad feeling about this."

"Me too," Eric said. He turned and called out to Rasheed. "Norm, pass the word: as of this minute the office is in emergency status. No one goes home. Anyone who wants to proceed to Woodward can do so. Everyone else remains in the office until further notice. You stay up here for now and keep checking on the news reports. Call me on my cell with any updates. Got that?"

"Got you, Eric," Rasheed said.

"Wilson, Nardella - you come along with McCoy and me," Dawson said.

"Jeez, Eric, if it's just a gas main, do I have to go, too?" Wilson said as we headed for the office exit. "I've got a hot date tonight."

"Yeah?" Angie said. "Got some new batteries for your love doll?"

"Hey, gimme a break, Peaches," Wilson said. "This is some nice, respectable babe my mom set me up with. Good Catholic girl."

"Really?" she said. "I hear they give the best head."

"Jeez-is, what a dirty-minded broad you are," Wilson said.

We hurried down the hall toward the elevator. I punched the button and a moment later the door opened. It was jammed with end-of-day passengers.

"Hey, wait a minute, Peaches," Wilson said as we pushed inside. "Aren't you Catholic?"

We rode down in the crowded elevator. Those of us in the FBI contingent stared grimly at one another, our eyes all simmering with the same question. Was this a terrorist attack?

On reaching the ground floor, we hurried across the lobby to the building's exits and headed up Michigan Avenue. With Woodward just four short blocks away, there was no point taking cars. We jogged up the sidewalk into the thickening cloud of black smoke pouring our way. The acrid stink of burning got stronger with each step. Fire trucks and EMS vehicles roared past us, the frantic whoops of their sirens echoing crazily off the towering downtown buildings.

When we reached Woodward Avenue, the scene from hell before us froze us dead in our tracks.

The explosion had taken place alongside Campus Martius, where north and southbound Woodward are separated by a broad boulevard that's a combination plaza and park. A southbound city bus and several cars around it were engulfed in ghastly cocoons of raging fire. The bus's rear had been blown to smithereens and the rest of its mangled hulk was a raging inferno. Inside the crackling yellow flames I could make out blackened cadavers twisted into horrifying, no-longer-human shapes. Around the bus were about ten hellishly-burning cars, the incinerated corpses of their drivers grimacing at us from behind their steering wheels. Outside of the inferno's periphery, bloody, smoking bodies and body parts lay scattered on the street and sidewalks.

"Sweet Jesus on crack!" I heard Wilson exclaim.

I glanced over and saw Nardella standing next to him, the back of her hand to her mouth. I followed their gazes downward. A woman's severed lower leg lay smoking on the sidewalk just in front of us, freckled pink flesh blistering above the red-painted toenails. I tore my eyes away, not wanting to gag and vomit, like the agent I heard just then behind me.

A ring of police cars, fire trucks, and EMS vehicles had already encircled the appalling scene. Sweaty-faced patrolmen were shouting, waving and blowing their whistles in shrill shrieks as they redirected traffic. Fire crews in their black helmets and green and yellow fire suits had hooked up their hoses and were just beginning to douse the flaming wreckage with streams of water. Emergency medical teams were scrambling out of their ambulances and pushing their way through the horrorstruck crowd on the nightmare's fringe, carrying stretchers and medical kits.

The sight of the first responders rushing to do their jobs jolted me out of my shock. I took a look behind me. Another dozen agents from the office had joined us and several more were running our way down Michigan Ave. I took a step toward Dawson. He was on his cell phone - no doubt calling the regional director with an onsite update. I decided to break in.

"What do you want us to do, Eric?" I yelled at him. Along with the roaring flames and steamy hiss of water hitting them, a disorienting cacophony of shouts, screams, sirens, and bullhorns were resonating through the intersection and nearby plaza

"For now, everyone just deals with victims!" he bellowed back. "Help get them to the EMS teams!"

As our FBI contingent began moving through the crowd, I suddenly froze again. Despite the fact that I was sweating profusely from the horrendous heat, a chill shot up between my shoulder blades.

Holy Christ! I thought. What if there's a follow-on bomb?

It was a technique I'd seen Iraqi insurgents use with devastating effect. They'd set off a powerful bomb in a market or square crowded with civilians. After that they'd wait until there were plenty of soldiers, police, and medical personnel at the site. Then they'd set off a second, often even bigger bomb that would decimate the responders and finish off the initial victims.

Cursing myself for not having thought of it sooner, I bulled my way out into the intersection. Frantically, I scanned the approaches for any large vehicles in the vicinity that might be carrying a follow-on device. Being as I'm six-six, I was able to see over most people's heads. The hair that had been prickling on the back of my neck only settled down when I'd confirmed there weren't any suspicious-looking trucks or buses parked or approaching.

I then got busy helping the other agents assist in aiding the survivors. Singly or in pairs, we took the arms of stunned victims who were staggering around, bloody or burned, and guided them to the medical techs or back to the EMS vehicles. We stooped down to check people lying on the pavements for signs of life. The living we picked up by their arms and legs and rushed to waiting ambulances. The dead we pointed out to the EMS techs, so they could cover up their bodies with the dark blue plasticized tarpaulins that would identify them for the morgue teams.

As if the horrifying sights around us weren't bad enough, a terrible stink hung in the hot, muggy August air over the plaza - a sickening potpourri of burning rubber, fuel, metal, plastic, and human flesh. Though I wasn't a hundred percent positive, I was pretty sure I detected the acrid stench of post-blast plastic explosives mixed in with them as well.

One thing was for certain: the rotten-egg smell that's added to natural gas was totally absent. This was no gas main explosion.

I'd just finished helping a woman whose hair had caught fire. Her hair spray had acted as an accelerant and the flames had burned her bald, searing her scalp into a mass of seeping, swollen pink flesh. She screamed and wept hysterically as I led her to one of the waiting ambulances.

I was returning to the intersection to look for more victims when my dead sister spoke to me.

Look over there, she said.

I stopped in the debris-strewn street, clamped my eyes shut, and blew out an exasperated breath.

Go away, Ofelia, I told her. *Not now, damn it!*

Over there, she insisted. Her voice sounded as if she were standing up close behind me, speaking into my ear in a soft but urgent tone.

When I opened my eyes again, something - don't ask me what - drew them toward the far side of Campus Martius.

A black Cadillac Escalade was parked at the mouth of a side street. As I watched, the SUV pulled out from the curb, turned right onto northbound Woodward, and headed away from the scene. The driver and any passengers were indistinguishable behind the Escalade's dark tinted windows. My eyes followed the car as it rounded the plaza and then went briskly up the boulevard. The distance and intervening wreckage prevented me from making out the plate.

Who was that? I asked her as the Escalade disappeared. But in her usual frustrating way, she clammed up after that.

I wasn't surprised Ofelia spoke to me. She's prone to doing it whenever there's death or dying nearby. Sometimes the things she tells me are helpful. But as often as not they either make no sense at all or end up being blind alleys that go nowhere. I blinked a couple of times, shook my head to clear my mind, and went back to work helping victims.

After a few more minutes it looked like all the injured survivors had either been rushed off or were getting medical assistance, so I decided to see what I could determine about the bus blast.

The fire department teams were still shooting streams of water onto the smoldering wreckage. I got in as near to the bus's mangled rear as I could without getting soaked. Up close I could see there was a twelve-foot deep crater in the asphalt below the area. But once again, there was no hint of natural gas smell from it.

After a couple of minutes Dawson and a handful of other agents came up and joined me.

"It was a bomb, Eric," I said, feeling more and more certain about it now. "Most likely some kind of plastic explosive - C-4 or Semtex. Probably mixed with white phosphorus to get this much fire."

"You're sure?" Dawson said.

"Damn sure," I said. "Which means we've got a terrorist attack here - a Federal crime. Do we take charge of the scene?"

Eric shook his head. "The regional director says to hold off for the moment. At this point we offer all possible assistance to DPD. Try to make sure they follow Federal-level protocols on evidence-gathering and crime scene management. I'll need to speak to whoever's in charge here."

A young black DPD cop was just then hurrying past. Angie Nardella flagged him down. Eric took out his shield and held it up to him.

"FBI, officer," he said. "Who's in charge of the scene?"

"Not sure who's in overall command, sir," the perspiring young cop said. "But my precinct boss is Captain Porter. He's over there."

He pointed toward a big, strapping black guy in a white uniform shirt standing in the center of the plaza. A steady stream of uniformed cops were running up to and away from him as he barked out orders. He had a cell phone in one hand and a bullhorn in the other. Our FBI group hurried over to him.

"Captain Porter?" my boss said as we came up to him. "I'm Eric Dawson, Special Agent in Charge at the local FBI office, and these are my people. We've got a probable terrorist attack here - a Federal crime. But we're going to need to rely on local law enforcement until we can bring in a full investigative team. Can I assume you'll be sealing off the scene and begin doing forensics?"

"Damn straight you can," Porter said. "I've detailed a squad of officers to keep the gawkers back and the media at bay. Soon as the emergency responders get done, I'm going to seal off the entire area. There'll be detectives from my precinct and three others here shortly. They'll do victim ID-ing and evidence-gathering. I've already alerted the state police lab up in Sterling Heights. They're going to send down some techs to help with the onsite work, and they're prepping to do a lot of incoming forensics analysis. The overflow we'll send to their Northville lab."

"Sounds like you're on top of things, Captain," my boss said with a grim, respectful smile. "Listen - do you have anyone with explosives experience coming here?"

"Yeah - Ellis Sidwell. He's DPD's main bomb squad guy. Just talked to him. He's contacting DDOT - the department of transportation. Telling them to stop all downtown bus service, evacuate the buses, and keep people clear until they're inspected for bomb plants. He'll be here shortly."

"Agent Johnson here," Eric said, nodding at me, "has explosives training and a good deal of bomb experience from his military duty. I suggest we have him and Sidwell work together when he gets here."

"Fine by me. For now, you and your people might as well stay here on the plaza. When the precinct detectives get here, they should have enough forensics gear to go around. You can share it."

While there was still plenty of frenetic shouting and running around going on, Porter was as much in control of the situation as anyone in law enforcement could be. Bands of yellow crime scene tape were being stretched around the intersection periphery and beat cops were keeping the growing crowd of gawkers back from the bomb site.

I saw that several TV vans were now parked on the edges of the plaza. I counted five cameramen following spiffily-dressed reporters around as they moved through the crowd, interviewing eyewitnesses. A few others were circling the wreckage, shooting video footage and pretending to not hear the cops trying to shoo them away.

After a couple of minutes, I saw a young, heavyset beat cop duck under the crime scene tape and run over to the plaza where we were standing. He waited to get Porter's attention while the captain was talking to someone in a low voice on his cell phone.

"Sir!" he said, a bit breathlessly, when Porter got off the cell. "Channels Two and Seven News are demanding a statement from the officer in charge!"

"Tell Channels Two and Seven to go shove a tire iron up their butt," Porter told him. "Sideways."

"Yessir!" the young cop said. He turned and began running back.

"Hold it!" Porter said, chuckling. "Come back here, officer!"

"Cancel that order," he said, as the young man returned. "Instead, you tell them this: In fifteen minutes Mayor Bling himself will be here. He'll have a statement for the media then. Now repeat that back to me."

"Yes sir. Mayor Bling - he'll be here in fifteen minutes. And he'll make a statement."

"Close enough. Now you go tell them that, son."

"Yessir!"

Porter chortled again as the young officer ran off. "Damn, I love rookies."

He turned to Eric. "Just talked to Candice Cartwright, the mayor's media whore - oops, I mean communications director. Bling and Chief Bardwell will be here shortly. They'll do a photo and video op - in front of a fire truck or ambulance, not the burnt-up bus or cars. They'll give a short statement and take maybe two or three questions. Bling and Bardwell will probably want you and me standing by them when they do, Dawson. You feebies know for sure this was a terrorist bomb?"

"Agent Johnson here says it was," Eric said, nodding my way. "That's good enough for me."

The precinct detectives and forensics techs showed up a few minutes before the mayor and chief did. So did DPD's head bomb specialist, Detective Ellis Sidwell. Eric and Porter formed everyone up into teams and told us to get started. When the bigwigs showed, the two of them went off to do their dog-and-pony for the media. The regular forensic teams began working with the morgue crews on the grim job of ID-ing corpses and gathering up body parts. Meanwhile, Sidwell and I and a couple of other bomb techs from the FBI office set to work doing the explosive forensics.

Sidwell was a fortyish, freckle-faced bulldog of a man, who looked like he did weight training. He spoke in a soft voice, with a strong southern accent. I soon discovered that, like me, he'd been on an Army Explosive Ordnance Disposal team, but had done three full tours of EOD duty to my one: two in Iraq and one in Afghanistan. When I heard that, it induced a kind of awe in me toward the man.

"Being around bombs doesn't make your stomach queasy?" I asked him.

He laughed. "Stomach? Naw. Hits me lower down. I've had to hose out my bomb suit more than once after a disarm."

We started off by examining the blown-out rear of the bus. The explosion had left it looking like a giant claw of fire-blackened metal, with wisps of gray smoke still rising up between its jagged talons. Its big diesel engine had even been blasted out of its compartment and had crashed through two cars behind it, hideously mutilating the occupants it had killed.

"We can see the explosion originated in the engine compartment," I said. "Which means they must've somehow planted the charge when the bus was being serviced."

"Makes sense," Sidwell said. "I seem to recall there's a big bus yard on the near west side. Probably where they do the servicing. I'll tell Porter to send a couple of detectives over there right quick. Check out the employees and see what they can come up with. Maybe they've got security cams that might've caught something."

While he went off to talk to the police captain, I crawled down into the still-steaming crater under the bus' rear. Although much of it was water-soaked, I found some dry areas. I picked up a handful of the smaller rubble. It was hot on my palm as I held it to my nose. Raw plastic explosives are scentless, but there's a characteristic after-smell. I was still sniffing at it when Sidwell came back.

"When I first got here I was pretty sure I could smell C-4 or Semtex after-blast in the air," I told him. "And possibly white phosphorus. This debris has the same smell."

"A shake and bake, then," he said as I climbed out of the crater. "Makes sense from the kind of damage we're seeing."

"Shake and bake" is GI slang for combining or alternating conventional explosives with incendiaries. It's a highly effective killing combo.

"One thing's for sure," I said as we began walking around with the retractable tape measure he'd brought, measuring out blast vectors from the epicenter. "This was no crude IED."

"No argument there," Sidwell agreed as he surveyed the scene. "Guys who built this bomb are at least semi-pro. They've had special ops-level training somewhere."

As I've already mentioned, I'd disarmed about a fifty IEDs during my tour of duty in Iraq, when I was an EOD team lead. Though highly lethal in their own right, there was no comparison to today's bomb. The device that destroyed the Woodward bus and surrounding cars was exponentially more powerful - the work of someone who had access to high-quality explosives and sophisticated technology for detonating them.

"Man, I just had a nasty thought," Sidwell said as we were tape-measuring the distance from the blown-out engine back to the blast epicenter.

"What's that?" I asked.

His eyes were grim. "How many more of these suckers do the sons of bitches have?" he said.

Our crime scene work continued well on into the night. Since most of the streetlights in the immediate area were blown out by the blast, big tripod-mounted floodlights were brought in and set up. They cast an eerie glow on the scene as the various law enforcement personnel crawled over, under, and around all the twisted and incinerated vehicles.

There were about thirty-five of us in all. Forensic specialists from the Michigan state police labs in Sterling Heights and Northville were there in force. A few others straggled in later, from labs as far away as Grand Rapids, to help out. Every bit of evidence we found was bagged, tagged, and logged. Both Dawson and Porter were adamant about keeping a tight chain of custody - making sure that correct protocols were followed so there'd be no evidence contamination.

I was thankful the work was just about non-stop. There was no time to spare to experience the rage, horror, and grief that might otherwise have overcome me. But I could tell they were there, alright. Churning below the surface of my mind and down deep in the pit of my belly.

Around 10 p.m. some downtown area vendors showed up with free food, coffee, soft drinks, and spring water for the folks working the scene. At the food truck I grabbed a sandwich and coffee and then went up to Dawson and Porter. Wilson and Nardella were with them.

"Anyone claiming responsibility yet?" I asked.

"So far, just the nutcases," Porter said.

"Charlie Sheen?" Wilson said. "Lindsay Lohan?"

"A couple have called the media," Porter went on. "A couple DPD. No one credible yet."

"I talked to Homeland Security in Washington a few minutes ago," Eric said. "They told me CIA found a Pakistani jihadist group claiming responsibility on their website. But they don't give it much credence. News reports on the bombing are already worldwide now. They think the group's just trying to make themselves look like they're hot stuff."

"There you go," Nardella said. "Pump up that resume."

Sidwell came up alongside me then, ham sandwich and spring water in his hands.

"So what've you two high-class bomb experts found out so far?" Porter asked us.

Sidwell shrugged. "Not much, unfortunately. Just that it was pro-quality work. Guy who built it is no amateur."

"Find anything in the debris that'll help us track the perps down?" Dawson asked.

"No," I said. "Other than the fact that they've somehow gotten their hands on high-grade military or commercial explosives and detonators."

"And they have the smarts to make some dang nasty cocktails out of them," Sidwell added.

"What about sources for the bomb materials? Could they be local?" Porter said.

"We'll work together with ATF to check it out," I said. "Start with Michigan and then work outwards, to adjoining states. Maybe even Canada, since it's right next door here. Some contractors have access to high-grade commercial plastic explosives. Mainly building demolition companies. It's all pretty tightly controlled - especially since nine-eleven. But it's probably worth making them double-check their inventories to be sure nothing's gone missing."

"Any chances of it coming from local military bases?" Dawson suggested. "Selfridge or one of the National Guard bases?"

"Not likely," I said. "Not the particular kind of ordnance they'd have on hand."

"Chances are the ATF and FBI guys will be able to trace down the manufacturer of the plastic component with spectrographic analysis," Sidwell said between sips of water. "They're required to put detection agents in all the explosives they produce. But that still won't tell us how it got here and got put into a sophisticated bomb."

"Right," I said. "The bad news is that I don't think we're going to get very far identifying the perps by doing bomb analysis. That's why I was asking about the responsibility claims. Letters or even emails to the authorities or media might be more likely to give us something we can use to track them down fast."

"Assuming they're credible," Dawson added.

"Do you guys think this bomb correlates with that one from last week?" Porter asked. "The one killed those hot rodders up in Warren?"

"There's no proof as of yet," I said. "But my guess is that they're related, alright."

"I agree," Sidwell said. "When I heard about that deuce coupe being blown up, it didn't seem to make any sense at all. But it does now."

"How so?" Porter asked.

"Practice run for this one," Sidwell said.

"I think blowing up that hot rod was the bombers' baby steps," I said. "This one today was a big, bad stomp saying 'Here we are!'"

"And the next ones," Sidwell said with a rueful grimace, "could be some real nut-kickers."

We all looked at each other grimly. But had no idea at the time how prophetic his words would prove to be.

Chapter 8   Nasty Surprise

Tuesday, August 16 - 4:20 p.m.

ON THE afternoon following the downtown bombing I was driving home, dog-tired from being up for the past thirty-some hours. As I made my way up the crowded Lodge freeway, I went over the meager progress we'd made.

Sidwell and I had worked the bomb scene until almost midnight. After that we went up to the state police science lab in Sterling Heights together. We spent the rest of the night looking over the shoulders of the forensic specialists and asking questions about the high-tech tests they were running on the evidence that had been gathered. One thing the techs came up with was bad news: the plastic explosive used was Semtex, rather than C-4. C-4 is a predominantly Made in USA product. The explosive being Semtex meant it was more likely sourced overseas - which would make it that much more difficult to track down the manufacturer.

Around 6 a.m. I went back downtown to the Federal building. When I wasn't in one of the emergency group meetings or phone conferences with DC that kept getting called, I was telephoning all my local counterterrorism contacts. None had the slightest clue about the perps or their motive. The bus bombing had taken everyone in the Detroit-area security apparatus by complete surprise.

By around 3:30 in the afternoon, I and most of the other agents were just about cross-eyed with exhaustion, despite all the caffeine we kept dumping into ourselves. That's when Dawson told me, Wilson, Nardella, and some of the other senior agents to go home, take a shower, grab a couple hours of sleep, and come back in at 9 p.m. in the evening.

On my way home I recalled that there wasn't much in the refrigerator of my Southfield condo, so I decided to stop at a neighborhood deli. Located in a strip mall, Have A Cow is owned and run by a congenial fifty-something couple named Solomon and Rachel Bronstein. When I went in, Sol was working the deli counter while Rachel worked the register. Rachel was ringing up a stooped, henna-rinsed lady who looked to be about ninety. The old woman stared at me as I walked past.

"So who's the big hottie *shvartser mentsh*?" I heard her say.

"Selma, you hussy!" Rachel hissed. "Be quiet! That's Agent Johnson. He's FBI."

"Izzat so? Hey, J. Edgar," she called after me. "You wanna come arrest me sometime?"

I turned back and gave her a sleepy-eyed grin.

"Only if you've been a bad girl," I said.

"I'm a pinko commie liberal," she rasped, putting a liver-spotted hand on her arthritic hip. "Through and through. Does that count?"

"Afraid not, ma'am. You've gotta be more evil than that."

She sighed and picked up her mesh shopping bag. "Story of my life," she said as she hobbled out.

"Hey, Sol," I said, approaching the counter. "How's the pastrami today?"

"To be honest, Mr. Johnson, a bit on the fatty side. I'd say go for the milk baloney or roast beef instead."

"Okay, make it roast beef. Three pounds, please."

He pulled the brisket out of the cooler and placed it on the slicer.

"You're looking tired, Mr. Johnson," he said as he began cutting. "I imagine you're working on that terrible bombing downtown?"

"Yeah," I said. "Was just about to leave work yesterday when the bomb went off. Heard it from our office up in the McNamara Building and went down there with some of the other agents to see if we could help."

"Bet it was some kind of nightmare," Rachel said.

"It was," I said with a nod, but without elaborating. "When we realized it was a bomb, we worked with the DPD to secure the scene and start investigating. Was at it all night and most of the day today. Heading home now to shower and grab a couple of hours sleep."

"We saw it on the TV news last night," Rachel said from the register, shaking her head sadly. "All those poor people killed. What a horror for their families. Breaks your heart."

"So who was it?" Sol asked. "Terrorists?"

"Seems the most likely explanation," I said. "But so far there've been no claims of responsibility. Credible ones, at least."

"Who would do some terrible, *meshuggeneh* thing like that?" he said, shaking his head as he sliced. "Some crazy Al-Qaeda or Hezbollah schmuck?"

"No idea as of yet," I said. "Could be foreign-based. Could be domestics with ties to foreign organizations. Or it could be completely homegrown. It's all conjecture at this point."

"You'll find them and stop them," Rachel said. "Sol and I have faith in you."

"Thanks, Rachel," I said. "It may not be me personally, but we'll get them, alright. I just hope we can do it before they claim any more victims."

After paying for my roast beef and a loaf of egg bread, I left the deli and headed off toward my place.

When I'd divorced three years back my ex, Vonessa, had gotten our house in Farmington Hills. Then she and her new husband had sold it and moved down to Atlanta. The Southfield condo I now lived in was bland but comfortable, with easy access to the freeway for my daily commute downtown.

I turned on the radio as I drove.

"Two more victims died in the hospital today, bringing the death toll from yesterday's devastating bus bombing to sixty-three. Authorities say forensic experts have now linked the Woodward bomb to the mysterious hot rod bombing in Warren last week. Community officials throughout metro Detroit are trying to dispel the sense of panic that many citizens are-"

Since radio news wasn't about to tell me anything I didn't already know, I switched over to a music channel. It was an oldies station, playing Marvin Gaye's "Inner City Blues." I let myself sink into its sinuous, elegant groove for the rest of the ride home.

As I was coming up to my condo complex, I recalled my words to the Bronsteins about stopping the bombers. What I hadn't let on to them was how shook up I felt inside about the Woodward bombing. In all the hectic busyness of the aftermath and the emergency status we were now on, I'd kept my feelings at bay. But now that I was away from the investigation, the weight of failure was tumbling down on me like a ton of bricks.

In the years since nine-eleven, the Bureau - along with plenty of other Federal, state, and local authorities - had successfully prevented any major terrorist attacks against our domestic population. But this one had gotten right by us.

I knew damn well feeling bad about what had happened was an unprofessional waste of time, but it wasn't something I could just turn off like a faucet. Ever since my sister was murdered - back when I was just a kid - I've lived my life with the sense that I could've and should've done more to stop innocent people from being victimized. And sure - I've brought a fair number of killers to justice over the course of that time. But it's always felt like it was too damn little, too damn late.

Look over there.

Ofelia's words and that black Escalade I'd seen on the far side of Campus Martius came back to me. What had she been trying to tell me? Were the bombers inside? Should I have run like hell across the plaza, commandeered a car and gone after it?

Or was I just giving myself one more reason to feel like a dad-blamed failure?

At the condo complex, I pulled into the lot and parked in my numbered slot. With briefcase and deli bag in my hands, I headed for my unit. I was coming up the walk when I froze in my tracks.

The front door was sitting wide open.

My groggy mind snapped awake and began racing. There was no way in hell I'd left it that way yesterday morning.

The only person besides me who had a key was Nadine Robinson - an ex-girlfriend I hadn't seen hide nor hair of in six months.

I remembered that the condo management company kept a spare key back in their office. One they might give to some repairman if there was an emergency problem at the condo. But there's no way they'd do that without notifying me first.

In the course of my career - first as a Chicago cop, and later as an FBI special agent - I've made plenty of enemies. Some of them extremely nasty people. It wouldn't be the first time some dirtbag I'd helped put away for a few years dropped by for an unannounced visit.

Keeping my eyes on the open door, I quietly laid down my briefcase and deli bag on the grass along the walkway.

I reached under the arm of my jacket, pulled my Springfield .45 out of its shoulder holster, and nudged off the safety.

With a two-handed grip, the barrel pointed skyward, I edged toward the condo door.

I stepped up onto the porch and squinted into the darkened entranceway. Head cocked, I strained to pick out any sounds of movement. But it was silent as a tomb inside.

I stepped over the threshold into the foyer and listened. Nothing.

The living room was a couple more steps to my right. When I got to the entrance, I leveled the Springfield and assumed a shooting stance. I swept left, then right. Nothing.

I brought the gun back to my shoulder, barrel again pointing up, and continued tiptoeing down the hall. The hardwood floor gave out faint but maddening creaks with every step.

When I reached the bathroom, I edged the door open with the toe of my shoe. The hinges gave out a long, munchkin-like squeak as it swung inward. No one behind the door. No shadows in the glassed-in shower. Clear.

Next was the bedroom. The door was open. I used my shoe to push it all the way back to the wall to be sure no one was behind it. Then I stepped inside, checked the closet and under the bed. Clear.

I passed the doorway to the basement. The door was open a few inches and a pair of yellowish eyes shone at me from the shadows at the foot of the stairwell. The Thing.

That's right, I silently told him. Hide down there in the dark, you worthless bag of skunk farts. But the fact was, I was glad he was safe.

The last room on the ground floor was the kitchen. As I crept up to it, my back to the wall, I thought I heard someone humming. The hum sounded female and disturbingly familiar. Tightening my grip on the pistol, I stepped into the open entranceway.

Seated at my kitchen table, in a frilly white bra and thong panty set, was Nadine Robinson - AKA Nasty Nadine - wife of Deputy Detroit Police Chief Harlan Robinson III.

The chair she was in was tipped back and her bare feet were up on the table. Her iPhone lay there as well, white audio cable running to the buds in her ears. She was humming along to the music it was playing. The sight of my drawn .45 didn't seem to faze her at all. She wiggled her pink-nailed toes at me in greeting.

"Hello, McCoy," she said, pulling the white buds out of her ears. "Remember me?"

Chapter 9   A Blast From The Past

Tuesday, August 16 - 4:45 p.m.

"UNFORTUNATELY, YES," I said, safetying the Springfield and slipping it back into my shoulder holster.

She pouted, pushing her lower lip out at me. It was as full, pink, and lush as I remembered it.

"Come on now, McCoy. I'm real happy to see you. Aren't you just a *tiny* bit pleased to see little old Nadine again?"

"Not particularly," I said.

She had her arms folded across her chest, purposely pushing up her generous décolletage until it was almost spilling out of the white bra. The lingerie looked French and expensive.

"Listen," I said. "I'm going back outside for a minute. While I'm doing that, you can get your clothes back on, hear?"

I went back outside and retrieved my briefcase and deli bag. I left the briefcase in the living room and headed down the hall. When I got back to the kitchen she hadn't moved. Still had her pretty little feet on my kitchen table and that same lecherous grin on her face.

"Damn it, Nadine-"

Shaking my head in annoyance, I walked over to the kitchen counter. Her hand snaked out and stroked my trousered thigh as I passed.

At the counter, I unpacked the roast beef and egg bread and began making my sandwich.

"Hey, honey man," she said to my back. "Do you remember our first time together?"

It wasn't the kind of thing you easily forget. That Labor Day weekend barbecue last year, at the Robinsons' big, fancy home in Palmer Woods. Must've been forty people there. With her in that outfit - skintight white shorts, orange halter top, and tall platform shoes - blatantly displaying her fit, luscious body. I'd asked her where the bathroom was. Told me she'd take me inside and show me. Her sweet, round behind swaying seductively as she led me upstairs to their elegant, oversized bathroom - all pink marble, with a huge Jacuzzi tub. I took a leak and when I came out again, she was standing there grinning. Led me back inside, locked the door behind us and knelt down. Drove me just about crazy before I pulled her to her feet and pushed down her shorts and the tiniest thong panties I'd ever seen. When I lifted her up onto the pink marble counter alongside the sink and spread her thighs, she was wet and ready. As we went at it, she was like a female cat in the grip of some wild, feverish heat. Snarling one second, whimpering the next. Arching, writhing, and clenching at me until she got off, biting down on the fleshy part of her hand to keep from crying out too loud.

"I remember," I said, not looking at her. Pissed that I'd fallen for her gambit and let myself get aroused.

"So how've you been these past few months, McCoy?" she said behind me.

"I'm doing just fine, Nadine. Except for this case I'm on right now, life is calm. Life is good."

"Got yourself a new girlfriend?" she asked.

"Not for a while," I said. "Probably why things have been calm and good."

I turned around and found her standing two feet away, leering up at me.

"Care for a roast beef sandwich before you go?" I said, doing my best to yank my eyeballs up out of her cleavage.

"Not the kind of beef I'm interested in at the moment, honey man," she said, glancing down at my crotch as she stepped closer.

Damn. I felt my face and body flush with heat. Those scanty strips of white against her voluptuous, honey-brown body. I'd almost managed to forget how drop-dead gorgeous Nadine was. I could feel my fingers twitching with desire to grab hold of her. To pull her close, kiss her, savor the feel of her in my hands, and then take her, right here and now. Maybe on that kitchen table...

"Listen, Nadine," I said, my mouth cotton-dry. "I think you better go. *Now.*"

"How come you gotta play so hard to get, McCoy?" she said. Putting her arms akimbo, she arched her back and thrust out her bosom at me. "We spend a few juicy minutes together making each other feel good. I leave. You stay. You're happy. I'm happy. What's the problem, honey man?"

"What about Harlan the Three?" I asked, using the standard Detroit cops' nickname for their deputy chief. "Otherwise known as your husband?"

She chuckled. "Honey, don't you worry none about Harley. Little old Nadine keeps him happy. Plenty happy."

"Not to mention half the DPD?" I said, hoping the insult would cool her jets a mite.

"Honey man, you know that ain't so. I get around alright, but I pick only the cream of the crop. Like you, daddy," she said, putting her hand on my belly.

"Nadine-"

Her hand began to move down.

"You want me to beg for it, honey man?" she said, moving in closer. "Is that what'll turn you on? 'Cause you know I'll do it. I'll get down on my knees right now and I'll-"

Just then my cell phone rang. Nadine got a startled look on her face and I stepped away from her. On the second ring I punched the answer icon and jammed it up to my ear.

"McCoy?" It was my boss.

"Hey, Eric. What's up?"

"There's an emergency meeting. I need you to get downtown immediately."

"Where to?" I said. "McNamara?"

"No," he said. "DPD headquarters. Thirteen hundred Beaubien. Fifth floor, the chief's office. ASAP."

"What's going down?" I began. But Dawson had already hung up.

I turned to Nadine. She had a disappointed smirk on her lips.

"That was my boss. I've got to head downtown right now. It's about the bombings."

She sighed. "Just about had you there, didn't I, McCoy?" she said.

"If it's any comfort to you, yes, you did. But why don't you head home to your husband now?"

"Well, for one reason," she said, "dimes to donuts old Harley's going to be the same place you're headed to."

I realized she was probably right.

"Then I guess you'll just have to find some other guy to keep company with. But I don't suppose that'll be too much of a problem, will it?" I said.

"Tsk-tsk, McCoy," she said, tossing her head. "Sticks and stones may break my bones, but insinuating I'm a slut will never hurt me."

"I've got to go," I said, pushing the oversized sandwich I'd made into a ziplock bag. "Put your duds on and get yourself out of here."

With an ironic smile on her face, she stood there in her skimpy undies and watched as I hastily opened and dumped a couple of cans of dog food into the Thing's bowl.

"Don't know what the problem is with that big old homely 'fraidy cat of yours," she said. "She took one look at me when I let myself in and scooted off down to the basement, like always. Never have understood why I terrify her so bad."

"It's a he, Nadine. A tomcat. Probably figures you're going to come on to him and runs for his life. Critter's got more sense than I did."

"Only tomcat I'm interested in around here is you, McCoy."

"Yeah, well my tomcatting days are over, Nadine. With you, at least," I said, heading out of the kitchen.

In the doorway I stopped and turned.

"And by the way," I added. "You can leave my house key on the kitchen table before you go. Then just close the front door. It'll lock behind you."

She put a forefinger to her luscious lower lip.

"Hmm - house key. House key. What *did* I do with that house key, I wonder?"

"I don't have time for this, Nadine. Leave it on the kitchen table when you go. And don't come by again."

She put one hand beneath a breast and the other to the crotch of her skimpy panties.

"Mmm - you *know* rejection turns me on, don't you?" she said, clenching her belly and grinding her hips at me.

"Nadine-" I began. But then realized it was pointless.

I spun around and hurried down the hall, sandwich bag in hand.

"Key on the table!" I called back to her, as forcefully as I could. "And don't come around here again, you hear?"

Desirable as she was, I wanted to be done with this damn woman. Wanted her out of my life, once and for all.

But the throaty giggle I heard from back in the kitchen did not sound promising.

Five minutes later I was on the John C. Lodge freeway, taking a healthy chomp out of my roast beef sandwich as I drove back downtown.

Around West McNichols, traffic became stop-and-go due to some road work up ahead. As I crawled along in the backup, my mouth twisted into a scowl at the thought of Nadine showing up at my condo like that.

After our session at the barbecue, I'd had a five-month affair with her. If that's what you'd call meeting for hot and heavy twenty-minute to one-hour sexual trysts at all kinds of crazy times and places.

I'd heard plenty about "Nasty Nadine" Robinson long before I actually met her. That she was a notorious cop groupie. That she kept a string of hookups going with two or three policemen at all times. That except for their all being cops, she didn't discriminate. Got it on with guys regardless of race, ethnicity, religion, or rank. Beat cops, detectives, officials - Federal, state, or local - any male with a police shield who happened to get her tingle going was fair game for Nadine.

Until that day at the barbecue, I'd had no intention of joining the crowd. But what I hadn't counted on was just how damned alluring she'd be in the flesh. It was one thing to say no in the abstract, but quite another to say it when confronted with that body, that face, and that horny "let's do it right here, right now" appetite of hers.

Eventually, though, it just got too weird for me. The fact that I was balling another man's wife began to stick too bad in my craw. For a while I rationalized it by reminding myself that Vonessa had put a nice, big set of antlers on me, back when I was married. But over time it all got to feeling too wrong. Too sleazy. Too dishonorable.

On that evening six months ago when I'd told her we were through being lovers, Nadine didn't seem surprised. She didn't argue or try to talk me out of it. Just laughed and pretty much sloughed it off.

"Your loss, honey man," she'd told me with a sassy smile on her face. "There's plenty other men-fish in the sea, you know."

"Yeah," I agreed. "Whole schools of them, I hear. But I reckon you know all about that."

For six months after that last meeting she'd kept her distance. No calls. No surprise visits. Even though she'd had my condo key all along.

So just what exactly had motivated her to come by and use it again today?

Chapter 10   Into The Weasel Cage

Tuesday, August 16 - 5:40 p.m.

1300 BEAUBIEN is the Detroit Police Department's headquarters. Built back in the Twenties, it was designed by Albert Kahn, the architect responsible for a passel of the Detroit area's signature buildings. Unfortunately, ninety years of city grime have turned the facade into a smudged gray eyesore, while the inside has grown more and more dilapidated. There were plans afoot to move the HQ into an abandoned downtown casino building, but that was at least a couple of years off yet.

I parked on the edge of Greektown, which is just around the corner, and went inside. When I got up to the fifth floor, I found Wilson pacing in the hallway. He was in one of his Seventies-style polyester leisure suits, this one a stylish zucchini-green number. He looked about as tired and strung-out as I supposed I did.

"Hey, Mojo," he said as I went up to him. Wilson was the only agent in the office who persisted in using the old nickname, despite my having repeatedly told him to cease and desist.

"What's up?" I said. "You been in there?"

"Yeah. Dawson's inside, with a bunch of bigwigs. I saw the mayor and some county execs come in the back entrance, under state trooper escort. I heard a rumor something big went down in the last couple of hours. But nobody's talking about just what it is yet."

"What are they waiting for, you think?"

"As I understand it, you."

"Me? Jesus, let's go in, then."

We hurried into the chief's office. It was more than a bit disconcerting to walk in and find Nadine's husband, Harlan the Three, standing there in his deputy police chief's blues. Especially when he spotted me and came over. He was a lanky dude, with a shaved head, mustache, and shiny, straightforward eyes.

"Good to see you again, Johnson," he said, smiling as he shook my hand. "Don't think I've seen you since our barbecue last year. There's a conference room just down the hall. We're about to get started. Been waiting on you."

"Sorry," I said, my face hot with discomfort. "Construction backup on the freeway coming in."

I tried to shake the weirdness of it as he led us down the hall. The guy deserves better than Nadine, I thought. Not to mention better acquaintances than me.

The conference room was a large, gray-walled space with windows that overlooked Beaubien. The shades were partially drawn to block out the bright early-evening sun. There were about twenty people in the room. Up near the front of the conference table sat Benjamin Bling, the mayor of Detroit. Given the Woodward Avenue disaster, I wasn't surprised to see him there. What did surprise me was to see all three of the area's county executives in the room. Seated beside the mayor was L. Sparks Cunningham, the Oakland County executive. Across from them I recognized Richard Sorenson and George Gates, the respective Wayne and Macomb County execs. Detroit proper sits inside Wayne, but the three counties together make up the overall metro area.

My boss was sitting next to Cunningham. He motioned for me and Wilson to take the two empty chairs across from him.

The only woman in the room was an attractive, high-strung-looking blonde who I recognized as Candice Cartwright, Mayor Bling's communications director. She was sitting at the foot of the conference table, in a navy blue business suit, glowering as she thumb-punched a message into her smartphone.

Everyone else in the room looked to be metro area municipal police chiefs, county sheriffs, or other senior public safety officials. Some I recognized, some not. Among those I did know was Joe Bardwell, the DPD chief, who stood up then at the head of the table and began the meeting.

"For those of you who haven't seen copies yet, I'm going to read the letter the mayor and the three county execs received today."

He held a sheet of paper and read from it.

"'Greetings, infidel, from Al-Qaeda in Detroit.'"

Eric, Wilson, and I exchanged glances, the same troubling question in our eyes. Al-Qaeda in Detroit?

"'By now you will have seen our handiwork,'" Bardwell went on. "Kowalski and Godwin in Warren, and the massacre on Woodward Avenue are just the beginning.'

"'We have hundreds of IEDs in our arsenal and dozens of devoted martyrs ready to place and detonate them.'

"'Detroit is a sick, dying city and we are eager to speed its death.'

"'But in deference to All-Merciful Allah, we are going to give you the opportunity to spare great numbers of your infidel citizens.'

"'Assemble fifteen million Swiss francs in thousand-franc banknotes and ten million euros in five-hundred-euro bills. Transfer the cash to us according to our forthcoming instructions and the bombings will cease.'

"'You have 24 hours to reply and 48 hours to come up with the money.'

"'In two days copies of this letter - including the addressees' names - will be sent to all local media outlets. It will thus be made clear to the public that you are culpable for the carnage that is coming, should you fail to meet our demands.'

"'We will expect your answer in tomorrow's Detroit News classifieds. The answer will be "To AQID - we accept your offer."'

"'To show that we mean business, the bombings will continue until the money is in our hands. The next one will be later today, in a suburban community. Many so-called "innocents" will die.'

"'We await your answer.'

"Signed, 'Al-Qaeda in Detroit.'"

Bardwell set the letter on the table and sat back down.

"There you have it, ladies and gentlemen," he said. "Twenty-five million in foreign cash to them in forty-eight hours. Or more bombings. The fact that they sent it to the three county execs, as well as the mayor here, makes it clear they're threatening not just the city, but the Greater Detroit metro area."

"How much does that money translate to in US dollars?" Mayor Bling asked.

"At current exchange rates, it comes to twenty-eight and three-quarter million, US," Candice Cartwright said, reading from her smartphone. She'd apparently looked it up online.

"Why do you think they're demanding foreign currency?" one of the municipal police chiefs asked. "Why not dollars?"

"Probably due to the weight, sir," I said. "Hundred dollar bills are our largest denomination. A million dollars in hundreds weighs about twenty-two pounds, so twenty-five million would weigh over a quarter of a ton."

"Could I see the letter, Chief?" I went on. "And can I assume that's a copy, not an original?"

"It's a copy," he said, passing it over to me.

"The originals were all dusted and sent to the state police lab for analysis," Eric explained as I read through the extortion letter. "In addition to the execs' or their admin people's fingerprints, there was another set of prints found. They were sent on to Washington a little while ago."

I frowned as I re-read the letter. Something about it was off.

"So what do you Feds know about this 'Al-Qaeda in Detroit' group?" one of the county sheriffs asked.

I looked up. Since I'm one of the counterterrorism leads at the local office, I caught Eric's eye and answered when he gave me a nod.

"Sheriff, the Bureau has a very extensive network of informants and operatives working the Detroit metro area. I can assure you this is the first we've heard of any such organization."

At that Candice Cartwright looked up from her smartphone.

"Could the FBI members present explain this kind of lapse in your intelligence efforts?" she said, her voice icy-cool.

"Duh - guess we were too busy downloading Internet porn and playing Grand Theft Auto," Wilson said. "Slipped right by us. You know how it is."

Cartwright stared stilettos at him.

"I really don't understand how you can sit there and smart-mouth about this, Agent," she said. "Seems to me the fact that sixty-some people are dead should be taken seriously."

"Oh, I do take it seriously, ma'am," he said. "What I don't take seriously is finger-pointing by self-appointed critics who don't know squat about what we're up against. Especially by self-righteous, bottle-blonde bimb-"

"I think what Agent Wilson means," Eric hastily interjected, "is that, while it's not well known, in the past several years we've successfully interdicted a half dozen terrorist plots targeting the Detroit area."

"But this one got by you," Cartwright said. "Obviously."

Eric spread his hands. "I concede the point, Ms. Cartwright."

"So do you think this Al-Qaeda in Detroit is some sleeper cell that's just surfaced?" Harlan Robinson asked.

"I suppose it's possible, sir," I said. "But from what I'm reading here, it sounds more to me like the primary motive is criminal extortion. The Muslim aspect may just be a red herring to throw us off."

"Red herring? What makes you think that?" Bardwell asked.

"The language, sir. Every jihadist communications I've ever seen contains some kind of very explicit political or religious rationale. Even though this one uses some Islamic terminology, in effect all it's saying is, 'give us money or we kill lots of people.'"

"So you're saying you think it's from a lone criminal or criminal gang, rather than from a jihadist group?" Mayor Bling asked.

"Based on what I'm seeing in this letter, that would be my guess, your honor," I said.

"But how can you be sure?" Bardwell asked. "What if it really is some jihadist cell? What if they're trying to get money to finance more attacks?"

"I wouldn't completely discount that possibility, Chief," I said. "But as I said, the lack of political or religious justification makes me skeptical it's a true Islamist threat."

Just then L. Sparks Cunningham, the Oakland County exec, piped up.

"You all realize Dream Cruise is just four days from now, right?" he said. He looked and sounded impatient and edgy, his jowly, pink face flushed with a bit of purple.

I stared at him, blinking. The truth was, in all the craziness of the past twenty-four hours, I hadn't even made the connection.

The annual Woodward Avenue Dream Cruise was scheduled for the coming weekend. It would draw over a million people to the various municipalities along the broad boulevard. There they'd either line up along the road to watch or "cruise" among the forty thousand-plus vintage and high performance autos that would go rumbling up and down several miles of Woodward's northern stretches, all of which lie in Oakland County. The possibility of an attack on a crowd that huge added a whole new level of gut-churning unease to what was already a bad situation.

"Sir, there's no direct threat to the Cruise mentioned in the letter," Ray Wapshot, the Oakland County Sheriff, pointed out to Cunningham.

"But the potential's certainly there," I said.

"Especially if they don't get this payoff they're demanding," Mayor Bling said.

"Maybe Dream Cruise should be cancelled this year, sir," I said to Cunningham.

L. Sparks' florid face went deathly pale. He looked at me like I'd just suggested he ax-murder his grandkids.

"Cancel Dream Cruise?" he said. You could see the mere notion was giving him a severe Maalox Moment.

"Matter of public safety, sir," I said.

"Isn't going to happen, Agent," he said, shaking his head. "Not something that brings fifty million much-needed dollars into the local economy. We'll just have to go all out on security this year. Do the whole blasted thing under armed guard if we have to."

He looked around at Sheriff Wapshot and the police chiefs of the various Oakland County municipalities. They all nodded. L. Sparks had been county exec since around biblical times, and none were about to contradict him.

"Besides," he went on. "Bombing's a Federal crime, right? Seems to me this whole bomb-threat thing is fundamentally a Federal government problem."

"I think Sparks is absolutely right," said Bling. "What kind of resources are the FBI and other Federal agencies going to devote to the search for these terrorists?"

For just an instant my eyes met Dawson's across the table. It was obvious what the local politicians wanted. To make sure the Bureau and other Federal departments took as much blame as possible for whatever death toll the bombers managed to exact.

"In addition to the sixty agents and technicians in our field office, there are twenty Federal special agents en route to Detroit as we speak, sir," Eric said. "From the CIA and Homeland Security as well as the Bureau. The specialists will include forensics experts and profilers, plus investigative manpower.

"When they arrive," he went on, "I'll be coordinating their efforts out of our office in the McNamara building. Agent Johnson here will be team lead on the investigation. Agent Wilson will be his assistant and backup. Both have training and experience in tracking down terrorists and mass murderers. Agent Johnson here has also had substantial experience with explosive devices."

"What kind of experience, Agent Johnson?" Chief Bardwell asked.

"Both military and Bureau training, sir," I said. "I attended the FBI Hazardous Devices School at Redstone Arsenal in Alabama. I also had training and a year of bomb squad duty in Iraq with my National Guard unit. All told, I've had extensive hands-on with both standard explosives and IEDs - that's improvised explosive devices."

"And he still has both of them," Wilson said. "Hands, I mean." Only one police chief chortled.

"In the course of my bomb work, I've also done a fair amount of post-blast forensics," I added.

"Did you do any of the forensic work on the Woodward bus blast?" one of the sheriffs asked.

"Yes, sir. Worked with Ellis Sidwell, of the DPD. We did onsite testing and analysis at the blast site. We also collected and transported a lot of forensic evidence to the state police crime lab in Sterling Heights. Same lab that did the analysis on the Warren hot rod bombing."

"What do we know about the MO on the bombings?" another chief asked.

"So far they've used powerful, relatively sophisticated explosive devices. Semtex plastic-based charges, mixed with white phosphorus for additional incendiary effect. Either taped or attached magnetically to the impacted vehicles. Detonation has been by remote control, either by line-of-sight electronic devices or possibly via cell phones."

"Excuse me, gentlemen," Mayor Bling said. "I know we've got a lot of law enforcement expertise here in the room. But rather than get into police work details, I'd like to focus a bit on some other aspects of the situation."

"The first thing I'd like to know," he went on, turning to Dawson, "is what does the FBI advise we do about the extortion demands?"

"We play along, your honor," Eric said. "We place the ad in tomorrow's paper agreeing to the payoff. When the bornbers contact us, we try to stall for more time. In the meantime, Federal, state, and local law enforcement go all out to identify them, track them down, and stop them."

"Fair enough," the mayor said. "Second. How do we deal with the media on this? What exactly do we tell them?"

"I'd suggest we tell them an extortion demand has been received," I said. "That'll assure people we're looking at terrorist criminals here, rather than religiously-motivated terrorists. It may help reduce potential violence toward the Arab and Muslim community."

"I don't know why you're so worried about the Muslim community, Agent Johnson," Cunningham said. "Seems to me there's still a pretty good chance there are some involved in this."

"That may be, sir. But as you probably know, metro Detroit has the largest Arab population in America. The vast majority are law-abiding citizens who want nothing to do with the radical jihadists. We don't need an upsurge of anti-Islamic or anti-Arab violence distracting us from the real mission here."

"Not sure if you heard," said Ed Wilkins, the Wayne County Sheriff, "but there've already been some assaults on local Arabs."

"And somebody threw a Molotov cocktail into an Arab-owned business in Clawson last night," said one of the police chiefs.

"Then I think your point's well-taken, Agent Johnson," the mayor said. "So let's get on to the third item. How do we come up with the money? The City of Detroit sure the heck doesn't have a spare twenty-nine mill lying around."

"Maybe you could dip into your election war chest, Ben," Cunningham said with a snarky grin.

Bling scoffed. "Chump change compared to what you've probably got in your kitty, Sparks."

"I don't think you need to worry about that, gentlemen," Eric said. "I've already spoken with a Bureau liaison to Treasury. They can provide the foreign currency, with markings on them that are only detectible under special fluoroscopic lights."

"You hear that, fellows?" Cunningham said with a chuckle, sweeping the room with a pointed finger. "You guys better watch out who you're taking money from."

"Goes for you too, Sparks," the mayor said, winking at Cunningham over his folded brown hands.

At this point the chumminess between the politicos was starting to get to me. Over sixty people were already dead, and it looked like there'd be more - maybe a lot more - very soon. But money and PR seemed to take priority over public safety with these guys.

I caught Eric's eye and glanced down at my watch. He nodded and broke into the chatter.

"Johnson, Wilson - why don't you two head over to the office and start getting things set up for the incoming task force members?"

"Yes sir," I said, as both Wilson and I launched ourselves out of our chairs.

I held up the copy of the extortion letter and addressed Bardwell. "Okay if I keep this, Chief?" I asked.

"No problem," he said.

"Thanks," I said. I noticed Candice Cartwright staring poison-tipped daggers at Wilson as we made for the door. "I'll call you with an update on the incoming agents when I get to the office," I said to Eric.

"Agent Johnson?" I heard behind me when we were out in the hall.

I turned and saw that Harlan the Three had followed us out of the conference room. He spoke quickly but earnestly.

"I've discussed it with Chief Bardwell and I just wanted you to know that DPD is ready to stand behind the Bureau with everything we've got - SWAT teams, forensics, detectives, beat cops - you name it. You guys are the experts. Just tell us what to do and it'll get done."

For about three long seconds I stared into the clear, decent eyes of the man I'd cuckolded more times than I cared to count.

"Thank you, Harlan," I said, pumping his hand, eager to get away. "We'll, um, be in touch."

"Thanks for getting us out of there, Mojo," Wilson said as we hurried toward the elevators. "It was like being trapped in a cage full of over-caffeinated weasels."

When we got down to ground level and started past the check-in counter, I noticed three cops crowded around a TV mounted on the back wall.

A bilious feeling went through me as I recalled the extortion letter's claim that more "innocents" would die today.

"Wait a sec," I said to Wilson. "Let's check this out."

We strode over to where the cops were standing.

"What's up?" I asked the nearest man, a sergeant.

His mouth was a grim line. "Another goddamn bomb," he said.

We looked up at the TV. The news announcer was staring at the camera, looking stunned. My stomach did flip-flops as I read the text scrolling across the bottom of the screen.

"BUSLOAD OF BOY SCOUTS FIREBOMBED IN NORTHVILLE TOWNSHIP. DRIVER, SCOUTMASTER, 14 BOYS DEAD. 'A BALL OF FIRE WITH TERRIBLE SCREAMS COMING FROM INSIDE,' SAYS EYEWITNESS. DETAILS UPCOMING."

"Holy mother of rat poop," I heard Wilson mutter beside me.

Chapter 11   Blandings And Dorn

Tuesday, August 16 - 6:25 p.m.

OUTSIDE, ON the porch of the DPD building, I called Eric on his cell. I didn't want to go back up there and possibly get tied up again with the pols and police chiefs.

"McCoy?" he said. "Hang on. I'm stepping out of the room for a sec."

"Okay," he said when he when he free of the conference room.

"There's been another bombing."

"We heard," he said. "Ed Wilkins, the Wayne County Sheriff, got a message on his Blackberry and announced it."

"Did everyone in the room puke?"

"Wilkins and Dick Sorenson, the Wayne County exec, looked like they were going to. The rest all looked relieved it wasn't on their turf."

"How do you want us to play it?"

"I need you and Wilson at McNamara to handle the incoming agents. Send Nardella and Rasheed out to the bomb site. I'll get to the office as soon as I can."

"Good luck getting out of there," I said.

By the time Wilson and I got to the McNamara Building, the contingent of special agents had already begun to arrive. A man and a woman were checking in at the admittance desk with Mabel Partridge, our office admin. The man had a laptop in his shoulder bag. The woman had one of those computer bags with wheels and retractable pull-bar. Wilson and I nodded at Mabel, swiped our access cards and hurried past them, figuring I'd do intros once they got cleared through.

Inside the office were another ten or so agents Mabel had already checked in. As Wilson and I were introducing ourselves, I was surprised to see one of the incoming agents had apparently commandeered Dawson's glassed-in office. He wore a snow-white shirt, blue-and-gold tie, and was seated behind Eric's desk. He was working two phones at once, alternating between Eric's desk phone and a cell in his other hand. After staring a few seconds, I noticed there was another man in the room. A short guy who was seated in the chair opposite the desk, scribbling notes on a leather portfolio pad.

"Who's Mr. Take-Charge?" Wilson asked.

"That's Morley Blandings," Ryan, one of the visiting agents, told us. "Guy with him's named Elliot Dorn. Blandings says he's about to be put in charge of the bomb investigation."

"What do you mean?" I said.

"We were all told to report to you for further instructions," Ryan went on. "But when we were on the plane coming here from DC, this Blandings guy must have recognized us as Bureau agents. He came over and told us he was going to be put in charge of the incoming agent contingent, and probably the entire investigation."

I watched the man in the office. He had the smug look of somebody who thinks they're a born VIP. I wondered if he was in there on the two phones managing, investigating, or politicking. I suspected it was mostly the latter.

But there was no time to deal with that kind of bullshit right now. It would be Eric's fight, once he got here - assuming he could extricate himself from the weasel cage over at Beaubien.

When the two agents who'd been checking in with Mabel entered, I gathered them all together. I didn't bother with the two self-appointed VIPs, who were leaning over Eric's desk having some kind of intense dialogue with one another.

"As you can see," I began. "There's not a whole lot of extra room in the main office. What we'll do is get you set up in the large conference room down the hall here. It'll seat about ten or twelve. We've got a network switch we can activate to give everyone computer and IP phone connectivity. We'll put out power strips so you can charge and operate your cell phones as well. There's a secure fiber connection into the office that gives us dedicated, high-bandwidth links back to DC and Quantico."

"We've also got a space-sharing agreement with ATF," I went on. "They're on the same floor as us, in the adjoining wing. They've got an emergency situation room with phone banks and extra computer and IP phone links. Those we can't fit into the conference room will have to link up there."

"What about lab facilities?" one of the agents asked.

"It's got limited equipment, but there's a lab room at the end of the hall. Anyone using it will need to have an ID card made up. The entrance door's got sensors that'll set off an alarm if anyone tries tailgating through it. Mabel out front can take care of making cards for you."

"What do we know so far about the bombings?" Ryan said as we led the group down to the conference room.

"They appear to know what they're doing, as far as bomb-building goes. The one yesterday was a pretty sophisticated device. Very compact in size, but with extremely powerful blast and follow-on incendiary capabilities. The devices used so far appear to be mixes of Semtex plastic explosive and white phosphorus. I'm pretty confident the latest one out in Northville will be the same."

"Any idea where the bombers are getting their materials from?" another agent asked.

"No. That's one reason all you extra agents are being brought in," I said. "There's a lot of phone-calling, interviewing, and data-mining to be done. If we can identify the manufacturer of the Semtex, we can start trying to trace who they've sold it to."

"Be difficult if it was someplace like Eastern Europe or Africa," Ryan said.

"I hear you," I said. "Anyplace there's a lot a corruption, there's the possibility sales and inspection documents will be phony. But at this point, it's our best shot at finding out where the explosives came from."

At around 7 p.m. Eric Dawson called. He was still stuck over at 1300 Beaubien.

"Have all of the out-of-town contingent come in?" he asked.

"Sixteen of the twenty are here," I told him. "I've got them in the big conference room and the overflow in the ATF emergency room. Mabel's arranged for their hotel rooms. There's a problem, though."

"What's that?"

"There's some guy here named Blandings who's commandeered your office. Him and-"

"Blandings? *Morley* Blandings?" He spat out the name as if it were some kind of insect that had crawled into his mouth.

"That's him. I hear he's making noises about being put in charge of the incoming agents. Maybe taking over the entire investigation."

"Why, that slimy, sneaky dirtbag. I should've known he'd pull something like this."

"Uh-oh. I take it he's an acquaintance?"

"Yeah, I know Morley. He was in my class at the academy. A smug, silver-spoon Ivy Leaguer. He's a kiss up, kick down type. He's plenty smart, but he puts most of it into politicking and polishing his resume. My guess is that he sees the Bureau as a stepping stone to bigger things - House of Reps or maybe even a Senate seat."

"Want me to boot his sorry butt out of your office?" I asked.

"Thanks, McCoy, but no. That'll just mean trouble for you. Morley's got big shot family connections and he's cultivated a lot of friends on Capitol Hill and DOJ. Cross him and you may end up running around in mukluks out of the Bureau's Juneau branch."

"Swell," I said. "By the way, he's got some ugly little horny toad with him named Elliot Dorn."

"Dorn's there?" Dawson snickered. "I'm not surprised. Dorn's his factotum."

"His what?"

"His Igor. Does all of Blandings' detail and dirty work for him. The actual boots-on-the ground investigative work, as well as the backstabbing and disinformation-spreading. He was in the same academy class. I think he saw Blandings as a rising star even then and attached his nose to the guy's butt. Been there ever since."

"Christ, Eric - how come we're getting saddled with a couple of sleazy career hounds, when we've got three bombs and over eighty people dead on our hands?"

"Unfortunately, politics in the Bureau are a reality, McCoy. I'm a relative amateur at it and Blandings is a pro. He lives and breathes that crap. The upside is that he's supposedly good at using other people to get results. He'll take most of the credit in the end, but I can live with that if we can bring these guys to justice quickly."

"Anyways," he went on, "until something official comes down, you're still in charge of the investigation, McCoy. Deploy the out-of-towners as you see fit."

"Okay, then. As soon as all the forensics and pathology experts get here, I'll get them working on the bomb evidence from the three blasts so far. I'll have one set of investigators doing background checks on the victims, to look for possible correlations. Have another checking out the explosive materials angles."

"Sounds good, McCoy. With any luck, I'll be there in another twenty minutes. Hold the fort down till then."

"You got it, Eric," I said.

While I was waiting for Dawson to show up, I took a call at my desk from Angie Nardella at the Northville bombing site.

The scout troupe bus bomb had gone off on Edward Hines Drive. Hines Drive is a two-lane that snakes through several of Detroit's westside suburbs. There's a narrow, miles-long park alongside the road that also serves as a flood basin for the branch of the Rouge River it follows. The Boy Scouts aboard were returning from a nature day field trip to several spots in the park.

Nardella reported that the bomb was the same "shake and bake" type used in the downtown bus attack: high explosives mixed with incendiary material. The blast had ignited the small school bus's fuel tank. The kids who weren't blown to bits by the initial blast were incinerated in the flaming holocaust that followed.

I didn't envy her and Rasheed having to view the bodies and wreckage. Not to mention deal with the parents who'd shown up - several of whom apparently began screaming expletives at law enforcement when they weren't shrieking over the hideous deaths of their boys.

When I came out of my cubicle I saw that Eric had finally arrived and was sitting in his glass-walled office with Blandings and Dorn. I tried not to stare too hard as I passed by. Blandings had surrendered his desk to Eric and now was seated in front of him. He was all congenial smiles as he spoke, his hands steepled in front of him - almost as if he were praying.

Praying that he'd get to climb over Eric's desk and take his job from him, I was willing to bet.

Like Eric, Blandings was in his mid-thirties. He was tall, with longish, dark, razor-cut hair, slightly gray at the temples. He looked more like a Wall Street stockbroker than a typical Bureau agent.

Dorn was a small, bug-eyed creature who looked like a cross between the actor Peter Lorre and a horny toad. He mostly kept his mouth shut during the conversation. Just stared at Eric with his buggy eyes and a little snake-like grin on his almost lipless mouth.

I had to push my resentment down as I walked on back toward the conference room to check on the agents there. It ticked me off that Washington was possibly going to bump Eric. Though I knew all the FBI regional offices - even New York, Chicago, and LA - are considered the boonies by the honchos in DC, the Detroit office had a damn good track record on solving difficult cases. It grated to think that Blandings' political connections could somehow override that.

When I came back out through the main office I saw Eric on the phone with someone. I continued on over to the ATF wing and spent some time helping out a couple of the agents we'd situated there with their network and phone connectivity.

When I got back into the main office, Eric spotted me and waved me in to his office.

"McCoy," he said. "I just got off the phone with the Regional Director. Morley's now in charge of the investigation. I'll be his backup and assistant. Elliot here will manage the investigative team. You'll be his adjutant and adviser."

I had to admire Eric's equanimity as he gave me the news. He said it matter-of-factly, but I knew he must be seething inside. I sure was.

"All the same to me," I said, as emotionlessly as possible.

Blandings gave me a smile that just about dripped with smarm. "Eric told me about the great work you did on getting that serial killer last year," he said. "Plus he says you've got in-depth expertise on explosives. We look forward to working with you."

"Whatever," I said. "The important thing is that we stop the bombings. ASAP."

"Absolutely, McCoy," Blandings said. "Eric also told me you've also been heavily involved in the Bureau's intelligence gathering on local Muslim extremists. What's your take on the bombings? Do you think this Al-Qaeda in Detroit is a sleeper cell that's been activated?"

"I'm trying not to make any assumptions. But the extortion letter they sent doesn't feel right to me."

"In what way?"

"It just doesn't give the feeling they're politically or religiously motivated."

"Really?" Dorn said. "Did you hear about the downtown bus number?"

"No."

"It was oh-nine-eleven. A pretty obvious reference to the 2001 attacks."

"Yeah, well - maybe too obvious," I said.

"DPD provided some security video from the yard where the transit buses are gassed up and maintained," Blandings said. "An unknown Arabic-looking guy went in there early yesterday morning, dressed as mechanic and showing false ID. Went in a couple of times previously as well. Here's a screenshot."

He handed me a printout with several grainy, black-and-white video stills of a guy in a mechanic's uniform, carrying a toolbox. He had dark, curly hair, a beard and mustache, and a swarthy complexion. None of the shots showed his features clearly.

Right then an agent rushed up and rapped excitedly on the office door. Blandings waved him in.

"We just got a positive fingerprint ID from Homeland Security," he said. "Prints on all four of the extortion letters match those from the immigration records of a guy named Ali Mohammed Al-Rafi. He's an imam, apparently - one of those Muslim priests or whatever. Has an address in west Detroit - 12079 Elmore Street."

Blandings steepled his hands again and grinned at Dorn.

"Elliot, looks like it's time for you and Johnson here to rock 'n' roll."

"By which you mean-?" I said.

"My plan is to have DPD and their SWAT team meet up with a small cadre of us at this Al-Rafi guy's house," Dorn answered. "We ask him real nice one time to let us in. If he refuses or delays, we send the SWAT team in. His fingerprints on the extortion letter give us enough probable cause to justify going in without a warrant."

"What if he resists?"

"We breach the house and subdue him. If absolutely necessary, we take him out. Arrest is highly preferable, obviously. We want to find out who else is in the cell."

"What if this place is their bomb factory?" I asked. "We could be jeopardizing a lot of people in the vicinity of the house."

"Good point, Johnson," Blandings said. "Can DPD provide a couple of bomb disposal techs to go in there along with the SWAT team, just in case?"

"I expect so," I said. "They've said they'll back us up every way they can."

"Then get on the horn with them now," Dorn said. "Tell them to get their teams to that Elmore Street address, ASAP. In one hour, if possible."

I pulled out my cell and called Harlan Robinson. Doing my best not to recall his wife in my kitchen in her scanty white undies, I gave the deputy chief the FBI's request. He assured me the DPD SWAT team and a pair of bomb techs would be there in an hour, at 8:30 p.m. I nodded at Dorn as I was wrapping up the call, and he gave me one of his snaky smiles.

"Something's off here, though," I said when I hung up.

"What's that?" Dorn asked.

"Does it really seem likely a group of terrorists smart enough to build and place sophisticated bombs would be stupid enough to leave fingerprints all over an extortion letter?"

"Sometimes smart people do stupid things," he said, getting up out of his chair. "Seen it a hundred times. Let's get our team together and get ready to roll."

I had my own thoughts about how the team should go about confronting Al-Rafi, but it was Dorn's show now, and he didn't ask for my opinion.

Before leaving, I went to my cubicle and placed a call to Amir X, one of our moles in the Islamic fundamentalist community. I didn't get through, so I left a message asking him to call me with whatever he knew about this Imam Al-Rafi. Then I strapped on my Springfield, grabbed a jacket and headed out of my cube to catch up with the others.

Mabel Partridge gave me a thumbs-up as I hurried past the admittance desk. I returned it and strode toward the elevators, my adrenaline pumping.

Chapter 12   The Bomb Factory

Tuesday, August 16 - 7:30 p.m.

"LOOK AT that, Bub," he says, smiling as he watches the images flash across the screen of his oversize flat screen TV.

One of the networks is airing another special report on the bombings and he's savoring the post-explosion video they're showing. Twisted, ash-covered vehicles, still sending up tendrils of smoke from their melted tires. Firemen wiping tears from their smoke-blackened faces. Black plasticized body bags lined up on a sidewalk. Grim-looking uniformed policemen and detectives walking back and forth behind yellow crime scene tape.

The pit bull is lying on his belly a few feet away, muzzle resting on his front paws. His good eye moves back and forth from the man to the screen, while his bad eye seems to be examining the ceiling.

"Eighty-two dead and counting," the man says, rubbing his hands together. "Well over my target minimum."

The local TV stations are going nuts over the dead Boy Scouts, playing video clips of the smoking school bus remains and wailing relatives over and over again. Meanwhile, coverage of the three bombings to date has gone national. It's on all the major networks and, as a quick check of the major online news websites has shown, the entire Internet hive is abuzz with it. Even the President has come out with a statement, reassuring the country that Federal, state, and local law enforcement agencies are addressing the apparent terrorist attacks in Detroit with every resource at their disposal.

Har-har.

Because the next group to die will be cops. Lots of them. With any luck, the prep work he did at the imam's place two nights ago will take out an entire SWAT team of them tonight. And if there are Feds among them, all the better. They'll die, too.

With a satisfied grin on his face, he picks up the remote and switches off the TV. He checks his watch. He's got thirty minutes before he needs to leave to watch the SWAT team massacre. He decides he'll do a bit more work on that special car controller device he's been working on.

The yellow dog gets up and follows the man as he leaves the TV room and heads out through the back door to his shop.

The shop is a big, gray aluminum-walled structure that sits behind the house. Thanks to the outsized, fenced-in lot, his nearest neighbor's home is an eighth of a mile away. With the multiple vehicles parked around it, his neighbors no doubt think he's some kind of self-employed truck mechanic or machinist. Driving by at night they may occasionally see lights in the shop's barred windows and hear the faint sounds of grinders or drill presses. But the chances of their suspecting what he's really up to have got to be nil.

At the steel entrance door, he punches in the code on the electronic keypad above the knob and lets himself and Beelzebub in. Once inside, he flips on the lights and disarms the security system. The shop has state-of-the-art alarms to keep out any prospective B&E types. The last thing he needs is some enterprising burglar browsing through his gear and inadvertently blowing himself, the shop, and everything for a half-mile around to bite-sized rubble.

After crossing through the machine shop, he keys in the code to the inner workroom. He opens the white metal door and lets the dog go in first. His workbench sits against the far wall. The room's other walls are lined with five sturdy steel racks. Three of them hold the two dozen bombs he's completed. Another holds his explosive materials and detonators. The fifth is full of the electronic gear he uses to make triggering mechanisms. Off to the left a computer and printer sit atop a small desk. Alongside it stands the metal file cabinet where he keeps his research materials and diagrams.

"It's frigging amazing what you can find on the Internet with the right keywords, Bub," he tells the dog, which has seated itself on the floor off to one side.

Although he got solid training in bomb and booby trap-making from VanBoort, that South African mercenary he worked with in Sudan, there's always more to be learned. New technologies, new electronics, new detonation systems. He spends several hours a week visiting obscure websites - some offshore, some domestic - that offer useful tidbits of technical information for the aspiring terrorist.

He sits down at the workbench, flips on a quartz lamp, and slips the fiber optic dentist's headlamp-magnifier onto his head.

With the pit bull on his belly watching him, the man gets to work on his latest device: a digital watch-based timer that will activate an electric servo-motor. Although the electronics work involves some attention to detail, the work has become largely rote for him. Enough that he can let his mind wander over the current situation as he clips, screws, and solders the piecework before him.

Ever since that fateful day in Fallujah, five years ago, he's been working on the Master Plan. The plan that will finally avenge the unspeakable thing that got done to him there.

There are plenty of douchebags who go around saying, "I don't get mad. I get even." But talk is talk and action is action. Other than Beelzebub, he's never said a single word to anyone about getting even. Instead he works at it. For one thousand, seven hundred and sixty days he's worked at it.

And now his Master Plan is finally in motion.

If all goes well - as he's dead certain it will - in a few days he'll be comfortably wealthy and be out of the US-of-frigging-A for the rest of his natural life.

Detroit - already a crippled and dying city - will never recover from the holocaust he's going to wreak on it. Despite the dogged stubbornness that has kept it alive through the slow-motion implosion of its auto and manufacturing industries, he has no doubt whatsoever the unimaginable horror he'll soon be inflicting will finally crush it. Turn it once and for all into a rusty, dust-covered ghost town, moldering away as the scavengers finish their looting, and the rats and the roaches, the pigeons and gulls, finally take over for good. And not just the old city, but all those suburban barnacles that have grown up around it, too.

"Gonna make you proud, pa," he mutters absently as he solders a tiny joint. Even though he hasn't spoken to the old fart in over eight years.

After thirty minutes worth of work on the controller mechanism, he checks his black special ops watch. Time to wrap up and get going. He locks up the workroom, arms the building alarm system and, with Beelzebub following him, exits the shop.

As he's about to climb into his black Ramcharger pickup, he notices the pit bull looking up at him expectantly.

"Sorry, Bub," he says. "Can't take you with me this time."

The wall-eyed dog gives out a surly growl of disappointment.

He's reluctant to tell Bub the real reason he isn't taking him along, which is that he's tired of cleaning up his slaver afterwards. Damn dog's saliva glands must work overtime. Drools worse than a frigging baby.

"Tell you what, dude," he says. "Why don't you go do a perimeter check? Bring me back some rabbit parts. Understand, boy? *Rabbit hunt.*"

The red at the center of his black eyes growing brighter, the dog's snaggle-toothed jaws open into a repulsive grin. The compound's oversized yard is already dotted with forty or fifty little mounds of dirt where he's buried the bloody remains of his bunny victims. Happily, he trots off.

After locking the gate to his huge, fenced-in yard, the man pulls down the long drive, recalling the surprises he has in store for all those stupid cops who are going to die tonight. At the end of the drive, he turns south onto the two-lane that will take him to the expressway, and from there to Detroit. With the sun getting low in the sky now, the dark shadow of the Night Runner stretches for almost fifty yards as he cruises down the highway.

By the time he gets onto the freeway, he's pushing the speed limit just a bit. He doesn't want to be late for the little party in westside Detroit he's arranged for tonight.

At 12079 Elmore Street.

Chapter 13   Sergeant Rock

Tuesday, August 16 - 8:30 p.m.

DUSK WAS falling as we approached the area off Michigan Avenue where Al-Rafi lived. The heavily Arabic neighborhood continues on into eastern Dearborn, which is another Arab-American enclave. I've heard the whole area referred to more than once as "Camel Town."

Dorn, Wilson, and I rode in one car, with Wilson driving. Four more special agents followed us in another.

Dorn sat in the center of the back seat and acted as if we were limousining him. I'd given him Harlan Robinson's number and, after informing the Deputy Chief he was now the lead investigator, he spent most of the ride issuing additional instructions for the Detroit Police teams.

It turned out Harlan the Three wasn't kidding about our getting DPD's full support. By the time our FBI contingent arrived at Al-Rafi's street, they had patrol cars already sealing off the block and we had to show our Federal shields to get past them.

As we came down Elmore, I saw the SWAT team's big, blue armored bus parked in the middle of the street. A massive red-and-white bomb containment vehicle sat directly behind it, looking like some sort of super-mean Brinks truck.

"Let's find out who they've got in charge here," Dorn said when we'd parked and gotten out of the two cars.

Ten steps away from the car, my cell rang. It was Amir X, the Islamic community mole I'd left a message for earlier. He filled me in on what he knew about Al-Rafi while our FBI team double-timed the rest of the way to 12079.

The large police presence had brought out a crowd of curious neighborhood spectators. We flashed our shields to the beat cops who were keeping them back, a few houses down in both directions from our target address.

As we approached Al-Rafi's place, I saw that it was an old brick two-story. A thick hedge ran along the front of the house and a narrow driveway led back to a small, white wooden garage. The house was a bit bigger and better kept up than most of the other homes on the block. SWAT team members in black Kevlar-vested uniforms and helmets were securing the perimeter and evacuating the homes adjacent to it, sending the occupants down to join the cordoned-off crowds.

"Who's in command of the SWAT team here, officer?" Dorn called out to one of the helmeted team members.

"Sergeant Rock, sir," the man said. "Roczinski, I mean. He's over there."

He pointed toward a scowling, lantern-jawed man who, except for being in a black SWAT uniform instead of military fatigues, bore an uncanny resemblance to the comic book GI. The only thing missing was the butt of a cigarette clenched in his tight-lipped mouth.

Roczinski was standing in the middle of the street with a couple of the team's techs. They were surveying the house with a tripod-mounted TGS unit - a thermographic scanner that would show heat signatures inside the building. Sgt. Rock was staring at a laptop computer connected to the scanner. He had a Bluetooth-type commlink device attached to his ear.

"Sergeant Roczinski?" Dorn said as we went up to him. "I'm Elliot Dorn, FBI. I'm the lead investigator and this is my team. I see you've got a thermo scanner there. What are you seeing inside?"

"We've got heat signatures on both floors," the SWAT sergeant reported. "Two on the first, one on the second."

"Any of them moving?" I asked as we all edged up to look at the laptop. Some fuzzy pink and orange digital blobs flickered on an otherwise deep purple screen.

"Negative," Rock said. "May just be appliances."

"Anybody try knocking on the doors to see if anyone's home?" Wilson asked.

"Two of my team banged on them loud enough to wake the dead," Rock said. "No answer."

"Are your men ready to go in?" Dorn asked.

"We're ready. Just waiting for the two bomb squad guys to finish suiting up."

"Ellis Sidwell one of them?" I said.

"No. They detailed him out to Northville, to do forensics on that bus blast."

"Listen, Sergeant," I said. "Do your men realize there's a high risk of this being an ambush?"

Dorn gave me a venomous look. "I already thought of that, Johnson," he snapped. "That's why I asked them to have the bomb squad guys go in as leads, front and back. They'll be in full protective bomb suits and have electronic detection equipment. The SWAT team guys behind them will have hazmat gear with them, in addition to their armor."

"Listen, Elliot," I said. "I just got a call from one of our undercover guys on this Al-Rafi. Says he's in his late sixties, a widower. Apparently a moderate, peaceable type. Known for teaching tolerance and strongly opposed to jihad. Be way out of character for him to be involved in bombing attacks."

Dorn snorted. "Or be good cover, if he's a secret jihadist," he said.

"All I'm saying is that this whole thing smells like a trap to me. Might be smart to send in just the two guys in bomb suits first. Check the place out thoroughly before anybody else goes in."

"No way, Johnson," Dorn said. "If there's a nest of jihadists in there, I want us going in with sufficient firepower to subdue or waste them."

I could see I wasn't going to get anywhere with this cocky little squirt.

"Look," I said to Roczinski. "Tell your guys to be damn careful going in there. Have them take their time."

Sgt. Rock smirked at me.

"We know our business, agent. We don't need the FBI nannying us."

"He's absolutely right, Mojo," Wilson piped up. "Shame on you for questioning their judgment."

"By the way, Sergeant Rock," he went on, "you did bring along plenty of body bags, didn't you? Enough for your whole team?"

The SWAT sergeant ignored him.

I looked around at the tense scene. The sky had gotten overcast and it was close to being fully dark now. Soon the cops would be going inside Al-Rafi's looming house.

I put my hand on my stomach. It was starting to feel like I'd just swallowed a live snake.

Chapter 14   A Face In The Crowd

Tuesday, August 16 - 8:45 p.m.

EYES GLEAMING with anticipation, he can feel his heartbeat tick up as he watches the police gathered outside Al-Rafi's house.

The fun's about to begin.

It's hard to see exactly what's going on down the block in the hazy August dusk, but he can make out at least some of it. Several cops are gathered around some sort of electronic equipment, set up on a folding stand in the street. They appear to be deep in discussion - no doubt ironing out how they're going to infiltrate the house. One of them is a big black guy in a white shirt. He wonders for a moment if he could possibly be McCoy Scumbag Johnson. But it's too dark to be sure, so he dismisses the idea. Not likely he'd that lucky, this early in the game.

Just then a tall Arab teenager edges in front of him. The kid smells like he just took a cologne shower. He's tempted to shove the young punk out of the way, but opts for discretion and changes his position instead. He's blending himself in with the crowd of people behind the police cordon. Most are Arabs, but there are enough Caucasians scattered among them to assure he doesn't stand out too much.

It's too bad he has to maintain the guise of curious and concerned citizen. Because what he really feels like doing is laughing. Dancing, even. Breaking into a little jig while he sings:

Die! Die! You're all gonna die! Gonna burn out your eyes! Gonna blow you sky-high! You stupid frigging dumbshit cops!

But unfortunately, dammit, he's got to stay cool.

Not that the cluster of yammering people he's mixed in with are acting all that serious. The older men and women are, looking grim and suspicious at the sight of all the cops as they lean their heads together, chattering in Arabic at one another in low voices. But the more youthful men all seem to have that young Arab male cockiness. Some are laughing, playfully punching and poking each other as they make smart-mouth comments in gangsta-style English.

The young Arab women and teenage girls around him are a weird mix. Some wear their hair free and are dressed in snug, graphics-adorned t-shirts and shorts that show off their tanned legs. By contrast, the more religious ones are wearing headscarves and either shapeless dresses or baggy sports clothes that look like exercise sweats. Regardless of their attire, at least two-thirds of the young females are ongoingly talking, texting, or checking messages on their cell phones as they watch the goings-on up the street.

Thirty minutes ago, when he first arrived, there was no one from the media present. So he'd pulled the disposable cell phone he'd brought along out of his jeans and speed-dialed four local TV stations, using the numbers he'd pre-programmed into it. Blabbing rapidly, as if he were an excited, dirt-dumb bystander, he'd blurted out his tip about the big police and SWAT team presence at the westside home of a Muslim imam named Al-Rafi. Fifteen minutes later the TV crews started showing up in their vans.

Now a reporter and cameraman are moving among the cordoned-off crowd, not far from where he's standing. The reporter is a dyed blonde who looks uptight and frazzled when she's off-camera, but who automatically puts on a journalist's pleasantly neutral face when the camera lights come on. She's interviewing crowd members. Posing questions into a mike and then holding it up to the interviewee's chins to get their answers. Apparently she's asking their opinion about what's going down.

Curious, he edges up closer to nose in on what's being said. He's careful to stay behind the cameramen so that he doesn't get videotaped.

"What do you think about what's going on here, sir?" the reporter asks one gel-haired youth.

"I don't know, man. Just came out here to party, you know?" the idiot says, adding a cretinous *hyuk.*

"Thank you," the TV reporter says. With a tepid smile frozen on her face, she moves on to another person. This one a young Arab woman in a headscarf.

"Hello, ma'am," the reporter begins. "And what do you think about what's going on up the street here?"

"I tell you, I don't understand it," the young woman says, shaking her head. "We're neighbors with Imam Al-Rafi. He's a very nice man. My family hasn't seen him for a couple of days. We've been worried about him."

"At least one anonymous caller said Mr. Al-Rafi's involved in the recent bombings that've occurred around Detroit, and that that's why the police are here. What do you think?"

The young woman frowns. "That doesn't sound like the Imam Al-Rafi we know."

Behind her some idiotic young Arab youths are mugging and making gangsta-rap hand gestures. One is rubbing his chin with his middle finger while he grins into the camera.

"Thank you," the reporter says. She moves on to a balding, white-shirted man in his thirties. There's a tight-jawed look of outrage on his bearded face.

"And what about you, sir?" she asks.

"It's police harassment," he says, jabbing with his forefinger as he speaks directly into the camera. "Pure and simple. Somebody sets off a few bombs and right away everybody thinks the Arab community is responsible."

"Who do you think is responsible for them, sir?" the reporter asks.

"What I want to know is, how come they're not surrounding houses up in Oak Park? I wouldn't be surprised if these bombings aren't some kind of plot by the Jews to make Arabs look bad. Maybe even Mossad is in on it," he says, referring to the Israeli security agency.

"Thank you, sir," the reporter says, moving on.

"Ask me!" a middle-aged woman says, waving her hand.

"All right, ma'am," the reporter said. "What do you think about what's going on here? And do you know Imam Al-Rafi personally?"

The woman has big, dark, earnest eyes, set in a hound dog's droopy, deeply-lined face.

"I know Mr. Al-Rafi," she says. "I knew his wife too, when she was alive. She was a *wali* - a saint. They're both saints. He's the sweetest man. He wouldn't hurt a flea!"

He sure wouldn't now, the man thinks, chuckling softly to himself as he moves away from the TV crew.

Given those body parts he's missing.

When he gets back to the row of policemen who are cordoning off the crowd, the man again scopes out the imam's house.

It looks like the party is about ready to begin. The SWAT cops have arrayed themselves around the house in a military-style formation, their M4 carbines at the ready.

A lot of good it'll do them - since there'll be no gun battles. No crazed jihadists shooting or hurling Molotov cocktails at them.

No. It'll be much sweeter than that. The team or teams are going to go inside. And getting in will be easy for them. They'll have to bust through the entrance doors, but that'll be a piece of cake with the mini-battering rams they'll no doubt have. If they're using bomb detectors they'll notice they're not working, but won't know for sure if it's due to the signal-jammers he's planted. After that, there'll be nothing to impede them as they move deeper and deeper into the trap. Their confidence growing. Their guard dropping. Until someone opens that refrigerator door - and all hell breaks loose. They'll try to go back. And when they do, they'll start breaking the reverse-sensing sensor beams.

Yes, he smiles. The going in will be easy.

It's the getting out that will be a bitch.

Abruptly the smile drops off his face. His brow furrows and his face gets hot.

The big black man he saw earlier has turned his way. The streetlights have come on and in the glow from the one nearest the cops he can see his face clearly now.

Motherdumping sonofabitch! It IS him!

McCoy Scum-Sucker Johnson!

He pictures the Glock he's left back in the Night Runner, but then curses himself. Dammit! He hadn't thought to bring along the silencer.

If he had, it would be *sooooo* easy.

He'd head back to the Night Runner for the Glock and silencer. Sidle away from the crowd and slip into the foliage alongside one of the house porches. Like that house over there, with the big hydrangeas. Screw on the silencer. Distance under a hundred yards. Close enough for a head shot. Steady his aim by resting his elbows on the porch concrete. Take careful aim and slowly squeeze off the round. *Thoop!* A small, dark red entrance hole appears in the frigging dickhead's nappy-haired temple. Exit wound is the size of a golf ball. Skull fragments and bloody gray brain matter spattering the other cops standing near the crud-sucker.

Crap! Crap! Crap! Why the *hell* didn't he bring that silencer?

For a moment, his faith in the Master Plan shimmers with doubt.

But then he gets hold of himself again.

The night is young. Soon the SWAT cops will be going inside the house. And when they do, they'll begin dying. Dying horrible, excruciating deaths. Deaths they won't ever, even in their worst nightmares, have imagined.

And maybe - just maybe - that big, black douchebag will be stupid enough to go inside after them.

And if he does - it'll be curtains for McCoy Effing Bastard Johnson.

Chapter 15 House Of Horrors

Tuesday, August 16 - 9:00 p.m.

"WHAT'S THE delay?" Dorn said, irritation in his voice.

"Roper? Cain? You guys ready to rock 'n' roll or what?" Roczinski said into his commlink.

As if in answer, two men in olive drab bomb disposal suits just then began climbing down out of the SWAT bus. They moved slowly in their heavy bomb armor. The gear looked military spec, which meant it weighed roughly ninety pounds. I hoped it wouldn't slow them down too much if they needed to get out fast.

"Are those videocams on their heads?" I asked, noticing the lenses mounted on their black, reinforced-fiberglass helmets.

"Yeah," Rock said, reaching down and tapping away at the laptop. "They transmit wireless." A pair of windows popped up on the screen, displaying the shadowy output from the two bomb squad guys' headcams as they waddled toward the house.

"Listen, do you have any spare headsets so we can listen in and talk on your commlinks?" Dorn asked the sergeant.

"No, but we can plug in a speaker and mike," he said. "Benson, set up an external speaker-mike combo for the FBI crew."

One of the techs operating the thermographic scanner hurried off and few moments later came back with a small speaker-microphone unit. He cabled it into some kind of transmitter box and the voices of the SWAT team started coming over the speaker.

"Radio checks," the sergeant said into his mike. "I want to hear everyone sound off."

When he was satisfied he had contact with all ten of the team members, he gave the go-ahead.

"Showtime, kiddies," he said into the mike. "Team Alpha, Team Bravo - get those mighty gonads of yours inside. But remember: take your time and give me a running rap on what you're seeing. And no talking all at once."

On Dorn's orders, they were sending in ten men in two teams. Four SWAT members to a team, each led by a body-suited bomb squad tech. Both front and back doors proved to be locked, so the teams brought up a pair of Blackhawk Monoshock battering rams. The rams quickly busted up the wooden doors, after which the bomb-suited lead cops kicked the debris clear and went in.

Just then my cell phone rang. Damn! I thought. I checked the number, but didn't recognize it.

"McCoy Johnson," I snapped into the phone.

"Agent Johnson? It's Bill La Borgia."

For a moment I stood there, cell jammed to my ear, too stunned to speak.

Willie the Pimp?

The caller was William F. La Borgia. AKA Willie the Pimp, AKA Billy Knuckles. Internet sex industry magnate and son of Detroit mafia kingpin Fiorello La Borgia.

I wasn't surprised that La Borgia had my number. I'd met with him a couple of months back, at some high-class country club in Bloomfield Hills. Gave him my card at the end of the interview.

But why the hell was he calling me now?

"Mr. La Borgia," I said, squinting at the SWAT team members who were cautiously following the bomb squad lead into Al-Rafi's house, "I'm in the middle of something extremely important right now."

"I totally understand, Agent Johnson. I won't take up much of your time."

"Listen, I can't talk-" I began.

"This'll just take a few seconds. I wanted you to know how appalled I am by these bombings. I mean, all those people downtown. And those poor kids-"

"Mr. La Borgia, I really can't-"

"Look, Johnson, I just want you to know that anything I can do to help stop these sons of bitches, you've got it, okay? As I'm sure you know, I've got a lot of money and resources I can bring to bear on-"

"Thanks, Mr. La Borgia," I interrupted, as I nervously watched the last of the SWAT cops disappear into the dark house. "But I don't think so."

"Anything. Anytime. Just call me. You've got my personal number, right? I gave it to you at our interview. You want it again?"

"No. I've got it, sir. Mr. La Borgia, I'm going to hang up now."

"I understand. Just remember, Johnson: Anything. Anytime. It's yours."

"Thanks and goodbye, sir," I said and hung up.

Christ, I thought. What the hell is La Borgia doing, calling me like this? Is he playing some kind of angle? Or does he honestly just want to help?

It was a distraction I definitely didn't need right now. I pushed the questions out of my mind and zeroed in on the laptop screen and the voices of the police team coming through the speaker. The screen wasn't showing much beyond flashlight beams on shadowy walls. Then I saw a blinking box appear inside a heavy-gloved hand.

I leaned forward and spoke into the mike. "Cain? Roper? Anything showing up on your bomb detection gear?"

"Negative. Just a bunch of static." I wasn't sure which of them was speaking.

"Same here," the other man said. "Don't know if there's just something in the structure that's interfering, or if there's maybe some kind of scrambler."

"But so far, so good," the first man said.

The fact that their bomb detection gear didn't seem to be working made the coiling in my stomach worsen. Was it just a malfunction? Or was there some kind of jammer in the house?

The team that had gone in the front door were climbing the stairs to the second floor. In one of the laptop's windows I could see shadowy shots of the stairwell, flickering and jumping as Cain, the bomb squad lead, trod up the stairs in his heavy gear, sweeping a flashlight around as he went.

The team that had gone in the back door was in the dark kitchen now. Roper's headcam swept past a white stove and refrigerator as he scanned the room with his flashlight.

"Shall I check out the refrigerator? I could use a bite to eat," he joked.

"Go ahead," Roczinski told him. "It'll maybe give us some clue whether the house is occupied. And if they've cleared out, maybe how long they've been gone."

On the laptop window we could see Roper's flashlight move up and down the refrigerator's face as he waddled toward it in his heavy gear. We saw his thick-gloved hand reaching out for the door.

Then the images from Roper's headcam became flashes of white, the lens seemingly dazzled by the refrigerator's interior light.

"What the hell?" came his voice over the intercom. "There're some things inside here, on the shelf. Looks like- HOLY SHIT!" he yelled. "IT'S A FRIGGING HEAD!"

His voice was kind of breathless now. "A frigging head! Covered in some kind of plastic, like - like frigging sandwich wrap!"

"Who is it?" I said. "Do you recognize it?"

"It looks like- Yeah, it's him, alright. That imam guy, Al-Rafi. And there are two big glass tumblers on either side. With a goddamn HAND stuffed into each of them!"

The headcam had apparently adjusted somewhat for the brilliant light inside the refrigerator. On the laptop we could now make out three shadowy, ghoulish shapes resting on a white rack.

I looked at Dorn. "There's your fingerprints on the extortion letters," I said.

He glared at me. "You think I don't know that?" he snapped.

"Listen, Roper," I said. "Do you see wires anywhere?"

There was silence for a few moments.

"Yeah. There's a pair running from under the head. They go back down inside the refrigerator. Jesus - there's blood running down from them. It's dripping down onto-"

"Christ!" I said into the mike. "Listen, Roper - don't touch that head! Or those wires! Okay? And don't shut that door! Do you hear me? Just back away slowly from the refrigerator. And whatever you do, don't-"

All at once the laptop window showing Roper's headcam video went blank white. A horrendous blasting sound came out of the little speaker, echoed by a muffled version coming from the house itself. I saw Roczinski grimace in pain and rip the commlink off his ear. But a couple of seconds later, his eyes gone panic-wide, he jammed it back on again.

"Roper!" he yelled into the mike.

"Down, sir!" one of the SWAT team men said. "He took the full force of it and it blew him across the room! He's on the floor!"

"Shit! Is he dead?" Roczinski asked.

"I don't know, sir! The front of his suit is chewed up pretty bad, and he's not moving!"

"Then get him out of there, dammit!" the sergeant yelled.

The other window on the laptop had become a blur of flashing light and darkness.

"Cain!" Roczinski said. "Where are you and your guys?"

"On our way downstairs to help out, Sarge!"

The sound of heavy boots clattering on wooden stairs came through the speaker.

I looked up then as a series of loud pops came from inside the house, echoed by the speaker. From outside they sounded like a bunch of cherry bombs going off.

Then the screaming started.

First came a long, blood-curdling shriek. It was followed by someone's hysterical yell:

"MY BALLS! MY BALLS! SOMETHING SHOT OFF MY FRIGGING BALLS!"

"Holy humping hamsters," Wilson muttered, shifting his stance nervously.

"What's going on in there?" Roczinski demanded into his commlink. "Copy me, dammit! What's going on?"

"It's Porter, sir. He's down! There was a report - like a small arm going off. Then something shot up out of the floor and into Porter's groin. He's bleeding bad, sir!"

"AAAAGGGGHHHH!" the man was screaming. "OMIGOD! MY BALLS ARE GONE! MY FRIGGING BALLS ARE GONE!"

"Help him, goddammit!" the sergeant roared into the commlink. "Get him out of there!"

He turned and bellowed at the medical team that was standing by a few yards away. "Up to that door, dammit! We've got injured officers coming out!"

The med techs raced towards the house. "Which door, sergeant?" one of them yelled. "Front or back?"

"Front!"

"Carson! Pahlaniuk!" he said into his commlink. "What's your status?"

"We've got him, sir! Moving him back towards the door now! In just a sec-"

There was another report over the commlink. This one louder, like a shotgun blast. Then came another bloodcurdling scream.

"AAAAAAGGGHHH!!!"

"OH SHIT! SHIT! SHIT!!!" someone yelled.

"What's going on?" Roczinski bellowed.

"Pahlaniuk's down, sir!" someone shouted. "Shotgun blast to his groin! Omigod, sir! His crotch looks like - like bloody hamburger!!!"

"I'm getting my ass *outta* here!" another voice said.

"Get your team out first!" the sergeant yelled. "Get your team out, officer! That's an order!"

"Screw that!" the man said. "I'm outta here! I'm not losing my-"

A low, weird *thwump!* sound interrupted him. The next thing that came out of his mouth was a horrendous shriek.

"MY EYES!!! I CAN'T SEE! OMIGOD, IT HURTS! IT'S ACID! FRIGGING ACID IN MY EYES! OMIGOD!"

"Who is that?" Roczinski yelled.

The only answer was more screaming and groaning over the commlink.

"Get in there! Get those men out!" the sergeant yelled at the med techs. They were standing on the porch, frozen, gaping through the smashed door at the hysterical screams of pain from inside.

"Ignore that order!" I called out to them. "Get off that porch!" They quickly complied.

Roczinski glared at me, bug-eyed with fury. "My men are dying in there!"

"Those techs'll never get out alive!" I yelled at him. "The whole damn place is booby-trapped! Do you have any more bomb suits?"

"In the van!" he said. "But there's no time. I'm going in there!"

"Don't be a fool, Roczinski!" I snarled at him. "Our only chance is to go in with bomb suits."

"Screw that!" Roczinski said. "I'm going in!" He took off toward the porch, strapping on his black SWAT helmet as he ran.

I turned to Wilson.

"C'mon!" I yelled. "We're putting on suits and going in there!"

"We are?" he said. Even in the dark you could see he looked ill.

Chapter 16   Kevlar Pajamas

Tuesday, August 16 - 9:15 p.m.

AS WILSON and I ran toward the big blue SWAT bus, I saw Dorn standing off to one side. Trickles of sweat were running down his horny-toad face as he chattered into his cell phone. No doubt calling Blandings, I thought. Giving him a heads-up on this world-class clustermuck he'd orchestrated.

We climbed into the bus. The spare bomb suits hung from big metal hooks on the rear wall.

"Are these pajamas one size fits all?" Wilson said as we yanked a pair down.

"If they're military spec, yes," I said, beginning to strip down to my skivvies. "There'll be Velcro straps to adjust the sleeve and pants lengths."

"Now the boots," I said when we were inside the heavy, Kevlar-lined shells.

We sat down on the bench that ran along the wall and pulled on the armored boots.

"Jeez-is! These things weigh a ton," Wilson complained.

"Actually, they're about eight pounds each," I said.

"Now the armor," I said, standing up.

We helped each other strap on and secure the belted chest and groin ballistic plates.

"I'm going for a double on these codpieces," he said.

"Gonna add a lot more weight - maybe give you a hernia," I said.

"Did you hear those guys in there? Screaming about getting their balls blown off? I'll take the hernia."

"Hmm - you may be right," I said, and strapped on a second groin plate over the first myself.

The last things to go on were the high-strength, reinforced-fiberglass helmets.

"What about the radio and video units?" he asked. "Do we attach them?"

"No time," I said. "Just speak up when you talk through the mouthpiece. I'll hear you."

"Yeah you will," he said. "Especially when I start screaming."

We latched the helmets into place inside the oversize collars of the bomb suits.

"What's with the big Dracula collars?" Wilson asked.

"They're to keep your neck from being snapped when a blast throws your head back," I answered.

"Gee, how reassuring," he said.

Wilson lurched and almost fell when we started for the door.

"Dang!" he said. "These suits filled with lead? I can barely walk in the damned thing."

"You'll get used to it," I said.

"Wanna bet?" he said.

We clambered down from the van and started waddling toward the house. I didn't let on to Wilson what I was really feeling - which was the same intense, fear-driven nausea I'd begun having near the end of my Iraq tour. The snake I'd felt earlier in my stomach now felt like it was desperately trying to escape. I did my best to ignore its gyrations as it did a frantic hula-dance down in my gullet.

"Where's Roczinski?" I asked Dorn when we were passing by the laptop and command gear.

"Went in. Something went off. Didn't come out," he said with an angry scowl.

"You realize you're dead meat?" he called after us as Wilson and I approached the porch.

"Thanks for the vote of confidence," I muttered inside the fiber helmet.

"Asshole," I heard Wilson say, as if completing the thought.

Chapter 17   I Like To Watch
Tuesday, August 16 - 9:20 p.m.

A THRILL goes through his muscular body as he watches the two men emerge from the police van in greenish bomb disposal suits and begin lumbering toward the house.

He's grinning broadly now, unable to suppress the almost ecstatic feeling of excitement that's buzzing through his mind and body.

Johnson's going to go inside the imam's house.

Which means the scum-sucker is dead. Finished. Kaput.

He can't believe his luck. No need now for a Glock and silencer and perfectly-aimed shot.

It'll be frigging exquisite. First, there's an excellent chance he'll have his genitals blown off by one of the crotch bombs or sawed-off shotguns that haven't yet gone off. Or maybe he'll catch a nice, friendly blast of sulfuric acid to the face. It may not go through his visor, but it'll blind him and get him stumbling around to where he'll likely trip one or more of the other booby traps.

Then, after the black bastard has experienced several minutes of horrendous pain - minutes that'll stretch out for what seems like hours - he'll slip the remote out of his back pocket and detonate the charges he's planted around the house's foundation. Tons of brick, mortar, wood, and metal will rain down as the house collapses on top of him. Mashing his internal organs to jelly as it crushes his body, snaps his bones, and caves in his frigging skull.

And even though it will all be over for Johnson far too quickly for his taste, he'll have the knowledge that that big, black son of a bitch has suffered the excruciating death he so richly deserves...

Chapter 18   Into The Meat Grinder

Tuesday, August 16 - 9:21 p.m.

ALTHOUGH THE helmet limited my hearing, I could still hear the sounds of groaning and whimpering as I stepped through the smashed front door.

When we were both inside, Wilson came up alongside me and we shined our flashlights around the scene. To the right of the foyer was a living room filled with Middle Eastern-style furnishings. Off to the left slightly was a stairwell. The bodies of two SWAT team cops lay atop one another at the foot of the stairs, not moving. Alongside the stairwell, a hallway led to the back half of the house. Three more bodies lay crumpled along the length of it, one of them in a bomb suit. Big dark pools of blood were soaking into the yellow-and-beige shag carpeting beneath all of them.

Cautiously, we edged over to the pair of bodies at the foot of the stairs. I knelt down, pulled off one of my heavy bomb gloves, and checked them for vital signs. There were none. As I looked up the stairway, I saw some gaping holes in the steps and adjoining wall, where the shotgun blasts or explosive charges that had taken them out had come from. Above one of the holes I noticed a faint red pinpoint glow.

"Wait a second," I said to Wilson. "I just had an idea. Turn off your flashlight."

"Did I ever mention I'm scared of the dark?" he said.

We turned off the big, black Maglites we were carrying and blackness enveloped us. I scanned all around me. The stairwell. The hallway. The living room across from us. As my eyes adjusted to the darkness, I began to see them.

"Look," I said. "See all those little red lights?"

"What're you talking about, Mojo?"

I took hold of his bomb-suit sleeve and pointed his arm toward a couple of the tiny orangish-red lights. They were so small, they didn't give out much more than a faint, telltale glow around themselves.

"They're LEDs," I said. "Light-emitting diodes being used as miniature motion sensors. That's how the booby traps are being triggered."

"Does knowing that help us?" he asked.

"Yeah. We work in the dark and watch for them. If we can, we go under or around them. If we can't, we use something to trigger them from out of range."

"Sounds like a plan," he said. "I think."

Leaving the flashlights switched off, we started down the hallway where the next three bodies lay. I scanned the floor, walls, and ceiling. I spotted a total of six of the tiny lights embedded in the two walls, all at about waist height, and pointed them out to Wilson.

"Let's get down and crawl," I said. "We can check the SWAT guys for vitals as we go over them."

As I clambered over each of the downed cops, I pulled off my protective glove and checked for pulses at their throats. There were none at the first two bodies. One of the checks left a sticky residue of blood on my hands. When I started crawling over the third guy, I heard a hideous, pitiful whimper.

"Officer," I said. "Can you identify yourself?"

"Roshinthkuh," he said in a gurgling moan.

"It's Roczinski!" I said.

"Sergeant Rock?"

"Yes. He's alive. Let's get him out of here."

"How do we do that, exactly?" Wilson asked.

"We stay low and drag him out. Push the other bodies aside and pull him out by his feet."

"Be fun in these suits, won't it? I'm already swimming in sweat inside this one."

After performing the grim task of shifting the other two cops' corpses against the wall, we each took hold of a foot and dragged Roczinski down the hall and through the living room to the house's exit. When we got him onto the porch, the med techs ran up and got him onto a gurney.

Dorn came up as they were wheeling him away. "Roczinski, eh? Did you find any others alive in there?" he asked.

"We're still looking," I said. "Going back in to check for more."

"Nice to know you're out here keeping score, though," Wilson said as we turned to go back inside.

We alligator-crawled down the hall again, past the two corpses we'd shoved aside. As we were passing what I took to be a bedroom, I heard another moan and some faint babbling coming from inside. Keeping my head low, I checked in the darkness for LEDs. I saw four of them scattered around the room, once again at waist height. I switched on my flashlight and saw a black-uniformed SWAT cop lying on his back a few feet away, clasping his blood-soaked crotch. The babbling stopped. His head jerked up. It was a young white guy. His face was covered in tears and his eyes were crazy-wild with pain.

"Turn that frigging light off!" he screamed at me.

I saw one bloody hand reach for the black leather holster at his waist.

"All right, man," I said, quickly switching off the flashlight. "It's off, okay?"

"Don't look at me!" he yelled.

There was just enough light coming in the window for me to see the .45 pistol he was holding. It was pointed directly at my helmeted face. I wondered how good the ballistics specs were on the acrylic visor.

"Chill man, I'm not looking," I said. "Listen, what's your name, officer?"

"Pitts," he said, his voice cracking. "Officer Jerry Pitts."

"We're gonna get you out of here, Jerry."

"My balls," he whimpered, ignoring me. "And my dick. They're gone. They're frigging GONE!!!"

"Listen," I said. "We'll get you out of here. They'll fix you up, Jerry."

"Fix me?" he said. "I'm already fixed, asshole! I'm fixed for good!"

I heard the soft click of a pistol hammer latching back.

"Don't!" I said, "That's an order, officer!"

"Tell my wife I said I love her!"

"Jerry! Chill out, man! Please! Think about-"

BAM!

I lay there in the bomb suit for a time, shuddering and sweating, while I got my nerves back together.

"I don't know that I blame him, Mojo," Wilson finally said. "I think I'd do the same."

"Whatever," I said with a sigh. "Let's keep moving. And stop calling me 'Mojo.'"

"Right," he said.

We continued crawling down the hall until we got to the kitchen. At the entranceway, I propped myself up on the elbows of my suit. The smells of dust, blood, and explosives were strong in the room, even through the helmet's hazmat air filter. From scanning the dark room, I could see that moving around would be a bear. There were a slew of the tiny, telltale LEDs, at a variety of heights.

When I switched on the Maglite it was immediately obvious that the worst of the carnage had taken place there. There seemed to be corpses everywhere. Although the number of bodies in the room were proof that several of the booby traps had already been tripped, there was no telling whether others would go off if we made the wrong move.

Wilson tugged on the leg of my bomb suit, and I shifted to one side so he could crawl up alongside me at the entrance.

"Boy, the fun never stops, does it?" he said, surveying the room as I swept the flashlight over the bodies. "Are any of them alive?"

"Don't know," I said. "Haven't heard noises from any of them yet. We'll have to check for vital signs."

"What I don't like," I went on, "are all the LEDs I'm seeing. They're at a bunch of different heights and directions. We're going to have to get something to try to trip them before we can move around safely."

"Yeah?" he said. "Got any ideas about what to use for a tripper?"

My mind raced through possible options.

"Maybe a curtain rod," I said. "Let's go back to the living room. We'll take down the rod over the picture window and bring it back here. Then wave it around in each section of the kitchen before we move into them."

"Okay," he said. "Let's do it before I drown in my own sweat."

We alligatored back to the living room. After double-checking to be sure we wouldn't trip any LEDs, we got up and yanked the ten-foot long curtain rod down off the wall. Light from the streetlamps and police vehicles outside poured into the living room. After pulling the curtains off the rod, we got down on our bellies again and crawled back to the kitchen.

"Let's do it in quadrants," I said at the entrance. "We'll start here."

Holding the rod in my heavy bomb gloves, I waved it around over the nearest body. Up and down and then side to side.

Nothing.

"Wag that thing some more," Wilson said. "Let's be sure."

I did and still there was nothing. We crawled over to the first body. He was face down on the linoleum floor. I pulled off my glove and reached around to check the pulse at the front of his neck.

"Dead," I said. Let's move on."

Two more bodies lay a few feet away. Wilson had dragged the curtain rod along with him. He extended it out over the pair of bodies and began to rotate it.

WHAM!

A booming shotgun-like blast exploded out of an adjacent cabinet.

"Yow!" he exclaimed, dropping the rod as a heavy load of buckshot or shrapnel spattered into the wall and counter above where we lay.

When Wilson lifted the curtain rod again, it was bent where it had taken the shot. He handed it to me.

"Here - you wag it this time," he said. "My hands are shaking too bad."

I resumed waving it over the two bodies. Up, down and around. Nothing.

"I think you cleared it," I said.

"How awesome of me," he said. "Let's get on with it."

We crawled forward. The two bodies were partly on top of one another. As we got close, Wilson flicked on his flashlight. The beam caught a face that was half-missing - apparently the guy who'd screamed about being hit in the eyes with acid. His SWAT helmet was off and the 9mm Glock he'd put to his temple was still in his hand.

"I wish I hadn't seen that," Wilson said, switching off the flashlight.

"Let's check the officer beneath him," I said.

"Okay. But watch out for post-nasal drip from this poor guy," he said.

I pulled off my glove and reached around to the throat of the man underneath. It came back wet with blood, but I'd felt a pulse.

"He's alive," I said. "Let's get him out of here."

Careful to avoid the acid residue, we shifted the body on top aside.

"Same drill as before," I said. "We drag him by his feet, staying in the quadrants we've tested."

"Gotcha," he said.

We pulled the man out of the kitchen, down the hall and out onto the porch. Again, the med techs rushed up and got him onto a gurney. In the light from the streetlamps his wounds looked pretty bad, but hopefully wouldn't prove fatal.

Dorn came up to the porch again. "Any more alive in there?" he asked.

"Not sure," I said. "We're working our way through the kitchen. That's where most of the bodies are."

"Need any support from us out here?" he asked.

"How about an ice cream cone?" Wilson said. "Tutti-frutti for me."

"With sprinkles on top," he added as we turned to go back inside.

Back on our bellies in the kitchen, I picked up the curtain rod and began waving it over Roper - the bomb tech who'd taken the refrigerator blast.

BOOM!

"Holy Miranda rights!" Wilson shouted as something shot out of a cabinet and hit the wall across the room. The explosion knocked out a drawer and it dropped to the floor, with the sound of silverware clattering. Then an ugly fizzing sound came from the opposite wall.

"Acid," I said as I resumed waving the curtain rod over the downed bomb squad tech.

"I prefer marijuana myself," Wilson said. "No flashbacks."

When we were sure there were no more booby traps to trigger, we crawled over to Roper. I flicked on the flashlight and swept it over his body. The front of the olive drab suit was charred black and badly chewed-up from the explosion. What with all the built-in and strapped-on armor, I couldn't tell if there was breathing or a heartbeat.

"Have to take his helmet off," I said.

I reached under the heavy bomb-suit collar and undid the helmet latch. Both of us then carefully pulled it over his head. There was blood coming from Roper's nose and ears, but when I felt his throat there was a pulse. Weak but steady.

"He's alive," I said. "But just barely. Let's get him out of here quick."

"Gonna be fun doing it with him in this ninety-pound nightgown," Wilson said.

"Hey, that's why we work out every day," I said.

"We do?" he said.

Again staying within the quadrants we'd checked, we dragged Roper out of the kitchen and down the hall. The extra weight of the man's bomb suit made pulling him out feel like a job for Schwarzenegger, if not Hercules. The insides of my own suit were like a sauna by the time we neared the front door.

"Sheesh, Mojo," Wilson said as we hefted him out onto the porch. "I think I've got a double hernia."

"Be sure to have the hospital check him for internal injuries," I told the med techs as they were loading Roper onto the gurney. "He took a high-velocity blast in there."

I looked around for Dorn before we went back in. He was nowhere to be seen. I figured he was off somewhere talking to Blandings, the two of them trying to figure out how to put some kind of positive spin on the debacle at Al-Rafi's house.

After crawling back to the kitchen, we waggled the curtain rod over the last two SWAT team bodies.

WHAM!

A loud charge blew out over our heads, showering us with broken bits of plaster and wood.

When the debris stopped raining down, I at first thought the ringing in my ears was from the explosion. Then I realized it was coming from an old yellow touch-tone phone mounted on the wall overhead.

Wilson gave me a nudge. "Probably one of your girlfriends," he said.

"Kind of doubt it," I said. "But I'd sure as hell like to know who's calling this number right now."

"Yeah? Well, I don't think I'd recommend putting that thing up to your ear."

He was right, of course. There was an excellent chance it'd be another booby trap.

To be on the safe side, I took the curtain rod and used it to knock the handset up out of its holder. There was no blast and the ringing stopped as the handset clattered down onto the linoleum floor. Its twisty yellow cord swayed as I crawled over to it. I picked up the handset in my gloved hand and awkwardly held it up to the side of my fiber helmet. I hoped the earpiece would be strong enough to resist a blast this close up, if there was one.

Silence.

I moved the handset down to the helmet's mouthpiece.

"Agent McCoy Johnson," I said into it and moved the handset back to my earpiece.

"Guess what, Johnson?" a man's voice said.

"Who is this?" I asked.

"Doesn't matter. In exactly one minute that damn house is going to be demolished. With you in it, asshole. You're going to be crushed like a frigging fly."

"How do you know my name?"

"Screw you, Johnson. I'll see you in hell."

"Who are you?" I began, but he cut me off with a nasty laugh.

"Fifty-five seconds, scumbag," he said.

The phone began humming at me as the line went dead.

I looked at Wilson and tossed the handset aside.

"We need to get out of here - fast!" I told him.

"What about checking out these other guys?"

I took a gut-wrenching look at the two remaining bodies.

"No time, damn it!" I said. "In less than a minute the house is going to blow! Get moving! Go! GO!"

Frantically, we crawled of the kitchen and down the hall, past the SWAT team members' corpses. I did a count-down as we scrabbled forward on our bellies inside the hot, heavy bomb suits. *Thirty. Twenty-five. Twenty. Fifteen.* We were at ten seconds when we reached the base of the stairwell and clambered to our feet.

BOOM!

The explosion blasted up out of the floor like a shotgun blast.

"AAIEEE!" Wilson screamed. Aghast, I watched him fall backwards onto the floor, clutching his groin.

"MY BALLS!" he howled as he lay there writhing. "OMIGOD!"

I looked down in horror at the smoking, shattered armor plate covering his crotch. Then I realized that the extra plate he'd put on beneath it was still intact.

"You're okay!" I yelled as I grabbed an arm and yanked him to his feet.

I was still counting. *Six. Five. Four.*

I looked around frantically. There was no time to reach the foyer and door from where we stood.

"THE WINDOW!" I bellowed. "JUMP!"

We bounded toward the living room's big picture window. Feeling death's icy breath on our hot necks, we reached it in what had to be a Guinness record for men sprinting in ninety-pound bomb suits. At the last possible millisecond we instinctively lowered our helmeted heads and dove.

Screaming like pair of madmen, we smashed into the plate glass just as the room behind us exploded in a hellish flash of white light.

Chapter 19   Shell-Shocked

Tuesday, August 16 - 9:40 p.m.

THE BLAST engulfed us, the shock wave slamming into my back like an ogre's fist. We burst through the disintegrating window, the sound of its shattering lost in the deafening roar that was propelling us outward.

Arms flailing, our bomb-suited bodies came down on the thick old hedge that ran under the picture window. The hedge trampolined us out over the front lawn, my fiber helmet flying off as I went head over heels in the air before landing, with a painful thump, flat on my back.

Behind me I heard a rapid-fire series of explosions follow the one that had blown us out the window. Even before they'd finished, there was a monstrous sound of cracking and crumbling as the walls of the house began to collapse.

Mindful that I was now helmetless, I frantically rolled over. Throwing my gloved hands over the back of my head, I pressed my sweaty face into the grass as the debris hit. I lay there trembling while a barrage of brick, wood, metal, and glass came crunching and spattering down onto my Kevlar-clad body.

When I finally dared lift my head, I saw a huge cloud of dust hovering in the darkness overhead, with the lights from the street lamps and police vehicles shining through it in hazy whorls.

Slowly and shakily I got to my feet, the suit feeling like it had tripled in weight. My mind was woozy and my body ached everywhere. I noticed something wet was running down the right side of my head and into my ear.

Dim blue figures were approaching. Blinking, I looked around for Wilson, the cloud of dust stinging my eyes.

"Thank you, Sweet Jesus," I heard him saying. "You're the best!"

I turned and through the haze saw him standing a few steps away, checking out his intact crotch. He'd taken his helmet off and was grinning down gleefully at the spare beneath his blown-out groin armor. Then he looked up at me.

"Hey, Mojo," he said. "You know what? You look like warmed-over elephant doody."

"That's about eggszhackly how I feel," I said, my voice slurring.

Dizzily, I turned around and gazed at the demolished house. I saw that - fortunately for me, Wilson, and the other bystanders - the explosions had mostly collapsed it inward. Then it struck me that this must've been exactly what the bomber wanted: a controlled demolition that would bring the house crashing down onto whoever was inside and make sure they were all dead.

Especially me, I thought, recalling the phone call.

He's in the crowd, I heard my dead sister say.

I blinked a few times. *Who is? What crowd?* I replied, my brain feeling like it was full of molasses. I turned my head but found my view blocked by the big bomb-suit collar.

He's in the crowd, Ofelia repeated. *Watching.*

When I rotated my body to take a better look around, the wooziness worsened. Instead of a crowd, all I saw was Dorn standing there. Three of him, actually.

"You look like you need medical attention, Johnson," the trio of horny toad faces said in unison.

"I'm fine," I told them, feeling myself wobble as I said it. "Couldn't be better."

I tried to add a smug grin, but the effort seemed to cause my knees to dissolve. I began toppling forward. In an oddly detached way, I watched the debris-strewn lawn rush up at me. But I was out cold before my face smacked into it.

Chapter 20   Waking Up In Heaven

Wednesday, August 17 - 4:25 a.m.

WHEN I came to again, I found myself staring into shimmering white light. The milky glow had a strangely peaceful and otherworldly quality to it.

Am I dead? I wondered. Was I transitioning into some higher realm or dimension? Was I about to see and meet God?

Only gradually did it dawn on me that I was in fact lying on my back, staring up at the murky radiance from a fluorescent light fixture with a translucent plastic cover.

When I tried to lift my head, a knife-like pain shot from the back of my neck up to the top of my skull. I groaned and let my head fall back. As the pain slowly dissipated, the face of a lovely brown female angel appeared to my right, leaning over me.

"Agent Johnson?" she said. "Are you awake?"

I stared at the angel for several moments. The light from the ceiling fixture was haloing her head, and the sense of being in some higher realm began to steal back over me.

"Am I in heaven?" I asked.

Her lovely mouth curved into a lopsided grin.

"Only if you think the Detroit Medical Center is heaven. Believe me, most folks don't," she said.

"Well, if you're not an angel, who are you then?"

"I'm Dr. Cummings. I was on ER duty when you came in."

"I'm in ER?

"You're out of ER. I just came up here to check on you."

"What's the matter with me?"

"Nothing much. Simple concussion. Severe laceration to the side of your head. Deep enough to score the skull and took fifteen stitches to close up. Three ribs probably cracked, but not fractured. A variety of abrasions and contusions. Other than that, you're fine."

As she was going over the damage toll, I became more and more aware of the fact that every inch of me felt like it had been pounded with a ball peen hammer.

"Sounds like I'm just ducky. How come I don't feel ducky?"

"Your body looks like it's taken a pretty traumatic beating over the past few hours. You'll be in pain for at least a couple of days. But to be honest," she added. "Compared to a lot of what I see coming into ER here - shootings, stabbings, car accidents - you're aces, my friend."

"I see your point," I said.

It was then that I happened to notice the clock on the wall behind the angelic doctor.

"Wait a minute," I said. "Is it 4:30 a.m. or p.m.? And what day is it?"

"It's Wednesday. 4:30 a.m. You've only been here a few hours."

"Shoot. That's few hours too many. I need to get out of here as soon as possible."

She shook her head disapprovingly.

"Listen, Mr. Johnson - I understand you're an FBI agent and that you're working on those terrible bombings. I even heard you're some kind of hero. But some bed rest right now would be a very good idea. Even for a hero."

"Believe me, doctor," I said. "I'd be all for that, if I had the time. But unfortunately I don't."

I made another attempt to lift my head. Again the pain shot up through it.

"Listen - could you possibly remove this Bowie knife somebody jammed into the back of my skull?" I asked.

"It's probably a combination of the concussion and a neck sprain. It'll subside. I'll write you a prescription for a few Vicodin. That should help."

"Thanks. Look, can you help me sit up? I think once I'm upright, I'll feel better."

"I can adjust the bed."

"No, I want to sit up."

"Okay, then. Here, take my hand."

As she pulled me up into a sitting position, I realized there was an IV unit alongside the bed, its tube running into my arm. I looked at the name tag on her blue medical outfit. *Dr. O. Cummings*, it said. I also noticed she wore a ring on her right hand.

Now that I was upright, she looked less like an angel and more like a woman. But so beautiful, she still seemed almost unearthly. I felt myself attracted to her in a strangely powerful way. A way I hadn't felt drawn to anyone in years. Or maybe ever.

"Damn, you're gorgeous," I said, staring directly into her eyes. They were medium brown, with flecks of jade green in them.

Her eyes skated away. I could see I'd discomfited her.

"I don't take flattery very well, Agent Johnson," she said. "And truth be told, I really don't appreciate it."

"Wasn't flattery," I said. "Just a statement of fact."

I nodded at the ring she was wearing. "Engaged?" I asked.

"Divorced," she said. "I like the ring, so I wear it. How are you feeling?"

I was right about feeling better once I'd sat up. My body was still riddled with aches, but the cobwebs were clearing from my mind.

"Better," I said.

"No dizziness?"

"None. Where's my clothing, by the way?" I asked. "Can't fight the forces of evil wearing this flimsy hospital gown. They'd just laugh at me."

"They're in the closet, but I really don't think-"

Wincing in pain, I swung my legs over the side of the hospital bed.

She frowned at me. "You're not kidding about getting out of here, are you, Agent? That really is a bad idea, you know."

"No choice, Doc. If it was up to me, I'd stay here and chat with you for hours. But this really is a matter of life and death. Last I heard, there are ninety people dead. Plus a lot more injured."

"I know," she said, looking grim. "I'm still treating over a dozen patients from the Woodward bus bombing."

"Can you take this IV thing out of my arm, then, and get me my clothing?" I asked.

With her brows furrowed she did as I asked, removing the IV and taping a wad of gauze over the purplish spot where needle had gone in. Then she brought me my clothes from the hospital room closet and laid them out on the bed.

"By the way, what's that "O" on your name tag stand for, Doctor?" I asked as I painfully got to my feet.

"Oprah."

"Hmm - not the most common name. Seems to me I've heard it before, though. Somewhere."

"Could be," she said. "I'm told there's this lady in Chicago's got the same name."

She backed away from the bed. "Listen," she said. "I'll step outside while you get out of that gown and get dressed."

"Might want to stay here, in case I fall down," I said. I wasn't really worried about it. I just didn't want her to leave.

"Then I'll turn my back," she said.

Her back side looked every bit as lovely as her front, I noted as she stood there facing away from me. More womanly than angelic, though.

"Do you ever date patients, Dr. Oprah?" I asked, pulling off the hospital gown.

"Wow," she said with a chuckle, shaking her head. "You sure do move fast, Agent Johnson."

"I really and truly don't, by and large," I said, as I began changing into my street clothes.

"But I'm in a peculiar frame of mind right now. You see, just a few hours ago I was surrounded by dead men - including some who'd died in the most god-awful ways imaginable - and I was in mortal danger myself. Coming out of that and surviving has got me feeling both very alive and very clear about what I'm seeing. And what I'm seeing is someone I want like crazy to get to know better."

"In a couple of minutes," I went on, tucking in my shirt, "I'm going to have to walk on out of here and go back to my job. I don't have time to be cool or suave or blasé, so I'm just going to say this straight out. When all this bombing madness is over, Dr. Oprah, can you and I get together some time?"

"I'm decent now, by the way," I added.

She turned around and gave me a level gaze.

"I genuinely don't know, Agent," she said. "As a rule, I don't date patients. So I'll have to think about it."

"Fair enough," I said. "Please do. Meanwhile, I've got to go now. Mind if I hug you?"

I could see the question had taken her by surprise, so I took advantage of her confusion to clasp her in my arms. I felt her body tense up at first, but then relax as I held her gently and rested my cheek against the top of her head. It felt good and right to have her in my arms. Maybe she felt it too, because her arms went around me and she tentatively hugged me back. I savored the feel of her against me as we stood there - even the stethoscope between her breasts.

"You're a strange man, Agent Johnson," she said, giving my back a gentle, un-doctorly stroke.

"I am," I agreed. "Sometimes, at least."

Reluctantly, I let go of her.

"Thanks for the hug, Doc. Got to run now," I said.

"Let me write you that Vicodin scrip," she said.

After quickly scribbling out the prescription on the bedside table, she reached into a pocket of her blue med jacket, pulled out a business card, and handed both to me.

"There may be complications from the concussion," she said. "If you start to feel strange - very dizzy or nauseous - give me a call right away, understand?"

"Yes, ma'am," I said.

Just before I turned to leave the room, I took her hand.

Her eyes looked back into mine, searchingly, as I drank in the sight of her face for a few more seconds. Damn, you're beautiful, I was thinking. But I kept silent this time, not wanting to make her uncomfortable again. Besides, it wasn't just her beauty that was captivating me. There was also that uncanny magnetism I'd felt from the moment I first saw her.

"Thanks, Doctor Oprah," I said. "I'll be in touch."

"Be careful out there," she said, giving my fingers a gentle squeeze.

"I will," I said.

"Promise?" she asked.

"Promise," I said.

On my way down in the elevator I called for a cab to take me back to the FBI office, so I could get my car. When I hung up the cell, it was a hell of an effort to push the lingering images of Dr. Oprah Cummings' stunning face, figure, and being out of my mind, but I did my best. I knew I had to get focused back on the job of finding the bombers and stopping them.

As I was going out the hospital exit, I spotted a newspaper box in the foyer. "HOUSE OF DEATH FOR SWAT COPS!" the headline read. Under it was the subtitle, "FBI Heroes Rescue 3."

I shook my head. It looked like Morley Blandings had somehow managed to turn the gruesome fiasco that had gone down at Al-Rafi's place into a PR win for the Bureau. And by extension, for himself.

Outside, as I waited for the cab I'd called to show up, the first light of dawn was just then breaking over the Detroit sky. I watched it with a dark look on my face, simmering inside.

As far as I was concerned, Elliot Dorn's call to send in those ten men all at once had been as rash as it was stupid. How many more asinine decisions like that would he and Blandings make before we tracked the bombers down?

And how many more lives would their bad calls cost?

Chapter 21   Gremlins And Gargoyles

Wednesday, August 17 - 5:30 a.m.

AFTER TAKING a cab from the hospital to the Federal building, I got into my government Chevy and headed back toward Elmore Street. As I drove west on Michigan Ave, the sky was just beginning to lighten in my rear view mirror, but the street lights were still on. There was only a trickle of traffic that early in the morning, which made it somewhat easier to focus on the swarm of questions about the bombings that were buzzing around inside my head. The foremost of them being: who the hell was that son of a bitch who'd telephoned me at Al-Rafi's?

Obviously it was someone who knew me and hated my guts. Someone who not only intended to kill me, but wanted to make me spend the last minute of my life in absolute terror, knowing that the imam's house was about to blow up with me and Wilson inside it.

But the maddening fact was, I didn't have a clue who the voice belonged to. While it had sounded vaguely familiar - like someone I might have heard once or twice in my life - I couldn't for the life of me place it.

One thing I *was* sure about was that he'd known I was inside the house.

He's in the crowd, I remembered Ofelia saying just before I conked out on Al-Rafi's lawn.

He'd been out there somewhere, amid the bevy of spectators who'd been at the scene. Though I hadn't paid them much attention, I remembered seeing TV crews there, behind the police cordons. I'd have to contact the local TV news departments later today and ask to view all the raw video footage they'd shot. Maybe I'd recognize the caller if they caught a shot of him and I saw his face. Assuming, of course, he'd been reckless or stupid enough to let that happen.

Dawn broke in the sky behind me while I continued down Michigan, the street lights winking off overhead as swaths of bronze sunlight began to spread over the shabby thoroughfare.

I began mentally clicking through all the criminals I'd put away over the fifteen years I'd been in law enforcement. First as a beat cop back in Chicago. Later as an FBI special agent in Atlanta and Memphis. And for the past eight years - aside from my twelve-month Iraq stint - in Detroit.

As I went through the mental snapshots, I tried to picture the perps at times I'd heard them speaking. Some I saw sitting sullenly handcuffed in the back of a car. Others when their eyes were shifting nervously while we grilled them in some interrogation room. Still others as I sat in courtrooms, watching them solemnly swear to tell the truth and then proceed to lie with as much cunning as they were capable of.

By the time I finished going down the list, I had to admit I felt reasonably satisfied about the number of criminals I've helped send up the river. They've ranged from corporate con men and child pornographers to big-time drug dealers and vicious serial killers. But the voice I'd heard back in that deadly, booby-trapped kitchen didn't match up with any of the faces in my memory.

I next tried to imagine who in that rogue's gallery could possibly have the explosives expertise our perp obviously had. None of the guys I'd put away had been involved in bombings or illegal munitions traffic. Maybe some of them had military or demolition company experience, though. I'd have to go back through my case files and do history checks on them.

One of the many things that nagged at me was that the whole setup had obviously been meant to kill cops. The bomber had murdered Al-Rafi simply to put his fingerprints on the extortion letter and lure the police there into the booby-trapped house. Why? Did he have some beef not just against me, but against cops in general?

And why were so many of the booby traps aimed at mutilating the cops' genitals? Was it simply that it was one of the most horrifying injuries you could inflict on a male? A perverse, sadistic form of cruelty? Or was there some deeper, darker reason?

And finally - what was up with that call from La Borgia, offering to help? Was it sheer coincidence that he phoned while I was at Al-Rafi's? Could he be involved somehow?

I glanced up at the rear view mirror and wasn't surprised to see the scowl of frustration on my face.

There were too damn many questions. And too damn few answers.

It was a bit after 6 a.m. by the time I got back to Al-Rafi's place. The demolished house was surrounded by yellow crime scene tape. But amazingly, there were no cops there on duty. No one guarding the site to prevent evidence contamination. And - unless they were hiding up in the trees with the squirrels - no one in plainclothes posted up and down the street to see if any interested parties might show up there. Another pea-brained call by Elliot Dorn, super-sleuth, I figured as I got out of my car.

I shook my head in disgust. The one upside was that at least I'd have total peace and quiet as I did my post-mortem lookaround.

I began by making a circular walk around the collapsed house's perimeter. I could make out the spots where they'd dug the corpses of the dead SWAT team members out of the rubble. I wondered how they'd located them and decided they most likely brought in dogs.

I decided to pick my way through the debris. As I stepped up onto the heap of broken bricks, shattered wood, and twisted metal, a disquieting notion came to mind. What if there were still some unexploded booby traps down there?

After that I took my time, scanning every place I was about to step before I put my two hundred-twenty pounds down on it.

A few minutes into my search, I came across a charred white metal panel in the area where the kitchen must have been. Probably a piece of the refrigerator, I thought. There was blood on it, and it bugged me that it hadn't been taken to the evidence labs. I wondered whose blood it was. Al-Rafi's? One of the SWAT cops? Testing could determine it.

"How come you're walking around in there?" I heard a young voice ask.

I turned. An Arab-looking boy was standing at the edge of the rubble, staring at me through a pair of rectangular black eyeglasses. He looked to be about ten.

"Howdy there, young man," I said to him. "You're up and about mighty early."

"It's summer," he said. "I get up when I want. I was gonna watch TV but I saw you out here. Are you a policeman?"

"Sort of. I work for the FBI. Do you know what that is?"

"Sure. Federal Bureau of Investigation. You guys are always on television, chasing serial killers and terrorists and mafia guys, like Tony Soprano. Are you on TV?"

"Nope. Afraid not."

"I saw you here last night," he said. "In your space suit."

"You did, eh?" I said. "So you were here last night when the house blew up?"

"Uh-huh. I watched it all from my bedroom window," he said. "Over there."

He pointed to the house directly across the street.

I frowned at him. "I thought the police evacuated all the surrounding houses."

"They did," he said. "I snuck back to watch. My room's upstairs. My ma just about killed me later."

"She should've," I said, wagging a finger at him.

"What happened to your head?" he said.

I touched the bandage over my ear. "This? Got a nasty scratch when that house came down."

Then a question occurred to me. "Before last night, did you ever see Mr. Al-Rafi from up there?" I asked.

"Sure. All the time. I have a table next to the window and I look out a lot. Like when I sit there drawing or playing games and stuff."

"Ever see anything unusual go on over here?"

"I saw a man go into his house three nights ago."

I froze, my breath stopping for a couple of seconds while I stared at him. "You did?" I said.

"Yeah. He parked his car up the street. A big black Cadillac Escalade."

Look over there. My dead sister's voice and the SUV I'd seen just after the Woodward bombing came back to me.

"You're sure that's what it was?"

"Sure I'm sure. That's my favorite car. I'm gonna buy one and pimp it out," he said. "When I grow up," he added.

"And you say this man went into Mr. Al-Rafi's house?"

"Yeah. He just walked over and went up the driveway to the side door. And then he went in."

"You said this was at night. What time?"

"I dunno. Pretty late - maybe midnight. I was supposed to be asleep, but I was playing this new game I got, with the lights off. It's called 'Gremlins and Gargoyles.' Have you ever played it?"

"Nope, sorry, I haven't. This man - you say he just went in? Like he had a key?"

"I couldn't see if he had a key or not. He just stood there in the shadows for like a minute or two. Then he went inside."

"Were there lights on in the house?"

"There was one light on upstairs, I think."

By this point I'd picked my way back out of the rubble and was standing in front of the boy. He was wearing tan cargo shorts and a Tigers t-shirt.

"What's your name, son?" I asked.

"Ahmad," he said. "Al-Jamal."

I took out my ID wallet and showed him my FBI badge.

"Ahmad," I said. "Look real close at this picture ID and the seal on it. This is to show you I am who I say I am. Don't ever trust someone who won't prove to you who they are. Understand?"

"Okay," he said.

"Good," I said. "Now, tell you what, son - how about you and I go get us some breakfast somewhere?"

After a couple of miles of driving around, I found a Denny's that was open. As Ahmad and I ate our pancake and turkey sausage breakfasts, I pumped him for as many additional details about Al-Rafi and the man who'd gone into his house as I could. Then I dropped the boy off at his home and headed back to my condo for a shower and change of clothes. On my way there I called Dawson on his cell.

"It's Johnson," I said when he picked up.

"McCoy? I thought you were at the DMC."

"They let me out. Listen, I think we've caught a break. Went back to Elmore Street and ran into this boy, Ahmad Al-Jamal. He saw a guy go into Al-Rafi's house three nights ago. Probably picked the door lock or jimmied his way in. I've got a partial description and a vehicle make and model."

"That's great. But how come you're calling me? You should be telling Dorn or Blandings."

"I figured I'd tell someone who might actually do something useful with it. Those two will just blow it off if it doesn't fit the picture they want to see."

"That may be, McCoy. But believe me, you won't be helping your career any by trying to go around Blandings. Stick with the chain of command."

"Listen, Eric - that Dorn guy of his is bad news. By the time they went in there I was pretty sure it was a trap and I told him so. Tried to get him to make those SWAT cops be extra careful about breaching the house. Instead, he blew me off. Let them all go in there like gangbusters, and now eight of them are dead."

"Well, the way they spun it to the media and Washington is that the DPD SWAT was overeager to go in there. But you and Wilson are the FBI heroes who risked life and limb to save the ones you could. Under Elliot Dorn's savvy direction, of course."

"You're kidding, right? Dorn was standing there with both thumbs up his butt, sweating like an Alabama pig. It was my idea to go in and get those guys out."

"I know. Wilson filled me in on what really went down."

"All right - whatever. I'm heading home now for a shower and change of clothes. I'll get into the office as soon as I can."

"Sounds good, McCoy. I'll tell Dorn and Blandings you're out of the hospital and you'll be coming in later. And that you've got some new information."

"Fine. I'm sure Beavis and Butt-Head will be tickled pink."

When I got to back to my condo complex, I parked my car and headed for the front entrance. As I was about to turn up the walk, I heard the short beep of car horn behind me. I looked around and saw a hot pink Corvette heading my way. Its smoked glass windows prevented me from seeing who was in it. I stood and watched the car ease over to the curb and pull up alongside me. The passenger side window began sliding down. Cautiously, I leaned over and looked inside.

Behind the wheel, wearing nothing but a lot of jewelry, a pair of suede cowboy boots, her seat belt, and a lascivious grin, sat Nadine Robinson.

"Hey there, honey man," she said. Her big brown eyes had their usual evil twinkle in them.

I sighed as I let myself drink in the sight of her voluptuous body. I wondered if Michigan had a law against driving naked. At least she had her seat belt on.

"Nice wheels," I said, nodding at the sleek, powerful sports car.

"A little birthday gift from sweet old Harley," she said.

"So what are you doing here, Nadine?"

"Just thought I'd come by and give my favorite FBI agent a discreet little reward for all his heroic efforts. Why don't you jump in here, McCoy?" she said, patting the beige leather passenger seat.

"I don't think so," I said.

"Come on, honey man. I'll take you for a ride on the freeway of love." Her fingers were fluttering suggestively over the Cadillac's gearshift lever and knob as she spoke.

"Not going to happen, Nadine. Go home to your husband."

"McCoy-McCoy-McCoy," she said, shaking her head as she pouted at me. "Whatever am I going to do with you?"

"You know what, Nadine? There *is* something you can do for me."

The pout became a devilish grin. "You just name it, honey man," she said, her voice husky, moving her shoulders in a way that made her heavy breasts sway.

"You can give me my house key back."

She put a finger to the side of her mouth and shook her head.

"Uh-uh. Not going to happen, McCoy," she said. "As they say."

"Listen, Nadine - what's going on here? How come you're all of a sudden so hot for us to get back together?"

"What if I said I missed that very special *manly* loving of yours?" she said. She was gripping the gearshift knob now, squeezing her thighs together and slowly rotating her hips on the leather seat as she grinned up at me. I noticed she'd shaved her pubes down to a little heart shape.

Damn. With a superhuman effort, I ripped my eyes from her ripe, undulating body and made myself focus on her leering face.

"I'd say you're lying and trying to con me," I said, squinting at her. "So why don't you tell me what you're *really* up to, Nadine?"

For just an instant I saw gears working behind the come-hither expression on that beautiful face of hers.

"Let's just say I like a *challenge*," she said.

With that, she touched a button on the Corvette's steering wheel.

"One of these days, McCoy," she said as the smoked glass window slid up, "you're going to have a lapse in that tired old Puritan morality of yours. And when you do, little old Nadine here's gonna take you straight to heaven's gate."

"Or hell's," I muttered as the window closed.

With a petulant-sounding chirp from its fat tires, the hot pink Corvette sped away.

As soon I opened the door to my condo, the Thing accosted me, yowling like some ungodly beast from a monster movie. He followed me to the kitchen, where I hastily opened and dumped out three cans of dog food into his aluminum bowl (he'd long ago torn up and eaten the original plastic one) and got out of his way.

Grimacing as I watched the nasty little sucker thresh through his dinner, I thought about Nadine's coming on to me again.

I was damn sure she wasn't just looking to reward me for being some kind of hero. She had something else on her agenda besides lustful fun.

But what in tarnation was it?

Chapter 22   Intuition

Wednesday, August 17 - 7:00 a.m.

"DAMN THAT motherdumping sonofabitch Johnson!" he says. He's glowering at the oversize TV, his blue eyes wide with outraged disbelief.

Beside him Beelzebub gives out an empathetic snarl that bares his jutting white teeth.

Furious, the man clicks off the TV and flings the remote at the couch. The pit bull follows him as he stomps out of the room and heads for the back door.

He thought for *sure* he'd taken out that big, black scum-sucker last night!

After his taunting call to Johnson, he'd waited for the minute to run out and then discreetly lifted and pointed the remote. With a quick press of the PLAY button, he detonated the explosives he'd planted around the house's foundation and joists. Shivers of pleasure went through him as he stood behind the police cordon a hundred yards away. With smoke and flames shooting out of the chimney and windows, the rumbling explosions ripped through Al-Rafi's place. Around him, the Arab women shrieked like banshees at the sight and sound of the old brick house crumbling down. A huge cloud of dust covered the scene and then wafted up the street to where he stood with the crowd. When it cleared, all that was left of the house was a pile of rubble, with cops and EMS techs just beginning to warily approach it.

For about twenty minutes afterwards he'd stood there amid the excitedly buzzing crowd, savoring the sight of the demolished home. With a leer on his face, he'd imagined Johnson's mangled body inside: ripped and torn and squashed, his innards spilled out like a gutted deer's.

Cued by seeing several other onlookers do it, he'd snapped a few photos of the scene with his cell phone camera - despite the fact that the darkness and distance made it unlikely he'd get any decent shots. Finally, he'd gone back to his pickup and driven home to the compound. Around midnight he'd crawled into bed, tired but deeply content, certain he'd finally done the big, black scumbag in.

But now, having just checked the morning TV news, he's found out that not only is the son of bitch still alive, he and that other FBI agent who'd gone in are being hailed as frigging heroes because they'd apparently saved three of the SWAT team members before the house exploded.

"Those bastards!" he grouses as he's crossing the apron of concrete that leads to his workshop. "How the hell did they get out of there in those effing bomb suits in less than a minute?"

Behind him the pit bull echoes his frustrated tone with a surly growl.

"Well, screw it," he said, as he punches in the code to unlock the shop. "One way or another I'll get that rotten, crud-sucking pig over the next couple of days."

Beelzebub's muzzle drops open in a toothy, approving leer as he follows him inside. The dog has to walk quickly to keep up as he weaves between the drill press, grinder, and welding equipment before keying his way into the inner workroom.

A four-wheeled handcart sits in the room's center, with a big plastic storage box on top of it. He removes the cover and sets it aside. After slipping on a pair of latex gloves, he goes over to the metal wall rack where his completed bombs are arrayed.

"Good old Simon Says," he says at the sight of them. Although he's never met the arms and chemicals dealer personally, they've had a long and lucrative business relationship. Maybe someday, after he's inflicted his holocaust on Detroit, he'll travel to Russia and pay a visit to Simonenko. Get trashed on Stoly and visit some whores together.

Each homemade bomb is in an aluminum casing, with neodymium-iron-boron magnets attached to one side. Gingerly, he begins picking them up from the rack, carrying them over to the cart, and placing them into the blue plastic box. As the box fills, he interleaves bubble wrap between the casings.

When there are ten bombs in the storage box, he attaches the plastic cover and latches it. He then wheels the cart out of the lab to the main shop area. He punches the button that brings up the electric entrance door and pushes the cart out to his waiting pickup. The black Night Runner draws admiring looks from MoPar truck freaks, but is otherwise a fairly discreet ride.

He drops the pickup's gate, hefts the box up onto the bed and secures it with four sturdy bungee cables. He then does a quick count of the canvas shopping bags that are stacked to one side. After closing up the gate, he brings down the shop door and climbs into the truck. He notices Beelzebub squatting on the pavement nearby, looking up at him with a grim expression on his homely dog's face.

"Not today, Bub," he says. "Go get yourself some more rabbits. *Hunt rabbits*, boy."

The pit bull's answer is an ill-tempered growl. He's unable to communicate that he seems to have completely decimated the neighborhood's population of white-tails. Or else the remainder have finally wised up to the fact that burrowing under the chain link fence into the big, grassy lot is a one-way ticket to death and dismemberment.

On his way down the driveway, the man passes the gravel utility road that makes a U in and out of his property. On it sit a white Chevy Suburban and a semi cab with a twenty-five-foot trailer. Both are packed end-to-end with green plastic barrels of ammonium nitrate - a little tribute to Tim McVeigh. This evening he'll begin the process of soaking the fertilizer with nitromethane and hooking up the detonators. He expects a spectacular body count when he deploys them tomorrow. But still nothing at all compared to The Big One he's got planned for Dream Cruise Day.

He turns onto the two-lane that runs past his place. As he heads toward Southfield Road, a glower crosses his face. Though he's doing his best to think positive and stay focused on the slaughter that lies ahead, the fact is he's deeply pissed off. He thought for *sure* he'd whacked McCoy Crapface Johnson at Al-Rafi's house. He also thought he'd take out a lot more SWAT cops. After all the work he'd put into murdering the imam, booby-trapping the house, and then wiring it to explode, only eight lousy cops were killed. He was sure he'd whack at least a dozen there.

But no use crying over spilt blood. Or in this case, lack of it. If things go reasonably well today, he'll give those shitheads in the media a hundred new victims they can jack off about. Not to mention a new horde of scarred and mutilated survivors.

Twenty minutes later he's exiting from the Southfield freeway onto I-94 west. This portion of the Master Plan calls for him to select ten random bomb targets. The only requirement is that he has to be sure they're spread across the entire metro Detroit area. After another ten minutes or so of driving westbound, he spots the exit sign for the city of Belleville. A flash of intuition tells him to get off the freeway. At the end of the turn-off, he turns onto Belleville Road and follows the winding two-lane toward the town, passing a scenic lake on the way.

On the edge of Belleville's smallish downtown shopping area, he notices a family-style restaurant off to his right. The name - Good Pickings - brings an ironic grin to his face. He turns into the parking lot, which is crowded with cars. As he's driving through the lot, he notices a slew of dusky-skinned men getting out of an old Ford van. They look Mexican or Central American and he figures they're probably wetbacks working as farm laborers or landscapers.

Hmm, he thinks. Very promising for body count.

He pulls the pickup into an empty slot and watches in the rearview mirror as the short, husky men go inside. He counts ten of them.

After climbing out of the Night Runner, he goes back to the bed and opens the gate. Quickly he slips on a pair of latex gloves, extracts a bomb from the plastic box, and slides it into one of the sturdy canvas "Be Green" shopping bags he's brought along. He then closes the gate and walks toward the dingy-beige Econoline with the bag.

Checking for onlookers, he takes out the bomb, drops the bag onto the asphalt, and lies down on his back atop it. With the casing on his midriff, he quickly scoots under the rear of the van. He lifts the casing up to the steel fuel tank. When it's an inch or two away, the casing's powerful magnets pull it up tight against the tank. Reaching around the side, he throws the switch that arms the detonator. Then he slides out from under the van.

Getting up, he removes the latex gloves, stuffs them into his jean pockets, and brushes off his back and shoulders. He then heads into the restaurant with the bag folded under his arm. Inside, he finds a seat near the wetbacks and orders a buffet breakfast. After piling a tray full of scrambled eggs, bacon, fruit salad, and juice, he seats himself and watches the Latinos. Despite the August heat, they're all dressed in head-to-toe work clothes, with dusty work boots on their feet. They chatter laconically in Spanish as they eat. After twenty minutes, the foreman, who seems to be the biggest and burliest, sends them out to the van while he checks over the group's bill.

Slugging down the last of his orange juice, the man gets up and hurries to the cashier station. He pays his tab and heads out to his truck. He tosses the canvas bag into the bed and climbs into the cab. In his rearview mirror he watches seven of the men climb into the van, a couple staying outside to smoke cigarettes while they wait for the foreman. He pulls out of his slot and turns onto Belleville Road. After about thirty yards, he makes a U-turn and brings the Night Runner to a stop on the opposite shoulder. Now he's aimed back toward the expressway and has a clear view of the restaurant parking lot.

When he sees the foreman come out, he removes the modified TV remote from the truck console. He watches as the remaining men climb into the beige van. When it begins backing out of the parking space, he punches in the detonation code.

Just as the van pulls up to the exit and is about to turn left onto Belleville Road, an old bronze-colored Mercury Marquis approaches from the opposite direction, its turn signal blinking. The car, obviously a restore job, looks to be late Seventies vintage. Inside it are a gray-haired boomer couple.

"Perfect!" he rasps with an excited chuckle as he aims the remote. When the Marquis turns and the two vehicles are beside one another, he presses the PLAY button.

BLAM!

The rear of the Econoline goes ten feet in the air, with flames and body parts shooting out through the blown-out doors and windows. The blast-force knocks the old Mercury onto its side, where it sits rocking as the van crashes back down, flames and black smoke pouring from inside. At the same time the Mercury finally topples onto its roof, a charred man crawls halfway out of the van's blown-out side door. Another, in flames from head to toe and screaming at the top of his lungs, steps on the first man's back as he comes leaping out. The burning man rushes toward the restaurant, but collapses on the asphalt not far from the entrance door, from which shocked-looking patrons have begun to emerge. They stare at the incinerating man in wide-eyed horror as he rolls around on the pavement, shrieking in agony. He notices several windows on the restaurant's facade have been blown in. Hopefully there'll be some collateral injuries inside from the flying glass. With any luck, someone will bleed to death or die of a heart attack and help push up the body count.

As he's watched the carnage, quivers of ecstasy have been running up and down his muscular torso and limbs. While he'd love to sit here longer and soak up more of the victims' evaporating life energy, he knows he needs to be prudent. Cars are passing the restaurant, slowing down to stare in horrified disbelief at the flaming wreckage. A couple of them pull off onto the shoulder in front of him, apparently thinking to offer help, but most continue on their way. He slips the Night Runner into gear and joins in with the passers-by.

Rolling past the wreckage, he can smell the pork-like aroma of human flesh, crackling and popping as it roasts over a puddle of burning gasoline.

When he's a quarter of a mile away from the scene, he hears the first sirens. They quickly fade as he follows the traffic past the lake and down the winding road back to I-94. He takes the eastbound ramp and merges with the traffic heading back toward Detroit.

It's a bright, warm, beautiful morning. With the sun now glaring in his eyes, he slips on his sunglasses. Behind the wraparound lenses, his eyes search the exit signs, awaiting the next spark of intuition that'll tell him where to plant bomb number two.

His lips purse and he begins to whistle. With each passing mile, the explosive crescendos of the Goodbye Detroit Symphony are booming louder and louder inside his head. Step by step, blast by blast, his deadly composition is unfolding.

And in just three days from now, he'll conduct its horrifically lethal climax.

Chapter 23   Showdown

Wednesday, August 17 - 9:00 a.m.

"HEY there, Mr. Hero," Mabel Partridge said when I approached the FBI office's check-in desk.

"Hold the accolades, please," I said, raising my hand. "Or I'll barf on you."

"Was pretty brave, what you and Wilson did last night," she said.

"Yeah - and there are still eight cops dead and their killer uncaught," I said. "So pardon me if I don't feel like celebrating how wonderful I am."

"I think Ted Danson and Peter Lorre are in there waiting for you," she said.

I chuckled at her characterizations of Blandings and Dorn. Physically, they weren't far off the mark.

"Showing your age, Mabel," I said. "Both those guys might just as well be dinosaurs today."

"Maybe that's why they're replacing me," she said.

"What are you talking about?" I said.

"Blandings called me in and told me he's bringing in some favorite admin of his from DC later today. Her name's Hannah Hochheuters."

I frowned. "What'll you be doing?" I said.

"Helping the out-of-towners that were brought in," she said. "Could be worse."

"True," I said. "Heckle and Jeckle in there could've made you their lead investigator."

"Now *you're* the one showing your age," she said with a smirk as I slid my access card and headed down the short hall to the main office.

Inside, I saw Blandings and Dorn in Dawson's usurped office. Blandings stood up and waved me in.

I resisted my urge to flip him the bird. Instead I gave him a "one minute" gesture with my forefinger and headed down to my cubicle, When I passed Wilson's cube he was leaning back in his chair, on the phone.

"Johnson just came in," I heard him say. "The rotten slacker."

At my desk I set down my briefcase and hung up my jacket. After removing my digital recorder from the desk drawer, I headed toward the glassed-in manager's office.

"Good work, McCoy," Blandings said when I finally sat down in front of him. "Elliot here told me what an outstanding job you did at the Al-Rafi scene."

"Guess you also told all the media about it," I said. "Since the whole world seems to know about it this morning."

"Well, we had to put out something to them. It was a bad situation, but thanks to you and Wilson, we ended up making the Bureau look good."

We? I thought.

"How's your head?" Dorn asked, indicating the bandage over my ear.

"Fine," I said. "Compared to what happened to those SWAT cops you sent in there, it's nothing."

The look Dorn gave me was lizard-cold, but Blandings spoke up before he could reply.

"The important thing, of course, is that you're alive and well," he said. "And Eric mentioned that you found out some new information on the case."

"That's right," I said. "Went back to Al-Rafi's house early this morning and ran into this Arab boy from the neighborhood. He saw some guy go into the house three nights ago. Was able to give me a partial description on the suspect and the vehicle he was driving."

"Was the guy he saw Arabic?" Dorn asked.

"No. Caucasian."

I saw Blandings and Dorn exchange glances.

"Age around thirty," I went on. "With a husky, body-builder's physique. Dark blond or sandy brown hair. Wore a black long-sleeve polo, cargo pants, and black high-top sneakers. Was driving a black, late-model Cadillac Escalade. I saw a similar car at the Campus Martius bombing."

Blandings frowned. "To be honest, McCoy, that doesn't really fit in too well with other information we've uncovered," he said.

"How old is this kid?" Dorn asked.

"Ten."

"You think a ten-year-old kid's statements are reliable?" he scoffed.

"I think this one's are. He lives right across the street from Al-Rafi's place. What's this 'other information' you mentioned?"

"There's a source in the Arab community saying an imam named Sayed Abdullah is behind the bombings," Blandings said.

I felt my brows knit.

I knew Abdullah. I'd even done tails on him a few times. He was a radical fundamentalist Muslim preacher who liked to rail against America as the Great Satan. He made no secret of his loathing for our culture and political system, but had always carefully avoided any overt calls for violence. We'd also never been able to conclusively connect him to any terrorist or support organizations.

"Who's your source?" I said. "I talked to all of mine on the morning after the Woodward bombing. None of them mentioned Abdullah."

"The tip came through a local talk radio host. Guy named Larry Lattimore," Dorn said.

"Larry Lattimore?" I said. "You're kidding me, right? The guy's delusional."

I'd listened to the guy's show once or twice. He was rabidly anti-Muslim and so far to the right he considered Limbaugh a commie stooge.

"We don't think so, McCoy," Blandings said. "Not in this case."

"Lattimore put us in touch with a concerned Arab citizen who's infiltrated Abdullah's mosque," Dorn said. "Apparently, the guy's a big fan of Lattimore."

"Which means he's a certified paranoid," I said.

"That's not our take," Blandings said. "We met with him this morning and he outlined a number of suspicious things Abdullah's been saying and doing lately."

"Such as?"

"Talking about the bombings being 'Allah's will.' Thanking him for killing so many infidels."

"Sounds like the same crazy bullshit Abdullah's been puking out for years, under that First Amendment prayer cap he wears," I said. "What's the informant's name?"

"Arthur Hakim," Dorn said. "He's Chaldean - Iraqi Christian. After Lattimore mentioned this Abdullah on one of his shows, Hakim got the idea to start cozying up to him. Pretended he'd converted to Abdullah's fundamentalist flavor of Islam."

I shook my head. "Listen," I said. "You've pulled Abdullah's file, right?"

"Sure," Dorn said.

"Then you know we've had people watching him for the past several years. That his phones are tapped, his house is wired, and we've compromised his son's personal computer. There's no question Abdullah's a religious fanatic and general dirtbag. But I still don't see him as part of this."

"Well, we do, McCoy," Blandings said. "Elliot here's putting tails on all his known associates and we've already got court permission to start monitoring all their calls - cell phones and land lines."

"And here's another kicker, Johnson," Dorn said. "Apparently, this Abdullah and Al-Rafi were enemies. For years the two kept putting out dueling religious opinions - *fatwas*, they call them. Which probably accounts for Al-Rafi being killed."

"How so?" I said. "You think Abdullah booby-trapped that house? Abdullah spends all of his spare time poring over twelfth century religious texts. He's so anti-modern, he probably doesn't know how to operate a toaster."

"Obviously, he's got helpers," Blandings said.

"Like who?" I said. "Listen, you've seen the file. None of his followers have been out of the country for any suspicious periods of time."

"Wrong," Dorn said. "One of them spent two weeks in Bahrain a couple of months back."

"What's his name?" I asked.

"Samir Hadidi," Dorn said.

"Sam Hadidi?" I said. "Fat guy? Runs a video store?"

"So you know him?" Blandings said.

"Saw him together with Abdullah once on a stakeout and checked him out afterward. Guy doesn't have the brains or the physical abilities to turn Al-Rafi's house into that hellhole we walked into. The son of a bitch who did it is highly skilled at both bombing and booby-trapping. Plus, like I told you, the man that kid saw go in there was Caucasian. Just like the voice on that call I got threatening to blow up the house was Caucasian."

"How can you be so sure he wasn't Arabic, if it was a phone call?" Dorn said.

"No Arab accent or inflection."

"I'm sure there are plenty of Arab Americans who have no accent or inflection to speak of," Blandings said.

"Yeah, but this guy did have an inflection - white male, midwestern," I said.

"Listen, Johnson," Blandings said. "I know you're a senior agent and I respect your opinion. But to us, the Abdullah connection makes the most sense."

"Okay," I said. "So what's your plan?"

"We tail him and every one of his followers - especially this Hadidi guy - non-stop, seven by twenty-four," Dorn said. "We tap every call. We use hidden shotgun mikes to capture every conversation. We slip in and plant spot mikes all around their homes. We catch every word, every grunt, every fart the dirtbags let out."

"Fine," I said. "But leave me out of it."

Blandings' gray eyes went cold. "What do you mean, McCoy?" he said. "You're Elliot's right-hand man. Second in command on the investigative team."

"I'm resigning from that position," I said. "Effective immediately."

"You can't resign," Blandings said.

"I just did."

"Then you might as well consider yourself resigned from the Bureau," Blandings said. "Effective immediately."

"I don't think so," I said.

"This is insubordination, Johnson," Blandings said, his eyes gone rock-hard now. "I won't stand for it."

"So you're going to can one of the 'Elmore Street Massacre Heroes'?" I said. "The day after he wipes the shit off the Bureau's face your buddy here smeared on it? I doubt it."

"Listen, Johnson," Blandings said, just about snarling now. "I make one call to the Office of Professional Responsibility right now, and you're out on your dumb, stinking black ass."

His face went white - so to speak - when he realized what he'd just said. Then it turned kind of purple when I pulled the little black Olympus voice recorder out of my pocket.

"Can I quote you on that?" I said with an evil grin. "To OPR?"

"You - um - that came out wrong. It- You know what I meant, Johnson," he spluttered.

I stood up.

"Listen, Morley," I said on my way to the door. "If you and Alice here want to jump down rabbit holes and waste twenty or twenty-five agents' time while more people get blown to bloody bits, that's your damn business."

"But I've got a bomber to catch," I said, and shut the glass door behind me.

I'd just gotten back to my cubicle when my cell phone rang. This time I recognized the calling number. I was tempted to just put him into voice mail, but my curiosity got the better of me.

"This is Johnson," I said.

"Agent Johnson? Bill La Borgia."

Willie the Pimp again.

"What can I do for you, Mr. La Borgia?"

"Listen - first of all I wanted to commend you," he said. "Getting those SWAT cops out of that booby-trapped house - that took some real *coglioni*. Or *cojones*, as the Latinos say."

"Was just doing my job, Mr. La Borgia. Now once again, what can I do for you?"

"You've got it backwards, Agent Johnson. The question is, what can I do for *you*?"

"Mr. La Borgia-"

"Hear me out, Johnson - okay? I've got a fair number of people who work for me, including a couple of very sharp private investigators. I'd be happy to put them at your disposal. They can do surveillance, research, interviewing - whatever you need. I've also got a private helicopter and pilot you can use, any time you want. Private jet too, for that matter. All on my dime, of course."

"And your motive for offering all these resources to the FBI is-?"

"Just trying to do my civic duty. These bombing are unconscionable, Johnson. An abomination. I can't sleep at night, thinking about them. I just want to do whatever I can to help stop them. And fast - before any more innocent people get killed."

"So you're just a concerned citizen, trying to help us out?"

"That's right. Is that so hard to believe?"

The truth was, I wasn't sure what to believe. Maybe he did sincerely want to help out. I knew from my investigation that La Borgia spent most of his time on his porn business and didn't have a wife or kids. Just a number of model-pretty girlfriends. But he was close with his family and apparently doted on his nephews and nieces - his three sisters' children.

"Tell you what, Mr. La Borgia," I said. "On behalf of the Bureau, I'll take your offer under consideration. I'll let my superiors know you're interested in helping us out. If they agree, perhaps we'll avail ourselves of some of the resources you've offered. I'll let you know. In the meantime, let me assure you that the Bureau - in conjunction with state, local and other Federal agencies - is doing everything possible to stop the bombings."

La Borgia sniggered into the phone. "And yadda-yadda-yadda, right? Okay, Johnson. I realize the FBI probably doesn't want to sully its hands by doing business with some sultan of sleaze like me. But the offer holds. Call me if you want any of the resources I mentioned."

"Thanks, Mr. La Borgia. Now I need to get back to work."

"Me too. *Arrivederci,* Agent Johnson. "And *buona fortuna* - good luck."

After hanging up my cell, I sat back in my chair and tried to figure out if the guy was gaming me or not.

About three months ago I got tasked with investigating a Detroit connection to the international sex slave trade. Attractive young women from Asia and Eastern Europe were being conned into traveling to America with the promise of jobs, only to find themselves forced into sex work on behalf of brutal criminal gangs. In the course of the investigation the name of La Borgia's Detroit-based outfit, Eros Unlimited, had come up.

However, the digging I did failed to show any direct connection between Eros Unlimited and the trafficking. And while some of the young women were indeed ending up as employees in the huge Internet porn, phone sex, adult dating, and escort services empire he'd built, there didn't seem to be any coercion involved. Apparently EU paid well, took a reasonable cut from its commission-based workers, and didn't employ any underage or unwilling girls. The only strong-arm techniques his outfit had a reputation for using were against prospective pimps and gangs who tried to horn in on the women's earnings.

In the course of the investigation I'd contacted a number of Detroit area sex workers as well as several local county and municipal law enforcement agencies. One of the contacts must've leaked word about it, because one day, about six weeks back, La Borgia had out of the blue called the Detroit FBI office and asked to speak to me personally.

When I got on the line with him, he invited me to interview him face to face. Even told me, with a sly laugh, that I was welcome to wear a wire. I accepted and we did it at some ritzy country club he belonged to up in Bloomfield Hills, one of Detroit's most upscale suburbs. Instead of the wire, I brought my little Olympus digital audio recorder and laid it on the table while we talked.

Bill La Borgia proved to be a charming, likeable guy in his early thirties. His father, Fiorello, was a longtime senior *capo* in the Detroit mafia - which the families themselves call "the combination" or "the partnership." The old man had made his initial fortune the old-fashioned way - gambling, prostitution, numbers, and protection, mostly. But over time he'd diversified into ownership or part-ownership of several legitimate companies as well. His vision for Bill, his only son, was that he go to business school and then come back and run the legit operations.

La Borgia told me it was while he was in college - Wharton, no less - that he'd foreseen the then-nascent Internet porn business was going to be huge. While he was still in school, he began setting up a network for the production, distribution, and sales of it. After graduating ("Third in my class," he'd told me, with a proud grin on his face. "Not bad for an ignorant wop from Detroit, eh?"), he went full-time into online pornography and caught the wave as it expanded into the multi-billion dollar industry it is now. Within five years he'd made several times the money his old man had in over thirty years of racketeering. All of it technically legit.

"'Sleazy but legal' - that's my motto," he told me as he spooned more pâté de foie gras onto a piece of toast.

"Very inspiring," I said as I fork-sliced the most expensive cut of steak I'd ever eaten. "Would look great on a family coat of arms."

"Willie the Pimp" was local law enforcement's nickname for him, due to his being in the sex trade. The name itself was something of joke, harking back to an old Frank Zappa tune. La Borgia's other nickname - Billy Knuckles - was the one used by his dad's *cosa nostra* crowd. He told me it came from his having a fistfight with another mafia *capo's* son when he was fourteen, in which he'd broken the other kid's nose.

But the Armani-clad guy before me at the interview certainly didn't display any kind of thuggishness. He'd brought along no heavies and there were also no veiled threats and no braggadocio. Instead he came across as smart, unpretentious, and almost happy-go-lucky. Made self-deprecating jokes about himself and his chosen calling. Even seemed to be environmentally conscious. Told me that he was an investor in some green businesses, and drove some kind of hybrid car. I found myself liking the guy, despite the fact that on a gut level I also didn't really trust him.

"By the way," he told me as we were finishing our lunch. "That guy whose nose I broke? Charlie DiFrancetti? We're friends to this day. He tells me that busted schnozzola was the best thing ever happened to him. Upped his credentials with all the families and got him lots of babes he never would've got 'cause he was too pretty. He's a big shot lawyer now, with the Teamsters Union."

I declined La Borgia's offer to pay for my lunch and covered my eighty dollar tab myself. As we walked around the country club's fountained, English-style garden afterward, I finally got around to asking the question that has been foremost on my mind.

"Who let on to you that the FBI was investigating you?" I said. "And who gave you my name?"

He spread his hands and grinned at me around the twenty-five dollar cigar in his mouth.

"Agent Johnson," he said. "The bird sings. The groundhog digs in the dirt. The entrepreneur looks out for his business interests," he said. "Afraid I can't tell you who whispered your name in my ear. Without a subpoena, at least."

My recollections of the meeting with La Borgia were interrupted just then by Wilson's "Holy crack pipes!" from the next cubicle.

"Hey, Mojo," he called over the wall. "Check out Clickondetroit dot com."

"Why?" I asked.

"Another bomb."

"Damn," I whispered as I pulled up the website.

Chapter 24   Buckle Up, Grandma

Wednesday, August 17 - 9:30 a.m.

"BREAKING NEWS: TERRORIST CAR BOMB KILLS TWELVE IN BELLEVILLE!" read the lead story's headline.

Belleville is a small, semi-rural community west of Detroit Metro Airport. Scrolling quickly down through the story, I saw that the blast had occurred in a restaurant parking lot about twenty minutes ago.

"Rasheed! Wiley! Cantor! Into Morley's office!" I heard Dorn bellow.

"Or vee set zee dogs on you, feelzy shvine!" Wilson hissed from his cube.

"Charming guy, that Dorn," I said.

"About as charming as stale body odor," he said.

I assumed Blandings was detailing the agents to go to the Belleville bomb site and, sure enough, I saw the three of them rush out of the office a couple of minutes later.

I continued checking the local news websites as more information trickled in. Apparently, the explosion took out a van full of landscaping workers who'd stopped for breakfast at some family restaurant. After eating, they'd come out, piled into the van, and were just about to pull out onto the highway when a powerful explosion ripped it and everyone inside apart. A fiftyish couple in a nearby vehicle had also been killed.

I hadn't even finished reading the latest update when another one popped up the on the screen above it. My stomach began to churn out bile as I read the scrolling headline.

"BREAKING NEWS: TEN DEAD IN ALLEN PARK INTERSECTION BLAST!"

"You know what, Wilson?" I said. "This is going to be another rotten day."

"And that's news?" he replied.

"Check Clickondetroit dot com again," I told him.

"Say it ain't so, Mojo," he said.

"Everybody to Morley's office!" came Elliot Dorn's shrill voice. "Now!"

Soon fifty or so agents, including Eric, were gathered outside of his usurped office. After keeping us waiting for four or five minutes while we watched Blandings talk on his phone and Dorn pace up and down in front of his desk, the two came out.

"As you've probably all heard, there've been two more bombings this morning," Blandings began. "One in Belleville less than an hour ago, and now one in Allen Park.

"Johnson, Wilson, and Nardella - I want the three of you to proceed to the Allen Park site. I want everybody else here to consider yourselves on standby. Be ready to head out of here on a moment's notice if there are any more bombings."

Grimly, everyone nodded.

"By the way, Johnson," he said in an aside to me, not bothering to hide the snideness in his voice. "Since you're no longer a lead investigator, I assume you'll have no objections to this field assignment?"

"None whatsoever," I said.

"Your first job when you get onsite," he went on, addressing the group again, "is to make sure the local police don't muck up the forensic evidence too badly. But your main job there will be to interview witnesses and survivors. We especially want to find out if there were Arab-Americans in the area prior to the explosions - this man in particular. His name's Samir Hadidi."

Dorn passed out photocopied sheets that had multiple grainy shots of Hadidi on them.

"And while we're at it," I said to the group, "we'll also want to check if a lone Caucasian male was seen in the area just prior to the blast. About six feet tall and thirty, thirty-five years old, with short blond or sandy-colored hair. Body-builder's physique and maybe wearing cargo pants, polo shirt, and running shoes. Possibly driving a black Cadillac Escalade."

"Suit yourself, Johnson," Blandings said, his voice cold.

"You got a photo of your guy, McCoy?" Angie Nardella asked.

"Unfortunately-" I began, but Blandings cut me off.

"I also want all of you to keep in mind there'll likely be media people at the sites. Be sure to look and act professional at all times, but I want absolutely no talking to them. Refer all questions and inquiries they may have back to the office. To me personally or to Elliot here. Understood?"

"*Jawohl, Übersturmbannführer!*" Wilson growled under his breath.

"Is that it, then?" I asked Blandings.

"That's it," he said, his mouth tight.

"Then let's move," I said to Wilson and Nardella. "People are dying while we stand here yapping."

"Don't worry about the looking professional part, Mojo," Wilson said as we hurried back to our desks to collect our gear. "We'll let you know if you've left your fly open."

"And I'll let you know if any flies come buzzing out of your mouth," Nardella told him.

"We'll take my car," she announced when we got to the parking structure.

"Wait a minute, Peaches - you're driving?" Wilson said nervously.

"That's right," she said, opening the door to her government Ford. "You drive and we'd be lucky to make it by nightfall."

"But on the other hand, we'd get there alive," he said as he took the shotgun seat.

"Buckle up, grandma," she told him.

Angie was notorious for her aggressive driving, but on this morning she appeared to be in full-bore kamikaze mode. After roaring down six levels of parking structure with tires shrieking, she shot out into Michigan Avenue without bothering to slow down and check for oncoming traffic. When the driver of the semi she'd cut off slammed on his brakes and leaned on his air horn at us, she stuck her snarling face out the open window.

"Kiss my patootie, pork-brains!" she bellowed up at the purple-faced man as we swung by his cab.

"This thing have air bags?" Wilson said as we shot west toward the Lodge Freeway.

"Yeah," she said with nasty chuckle. "The two inside your chest."

After a few blocks, we made a screeching turn onto the Lodge's entrance ramp and barreled down into the freeway traffic. We were doing ninety when we took the turnoff bridge onto I-75 and began heading southwest. At one point a blue Michigan State Police cruiser pulled up on us with their light bar flashing. But apparently they saw the federal government plates, because they quickly backed off.

Wilson, meanwhile, had turned on the car radio to listen for more news updates. We'd just made our exit off the freeway and gotten onto Southfield Road when the bulletin came out on the morning's third bombing.

"Uh-oh," Wilson said. "Another one?"

He turned up the radio. This one was in Garden City - about a dozen miles north and west of the site we were headed to. Apparently the car bomb had decimated a bunch of shoppers at a crowded strip mall. I felt a fresh knot tie itself in my belly.

Nardella was coming dangerously close to other cars as she wove in and out of the highway's heavy morning traffic. She had a murderous sneer on her face.

"Those rotten, sonofabitch bombers," she said. "I'd like to cut off their stupid, stinking balls with a linoleum knife and wrap them around their buzzard necks like a bowtie."

"Is that a direct Emily Post quote?" Wilson said. "Or a paraphrase?"

"Emily can bow down and kiss my cellulite," she said.

We turned off of Southfield and were drawing near the Allen Park site now, blowing through a neighborhood of small, single-story brick homes.

"Jeez, Peaches - are you by chance at some kind of low ebb in your biorhythm today?" Wilson asked, clinging to his seat.

"Are you by chance at some kind of low ebb in your IQ today?" she said.

"Hey, I'm just saying," he said. "You know, I took this PMS sensitivity training class a while back. They said it's best to talk openly about the heartbreaking symptoms."

"What makes you think I'm PMS-ing?"

"The fact that you're doing seventy miles an hour in a residential neighborhood while mumbling a steady stream of obscenities to yourself?" he said.

"Perfectly normal behavior," she said.

"For a psychopath," he muttered to his window.

Up ahead I could see plumes of black smoke rising over the next stop-lighted intersection. Nardella had to stand on the brakes when we came up to the rear of a long traffic backup. After twenty seconds of sitting at a dead stop, she began scooting in and out of the oncoming traffic lanes to get closer. When people started honking their horns at us, Wilson and I held up our FBI shields to the windows. Angie just held up a finger.

As we got closer, I saw that there were three yellow fire trucks, a couple of ambulances, and about a half-dozen police cars scattered around the intersection where the bomb had gone off. Near the corner a row of black-bagged victims were lined up on the grassy area between the road and the sidewalk. Nardella spat out another string of expletives while we drove past the body bags and parked on the edge of the scene.

When we climbed out of the car, the scent of burning hung heavy in the hot summer air. I looked at my watch to note our arrival time. It wasn't even 10:30 a.m. yet and already there'd been three more deadly bombings. With a sinking feeling in my gut, I gave in to the virtual certainty that this was going to be another very long and gruesome day.

"I hope to God you're not going to make your usual pea-brained, pseudo-funny comments," Angie said to Wilson as we strode toward the crowd of Allen Park police officers who were controlling the scene.

"Hey, gimme a break, Peaches," he said. "It's my *Witzelsucht.*"

"'Vitzel-sookt'?" she said. "What in bloody hell is that?"

"Think I've heard of it," I said. "Isn't that the mental condition where you can't stop yourself from making dumb jokes at inappropriate times?"

"Yeah," he said. "Some psychologist once told me it's probably from the time my drunk uncle dropped me on my head as a baby."

"Only one time?" Nardella said. "Sure he didn't dribble it all the way down a basketball court?

"Hey, come on, Peaches. I can't help it if I've got a warped sense of humor."

"And by the way, honeybunch," he added, sidling closer to her as we approached the big cop who seemed to be in charge. "Have I ever told you you're even more beautiful than usual when you're PMS-ing?"

I managed to keep Nardella from ripping out Wilson's throat by hastily intervening between them and introducing us to the officer in charge of the scene. He was an Allen Park Police sergeant named Joe Yates, a fiftyish guy with a stubble of gray hair on his head. He looked like he normally had a florid face, but at the moment it was greenish, with some purple here and there.

"You Feds missed the good part," he said, with a rueful edge. "Cleaning up the body parts. Morgue guys just left with them."

"Those guys have all the fun," Wilson said.

"Jesus," Yates went on, shaking his head. "I've seen some nasty crap in my career, but never anything like this. Lost my cookies after I accidentally stepped on some kid's decapitated head."

Wilson gave a sympathetic nod. "That'll do it every time," he said.

As I looked around, I saw that Yates and his team had totally botched up and contaminated the bomb scene. For forensic purposes, he should've completely closed off the intersection where the explosion had occurred and re-routed traffic through side streets. Instead he'd had a private wrecker crew come to the site. They'd towed the smoking remains of the half-dozen vehicles that were destroyed off to one side and were now dragging or sweeping the debris up to the curbs. Traffic was moving in three of the road's four lanes. Slowly, of course, and with plenty of rubbernecking.

A quick visual of the demolished cars told me that one ripped-up yellow hulk, its make and model unrecognizable, had been the epicenter.

I asked Yates if they'd recovered any license plates. He said they'd found one attached to a fragment of bumper and had run a check with the state license bureau. The plate was registered to a Toyota Sequoia SUV owned by a Ronald C. Carpenter of nearby Lincoln Park. They'd called the Lincoln Park police and they were on their way now to the address.

I asked him if there were any witnesses or survivors present we could talk to. He pointed to a small cluster of people standing off to one side, who appeared to be giving statements to a uniformed female cop.

On our way over to them, I watched the TV crews that had shown up shortly after we did. One cameraman was videotaping the aftermath, while a second followed a head-shaven black guy in a white shirt and tie who was looking for likely candidates to interview.

When we came up to the witnesses, we asked the officer, whose name tag read Webster, if we could run a few questions past the group.

"Folks, did any of you see anyone or anything suspicious prior to or just after the explosion?" I asked. "Car driving away fast? Person standing around observing? Possibly making a cell phone call?"

They all shook their heads.

"I was driving along, minding my own business," an older man with a piece of gauze taped to his forehead said, "when this yellow SUV a few cars ahead of me just blew up like a giant firecracker. Scared the bejesus out of me. Jammed on the brakes and smacked my head on the steering wheel. My heart's still missing beats."

"But you didn't see anything odd, either before or after?" I asked.

"No sir, I sure didn't."

"There are a couple of persons of interest we're investigating," Nardella said. "One is a heavyset Arab man, about forty. Here's a picture."

She held up the sheet with the photos of Sam Hadidi that Dorn had given out in the office. "Anyone see this man, either before or after the explosion?"

One after another, they squinted at the sheet and shook their heads.

"How about a Caucasian man, about thirty, thirty-five with short blond or light brown hair," I asked. "Possibly in a black Cadillac Escalade?"

"You know, I did see a guy who kind of looked like that," said a young woman who was holding a baby on her hip. "But he wasn't in an Escalade. He was in a black pickup truck. A Dodge, I think."

"Do you remember anything more about him?" I asked.

"Not really. After the explosion, everyone who was okay was sitting there in their cars, kind of stunned, you know? Some people got out to help, but others just waited a bit and then drove away. I'd got out of my car and was standing there in the street when I noticed this one guy drive by. He had this strange look on his face. Most of the people going by were looking shocked or whatever. But he had this weird grin on his face like he thought it was all a big joke or something."

"Can you tell us any more about what he looked like? Anything distinguishing about his face?" Nardella asked.

"Not really. He looked - I don't know - kind of military."

"Would you be willing to work with a police artist to try come up with a picture?" I said.

"Sure," she said. "Soon as I can get a babysitter."

Just then Yates came over to where we were standing. He looked like he was getting his natural ruddy color back, but his mouth was tight.

"You Feds hear the latest?" he said.

"What's that?" I said.

"There's been another bombing."

"The one up in Garden City?" Wilson said. "We heard."

"Nope," he said. "This one's in Redford."

"Sweet Jesus in the outhouse," Wilson said.

Spewing saliva as she spoke, Nardella let out a string of obscenities that would make a sailor blush. Her lurid invective brought double takes from most of the crowd, including Yates. "Excuse me, ma'am?" he said.

"We'll have to ask you folks to excuse Special Agent Nardella here," Wilson said. "She's got a bad case of PM-"

Spotting the homicidal gleam in Angie's eyes, I interrupted him. "She's having a real bad day," I said hastily.

Thumbs tucked into his heavy black police belt, Yates slowly turned and surveyed the bomb scene.

"Shit fire and save the matches, man," he said, shaking his grizzled head. "Who isn't?"

I was watching a fire truck roll through the explosion-blackened intersection when I pulled out my cell and called Morley Blandings. He answered on the third ring.

"Who's this?" he snapped. Apparently the day's bad news was making it difficult to maintain his customary smarm.

"Johnson," I said. "I wanted to report that a witness here spotted somebody suspicious leaving the scene. A white male in a black pickup truck who matches the description of the guy that Arab boy saw back on-"

Blandings cut me off. "Never mind that," he said. Did anyone see Hadidi there?"

"No, damn it," I said. "We showed them the pictures. No one saw him. We-"

"Well, someone in Belleville saw an Arab in the vicinity near the time of the blast," he said. "Description's vague, but Elliot and I think it was probably Hadidi."

"Wait a minute," I said. "I thought you and Dorn had your people glued to Abdullah and Hadidi's fannies. Were surveilling their every fart, as I recall."

"Somehow Hadidi slipped out of his place without being seen. Now the dirtbag's out there somewhere. No doubt planting bombs and laughing at us."

"Look," I said. "Just in case you're wrong, how about getting out an all points bulletin out to all the local police departments to look for the Caucasian in the black pickup. He-"

"I'm not going to waste the Bureau or local police's resources on your wild goose chases, Johnson. You want to call them yourself and make a fool of yourself, go right ahead."

The line went dead. The sucker had hung up on me.

"Why you arrogant, scum-sucking, Ivy League asshole!" I yelled at the dead phone.

I looked around and saw everyone nearby was staring.

What's the problem, Mojo?" Wilson said. "You PMS-ing too?"

"Might as well be!" I said as I stomped away.

Fuming, I strode up the street a ways to cool down. Which was easier said than done with the hot August sun blazing down on me.

Then I got an idea. I called Mabel Partridge back at the office. I knew she'd have contact numbers for all the local police forces, and she quickly agreed to call them and get APBs out on the military-looking white guy in a black Dodge pickup truck our witness had seen. We both knew it wasn't much to go on, but it was better than nothing.

I headed back toward the cluster of cops, agents, and witnesses. My stomach was rumbling, less from hunger than from anger, nausea, and frustration. It wasn't even 11 a.m. yet, and the bomber had already hit four different communities. Almost certainly he was still roaming around out there, searching for his next innocent, random victims.

Where would the crazy, murderous son of a bitch strike next?

Chapter 25   The Purple Vomit Comet

Wednesday, August 17 - 11:55 a.m.

HE WATCHES intently as the family climbs into the white Pontiac Aztek van. Well-dressed in predominantly white casual clothing, they're dark-haired and fair-skinned, with features that suggest some Balkan or East European ethnic group. There are two thirtyish women, a trio of pre-teen girls, two smaller boys, a baby, and an old grandma. Nine in all: an excellent base number. They're parked near the busy crosswalk that leads into the mall. He sees the brake lights come on as the woman who's gotten behind the wheel puts the van into gear.

He does a quick re-check to make sure there's no one in the vicinity of his pickup. The universal remote is in his hand and he's already programmed in the trigger code. As the van backs hesitantly out of the parking slot, he waits until there are about eight or ten people in the crosswalk nearby. Then he aims the remote and presses the PLAY button.

WHAM!!!

Whitish-gray smoke and body parts burst from the blasted-out door openings as the white van jumps up off the ground. Some nearby pedestrians are flung through the air, at least one of them decapitated by a flying sheet of metal. Then the van comes back down, flames flickering from the interior as is rocks from side-to-side on its blown-out tires. After a few seconds there's a follow-on explosion when the gas tank ignites.

After allowing himself a couple of minutes of shuddering pleasure, he pulls out of his spot and loops over to the exit drive. A silver Mercedes Benz is sitting there, the fortyish woman inside looking aghast as she stares back towards the blazing Aztek. Calmly, he goes around her, signals, and turns right onto Orchard Lake Road.

As he heads south, he checks the rear view and side mirrors. A black, fifty-foot wide mushroom cloud is rising up from the flaming wreckage. He moves over to the left lane and makes a turnaround to go north, so he can check out the blast site once again. When he hears sirens behind him, he pulls off to the side and courteously stops to make way for the pair of Farmington Hills police cruisers and trio of EMS vans that go roaring past. He's highly impressed by how fast they've responded. When they've gone by, he continues north, eyeballing the chaos around the burning van as he passes the mall again. After another half-mile, he makes a double-right to get onto Northwestern Highway.

He checks his watch. It's just shy of noon and he's ahead of plan, having already set off five of the ten random bombs he's planned to detonate today. He decides he deserves a lunch break and continues down Northwestern to 12 Mile Road. After taking the turnaround, he heads east on 12 Mile for a ways and then pulls into the parking lot of a Ram's Horn Restaurant.

On his way in he buys a Detroit News from the red box at the entrance. The paper's headline is "BOMBERS STRIKE AGAIN!" With a satisfied grin on his face, he continues on into the restaurant. A pimply teenager in a white shirt seats him and brings him a glass of water. While he's waiting for the waitress, he quickly browses through some of the earlier bombings' gruesome details. Then he goes to the classifieds. He runs his fingertip down the column until he sees the ad.

'To AQID - we accept your offer. Can we talk?'

He gives a petulant snort. Someone had gotten creative and appended the 'Can we talk?'

The addition of the phrase annoys him. Was some son of a bitch trying to be a wise guy? Were they attempting to get him to call ahead of schedule, so they'd have more opportunities to track and locate him?

Well, whatever their intention, it isn't going to work. He'll stick with his own goddamn schedule and follow the plan. For one simple reason - because the Master Plan *rules.*

"Reading about those awful bombings?" a woman's voice says.

He looks up. The Ram's Horn waitress is a thirtyish redhead, fair-skinned and freckled. Shapely and pretty, but with weary green eyes.

He frowns and shakes his head. "Awful," he says. "Just awful. Hope they catch those terrorist animals soon."

"Me too," she says, before taking his order.

He watches the waitress' behind twitch as she walks away toward the order station. It's interesting looking at women the way he does now. Without the slightest iota of desire. A few years back, he'd have scanned her up and down and wondered what it would be like to screw her. Now he sees her with what seems like total objectivity.

When she was writing down his order, he'd noticed her wedding ring: cubic zirconium, from some suburban mall jewelry store. Good figure on her overall, but a bit of a belly from the two or three kids she no doubt has. Looks Irish, so probably raised Catholic. Uses birth control, but haphazardly or ineptly. Fundamentally a breeder and nurturer. Would prefer to be home, being a housewife and mother, to working a waitress job. But money is tight. Husband probably a factory or construction worker. Rough times for working class shlubs like him. Maybe laid off and collecting unemployment. The guy at home, playing at being Mr. Mom, caring for the kids when he isn't watching TV or jacking off to Internet porn while they nap.

Despite the rage that often rises up in him about the way he is now, he has to admit there are certain advantages to no longer having sexual urges. A lot less time spent distracted by the sight of well-formed tits and asses and legs, and even sometimes faces. Time you can put into planning, scheming, concocting, and acting.

There's a certain Swiss clinic he intends to visit once he's got the money and has it all safely stashed in offshore accounts. The clinic's actual specialty is sex change from female to male, but they've supposedly also had excellent results on men who'd had their genitals mangled or destroyed in auto or industrial accidents or military combat.

The thing he has between his legs now is a lifeless and sensation-less prosthetic. He's not even sure why he bothers to wear it.

He'd used it once with a prostitute, just to see what it would be like. He'd forewarned her about what to expect. At first she'd looked creeped out by it. Then, when he was using it on her, she did a lot of groaning and grinding - probably the usual act she put on for her johns.

The redheaded waitress brings his meal then.

"Can I get you anything else with that?" she asks, giving him a cordial smile.

He shakes his head and, after watching her ass again as she walks away with the same disinterest as before, digs into his meal. Killing has always seemed to stimulate his appetite. He'd noticed it years ago, first during his stints as a mercenary in Sudan, and then again later, when he was working for Blackwater in Iraq.

As he forks salad into his mouth, his mind goes back to that Inkster prostitute he'd screwed with the prosthesis. She'd have been fine if she'd just put her red spandex outfit back on and left. But as he was zipping up his trousers, she'd had the nerve to look over and smirk at him.

That was enough. After calmly returning her snide little smile, he'd finished buckling his belt and then motioned her over. She must've had an inkling she'd messed up, because she came up to him hesitantly, looking nervous. Maybe she saw the cold glint in his eyes that meant she was already as good as dead. She had long black hair. It was easy to grab it and pull back her head, baring her throat for the switchblade he'd palmed and flicked open. After slitting it deep so she couldn't call out, he threw her down on the bed and gutted her while she frantically gargled up blood. Afterwards, he went to a Target and bought a couple of cheap wheeled suitcases. Squeezed her hacksawed body into one, and the bloodstained bedclothes, clothing and towels he'd used to wipe up into the other. Then waited till dark before dumping them into one of those stagnant, lily-covered mini-lakes off of Edward Hines Drive.

It was when he'd killed the whore that he realized he was capable of a different kind of orgasmic ecstasy. Sometimes he thought of them as "killgasms." It's the feeling you get when you snatch someone's life from them - ideally, in as sudden and brutal a manner as possible. For a couple of minutes afterward you can absorb their life energy as it leaves their body. He couldn't explain the physics or biology of it, but it was almost as good as sex. In some ways, even better.

Roxy, he thought, belatedly recalling the prostitute's name. So long, Roxy. The sex wasn't shit, but the killing was a real ball.

After declining the redheaded waitress' dessert request, he leaves three bucks behind on the table and goes up to the register to pay his bill.

Outside, he walks over and gets into the pickup truck. He takes another pair of latex gloves out of the box in the console and slips them on. He then opens the glovebox and selects one of the several disposable cell phones inside.

Climbing back out of the pickup, he opens the cell and presses *1 to speed-dial the number he's programmed into it.

"Young Municipal Center. How can I direct your call?" a woman's voice says.

"This is Al-Qaeda in Detroit. Put me through directly to the mayor's office."

"Yes, sir!" she says.

A few seconds later another female voice comes on. "This is Candice Cartwright, the mayor's communications director. How can I help you?"

He was initially thinking he'd demand to speak directly to Mayor Bling. But he wants to keep this short and remembers seeing this blonde bitch on TV. She'll do.

"This is Al-Qaeda in Detroit," he says, adding a guttural tone and vaguely-Arabic accent to his voice. "We have received your message accepting our offer. We will contact you tomorrow with instructions for delivery. That is all for now."

"Wait a minute," the woman says. "Could you repeat that?"

His lips twist into a sneer. She's trying to keep him on the line so the call can be traced.

"I said you're a stupid infidel bitch. You got our message, whore. Deliver it."

With that he ends the call, kills the power, and, after checking to see no one is watching, heaves the cell phone back into the patch of trash-strewn woods that stands behind the Ram's Horn.

Back inside the pickup truck, he starts the engine but sits there for a time. His recollection of killing the whore has linked back to another event in his memory.

That dark, stinking room in Fallujah. Nose pressed into some kind of rough fabric that smells of stale sweat and various human orifices. Lying on the cot on his belly, the brutally-tight nylon ties digging into his bloody wrists behind his back. The voices of the men. Especially the one with the nasty laugh. And from a couple of rooms away, the voice of the woman who'd led him here. Kaleela - translates to "Sweetheart." His favorite whore. Up until the day she betrayed him.

After taking turns urinating on him, they'd pulled down his trousers and shorts. Burned his ass-cheeks with cigarettes. Hot-boxed one and then shoved the tip into his rectum. Then they'd worked his toes and the soles of his feet with plastic butane lighters. Then came the power drill. Once into the backs of his thighs. Once into each of his shoulder blades. Once up his ass.

Then they started pushing the whirring drill into his right ear. Scored and bloodied it and left him partially deaf there, but didn't drive it into his skull and kill him, as he'd expected they would.

Throughout the whole ordeal there wasn't a single question or demand. It wasn't about interrogation or ransom. It was about vengeance. For someone's dead kid, apparently. Even though all he did was sell the weapons that were used. The other reason was sport, of course. A few hours of manly amusement on a hot autumn night in Fallujah.

But all the preliminaries - the cigarettes, the lighters, the drill - were nothing. Nothing compared to what the laughing man did later.

With the commando knife.

He looks up at his eyes in the rearview mirror. Mixed in with the blue he can see flecks of red. Tiny flecks of bloody crimson.

And all because of that son of a bitch Johnson.

As he's pulling out of the Ram's Horn lot, he recalls that not far away down 12 Mile there's an oversized movie theater - a 20-screen megacomplex. An idea occurs to him. It's not in the Master Plan, which only calls for car bombs today. But the opportunity seems too good to pass up. After a short cruise, he pulls into the huge theater parking lot. Noting that it's gratifyingly crowded, despite it being midday and the middle of the week - school's out for the summer, after all - he parks the pickup.

The problem will be getting the bomb inside unseen. Fortunately, he still has several of the sturdy canvas "Be Green" shopping bags he'd bought last week at a local supermarket. He opens the rear gate of the pickup, removes one of the ten-pounders and throws the switch that arms it. Since he won't have line-of-sight to detonate the bomb, he'll have to use a timer. He plugs in an AAA battery, clicks through the digital display, setting it to six hundred seconds, and then starts the timer.

Ten minutes to get in there, place it, and get out again.

With the counter now decrementing, he strides toward the entrance to the complex. Inside, he finds the ticket counter is a large, circular booth at the center, with a half-dozen cashiers working the windows. The names of the films mean nothing to him, so he stands behind a big group of tweenagers to see which one they're buying tickets to. Something called "The Purple Vomit Comet" seems to be the hot item. When his turn comes, he sets the Be Green bag down and pays for his ticket. Then he follows the group of youngsters toward the theater showing the film.

A sullen black teenager with cornrowed hair is taking tickets at the entrance.

"What you got there?" the kid says, nodding at the bag, when he holds out his ticket.

"Brought my own popcorn," he says with an ironic grin.

"Ain't allowed," the boy says.

"Tough shit," he says, pushing the ticket into the boy's hand and stepping past him.

"Skanky mutha," he hears the ticket-taker mutter behind him as he goes in. But the kid's voice is more sulky than angry. He's not likely to get a manager and make trouble.

Inside the theater, he takes stock of where the tweeners are seating themselves. The heaviest concentration are in the first few rows, where the curved screen completely fills their field of vision. He ambles down the aisle. There are a handful of other adults in the dimly-lit room. Enough to where he doesn't look totally out of place here.

Not that it matters. Half the tweenagers are gabbing and giggling excitedly at each other, while the other half are reading, texting, or playing games on their cell phones. A few gape at him as he enters the aisle behind the biggest group, moves down to the middle, and seats himself. But after some snarky comments are exchanged with the friends beside them, their fly-like attention span quickly flits on to other things.

He sets the Be Green bag down between his knees. Leaning over, he folds the handles down over the top of the bomb, sets it gently on its side, and pushes it under his seat.

He checks his watch. Five minutes have elapsed since he started the timer.

He gets up and is starting to go back down the row of seats when it occurs to him that the metal base of the theater chair might seriously dampen the effects of the explosion. Hastily, he returns to the seat, pulls the bag out and sets it on top of the cushion. Then he heads up the aisle again, his passage causing another round of early-adolescent gawks and giggles.

When he walks out of the theater, the ticket taker is standing there. The boy stares at him sullenly, his mouth hanging open.

Crap! he thinks, his cheeks suddenly flushing with anxiety. I've made a mistake. This goddamn kid will remember the bag and be able to describe me to the police.

He notices a sign indicating there are restrooms nearby and goes to the men's room to figure out his next move. Four minutes left, his special ops watch shows when he checks it.

There's one boy in the blue-tiled bathroom, standing in front of the mirror, teasing his gelled hair into some kind of idiotic, rooster-like style. But he leaves shortly after the man comes in.

He stands there for several moments, clenching his fists, furious with himself now for being so reckless.

Then the door opens and the skinny ticket-taker walks in.

Allahu Akbar, he thinks, eyes going bright. Perfect.

"Yo, dude," he says, grinning at the boy. "Come here."

"Huh?" the kid says, already reaching for his zipper as he heads for the urinals. "You talking to me?"

"I am," he says, striding up to him.

"What you be-?" he begins.

But he already has his hand over the kid's mouth and a moment later his powerful arms are giving him a body slam, cracking his braided head hard against the tile wall. The kid goes limp and it's a piece of cake to drag him toward the shiny aluminum toilet stall, one muscular arm clenched around the boy's throat while the other twists his head in a three-quarter turn that audibly snaps his neck.

Inside the stall, he seats the ticket-taker's skinny body on the toilet and folds his legs back so they'll be out of view. The boy's sightless eyes are open, the expression on his face one of dull surprise. After latching the stall door, he quickly clambers up over the metal wall, drops onto the toilet seat in the next stall, steps down, and walks out its door.

As he hurries out of the bathroom, he passes two entering boys who are too busy laughing over some kid joke to look at him.

Striding rapidly now toward the movie complex's doors, he checks his watch again. Two minutes. He double-times it out of the building and through the lot to his pickup.

He's got his window rolled down and is just about to pull out onto 12 Mile when he hears the explosion: a low-pitched *ka-chunk!* from back inside the outsized building. He closes his eyes for a moment and lets a shiver of bliss ripple through his body.

With a satisfied grin on his face, he then slips into an opening in the heavy midday traffic and heads east. He realizes that planting the bomb in the theater has had one major drawback: no visuals of the carnage. In his mind he tries to picture the aftermath inside the theater. Swirling smoke and piles of smoldering debris. Youthful corpses and bloody body parts strewn beneath the shredded screen, on which scenes from the brainless movie continue to flash. There are shrieks and screams. There is uncontrollable weeping and general hysteria.

Then he finds himself wondering: what will the tweenage survivors be texting to all their stupid friends as they gaze in shock at the bleeding and dismembered young bodies all around them? WTF? OMG? OMFG?

The image of them clutching their smartphones and texting away, covered in blood and gore, starts him giggling. He tries to stifle it, but the more he attempts to suppress his laughter, the more it seems to well up within him. Soon he's shaking with it - the convulsions so bad he can barely keep the Night Runner in its lane.

He's glad when a red light stops him at Telegraph Road, giving him an opportunity to catch his breath and wipe the tears from his eyes. He's just about recovered his cool when the acronym pops into his mind.

"LOL!" he manages to sputter, just before another jag of laughter overcomes him.

Chapter 26   An On-The-Spot Rhinoplasty

Wednesday, August 17 - 12:10 p.m.

THE FIFTH bomb of the day went off at a mall on Orchard Lake Road, in Farmington Hills. I'd just gotten off the phone with the lead agent down at the Garden City site when Yates gave us the news. Despite my reluctance to speak to the arrogant pighead in charge of the investigation, I called Blandings again. Told him we were finished up in Allen Park and suggested Wilson, Nardella, and I go up to the Farmington Hills site.

"By the way," Morley said gloatingly. "At the Garden City bomb site some citizens reported a suspicious Arab couple in the area just prior to the car bombing there."

"Yeah, I just talked to Woods about it," I said. "Told me some folks reported them coming out of a market just before the explosion. Guess they thought they were suspicious because the woman wore a head scarf. Garden City cops found out they were regular shoppers at the market. Got their name and address from receipts at the market and went to their house to interview them. While they were there some redneck biker types started gathering around the house, so the cops took the family into protective custody. Good thing, apparently, because it seems somebody firebombed the house shortly after the police left."

"I see," Blandings said, his voice tight.

Oops, I thought, only then realizing that Woods must not have called Blandings or Dorn yet with his latest updates. I regretted having no doubt just set him up for a butt-chewing by Tweedledum and Tweedledee.

"All right," Blandings went on. "You three get over to the Orchard Lake Road site. Make sure you press hard on whether anybody saw Hadidi or other suspicious-looking Arabs in the area before the bombing."

"Your wish is my command, sire," I said and hung up.

As Nardella drove us up to Farmington Hills, I decided to give my mind a break from all the murder and mayhem and spend five delicious minutes thinking about Oprah Cummings.

Even though I was up to my ears in the life-and-death matters at hand, I hadn't forgotten that moment I woke up in that hospital bed and saw her face for the first time.

160

Crazy as it seemed, in those few minutes we'd spent together at four-thirty in the morning, there in that hospital room, something had happened to me. Something I couldn't even begin to explain to myself.

I'd never before in my life had a "love at first sight" experience. Fact is, the two or three times I've genuinely fallen in love have always been on the coattails of lust. On some rainy morning when I'd wake up next to a woman and realize I'd come to care about a lot more than just having good times and good sex with her.

But when I opened my eyes and saw Oprah that morning, I'd had the strangest sense of déjà vu. It was as if I'd had an image of her somewhere inside me, all my life. Hidden in some shadowy corner of my mind and soul. And then suddenly - in that antiseptic-scented hospital room - there she was.

And it wasn't just the way she looked - though her face and figure seemed just about as beautiful to me as a woman's could possibly be. No - there was something else. Some indefinable thing about her that came from the depths of her being. Some kind of strange, almost angelic energy that had immediately enthralled me. Truth is, I've sometimes wondered if certain people were angels from heaven without their even knowing it, and I strongly suspected this was the case with Dr. Oprah Cummings.

I checked my watch and sighed. My five minutes for basking in thoughts of her were up. Time to get back to "the real world." I noticed we were on I-275 now, heading north. Nardella seemed to have chilled out, and was driving at a brisk but not hair-raising speed.

"So what's with that grin on your face, Mojo?" Wilson asked from the front passenger seat. "Used to see that same expression on Bowser, our old Airedale, when he'd sniffed out some nice kitty bon-bon."

I looked at him and smiled. "Just thinking about somebody I hope to be with when this is all over," I said.

"Not that Nadine Robinson floozy, I hope," Nardella said.

"No," I said, frowning. "That's long over. Damn, though - does the whole field office know I was messing around with Nadine?"

"Don't worry," she said. "I was having lunch at the Book-Cadillac one day a few months back, and saw you get into an elevator with her. Haven't said a word to anyone up to this minute."

"I wish Nadine Robinson would mess around with me," Wilson said wistfully. "That woman is one smoking hot babe."

"Listen to him," Nardella said. "You don't have a chance, Wilson. I hear she only likes studly men. Not wieners."

"Hey, I'll have you know I answered this great penis enlargement email offer a while back," he said.

"I wish they'd stop sending them to me," Nardella said, shaking her head. "I get them all the time, too."

"Well, I bought the product they were selling and it's added three inches to my endowment," Wilson said.

"So you've got, like, four now?" Angie said with a giggle. Her hormonal tsunami seemed to have crested and subsided over the past hour, and she was now getting back to her more normal self.

"Listen, Peaches - I'll have you know I'm virtually the new John Holmes," he said.

"'Virtually' being the operative word there," she said. "Like totally in your imagination."

"Maybe you could get a job with Willie the Pimp's outfit," I said. "Be some high-paid studmuffin in his porn films."

"You heard from him again, by the way?" Wilson asked.

"Called me this morning, offering to help out."

"What's with that guy, do you think?"

"No idea," I said.

"I can see it now," Nardella was musing. "Long Floyd Wilson and his sex doll Cynthia in 'If Only I Could Find It.'"

"Hold on," I said to Wilson. "Floyd? That's your first name?" In all the years we'd worked together, I couldn't recall hearing it before.

"A filthy rumor," he said. "I suggest you ignore it."

"You just try me sometime, Peaches," Wilson said, turning back to Nardella. "I'll show you G-spots you never knew you had."

"G-spot, shmee-spot," she said. "I'd settle for a dork who doesn't just roll over and make me sleep on the wet spot while he snores like a warthog. But I'm sure that excludes you."

"That's true," Wilson said. "I snore like a walrus, not a warthog."

He turned around in his seat to me then.

"So you were with Nadine Robinson? Man, I'd drag my testicles over ten miles of hot asphalt with broken glass embedded in it, just to sniff the bicycle seat she sat on for five minutes a year and a half ago."

"Hear that, Angie?" I said. "Who says men aren't romantic?"

"Please," she said.

"So what's this Nadine babe like in the sack, Mojo?" Wilson asked. "She really hot stuff?"

"I'm not going there," I said. "And stop calling me Mojo."

"Right," he said.

The Orchard Lake Road bomb had gone off in a shopping mall parking lot, near the mall's main entrance. A crowd of people were gathered around the blast location, which was sealed off with a circle of crime scene ribbon. Nardella parked on the edge of the lot and the three of us got out.

"How about trying to control that *Witzelsucht* crap of yours while we're here?" Nardella said to Wilson as we walked toward the restricted area. "Out of respect for the victims."

"Gimme a break, Peaches," he said. "It's my coping mechanism. Helps me deal with the horror."

"The horror of being you?" she said.

As we approached the scene, I could make out a badly blown-out white van and a couple of other burned-up cars nearby. After showing a Farmington Hills cop our Federal Agent shields, we went under the tape and over to the officer in charge, a Lieutenant Killcullen. He was a lean, freckle-faced guy in his forties.

"What do we know so far, Lieutenant?" I asked him after we'd introduced ourselves.

"Fourteen dead," he said, his voice tight with disgust. "Nine of them from the same family. They were in that van over there. Two adult sisters, their mother, three teen girls, two younger boys, and a baby, for Christ's sake. The other five were nearby pedestrians. They took eight more victims down the road to Henry Ford Hospital, in West Bloomfield. Understand three of them are still in ER, in critical condition."

Wilson gave a rueful shake of his head. "Holy mother of bat farts," he said. Nardella glared at him.

"Any witnesses?" I asked.

"Six that are still here," he said. "Officer Campbell over there is taking depositions. I've got two more officers over at Henry Ford, getting statements from the ones who aren't critically injured."

"Do you know if any of them reported seeing suspicious people around, prior to or after the bombings?"

"No, I don't. You'll have to talk to them."

"Are those family members over there?" Nardella asked, nodding at a cluster of people amid the bystanders who were weeping and hugging one another.

"Yeah," he said, looking over at them. "They're from the van victims' family, the Djugashvilis. Georgians, apparently."

The older women in the group were bawling and literally tearing out lengths of their hair, while the younger ones talked or texted grimly into their phones. The men stood together, several with tears running down their faces, cursing and chain-smoking. Occasionally one man would hug another when he broke into mournful, disconsolate sobs.

As we were heading over to the spot inside the yellow tape where Officer Campbell was deposing the witnesses, one of the distraught family members called out to us.

"Mr. Police Detective!" the man said. He was balding and heavyset. The front of his white shirt was stained with tears.

"Yes sir?" I said.

"What's this about? Who did this to us? Why would they do such a thing?" he asked, holding out his hands. His voice was heavily accented.

"I don't know, sir. I wish I did."

"Your family doesn't have any enemies, does it, sir?" Nardella asked.

"Enemies?" he said. "We're not drug dealers. We're not criminals. We own a couple of shoe stores, for God's sake!"

A red-faced, middle-aged man was standing near the Djugashvilis, kibitzing. He was wearing a baseball cap with an American flag patch front and center on it.

"It's those goddamn Muslims," he interjected, jabbing his finger. "Those goddamn Muslim terrorists!"

"We don't know that for sure, sir," I said.

"Hogwash," he said with a sneer. "Listen to Larry Lattimore instead of the lamestream media. Goddamn frigging Muslims are plotting to kill us all!"

Ignoring him, I put my hand on the heavyset man's shoulder. "Sir, we're sincerely sorry about your loss," I said to him, gravely. "But we've got to get back to work."

We continued on over to where the half-dozen witnesses were standing. I asked if they'd seen anyone or anything suspicious either before or after the bombing. The answers were negative. We showed them the pictures of Sam Hadidi. More negatives. I gave them the description the boy Ahmad had given me of the Caucasian male he'd seen going into Al-Rafi's house. Negatives again.

Three strikes and we were out.

As we were finishing up with the witnesses, I noticed that a small crowd had gathered around the man with the flag cap.

"You better wake up, people!" he was saying. "Those goddamn Muslim terrorists are all around you. Plotting and scheming and planting more bombs. Goddamn frigging bastards like him!" the man said, pointing to a middle-aged man in a turban man who was walking by with his wife and young son.

The turbaned man stared at him dispassionately.

"Hey, Mohammed!" the flag-cap man said. "Why don't you get your lazy, foreign ass out of our country?"

The man in the turban's eyes narrowed, but he kept on walking, the wife and son instinctively moving closer to him.

"Did you hear me?" the man said. "Why don't you take your stupid kid and your dumb, ugly wife and get the frigging hell out of our country?"

The turbaned man turned around, stopped and glared at him. Then he spat on the sidewalk in the flag-cap man's direction.

"Did you see that? The terrorist bastard spits at us!" he yelled. "Goddamn Muslim scumbag!"

"We're not Muslims, you idiot," the turbaned man called out to him. "We're Sikhs."

"Yeah, you're sick alright. You're a sick Muslim motherhumper!" the man said.

By this point I'd gone under the yellow tape and was moving toward the flag-capped man. I saw the Sikh man shake off his wife's hand as she tried to pull him away.

Looking to head off trouble, I got between them.

"Sir, I think you should calm down," I said to the flag-capped man. "In point of fact, the Sikh religion has nothing to do with Islam."

"Says who?"

"Says anyone with half a brain," the turbaned man called out to him. "Which excludes you, of course, you numbskull."

"Hey, screw you, you frigging camel jockey!"

"Listen, sir," I said. "You'd better chill out, or-"

"Chill out?" he said as he spun on me. "Who the hell you telling to chill out, you frigging nigger?"

My vision narrowed down to where it seemed as if I were looking at the man's flushed face through a section of pipe. I didn't even realize I was about to give him an on-the-spot rhinoplasty until I saw what looked like a charcoal fire starter shoot past my cocked fist and jam into his upper arm.

The flag-capped guy's mouth and eyes went wide as saucers and he began to topple backwards.

Gunslinger-fast, the husky female cop who'd tasered him holstered the device, caught the guy's toppling body, and eased him down onto the pavement. He lay there with his mouth open, arms and legs jerking, his eyes bugged out like an insect's.

"When he comes to, cuff him and take him to the station," I heard Killcullen say behind me.

"What charge, Lieutenant?" the female cop said, looking up from alongside the twitching man.

"Disturbing the peace," he said.

"Too bad being an asshole isn't a felony," Wilson said. "They could send this creep up for life."

Just then another Farmington Hills cop came running up to us.

"Captain Killcullen, sir!" he said breathlessly. "There's been another bombing! A movie theater full of kids in Southfield!"

Wilson opened his mouth, but shut it at the sight of Nardella's homicidal glower.

Scream Cruise

Chapter 27   1-800-I-Gotcha

Wednesday, August 17 - 5:30 p.m.

POINTING THE remote, he switches on the oversize flat screen TV and begins clicking through the channels. The local stations are just beginning to broadcast their early evening news reports.

At first a smile of satisfaction crosses his face when he confirms that the lead stories on every station are his latest bombings. But then he gets impatient.

"Come on, you idiots," he says as he cycles through the channels. "What's the damn body count?"

"Police have tallied over a hundred dead," one station reports.

"'Over a hundred,'" he scoffs. "How about an actual number, you worthless dipshits?"

Finally one of them gives a hard count: one hundred twenty-three dead and seventy-eight severely injured - nineteen of them in critical condition.

"Hot damn!" he says as a smile lights his face again. He's averaged over a dozen dead per bombing!

Grinning broadly, he glances looks down at Beelzebub. The dog is lying on the carpet, idly gnawing on the Chatty Chelsea infant doll he'd bought him for a chew toy.

"Hear that, Bub?" he says. "One hundred twenty-three whack jobs. Decent. *Very* decent."

After releasing the pudgy vinyl baby and lapping away the slaver from his jaws, the dog growls up at him agreeably. "Da-da!" the doll says from between his paws.

The man clicks through the channels again, savoring the images he sees when the camera cuts away from the chattering, concerned-looking newscasters to shots of the carnage he's wrought. Shots of smoking wreckage and zipped-up body bags. Shots of weeping relatives and distraught bystanders. Shots of stressed-out-looking cops and firemen, with cuts to grim-faced police officials and municipal authorities.

He finds himself almost in awe at how well the Master Plan is working. In one day he's managed to spread an icy blanket of terror over the entire metro Detroit area, upping the paranoia quotient tenfold. Now no one can

168

kid themselves into thinking they're safe by telling themselves it'll happen to some poor schmuck across town, but not to them. Now they'll all realize that it can happen to anyone, anytime, anywhere.

Click-clack-click-*boom!* Like a well-oiled machine, today's installment of the Master Plan has ratcheted along from one step to the next. Cold, clean, and heartless. Leaving behind a trail of death for his randomly-chosen victims.

At this point he notices a scrolling message across the bottom of the news program he's tuned to. "AL-QAEDA IN DETROIT TERRORISTS DEMAND $25 MILLION FOREIGN CASH PAYOFF!" it says.

The headline piques his interest. Today is the day all the major local media outlets will have received copies of the extortion letters he'd sent to the asshole mayor and county execs.

He sits down on the couch and clicks around through the TV stations again. A couple are showing images of the letters, including close-ups of the addressees and his "Al-Qaeda in Detroit" signature. He turns up the sound to listen. As he's watching one of the reports, another messages slides across the bottom of the screen. "STAY TUNED: MAYOR BLING AND COUNTY EXECS TO HOLD NEWS CONFERENCE AT 6:00 P.M."

"News conference, eh?" he says, glancing at the pit bull. "This should be interesting."

Shortly before 6 p.m. the newscaster says "*We take you now live to a news conference at Detroit's Coleman A. Young Municipal Center - formerly the City-County Building - where Mayor Bling and the Wayne, Oakland, and Macomb County executives are about to hold a news conference.*"

The video cuts to a blue-curtained stage lit to glaring brightness by off-screen video camera lights. A pair of American flags droop from brass stands in the background. In the center is a podium with the city's Spirit of Detroit emblem on the front. To the left stands Benjamin Bling, the city's mayor, and to the right L. Sparks Cunningham, the Oakland County executive. Dick Sorenson and George Gates, the Wayne and Macomb County execs, stand slightly behind them.

Bling is the first to speak. Taking hold of the microphone atop the podium, he leans forward and reads a prepared statement, periodically looking up into the cameras. "*Good evening, fellow Detroiters,*" he begins.

"As you all know, the metro area has been subjected to a series of horrendous bombings over the past several days. A group calling itself 'Al-Qaeda in Detroit' has claimed responsibility and has demanded that local authorities pay what is in effect a ransom to purchase the safety of our citizens.

"In the interests of that public safety, it has been decided, in conjunction with state and Federal authorities, that Al-Qaeda in Detroit's demands will be met.

"Needless to say, we do so very reluctantly, but with the hope that our adversaries will be true to their word and stop these terrible bombings immediately.

"That's all I have," he says, stepping back.

Cunningham then takes the mike.

"I just want to add a couple more things to what Mayor Bling said," he says.

The camera then cuts to a close-up. You can see his jowly, pink face sweating from the hot TV lights.

"The first is this: while payoffs to thugs go against everything I believe in and stand for, the safety of our citizens is our first priority. We've agreed to pay off these terrorists for one reason only. To stop the bombings and ensure that the public is kept secure.

"But I also want the bombers to know something. We're going to get you. We're going to make you pay for all the needless death and suffering you've inflicted on so many innocent people."

At that the man all but leaps up off the couch and strides up to the oversize television. The demonic grin on his livid features is huge.

"You're threatening me?" he says to the county exec's two-foot high face on the screen. "I love it!"

"According to Morley Blandings, the FBI agent in charge of the bombing investigation," Cunningham goes on, *"Federal authorities are closing in on the Islamist terrorist group responsible for these horrifying bombings. Arrests are expected at any-"*

"What about Dream Cruise, Mr. Cunningham?" an unseen reporter calls out from offscreen. *"Any chance it'll be cancelled this year?"*

"Absolutely not," Cunningham says flatly, shaking his head. *"The Dream Cruise is a signature event for Oakland County and the Detroit metro area. This year, the security level will be the highest it's ever been.*

"Something people may not know," he goes on, *"is that security for the Cruise has always been a top priority for our administration. But this year, in addition to the increased law enforcement presence you'll see along the Dream Cruise route, we've also got a special number for citizens to call if they spot anything suspicious.*

"If you attend the Dream Cruise and notice something that doesn't seem right to you, just call this eight hundred number," he says, holding up a bumper sticker-sized sign that reads *1-800-I-GOTCHA.*

"Now let me stress something very important. Prank calls will not be tolerated. Make a prank or frivolous call and you'll be ticketed and given a stiff fine. But if you have what you believe is a legitimate suspicion about someone or something you've seen, don't hesitate to contact the authorities.

"Just call this number," he says, holding up the sign again. *"That's one eight hundred, I gotcha."*

With a sneer on his face, the man clicks off the television and turns to the yellow dog.

"Did you hear that, Bub?" he says, shaking his head. "What a worthless pile of steaming bullshit."

Beelzebub lifts his oversized head from the chewed-up infant doll. His good eye is focused on the man, while his bad one appears to be doing figure eights in its socket.

"Wait till that pus-brained old fart comes in to work tomorrow morning and sees what I've got in store for Oakland County," the man says. "He's gonna wish to hell he never frigging woke up."

"And as for Morley Blandings..." he goes on, chuckling as he recalls how amazingly easy it had been to penetrate the McNamara Federal Building a couple of months back.

All he'd had to do was find out the name of the after-hours cleaning company and then get a job working there for two weeks under an assumed name. A discreet visit to the telecom closet up on the twenty-sixth floor one night was all he'd needed to install the tap and wireless transmitter. Since then he could sit in the Night Runner or Escalade and listen to calls from the Agent-In-Charge's office from a couple of blocks away.

"That Dawson seemed reasonably sharp," he says to the dog. "But this Blandings dude is a real asshole. Spends most of his time yacking with the media or his cronies in Washington about the great job he's doing. When he isn't ordering food from that catering company-"

At which point the man's eyes light up with an evil gleam.

"You know what, Bub?" he says. "I've got me an idea. I think I'm gonna pay that FBI office downtown a visit. A little *surprise* visit. What do you think, bad boy?"

The pit bull looks up at the man with a grotesque, toothy grin. And then goes back to contentedly chomping on Chatty Chelsea.

"Ma-ma!" the doll squeaks happily.

Chapter 28   Memory Glitch

Wednesday, August 17 - 8:00 p.m.

"TEN GODDAMN bombings in one day!" Elliot Dorn raged. "One hundred twenty-three people dead in one day!"

"A hundred twenty-five," Wilson whispered alongside me. "Two more of the criticals died."

It was evening and we were back at the McNamara building. The last bombing of the day had occurred around 4:30 p.m. The bomber had switched to the east side in the afternoon and had once again slaughtered innocent victims in several more suburban communities. A general meeting had been called and we were all standing outside the glass office Blandings had usurped from Dawson, listening to Dorn dress us down like a drill instructor chewing out a bunch of raw recruits.

"This is totally unacceptable, people!" he all but shouted. "These slimy terrorist dirtbags are making the Bureau look like a collection of useless idiots. Morley here sends three agents to every single site, and every damn one of you comes back empty-handed. No clues. No fingerprints. No suspects. Nothing!"

While Dorn raved on, his pale, reptilian features purpled with fury, Blandings was standing there looking at us in a serious but also empathetic way. As if he saw us as errant but well-meaning schoolchildren, instead of the poop-for-brains incompetents Dorn was calling us.

"Gee, I get it," Wilson muttered in my ear. "Good cop, bad cop."

"Right," I whispered back at him. "Now Morley's going to tell us how much he respects our efforts, but that we've just got to do better."

Dorn was launching into yet another tirade, about how we were all worthless leeches dangling from the taxpayers' collective scrotum, when Blandings raised his hand and interrupted him.

"Ease up, Elliot," he said, giving us a sad but forgiving smile. "These agents have been through a lot today."

On cue, Dorn receded to the background while Blandings stepped forward, his hands steepled in front of him.

"The fact is, ladies and gentlemen," he said, "some days you give it everything you've got, but in the end come up with snake eyes. You're like

Sisyphus in that Greek myth. You push that huge rock all the way up the hill, but at the end of the day it just rolls back down again and crushes your toes. You move a mountain, but underneath all you find is a molehill."

"Huh?" Wilson said.

"I don't get it either," I whispered. I knew that, like everyone in the room, Blandings had gotten virtually zero sleep for the past two days. Maybe that's why he seemed to be rambling, with some of what he was saying making almost no sense at all.

"My point is this," he went on. "We did our absolute best today. But we didn't get the job done, did we? Today the bad guys won and the good guys lost. The black hats fished and the white hats cut bait. That's the unvarnished truth of it, and it's a crying shame."

"Guy's metaphors are a whole new can of worms," I heard Wilson mumble.

"But I want you agents to know something," Blandings went on. "My faith in you is unshakeable. I know what you're made of and I'm one thousand percent confident we're going to get a break soon. We're going to find the terrorist scum who made the Bureau look bad today."

"Wait a minute," I muttered to Wilson. "Is that what happened today? They made the Bureau look bad?"

"Right," he whispered back. "Never mind they blew the crap out of a hundred twenty-five innocent people."

"So all I'm asking, ladies and gentlemen, is that you redouble your efforts. Go after these jihadist scum with everything you've got. You're America's law enforcement elite. Get out there and show our citizens what we're made of!"

You could tell Morley enjoyed hearing the sound of his own voice, and his pep talk went on far longer than it needed to. When he finally wrapped it up, Dorn applauded vigorously, apparently to cue the rest of us. There was a smattering of hand-clapping before we all drifted back toward our cubicles.

"Guy's a legend in his own mind," Nardella said.

"I give him credit," Wilson said. "He managed to get Mom, Dad, God, country, duty, and honor into it. All he missed was the apple pie. Or is it cherry? I can never remember which."

"Not to mention the two hundred seven dead and God-knows-how-many wounded so far," I said. "Guess he didn't feel they'd be a motivator."

The truth was, I felt like hell about the lack of progress I'd made today. And I'm sure all the other agents did as well. After all, it was our job to prevent this kind of terrible crap from happening. And we'd failed miserably.

Using the mobile kit in the trunk of Nardella's car, I'd done what bomb forensics I could at all three of the blast sites we'd been at: the Allen Park intersection, the Farmington Hills mall, and the Southfield movie theater. While I'd confirmed that the same type of explosive devices were used at all of them, I'd come up with nothing that would break or even advance the case. We did bag some evidence and drop it off at the state police lab in Sterling Heights. But I'd already dusted the most promising debris for fingerprints and hadn't found even a partial. It was obvious our bomber was being scrupulously careful about leaving any behind.

The thing that was most driving me crazy was that I still couldn't place the man who'd called me in Al-Rafi's kitchen. All day long I'd kept going back to the vaguely-familiar voice in my mind. Replaying the threatening words I'd heard through the earpiece of my bomb helmet and trying to match a face and name to them.

"McCoy - Wilson - Nardella."

We halted as Eric Dawson came up to us outside our cubicles.

"How about if the four of us get together in my office and do some brainstorming?" he said. "Maybe we can come up with some new angles on the case."

"Fine by me," I said.

"I'm game," said Angie.

"How about five minutes from now?" Wilson said. "I need to go bleed my lizard."

"Sounds good," Eric said. "See you all in five minutes, then."

I decided to use the short break to call Oprah Cummings. I walked over to one of the windows and looked down at Michigan Avenue where it led to Woodward. It hardly seemed possible that only a little over forty-eight hours had passed since we'd run down the street and confronted the horrors awaiting us at Campus Martius.

I pulled the doctor's business card out of my wallet. I dialed her number and memorized it while it rang.

"Dr. Cummings," she answered.

"It's me," I said.

"Agent Johnson?"

I smiled. I'd made enough of an impression that she remembered my voice.

"Hi, Doctor. I'm just checking in with you."

"Are you having any problems?" she said. "Any of that dizziness or nausea I mentioned?"

"No, ma'am. I'm feeling fine."

"Did the Vicodin help?"

"To be honest, I never got around to filling the prescription. Been chewing aspirin instead."

"Well, be careful you don't take too many. They can irritate your stomach lining. But you're feeling basically alright?"

"I am."

"Good. I've been worrying about you. A little."

"I'm glad to hear that. I've been worried about you, too."

"Worried about me? Why?"

"Afraid you might think what I said yesterday morning - about our getting together when this is all over - was just the raving of a concussion-addled mind. Have you given it some thought?"

"I have, Agent Johnson."

"Please call me McCoy."

"Alright - McCoy, then. The fact is, yes, I have given it some thought. But I haven't made up my mind yet."

"Fair enough. I'm happy you haven't decided against it."

"Let me be frank, Agent - I mean, McCoy. My marriage didn't end in the happiest way possible. I caught my husband cheating on me, and it was, well, pretty devastating."

"Yeah," I said. "I know. Same thing happened with me."

"Really?" she said.

"Yes," I said. "Small world, isn't it?"

"I suppose what I've done in reaction to that," she went on, "is lose myself in my job. I work sixty to eighty hours a week, which means I basically live here at the DMC. But weird as it seems, I love it."

"Well, I work some pretty crazy hours myself, Oprah. Okay if I call you that, by the way?"

"I think so. Yes."

"Good," I said. "Listen, Oprah, to me it sounds like what you do is more than a job for you. It's who and what you are, through and through. Well, being with the Bureau is the same for me. Some people can't understand that - my ex, for instance. I think maybe you and I are a lot alike that way."

"Do you think so?" she said. "Or are we maybe just kidding ourselves? About what we need in life?"

"Whoa," I chuckled. "That's a very big conversation. And one I'd love to have with you soon. But unfortunately, I've got to run now and get to a meeting. I just wanted to touch base for a minute and let you know you're in my mind. Whether you want to be there or not."

"Well, thank you, McCoy. The truth is, you've been in mine too."

"Really? That's good to hear. Look - I've got to go now. Talk to you soon, I hope."

"Alright," she said. "Call me again when you can."

"I will. Be well, Oprah."

"You too, McCoy."

I hung up. As I hurried off toward the meeting, I realized my heart was pumping hard in my chest and I felt about a thousand percent better. That mundane little conversation had energized me more than a six-pack of Red Bull.

With Blandings and Dorn taking over his office, Eric had moved into a small conference room off the hallway leading back to the field office lab. His laptop was on the table and there was a whiteboard on an easel off to one side.

"Nice broom closet," Wilson said as we entered.

"It's actually not so bad," Eric said. "At least I don't feel like I'm sitting in a fishbowl all day."

"Any luck remembering the phone caller from back at Al-Rafi's house?" he asked me when we'd sat down.

I gave a rueful shrug. "Unfortunately, no - and it's driving me crazy. Sometimes I'm right on the verge of seeing the guy's face. And then," I said, snapping my fingers, "it just evaporates."

"Obviously it can't be someone you knew very well," Nardella said. "Has to be somebody you had a fleeting encounter with."

"Maybe a public restroom somewhere?" Wilson suggested. "Some airport maybe, like that Senator what's-his-name?"

"Thanks for the memory jog, but I don't think so," I said.

"We'll let that go for now," Eric said, standing up and going over to the whiteboard. "Let's list what we've got so far. You want to start, McCoy?"

"Okay. Here's what we've got, as I see it," I said. "Number one. Somebody who's highly-skilled at bomb-making and booby-trapping. Number two. Somebody who knows me and hates my guts - but who I can't even remember. Number three. Somebody who may have had it in for this Imam Al-Rafi. Number four. Somebody looking to extort a big payoff from the bombings. Number five. Somebody who has no qualms at all about killing people to get what he wants."

"Make that killing *lots* of people," Angie amended.

"I stand corrected," I said. "So what else am I missing?"

"Somebody who hates Detroit," Dawson said, adding it to the list.

"That's right," Wilson agreed. "Remember that 'Detroit is a sick, dying city and we want to help it die' stuff in the extortion letter? What's up with that? How come this swizzle stick hates Motown?"

"We keep saying 'somebody,'" Eric said. "Like we're assuming it's one person and not a group. Doesn't it make more sense to suspect there's a gang involved? Or a terrorist cell, the way Blandings and Dorn are supposing?"

"I'm basically going by my gut and by what that boy, Ahmad, told me," I said. "That a lone non-Arab guy went into Al-Rafi's house two nights before he lured us there. That'd give him plenty of time to kill Al-Rafi, cut off his head and hands, use the hands to put fingerprints on the extortion letters, and then plant all the bombs and booby traps. Plus there's been a time gap between all the explosions. Enough for a lone guy to do them all. If this was a terrorist cell, you'd expect them to do some coordinated bombings."

"By the way - what was with all the ball-busting booby traps at Al-Rafi's?" Wilson said. "Whoever set them is one sick mashed potato."

"Fear factor?" Nardella said. "You guys tend to be kind of sensitive about your thingies."

"'Thingies?'" Wilson said. "Listen, Peaches, they don't call them 'family jewels' for nothing."

"Maybe it's just a generic hatred of law enforcement agents," Eric said.

"Could the guy be some perp you sent up, McCoy?" Nardella said. "Maybe a long time ago? Someone who finally got out on parole?"

"Nobody that I can think of." I said. "I've always tried to keep track of when the offenders I've helped send up are paroled. But while there are a few candidates I can think of who'd probably love to see me dead, I don't make any of them for our bomber."

"What about the video the TV stations shot that night?" Wilson asked. "You thought the perp was probably at the scene and might show up in their shots of the bystanders."

"I got their production people to send over all the raw footage on DVDs - fortunately, they all shoot digital now. I was going through them just before Dorn and Blandings did their dog and pony show out there. But so far I haven't seen anyone in them who's rung my memory bells."

Just then the door opened and Elliot Dorn poked his head inside. He gazed around at the four of us with a "gotcha" smirk on his horny toad face.

"What is this? Some kind of cabal?" he said.

"Just trying to figure out what species you belong to," Wilson said.

"Actually, we're doing some brainstorming about the case," Eric said.

Maybe it was due to Wilson's comment, but I half-expected a forked tongue to come flicking out of Dorn's mouth as he spent a few seconds coldly looking us over.

"We just got word from the mayor's office down at the Municipal Center," he finally said. "Apparently Al-Qaeda in Detroit contacted them a few minutes ago about the payoff. They want the money to be delivered tomorrow afternoon."

"By who?" Eric said.

"An FBI special agent," Dorn said.

"Anyone in particular?" I asked.

"Yeah," he said, giving me one of his lipless grins.

"You."

Chapter 29   White Light
Thursday, August 18 - 8:50 a.m.

A SELF-SATISFIED smile crosses his face when he spots the approaching taxicab.

He's in the midst of the Oakland County government complex, standing near the entrance to the Sixth Circuit Court. Behind the wraparound shades, his sky-blue eyes take in the surrounding buildings.

He checks his watch. Another hour and ten minutes, he thinks, and this will be ground effing zero.

The cab, a black Lincoln Town Car, pulls up toward the court building. He waves to the driver and heads toward the curb.

He's wearing a big, blond handlebar mustache, a red head scarf, and sleeveless black muscle shirt. A heavy coating of artificial tan has turned the exposed skin of his face and body-builder's arms a burnt orange color. Jeans with a key chain and a pair of black, scuffed-up cowboy boots complete the outfit.

In a biker's slightly bowlegged amble, he walks up to the taxi and climbs in.

"Where to?" the driver asks.

"Telegraph and Square Lake, man," he says, adding some redneck twang to his voice. "You know where that is?"

"Sure," the driver says.

As they're pulling away from the circuit court curb, he gazes at the parking lot to his left. First he checks out the white 1999 Chevy Suburban parked at the far end of the lot. Then his gaze swings over to the twenty-five-foot-long semi trailer that's sitting about a hundred feet from the court building's entrance. Using a phony company name, he'd paid a private contractor to pick it up from behind a mall in Waterford and drop it there at 6 a.m. this morning. When they turn out of the lot and head up the complex's service drive, he resists the urge to turn around in his seat and grin back at them fondly again.

The driver looks and sounds Balkan. Albanian or Romanian, maybe. Which is good. It'll make it easier to fake the redneck inflection.

"Man, them sum-bitchin' Oakland County judges sure are a pisser," he says with a scowl.

"That right?" the driver says.

"Damn straight, man. One lousy DUI and that rotten judge took my frigging license away for ninety frigging days," he says. "Ain't that a bitch?"

"Sorry to hear that," the driver says.

"How the hell am I supposed to get to my job, man? Hitchhike? Shit, would you give me a ride if you saw me hitchin'?"

"Maybe you can take a cab to your job," the driver says.

"It's twenty frigging miles each way, man. Cab rides'll cost me a small fortune."

"Maybe some co-worker, he can bring you?"

"None of them live around me. Most of them are jungle bunnies anyway. I wouldn't ride with them if you paid me."

The driver was silent.

"Man, I don't know what this frigging country's coming to," he says. "Man can't drink a few beers, get a little tipsy, and ride home to bed without John Law busting your butt. Just 'cause I scared the living crap outta some teenage punks when I almost ran 'em over. Frigging punks get on their goddamn cell phones, call the frigging cops, and the next thing you know some foreign-looking bitch judge pulls your damn license for ninety frigging days."

How come I get all the redneck loser assholes as my fares? the taxi driver is thinking.

"That's tough, my friend," he says aloud.

Back in the parking lot, a green light blinks on the digital watch-based timer mounted inside the Suburban's glovebox. The starter begins to crank over and a moment later the engine catches and comes to life. Then an orange LED flashes atop the electric motor mounted on a steel pedestal where the console once stood.

There's a rumbling whir as the motor causes one machined aluminum lever to depress the brake while another shifts the automatic transmission lever sideways and back into low gear.

As the white Suburban begins to creep forward there's a loud *clack* when the brake is released and the whirring electric motor causes a third lever, weighted with a block of lead, to drive the gas pedal flat to the floor.

Giving out a powerful moan, the huge white SUV surges down the lane that leads straight toward the Sixth Circuit Court's entrance. A forged-steel steering wheel lock keeps its driverless aim true as it roars toward the court's multiple glass entry doors.

Just beyond the marble-walled lobby, four Oakland County Sheriff's deputies are manning the court building's metal detector and bag-scanning systems. As visitors come in, they're obliged to put car keys and other items that will set off the detector's alarm into plastic baskets before they walk through.

One of the deputies is rotating a set of the emptied baskets back to the check-in counter when he hears the sound of an engine running full-bore. He looks up and sees the huge white Suburban screaming toward the court building.

"HOLY SHIT!" he bellows. "GET DOWN!"

But instead of diving to the floor, the deputies and dozen or so visitors stand there in paralyzed terror while they watch the Suburban strike the curb, go airborne for twenty feet and slam into the entranceway.

For an instant there's a tremendous crash, with broken glass and metal hurtling across the lobby. Then there's nothing but white light as the nitromethane-laced barrels of ammonium nitrate inside the Suburban detonate and death's raging hand swoops out and obliterates them all.

"Did you hear something just now?" the cab driver says, referring to the low-pitched but clearly-audible *whump* he's just overheard, somewhere in the distance behind them.

The man in the back seat gives a dumb-sounding chuckle. "Sorry, man," he says. "Guess I must've farted."

He lifts and muscles his powerful tanned arms in a contented stretch. In the rearview mirror he can see the cabbie frowning.

Unable to sustain his surly act, he smiles to himself. It had taken a while to figure out a good way to take out responders, the way he'd seen the insurgents do so successfully back in Iraq. He remembers especially well that incident he'd witnessed in a small town outside of Tikrit...

His Blackwater team had gotten the job of escorting some government big shot to meet with the local sheikh. On their way to the sheikh's compound, they'd passed through the town square - a busy, open air market. While the meeting was going on, the sound of a loud explosion could be heard from back in the town's center. The sheikh insisted the party go there to see what had gone down.

When they got to the square, they were told a suicide bomber had blown himself up in the midst of the crowded market. About twenty people were dead and another fifty were injured. A big contingent of police, medical workers, and helpful civilians were trying to clean up and investigate the bloody mess.

As they were all rushing around, yammering in raghead, he noticed a young man appear at one of the little side lanes that led into the square. He looked to be in his late teens or early twenties. He wore an ankle-length white robe, and over that a white garment that was like an overlong vest. You could see his torso looked too thick for his face, and he instantly guessed the guy was another suicide bomber.

Someone else in their party must have spotted the young dude at the same time, because all of a sudden the guards began hustling the sheikh and visiting bigwig away from the scene. Interestingly, they'd done nothing to warn the people in the square. He'd backed away with them, but kept his eyes trained on the young man. His movements were tentative and almost timid at first. But the closer he got to the middle of the devastated market, the faster and bolder his steps became. When he was right in the midst of the crowd of police and aid workers, he reached inside the robe.

An instant later he saw the dude's head and arms fly outward from the smoky blast, along with the limbs of several men near him. The bomb must have been loaded with shrapnel, because all around the square people began toppling over, riddled with bloody holes. A tiny piece even hummed past his head and struck the wall behind him, sending out a spatter of stucco fragments.

For almost a minute he'd stood there, stunned with admiration for the sheer, cold-hearted beauty of it. By his estimate, the second blast claimed half again as many victims as the first. The majority of them cops, medical workers, and dumbshit good Samaritans. Then his team boss yelled at him and he got out of there.

His mind snapping back to the present, he looks around then at the heavy traffic on Telegraph. Another mile or so and he'll be at the Square Lake mall.

In some ways, it's too bad his is a one-man show. A shame that he doesn't have a bunch of pathetic fundamentalist cretins under his command, like whoever planned the one-two bombings he'd witnessed. Imagine having a dedicated corps of fanatics at your disposal. Dog crap-stupid pea-brains who sincerely believed that blowing themselves to hamburger will win them seventy dark-eyed virgins in the afterlife.

But that's okay. He's figured out a way to get the same results - and on an even bigger scale.

He checks his black special ops watch.

As he's going to demonstrate in just a little bit under an hour from now.

Chapter 30   Hulk Hogan's Kid Brother

Thursday, August 18 - 9:15 a.m.

I LEFT the FBI office around 4 a.m. Wednesday night, after Blandings and Dorn finally ordered all of us to go home and get some rest. Now it was Thursday morning and I'd just gotten onto the Lodge freeway to head downtown. When I turned on the radio and heard the news bulletin about the Oakland County government complex bomb, I pulled off at the next exit. While doing my turnaround, I called the field office and spoke to Blandings. He'd already heard about the bombing and, needless to say, wasn't exactly thrilled about it. I told him I wasn't that far away from the site and was going up there. He sullenly okayed it.

After getting back on the freeway, I caught the linkup from the Lodge to westbound I-696, got off at Telegraph, and headed north toward Pontiac, the Oakland county seat. Traffic moved well up through the Bloomfields and Pontiac, and got backed up only as I approached the turnoff into the county complex.

Sheriff's deputies and state police were screening everyone going in and out of the service drive. When my turn came, I showed them my FBI badge and they waved me through.

I'd been to the Sixth Circuit Court in the past for various cases, and headed right for the building with the oversize number 1200 at the top of its south facade. There was no visible damage to that side of the building. It was only when I got to the far side and turned into the north lot that I saw the collection of police cars, fire trucks, and a couple of lingering ambulances near the shattered and blackened entrance.

I parked my car on the edge of the lot and made my way toward the group of policemen standing near the entrance. Crime scene tape had been run midway through the parking lot, about a hundred feet from the blast epicenter. A large crowd of people were milling around outside the tape. Evacuees from the court building, I figured, as well as curious workers from the several nearby offices in the complex.

As I walked across the lot, stepping over fire hoses, something struck me as strange. There was a medium-sized semi trailer parked in the lot, just inside the yellow tape perimeter. It was cab-less, the front resting on its large, flanged metal feet, the rear on its eight truck tires. It had a big red, white, and blue *American Food Services* logo on its side. A refrigeration unit was puttering away on the front.

Hulk Hogan, my dead sister said as I walked by the trailer.

Thanks, Ofelia, I said. *Very helpful*. Sometimes her ghostly little hints made no sense at all.

Hulk Hogan, she repeated.

Coming up to the cop conclave, I saw that they were a mixed bag of county, city, and state law enforcement. Uniformed Oakland County sheriff's deputies predominated, but there were plenty of detectives in white shirts or casual outfits as well. As I drew near, I took in the destruction. The fragmented remains of a white vehicle were scattered across the concrete plaza at the front of the building. The glass and metal entranceway had been demolished and the lobby beyond it was a heap of smoking, ash-gray rubble. Huge black scorch marks ran up over the six-story face of the heavily-damaged building, all the way to the top. Every window in the adjoining wings also seemed to have been shattered by the blast. I wondered if many people in the offices had got torn up by the blown-in shards of glass.

Standing in the middle of the cop assembly was Ray Wapshot, the Oakland County Sheriff. He'd been in the Beaubien meeting on Monday. Over the years I'd gone to him for assistance a few times, the last being when I was doing the sex trade investigation on Willie the Pimp. Assuming Wapshot would be the officer in charge of the scene, I went up to him.

"Sheriff," I said, reaching out to shake his hand.

He looked a bit startled to see me there. "Johnson? What the hell are you doing here?" he said. "I mean, how'd you get here so fast?"

"Heard about it on the radio and came right up," I said. "There'll be other agents here shortly. How are you doing?"

He shook his head. "What a shit storm. Cunningham just left. He's going bonkers. Calling Homeland Security in Washington, and basically trying to rip everyone in sight a new butthole."

It was easy to picture L. Sparks Cunningham going ballistic over the bombing. His county exec office was in the complex, on the other side of Telegraph. He'd been bombed in his own backyard, less than twenty-four hours after assuring TV viewers the bombings would stop, the culprits would be caught, and that Saturday's Dream Cruise would go on as scheduled.

"Got a question for you, Sheriff," I said, indicating the parking lot. "What's that semi trailer doing there?"

Wapshot frowned. "No idea. Wasn't here yesterday. Why?"

"Is there anyone here from the maintenance or food service departments we can talk to about why it's sitting out there?"

His eyes swept over the crowd around us. "There's Dawn Carpelli, the building manager," he said. "We can go ask her."

We headed toward a heavy-set blonde in a leopard print pantsuit, who was talking to a fire department official.

"Ms. Carpelli," I said. "Do you know anything about that semi trailer that's parked out in the lot? Were you expecting any kind of food service delivery today?"

"No," she said. "Saw it on my way in this morning, but I don't know why it's out there. Why do you ask?"

My blood ran cold. Up till then I'd been suspicious, but figured I was probably being paranoid.

"Do you know the exact time the car crashed into the building?" I asked Wapshot.

"Time of detonation, they tell me, was 9 a.m. on the nose."

My mind was racing. If I'm a bomber and I'm targeting responders to a first explosion, I asked myself, how much time do I wait before setting off the second blast?

Fifteen minutes and you'll get a bunch of firemen and ambulance techs. Thirty to forty-five minutes and you'll get a mix of police and firemen. At one hour the fear quotient will have dropped and you'll get a passel of police, including detectives, plus possibly forensics specialists and senior officers. Not to mention maybe some civil authorities and the crowd of gawkers who by now will have been lulled into believing the danger has passed.

I checked my watch. 9:58 a.m. "Holy Jesus!" I said.

I grabbed Wapshot's arm. "We need to get everyone out of the area - now!" I said, my eyes boring into his.

"What are you talking about, Johnson?" he said, frowning back at me.

188

"It's a setup!" I said, pointing at the semi trailer. "Ramming that first car into the entrance was the first phase of the attack. Its real goal was to get a big crowd of police responders, authorities, and kibitzers onto the scene. Now that thing's going to blow up and wipe out everyone in the vicinity. We need to evacuate this area immediately!"

"Holy crap!" the sheriff said. "If you're right-"

I realized I didn't have time to do any more convincing. Better to just raise an alarm and get people moving ASAP.

"EVERYBODY OUT OF HERE!" I bellowed. "NOW! GET AS FAR AWAY FROM THAT TRAILER AS YOU CAN!"

I turned to the group of cops near the building entrance.

"IN LESS THAN TWO MINUTES THAT TRAILER'S GOING TO BLOW!" I screamed. "RUN OR GET DOWN! AND GET PEOPLE OUT OF HERE!"

Then I took off toward the lot. There were maybe a hundred curious bystanders from the complex milling around behind where the crime scene tape was stretched - many of them right next to the trailer. Another hundred onlookers were standing on the sidewalk that ran parallel to the curving service drive, only twenty or thirty yards from the trailer. Every one of them, I knew, was in mortal danger.

I raced toward the crowd in the lot, waving my arms. "GET OUT OF HERE! RUN OR GET DOWN! HURRY! THAT TRAILER'S GOING TO BLOW!" I screamed.

Most of the people began running, some of the women squealing in terror. A few of the gawkers just stared at me with their mouths open, maybe thinking I'd lost my mind. Behind me, I heard other cops now yelling at people to get clear. I glanced back and saw that people were running away in the opposite direction as well, along the adjoining building wing.

I looked at my watch. 9:59:30 a.m.

I continued to furiously bellow and wave my arms, as people scattered in front of me. "GET AWAY!" I screamed. "GET DOWN OR GET AWAY!" By now my voice was so dry and hoarse from screaming, I wondered if I hadn't blown out my larynx.

Reaching the stretch of grass at the edge of the lot, I looked at my watch and saw 9:59:58 a.m. 'DOWN!" I screamed one more time, diving onto my belly and clasping my hands over the back of my head. I lay there gasping, drenched in sweat.

And nothing happened.

Around me the crowd sheltering themselves on the ground remained silent. The only sound was the faint putter of the refrigerator unit on the truck, a hundred feet away.

And still nothing happened.

I heard some nervous tittering from people lying nearby. There was some weeping too.

"STAY DOWN!" I yelled with what was left of my voice.

There was more nervous laughter.

I looked at my watch. It was now 10:01 a.m. I watched the second hand sweep around. 10:01:15. 10:01:30. 10:01:45...

And still nothing.

The uneasy giggling around me began turning into mocking chatter.

I could feel my face getting hot. Had I completely called it wrong? I glanced back over my shoulder at the trailer-

And at that exact instant it blew.

Reflexively, I jammed my face down into the dirt again, the blinding flash leaving nova-like stars pulsing behind my closed eyes. The earth shifted under my clenched belly and groin as shrapnel whistled past, inches over my head. Then the shock wave scraped over my back like the hot, searing swipe of some hellhound's paw. I felt my bladder wanting to give way and had to fight to keep from wetting my trousers.

I lay there for a minute or so after the blast, my stomach up in my throat, before I shakily got to my feet. There was a huge cloud of dust over the scene and a big gray mushroom cloud rising up a couple of hundred feet in the air. Most of the people there were still on the ground, but had lifted their heads and were gazing around, their faces wary. A number were writhing in pain where they lay, obviously wounded. Two or three weren't moving at all. When I looked at the nearby trees lining the road, I saw that a couple had cracked and toppled over, and that the trunks, leaves and branches of all of them were badly shredded.

The trailer had doubtless been stuffed with ammonium nitrate. But it must also been loaded up with a huge amount of shrapnel - metal shavings, ball bearings, and bits of scrap metal that the powerful explosion had turned into tiny but potentially lethal missiles.

I wondered what the two-minute delay had been about. A mistake? An arbitrary choice to add them? Or perhaps a problem with the timer? I figured I'd never know unless I got a chance to interrogate the bomber - which sure didn't look like it was going to happen anytime soon.

I heard the wail of ambulances then and saw several coming down the service road toward the lot. In their midst was a white government Ford. It pulled off to the side of the service drive near where I was standing, and Wilson and Angie Nardella jumped out.

"Jumping Jesus, Mojo," Wilson said, gazing around. "This place looks worse than my back yard. What the hell happened? Was there a second bomb?"

"Yeah," I said. "Somebody parked a semi-trailer full of AN and shrapnel in the middle of the lot."

"A super-sized fragmentation grenade," he said, looking around at the shredded trees. "Cute."

"Not so cute for the people who haven't gotten up," Nardella said.

EMS techs from the ambulances were rushing up to help the people who were still down on the ground, writhing and moaning.

Then I spotted Sheriff Wapshot coming our way.

"Holy Christ, Johnson," he said as he came up to us. "It sure as hell was lucky you figured out that trailer was a bomb. This whole place would be a goddamn slaughterhouse."

"Made me edgy as soon as I saw it," I said. "Using follow-on bombs was a favorite tactic of the insurgents back in Iraq, when I was-"

I halted in midsentence and stood there with my mouth agape.

The three of them stared at me.

"What is it, McCoy?" Nardella asked.

"Iraq!" I said. "That's where I heard that voice - the caller in Al-Rafi's house. The one who said the house was going to blow in sixty seconds."

"You recognize the voice now?" Wilson said. "Who was it?"

I sighed in chagrin.

"No, damn it," I said. "I still don't remember exactly whose voice it was. But I'm *positive* it was someone I heard back in Iraq."

"Jeez-o-pete, Mojo," Wilson said. "Why the heck can't you remember?"

"I don't know," I said. "Maybe it was that damn concussion I got back in the house."

"What if I took off my shoe and gave you a nice thump upside your head?" Wilson said. "On the opposite side, maybe?"

"Thanks for the offer," I said. "But I don't think so."

"Hey, just trying to be helpful," he said.

As we worked the post-blast investigation, we found out that, in addition to the sixteen people killed in first attack, two more had died from the trailer bomb. One was an electrician from the complex who'd gotten up off the ground right before the blast, apparently thinking it was all just a false alarm. A dozen pieces of shrapnel had gone through his body. The one that went through his left eye and brain killed him. The other was a woman who'd been lying on the ground, but caught a fluke hit from a ball bearing that had caved in her temple. Another eighteen victims had sustained a variety of shrapnel wounds, ranging from mild to moderately serious.

I suppose I should've felt gratified that I'd helped prevent what could've been major carnage. But the main feeling I was left with was one of frustration. After gathering the crowd together, we asked for anyone who might've spotted anything suspicious to come forward. A half-dozen people volunteered that they'd seen things out of the ordinary. But when we took them aside and questioned them in more detail, none seemed to have anything useful to offer. One even said she'd seen the Angel of Death hovering over the circuit court building early that morning when she'd gone into work. Said he wore a long white gown, was wielding a fiery sword, and looked kind of like Kelsey Grammer, but with longer hair.

"Gee, maybe the bomb was Kirstie Alley exploding," Wilson said.

Then I remembered what Ofelia had said to me earlier, when I'd first noticed the trailer.

"Folks," I said to the group. "This may sound crazy, but did anyone see someone who looked like Hulk Hogan hanging around prior to either of the bombings?"

"Hulk Hogan?" Nardella said.

192

"Just a wild hunch," I replied.

"I did," a full-figured young black woman said.

"You did?" I said. "When did you see him?"

"About ten minutes before that car crashed into the building. I was up in my office looking out the window and I saw this fella down by the entrance. He got into a taxicab and drove away. I laughed when I saw him. Looked just like that Hulk Hogan dude, except maybe not quite as big. More like his kid brother, if he has one."

"You say he got into a taxi?" I said.

"Uh-huh. A black one," she said. "A Lincoln, I think."

We checked with local cab companies and found that Midnight Cab Service out of Pontiac used black Lincoln Town Car taxis. We also determined that one of their drivers had picked up a fare at the court building that morning. They gave me the cabbie's cell number and I called him. His name was Zlatko Markovic. He confirmed that he'd picked up the Hulk Hogan lookalike at the Sixth Circuit Court shortly before 9 a.m. He'd then dropped him off at the shopping mall at Square Lake and Telegraph. He said the guy had sounded like a not-very-bright redneck biker type. Spent half the ride bitching about having his license pulled, the other half staring off into space like he was stoned. When I asked if he'd said or done anything strange, he said the guy made a kind of joke when they'd heard the explosion: he apologized for farting.

Ofelia's hints were sometimes so oblique they were just about useless to me, and until that moment I'd been increasingly sure the downsized version of Hulk Hogan wasn't our guy. But the fart joke seemed to fit the profile I was beginning to put together in my mind of our bomber: a malicious bastard who hated cops and probably any other kind of authority figure. Smart in a devious and manipulative kind of way. Good with his hands. Excellent practical understanding of mechanics and electronics, along with first-hand experience at bomb and booby trap-building. And able to effectively alter his appearance when he wanted to.

Ahmad, the boy on Elmore Street, and the ticket seller at the Southfield cineplex had described a muscular but otherwise non-descript white guy - evidently our suspect as he actually looked. But the bus yard shots of an Arab or Pakistani-looking man and now the Hogan-lookalike that our witness was reporting showed that he liked to use disguises at times. And that he was good at them.

I knew from my own experience doing surveillances that the trick to disguising yourself is to add elements to your looks that stand out to people. That way they remember the false distinguishing features and overlook the real ones.

It was obvious now that we were dealing with someone who could disguise himself effectively - maybe even expertly - if he thought it was advisable or necessary.

Which left me wondering: what kind of face would our bomber show up wearing next?

Chapter 31 Catering Service From Hell

Thursday, August 18 - 12:15 p.m.

IT WAS shortly after noon by the time I got in to the McNamara building. I was alone. Wilson and Nardella were dropping off evidence from the Oakland County court site at the police lab in Sterling Heights. As I came out of the elevator on the twenty-sixth floor and went into the FBI office, I was surprised to find the admittance desk empty. Blandings had replaced Mabel Partridge, who normally manned the desk, with a woman named Hannah Hochheuters he'd brought in from DC. She was a heavyset blonde with grim, dishwater-gray eyes. In contrast to Mabel's efficient good cheer, Hochheuters had the menacing demeanor of a concentration camp guard.

Although it was highly unusual not to have someone staffing the check-in desk, I assumed that she'd gone for a quick bathroom break, so I swiped my card and continued on in.

As I walked toward my cubicle I saw that Blandings and Dorn were having lunch inside the glass-walled manager's office. A tall ponytailed guy in a white food service jacket and cap was serving them, taking styrofoam cartons off a shiny metal cart and placing them on the oversized manager's desk. Instead of going down to the basement food court or one of the downtown neighborhood restaurants, Blandings preferred to have his meals brought in by some upscale local caterer.

As I was passing by, Blandings glanced at me. I saw his lips move then as he made some comment to Dorn. Both Dorn and the guy with the ponytail turned their heads to look at me - Dorn with one of his snaky smiles on his lips, the other man's face impassive. I noticed the catering guy had one of those mini-goatees that consist of just a dark tuft of hair under the lower lip.

At my cubicle, I took my laptop out of my briefcase and sat down at the desk. As I was waiting for the laptop to boot up, I felt a frown creasing my brows. What was it about that catering guy's face?

I got up and went out of my cube. The caterer was gone and Blandings and Dorn were sitting in the glass office, eating their lunches.

I don't know if it was a hunch or instinct or whatever, but I decided to go after the catering man and check him out.

Blandings and Dorn stopped eating and watched me with cold curiosity, plastic utensils suspended in their hands, as I hurried by.

When I was coming out of the hallway that led into the main office, my eye caught something under the admittance desk. Leaning over, I saw Hannah Hochheuters was squeezed into the leg space under it. She was in a sitting position, facing outward, with blood draining down over her nose from the dark hole in her forehead.

Reaching into my shoulder holster for the Springfield, I ran out past the desk. I saw the ponytailed guy with his cart, standing in front of one of the elevators.

"Hold it right there!" I yelled.

His answer was to turn on me and raise something in his right hand to waist level - a forty-caliber Glock with a silencer on it. The gun gave out a *thoop!* and a small portion of the Formica-topped counter I was standing next to exploded.

I dropped to one knee and, with a two-fisted grip, aimed and fired three shots in rapid succession as he was ducking behind the cart. The bullets whanged off the metal cart and then ricocheted again off the hallway's marble walls.

When I saw the silencer appear at the side of cart I dropped and rolled. Again I heard the air-gun spit of the Glock, followed by the sound of spattering marble behind me.

I heard a ding from the elevator and saw the doors slide open. He raised his torso to push the cart into the elevator, trying to keep it between himself and my .45. For an instant the top of his head was in my sights. I aimed just under the white food service cap and was about to squeeze off a round that would blow off the top of his skull. But just then a deafening *WHAM!* from back in the inner office startled me and my shot went wild. A moment later the catering man disappeared into the elevator.

I got to my feet and spent a few nanoseconds deciding what to do next.

I didn't know the number to the ground level security desk, but recalled that Mabel had the extension posted on the admittance desk phone. I ran back to the desk and picked up the handset, being careful not to kick or step on Hochheuters' lifeless body. Dark gray smoke from the office billowed toward me as I punched the four-digit number.

"Security," a man answered in a bored voice.

"This is Agent Johnson up on twenty-six. Tell the U.S. Marshal's office in the building there's an armed and dangerous man coming down the elevator as we speak. He's just set off a bomb up here. He's a Caucasian in a white caterer's outfit, with long, dark hair in a ponytail. He's killed at least one person up here and he may be the Al-Qaeda in Detroit bomber. Sound the building alarms and stop him, damn it!"

"Yessir!" the man said, no longer sounding blasé.

I slammed the handset down and ran back through the smoke-filled entrance hall to the main office. The glass walls and door of the agent-in-charge's office were completely blown out and debris was everywhere. Three other agents were standing inside the smoky ruins.

A quick look at the shredded bodies of Morley Blandings and Elliot Dorn was all I needed. The pony-tailed catering guy had obviously left a fragmentation grenade in the room. In one of the styrofoam dessert containers was my guess. One of Blandings' arms and half of his head were gone. What remained of his blue-shirted, Armani-clothed body was speckled with oozing crimson holes. Dorn's Peter Lorre features were now a ghastly crater of toothy pink mush. Like Blandings, his torso was peppered with a hundred seeping wounds.

"I'll call the morgue. No point calling an ambulance," I heard one of the agents mutter as I turned to run back out of the office.

I took the elevator down to the main floor. When I ran out with my drawn Springfield I found myself confronted by a dozen Federal marshals in blue Kevlar vests aiming a variety of weapons at me. A loud alarm was alternately whooping, honking, and buzzing, its obnoxious sound echoing through the big entrance lobby.

"Freeze!" one of them yelled at me. "Drop your weapon!" yelled another.

Instinctively, I raised my arms over my head. "Where the hell is he?" I screamed back at them. "The guy I called down on?"

"We said drop it, asshole!" one of the marshals bellowed at me, his voice hoarse.

"I'm FBI, you idiots!" I yelled back at them. But in deference to the twelve weapons and twenty-four geeked-up eyeballs gaping at me, I turned the barrel of my .45 toward me, squatted, and cautiously set it down on the marble parquet floor.

"Damn you!" I growled at them as I stood back up. "I'm Agent McCoy Johnson! I'm the one who called down the alert!"

"That's Johnson, alright!" one of the marshals said. "I recognize him!"

"I told security to stop an armed guy in a caterer's outfit with a ponytail!" I said, my face hot with fury. "You don't mean to tell me you *missed* him?"

"No one meeting that description came out, Agent," one of the marshals said.

"The service entrance!" I said. "He must've gotten out on another floor and gone back out the back way! Two of you follow me!" I said, bending down to retrieve my Springfield.

"Hold it!" one of the marshals said. "Stay away from that weapon!"

I gave him a murderous glare. "You cretin!" I said. "The goddamn Al-Qaeda in Detroit bomber is getting away while you obstruct a Bureau agent! I'll have your *balls*, you nitwit!"

The marshal who'd recognized me stepped up alongside me and turned to the others.

"I know him, damn it! He's FBI!"

He bent down, picked up my pistol, and handed it to me.

"Let's go, sir!"

The marshal and I turned and ran toward the rear of the lobby.

"Do you know how to get back to the service entrance?" I asked him.

"This way, sir!" he said and led us down a hallway.

As we ran, I heard heavy steps behind us and, with a glance back, saw that several of the armed marshals were following.

When we got to the rear of the building, there was a *To Loading Dock* sign on one of the doors. We pushed it open and rushed into an office. Inside, two men lay on their backs on the floor, one in jeans and black polo shirt, the other in a guard uniform. Both had oozing red holes in their foreheads.

We burst out of the far office door and onto the concrete loading dock. A yellow van that said *Papa Vittorio's Catering* was just turning west onto Howard Street. I got two shots off at the rear of the vehicle before it disappeared from view. I caught the catering company's phone number on the back of the van, but couldn't make out the license plate number.

I whipped out my cell phone and dialed 911. I told them to contact the police and get an all points bulletin out on the catering van.

Then I called Papa Vittorio's and asked for the manager. When he came on, he told me they'd sent a man named Hector Ramirez to make the delivery. They described him as being about five-seven, heavy-set, with short hair and a mustache. I told him the van had been hijacked and police were searching for it. I didn't tell him Hector Ramirez's chances of being alive were about zero point zero.

As I was walking back into the shipping office where the two dead men lay, my cell rang.

"Johnson," I snapped, figuring it would be a callback from DPD.

"McCoy?" an angelic voice said. "It's Oprah Cummings. I made that decision about our getting together. Want to do lunch?"

Chapter 32   The Voice From Al-Rafi's Kitchen

Thursday, August 18 - 12:25 p.m.

AFTER A few moments of being totally boggled by the timing, I told Oprah that, while there was nothing I wanted more than to bask in her presence again, things were just too damn crazy at the moment.

"But you're alright?" she said.

"Yes, thanks," I said, thrilled by the concern I'd heard in her voice. "Listen, can we get together later for dinner?" I said. "Meet in Greektown, say?"

"Afraid not. I have to work this afternoon."

"Then let's try for lunch again tomorrow, okay?"

"Sure, as long as it's not too late."

My cell gave off its call-waiting tone - no doubt my callback from the DPD.

"I've got to go now. There are- It's not pretty here," I said, looking down at the two dead men on the shipping room floor.

"I understand. See you soon, I hope," she said.

I took the call from DPD. It was a sergeant from the local precinct. I told him about the missing catering service man, and gave him the description the manager had given me. He told me all the downtown precincts were already on alert for the van.

I hung up the cell, my head spinning with a bizarre mix of cop-chase adrenaline and romantic elation.

Back up on the twenty-sixth floor, workers in dark blue jackets that said *Morgue* on the back were wheeling the bagged bodies of Hannah Hochheuters, Morley Blandings, and Elliot Dorn out of the FBI office. As I stepped aside for the gurneys, I saw Dawson, Wilson, and Nardella up ahead.

Wilson was looking at the blown-out agent-in-charge's office. "Ding dong," he said. "And that's all I have to say on the subject."

I got what he meant: the wicked witch is dead. While I certainly didn't feel like celebrating their horrible demises, I had to admit I wasn't disappointed to have Blandings and Dorn out of the way.

"The regional director called," Dawson told me. "I'm back in charge of the bombing investigation. Which means you're lead investigator again, McCoy."

"Thanks," I said. "I think."

Angie Nardella was shaking her head. "I still can't believe it," she said. "How the heck did the bomber circumvent security? First downstairs, and then up here?"

"Probably got past the service entrance guard downstairs with no problem," I said. "They've had catering people coming to the building since the day after Morley got here. My guess is that when he got to the admittance area up here, Hochheuters took issue with his ID. So he put a bullet in her head and stuffed her under the desk. He had a Glock with a silencer on it, so no one would've heard. Plus most people in the office were already downstairs in the cafeteria. He went inside, served lunch to Blandings and Dorn, and as he was leaving pulled the pin on a fragmentation grenade. Or maybe planted some kind of homemade custom device."

"How did you end up confronting him?" Eric asked.

"There was no one at the check-in desk when I came in, which I thought was weird. Then, when I got inside, I saw a ponytailed white male serving lunch to Morley and Elliot. Had a hunch something wasn't right about the guy and followed him out. That's when I spotted Hochheuters' body. When I ran out and told him to halt, he took a shot at me. I returned fire, but the food cart he had with him blocked my shots. Had him in my sights when he was going into the elevator, but the bomb or grenade blew then and I missed the sucker.

"I called down to security to stop him, but he must've got out on the second floor - that's where they found the food cart he had. Went down the stairs at the back of the building and killed the shipping clerk and guard on his way out. Maybe he thought they had too good a take on his face."

"How about you?" Nardella said. "Did you get a good look at him?"

"Not really. He had long, dark hair pulled back in a ponytail and some whiskers under his lip. Both probably fake. He glanced at me when he was in the office, but then turned away. Out in the hall everything happened too fast. He did look vaguely familiar - but I couldn't place him."

"Did he say anything to you?" Wilson asked. "So you could tell if it was the same guy who called back at Al-Rafi's house?"

"No. Probably spoke to Morley and Elliot, but he didn't say a word to me. Dimes to donuts, though, it was our bomber. As far as height, weight, and build go, he fits the description of the guy that boy Ahmad, our Allen Park witness, and the ticket-seller at the Southfield movie theater all saw."

"How do you think he knew about Blandings using the catering service?" Eric asked.

"I don't know," I said. "Maybe he's been doing visual reconnaissance on the building. Or he may be a phreaker - knows how to hack into phone calls."

"Bastard's a real renaissance man, isn't he?" Nardella said.

"A regular Leonardo da Scumbag," Wilson said.

"Wait a minute," Dawson said. "You're saying you think he may be hacking into our phone calls?"

"It's possible," I said. "We should have a communications tech check our telecom closets and make sure they've haven't been breached and tapped. Probably wouldn't hurt to go through the employee files on all the people doing maintenance in the building, just in case he's infiltrated us that way."

"I don't believe it," Nardella said. "I thought this building was supposed to be super-secure."

"First couple of years after nine-eleven, everything was tight as a drum," I said. "But years going by with no incidents have made people lax. Then they privatized the security guards. So now you've got low-paid people with minimal training and motivation guarding the entrances."

My cell rang. I flipped it open and answered.

"Agent Johnson? It's Harlan Robinson. I just wanted to let you know our officers found the catering van you reported. It was abandoned in an alley, six blocks from your building. Did you want to come over and view it?"

"Not personally, but I'd like to send a couple of Bureau techs over to check for evidence. Was the caterer's uniform left inside, by chance?" I asked.

"No" he said.

"You may want to have your officers check around the area - trash cans, dumpsters, etcetera - and be sure he didn't get rid of it nearby. From what I've seen of this guy, it's not likely. So far he's been too smart to leave any fingerprint or DNA evidence at his crime scenes. But maybe he was in too big a hurry this time."

"Will do," he said. "I'll call you with updates. And I'll tell our men to expect your techs at the alley."

"Thanks, Chief," I said. "Talk to you later."

As I hung up, the images of Nadine in my kitchen and nude in that pink Corvette of hers flashed through my mind. I had little doubt that each time I'd shut her down, she'd gone off to visit another one of her boyfriends. Once again I found myself wishing Harlan weren't such a decent dude.

"Alright, team," Eric said. "Let's head back to my office and figure out our next steps."

The four of us went to the small conference room where we'd held our brainstorming session the night before. We'd barely sat down when my cell phone rang. It was Harlan Robinson again. The DPD officers searching the alley where the van was found had discovered a corpse in a dumpster. A heavy-set Latino male. Almost certainly it was Ramirez, the missing catering guy. Grimly, I thanked him and hung up.

"They found the guy from Papa Vittorio's - dead," I told the group.

"Our boy's really on a roll today, isn't he?" Nardella said.

"I'd like to roll one of his bombs up his you-know-what," Wilson said.

"Let's get started," Dawson said. "McCoy, the bomber has designated you as the drop person for the money and it's supposed to happen today, correct?"

"Right," I said.

"Then that's likely to be our next shot at getting the guy."

"Which reminds me," I said. "Do we even have the payoff money ready yet?"

"It's in the security vault down on the IRS floor. Two Treasury agents flew up with it and brought it into the building early this morning."

"Do we have a tracking mechanism for it?"

"Yes," he said. "It's in a heavy-duty plastic casing. There's a hidden compartment integrated into the casing for a transmitter. The transmitter has a seven-mile range and will be tracked from a Bureau helicopter that has receiving gear."

"And the bills are all marked?"

"Affirmative. Completely invisible, unless you use a fluoroscope set to a particular frequency."

"Then what's our next step?" I said.

"We wait for the bomber's call. He'll give us a drop-off location. With the transmitter in the money briefcase, we should be able to track you to within a few yards, wherever you go."

"What I'm concerned about," Nardella said, "is that, even though we don't know why, this guy hates your guts. Which means he's probably going to use the drop-off as an opportunity to kill you."

"Goes without saying," I said. "The only thing is, he won't do it till he has the money in hand. So up to that point I should be safe."

Just then Dawson got a call on his cell. He listened for a minute, then said "Got it." He gave the caller a cell phone number I recognized as mine and hung up.

"That was the mayor's office," he said. "The bomber just gave them his first instruction for the payoff. He wanted your cell phone number."

A few seconds later my cell phone rang. I flipped it open and put it to my ear.

"Agent Johnson? Bill La Borgia," the caller said.

What the hell? We'd just given out my cell phone number to the bomber. And now, not even a minute later, I was getting a call from La Borgia?

I scribbled "Willie the Pimp???" on a sheet of notepaper and showed it around to the other agents in the room as I talked. They all frowned or did double takes.

"What can I do for you, Mr. La Borgia?" I said.

"Since I haven't heard back from you, I thought I'd give you a call. Let you know my offer still stands."

"I see. Well, thank you, sir. But the fact is, I mentioned your offer to my superiors. And for now, at least, they're not interested in taking you up on it."

"Really? That's too bad. Because I'd genuinely like to help."

"I understand that, sir. But I think you can probably see that, from the Bureau's point of view, it'd be highly irregular."

"Alright, Johnson. I guess I know when I'm not wanted. I just hope the killing stops soon," he said.

"Me too, sir. Goodbye now," I said and hung up.

"What's with this guy?" Wilson said. "How come Mr. Internet Porn King is all of a sudden Mr. Helpful Citizen?"

"You're asking the wrong guy," I said, shaking my head, "because I truly don't know. On one level, I think he's sincere about wanting to help out. But on another, I have this gut feeling there's some kind of angle he's playing."

"Maybe he's looking for some good, pre-indictment PR," Nardella said. "Did you get any felony leads on him from that sex trafficking investigation?"

"No. That's the ironic thing," I said. "He's involved in a lot of stuff that's seamy as hell, but nothing that's blatantly illegal, as far as I could tell."

"Maybe we should take him up on some of those resources you said he offered," Wilson suggested. "Use that private jet of his to take me down to Cancun, so I can lie on the beach and get this case figured out. I do my best thinking when I'm surrounded by suntanned girls in thong bikinis."

"Or take me to Paris," Nardella said. "I do my best thinking sitting in cafés, smoking and drinking espresso after I've just blown a month's salary on designer clothes I'll never wear."

My cell rang again and I flipped it open.

"McCoy Johnson," I said.

"Hello, asshole," said the voice from Al-Rafi's kitchen.

Chapter 33   Runaround

Thursday, August 18 - 3:00 p.m.

DAMN! I thought. There was a tantalizing familiarity to the voice, but I still couldn't place it.

"Here's your first instruction, snatchface," he said. "Bring the money to the lobby of the Municipal Center downtown - alone. I'll give you your next instruction when you get there, dog-dick. Be there in twenty minutes or I abort the drop."

The line went dead.

"Christ!" I said, jumping up from my chair. "I need to grab the money and get down to the Young Municipal Center in twenty minutes or he aborts!"

"Alright, let's go down together," Eric said. "I'll try to speed up the sign-out."

Dawson got on his cell with the manager of the IRS office while we double-timed out to the elevator and went down to the seventeenth floor. Gaining entry and getting the security staff there to rush the transfer of a case containing almost twenty-nine million dollars' worth of foreign currency was a challenge, to say the least.

While I was waiting for the sign-out to be completed, I made an emergency call to Harlan Robinson, explained the situation, and asked him to provide a high-speed escort to the Young Center. I was just hanging up when a sweating IRS agent brought out the money case. It was a rectangular black plastic briefcase the size of a lawyer's trial bag. Even with the Swiss and EU cash in large-denomination bills, it weighed over fifty pounds. Hurriedly, I lugged the case out to the elevators.

By the time I got down to the Federal Building lobby with the money case, fifteen of the allotted twenty minutes were gone. But Robinson had come through. There were three white DPD police cruisers lined up on Michigan Avenue. A white-shirted police captain waved me into the middle car and we screeched off up the broad street.

With sirens whooping wildly, we roared the four blocks to Woodward and turned right. About a dozen cars were stopped ahead of us at the next light and there was a solid wall of traffic coming the opposite way. Honking his horn non-stop, the driver of the lead DPD car pulled up over the curb and onto the sidewalk. The remaining two followed him and together the three cruisers sped up to the intersection, scattering a host of astonished pedestrians as we whooped on by them.

At the intersection, we banged back down onto the street again and blasted up Woodward, sirens still wailing, as startled-looking drivers in the heavy midday traffic shifted over to let us by.

We made it to Jefferson with less than a minute to spare. I yelled out my thanks to the captain and hightailed toward the Coleman A. Young Municipal Center, cradling the heavy money case in my arms.

I'd just made it inside the door when my cell phone range.

"Johnson," I said, breathing heavily from my sprint. I noticed a bunch of people in the lobby were staring at me.

"So you made it, a-hole," the voice said. "Good. Now take the People Mover to the Greektown Casino. Then go down to the entrance and stand outside. You have fifteen minutes, craphead." The line went dead.

I noticed three policemen walking warily towards me as I stood there in the busy lobby, panting, drenched in sweat, and clutching a bulky black case to my midriff.

I took a couple of steps toward them, but halted when I saw them hover their hands over their weapons.

"Excuse me officers," I called out to them. "Where's the nearest People Mover station?"

"You from out of town, sir?" one of them asked me.

I didn't have time for explanations. "Yes, sir," I said. "I'm late for an appointment. Where can I get on the People Mover?"

Thankfully, the question seemed to assuage their suspicions.

"Go out of the building and down to the Millender Center," one cop said, pointing east. "The station is up on level five."

"Thanks!" I said. "And God bless!" I added, giving them a reassuring wave as I rushed out.

I sprinted down the sidewalk that runs along Jefferson Avenue. People were stopping and turning to stare as I hot-footed it past them. More than one laughed and made sarcastic comments I was too preoccupied to catch.

At the Millender building, I took the elevator up to level five, bought a token and impatiently waited a couple of minutes for the next train. When I got on, there were more stares from the Mover's passengers - at me, the bag, and my sweat-soaked clothes. After two stops I got out at the Greektown Casino. I took the elevator down to the main entrance level and went outside.

My cell phone rang.

"So you made it, eh, butt-wipe?" he said with a nasty laugh.

"I made it," I said, keeping my voice neutral and not adding the expletives I was thinking.

"You see that bicycle chained to the railing over there?"

I looked over and saw a dilapidated Schwinn chained to one of the handrails along the steps leading into the casino.

"I see it."

"There's a key in the bottom of the seat. Unlock the chain and ride the bike to Eastern Market. And since I'm such a nice guy, cheese-brain, I'm even going to give you directions. Take Lafayette over I-75 to Orleans Street and turn left. Take Orleans Street all the way up to the market and look for a black 1992 Buick Landau hearse. You've got fifteen minutes, manure-brains."

When he'd hung up, I let loose with the string of curses I'd been holding back. They drew some stares and double takes from the people coming in and out of the casino. I went over to the bike, found a key lodged under the seat, and unlocked the heavy-duty chain. Then I walked the bike down to the sidewalk, climbed on and began pedaling.

I'm six foot six, two hundred-twenty pounds, and the old Schwinn was dramatically undersized for me. There was no doubt in my mind humiliation was part of the bomber's scenario as I pedaled through the dense Greektown traffic and took Lafayette over the I-75 bridge. Orleans was the second street east of it, so I hung a left and headed north toward the market. It wasn't easy riding the undersized bike while carrying a fifty-pound briefcase packed with twenty-five million in foreign cash. The sun was beating down on me like a blowtorch and the humidity must've been around ninety-five percent. By the time I got to Eastern Market I could smell my own stink, even in the rather gamy odor that permeates the market year-round, but especially in the summer months.

Up ahead of me I spotted a black Buick Landau hearse parked at the curb. I checked my watch. The fifteen minutes was just running out when I drew near to the funeral car and my cell rang. I stopped, balancing on the bike as I pulled out the phone and answered.

"Open the hood of the Landau, snot-for-brains," he said. "The key'll be in a magnetized case near the radiator. Drive to Belle Isle. When you're midway over the bridge, stop and pull over. You've got another twenty minutes, crapface."

Cursing him again, I propped the bike against a street sign, popped the hood on the Buick, and found the key. Then I unlocked it, put the case with the money on the passenger seat and got inside. I put the key in the ignition, but found myself hesitating for a second. Would this dirtbag be crazy enough to blow up twenty-nine million dollars' worth of cash just to get even with me?

It didn't seem likely, despite the fact that he was obviously a homicidal maniac. Nevertheless, a fresh wave of sweat joined the rivulets that were already pouring down my body from the bike ride as my trembling hand turned the key.

The car cranked over and started normally.

The first thing I did after peeling away from the curb was switch on the hearse's air conditioning full blast. I got back over to I-75 as fast as I could, squealed up the entrance ramp, and went roaring down the freeway at almost a hundred miles an hour. Only one asshole in a BMW passed me by the time I came to its end at Jefferson Avenue.

I turned left on Jefferson and did fifteen over the limit as I headed east. I wasn't sure what the exact mileage was to Belle Isle, but knew that I'd have to break traffic laws to get there on time. There are a lot of stop lights along Jefferson, and when I caught them, I watched for openings and blew on through. Rather depressingly, I noticed copycats in my rear view mirror doing the same.

Belle Isle is a 980-acre island park in the Detroit River. It's reached by taking a multi-lane bridge that extends from East Grand Boulevard out to the island. As I was coming up to the turn that would put me onto the bridge, I checked my watch and saw that the twenty minutes had already expired. I gunned the Buick hearse and made the turn on two wheels, tires shrieking and horn blaring.

My cell phone rang. This time the bomber's voice had a strange, echoey sound to it.

"Are you there, dung-hole?" he said.

I realized he had to be somewhere where he couldn't see me, but figured I couldn't take a chance on lying.

"Be there in five seconds," I said as I crossed over into an oncoming traffic lane in order to streak past several sluggishly-moving cars.

When it looked like I was midway to the island, I pulled over to the right lane and slammed on the brakes.

"I'm there," I said.

"Nice work, dick-head," he said in that same echoey voice. "Now get out of the car. Stay on the phone and bring the money case with you."

As I climbed out of the hearse, I realized what was about to go down. He was down in the river, probably under the bridge, in a diving or scuba outfit with a radio-phone attachment. He was going to have me toss the case over the railing and into the water.

And then he was going to blow up the funeral car and kill me as he swam away.

"Come around to the bridge's guard rail, butt-wipe," he said.

I did as he told me, but also began moving away from the Buick. There's no parking on the bridge, and people were staring at me with a mix of curiosity and ire as they drove past the lane-blocking hearse.

"Are you at the guard rail?"

"Yes."

"Okay, scum-face," he said. "Now toss the case into the river and then wait for my next command."

Right, I thought.

I took hold of the briefcase's handle with both hands and spun around in a circle to gather momentum, as if I were doing a hammer throw. After a couple of spins I heaved the bulky case up over the guardrail, as high as I could - hoping to gain a couple of extra seconds before he'd see it hit the water and detonate the hearse.

Then I ran for my life.

I'd made it about eight yards away from the Buick hearse when I heard the splash of the case hitting the river water and got a couple more behind me before it blew.

The blast impact slammed into my back and sent me into a headlong dive. My arms flailed as I flew through the air, but I managed to tuck them under my face and chest before I came down and struck the pavement. It felt as if a quarter-inch of flesh was getting scuffed off my knees and forearms as I slid for several yards on the hot concrete. Just as I was coming to a stop, I heard a deafening squeal of brakes. A moment later a car screeched to a halt with its hot underside over my head and shoulders.

And it was then - as I lay there panting and bleeding on the Belle Isle Bridge, with the stink of scorched brake pads and burning rubber in my nose, my brain being broiled by the blistering-hot engine rumbling inches over my head - that it came to me.

The name of the man who'd called me at Al-Rafi's house.

The name of the Al-Qaeda in Detroit bomber.

Sonofabitch! I thought. *Him?*

I knew I had to tell Dawson and the others immediately. But there was a major problem. I was in excruciating pain and I could tell I was rapidly going into shock. My heart was racing and my breathing was shallow. Despite the heat from the pavement and the engine overhead, my sweat-covered body was starting to feel cold and clammy. Darkness was rising up all around me, trying to envelop me. Then I heard my dead sister's voice, from somewhere nearby.

Hi, McCoy, she said.

Hello, Ofelia, I answered.

You've come to join me at last, she said.

No, I told her. *Not just yet.*

Yes, you are, she said. *You're right here.*

I felt her cold, invisible arm slip around my shoulders. A shudder went through me as the chill from her touch moved down through my body, numbing away all the hot, burning pain.

Come on, McCoy, she said. *Let's go.*

No, I said. *Let me go, Ofelia. I need to stay here.*

But I could feel her pulling me tighter. The icy cold seeping deeper and deeper into my body and being.

Come on, little man, she whispered. *Come with me.*

No! I said. *Let me go, Ofelia!*

Why? she said. *Why not come with me?*

Because I've got to stop him, I told her.

Who? she asked.

J. J. Nails! I said.

Chapter 34   Nail In The Coffin

Thursday, August 18 - 4:30 p.m.

A FAINT trail of bubbles rises up from the river as the scuba diver draws near to the dock.

Then his goggled head breaks the surface. He scans the dock area and, seeing no signs of movement, kicks his finned feet up and down to bring himself to the shoreline. At the water's edge is a tiny stretch of sandy beach with a rock wall behind it. A red duffel bag sits on top of the wall. He emerges from the river in his wetsuit and oxygen tank, carrying the black plastic case by its handle. Attached to the case is a camouflage-shaded flotation pack. After sloshing through the shallows, he walks up onto the mini-beach, his flippered feet flapping wetly on the sand.

At the rock wall, he sets the case down and strips out of his scuba gear. The house's back yard, which slopes down steeply to the river, has high, thick hedges on both sides. They shield him from being seen from the adjoining yards as he hastily removes the oxygen tank, radio-phone unit, flippers, and wet suit.

When he's down to the pair of shorts and t-shirt he has on under his diving gear, he removes the flotation pack, undoes the case's snaps, and opens it. His eyes gleam with satisfaction as he smiles down at the banded stacks of bills. Then he unzips the red duffel and quickly transfers the cash from the case to the bag.

Through the trees that keep the yard shrouded in shade, he hears a helicopter's choppy drone overhead. He turns around and looks up, sneering. Obviously, they've violated his instructions and hid a transmitter in the case.

Fortunately, he'd anticipated the transmitter in his Master Plan and already has a strategy to deal with it. He snaps the empty plastic case closed, carries it out onto the short, wood-planked dock that extends out from the house's back yard, and steps down into the twelve-foot boat tied up to it. He pushes the case under the seat at the boat's middle, starts up the outboard motor and, with a length of heavy clothesline, ties the tiller into mid-position. He slips a clamp over the tiller, twists it until the revving engine is causing the boat to strain against its tie lines, and tightens the finger-levers on the clamp so that the engine is giving out a mild but steady roar. He then climbs back onto the dock and releases the lines.

Freed from the straining ropes, the boat spurts away from the dock. He watches it putter out toward the river's center, the current carrying it downstream somewhat, as he goes back over to the stone wall. There he grabs the duffel bag and diving gear and heads up the steep stone walk that leads to the house's rear. Nearing the back porch, he cuts over to the driveway where his Night Runner sits behind a ten-year-old beige Cadillac. He tosses the duffel bag and diving gear into the pickup's cab, climbs in, and begins to back out.

As he's passing the orange brick house's living room, he looks in through the side window and sees the old black guy who's sitting there on a green vintage couch. He's in linen shorts, sandals, and a Hawaiian shirt. He's got a big flat-topped straw hat on his gray-haired head that obscures the blood dripping from his face. Nearby, a woman's bare, brown legs are visible on the floor.

When he reaches the end of the driveway, he leans over and looks up through the windshield. His mouth twists into a snide grin as he sees the helicopter heading out over the river.

He then drives up the short block to Jefferson Avenue and turns left. He takes his time, easing into the right lane so the more impatient drivers can get by. He's in no hurry. When he gets to East Grand Boulevard, there's a bit of a backup due to the apparent traffic problem out on the Belle Isle Bridge. When he finally gets to the intersection, he can see that the road to the island has been closed and there's a cluster of police and fire vehicles out in the middle of the bridge.

A blissful smile crosses his face as he continues up Jefferson. A feeling of total satisfaction has settled over his being - better even than any of the hashish or heroin highs he used to enjoy, back in his mercenary days.

After five long years, he's finally gotten his payback for what got done to him in Fallujah. Hundreds are dead - including McCoy Bigmouth Sonofabitch Johnson - and he's got twenty-five million in euros and Swiss francs sitting alongside him.

Very soon now - after his visits to those clinics in Mexico and Switzerland - he'll be setting off on his world tour. A tour that will take him to many, many exotic and luxurious places.

But not before he carries out the last couple of steps in the Master Plan.

Tomorrow he'll spring that nice little surprise over in Dearborn. It should account for a couple hundred more dead, minimum. It was going to happen anyways, of course, but decides he'll consider it his payback to the Feds for their bullshit transmitter in the money case.

And then Saturday - Dream Cruise Day - will come The Big One. The one where he'll live up to his name and pound the final nail into the coffin. The coffin holding the rotting remains of what was once a city called Detroit...

Chapter 35   Interlude

Thursday, August 18 - 9:00 p.m.

THIS TIME when I came to and saw the shimmering white light in front of my eyes, I knew right away it wasn't some heavenly afterlife awaiting me. I was back in the DMC, once again lying flat on my back on a hospital bed.

"Oprah?" I said hoarsely.

And like magic her gorgeous face was there again, once more haloed by the overhead light.

"McCoy?" she said.

"Am I in ER?" I asked.

"You were," she said. "You're up in a private room now. Seems like you're getting to be a regular here."

"Well, at least I get to see you this way," I said. "How am I doing?"

I had to ask because I wasn't feeling much of anything throughout my body. Just a kind of strange, tingling numbness. Along with it was the remainder of the chill I'd felt when Ofelia put her cold, lifeless arm around me. I also had the sneaking sense my dead sister was still lurking somewhere nearby.

"To be honest, you're a bit worse than last time," Oprah told me. "I spent an hour pulling bits of glass and metal out of your back and sewing up the entry wounds. Plus you've got some really serious abrasions on your arms, chest, and knees."

"But on the upside," she went on. "We did a CAT scan. Amazingly, there's nothing broken and no apparent internal injuries."

"How come I feel like my body's gone, and all I've got left is my head?" I asked.

"Anesthesia and pain-killers. When they wear off you're going to feel like you got kicked down the length of a football field."

"Sounds awesome," I said. "Can hardly wait."

Fighting against the numbness, I began struggling to push myself up on my elbows, forcing my muscles and bones to obey me.

"What are you doing, McCoy?" she said, sounding annoyed.

"Trying to see a clock," I said. "What time is it?"

"Around 9 p.m."

"Listen," I said. "Are there any Bureau people here?"

"FBI people? Yes. A man named Dawson who says he's your boss. And two other agents, a man and a woman."

"Send them in, please. I need to talk to them."

"I don't think that's a good idea at all. I told them I'd give them updates on your condition, but they couldn't see you."

"I have to see them. I've got some extremely important information they need to know about the bombings case. It's life-or-death important, Oprah."

She frowned, biting her lip in an adorably un-doctorish way. "You're sure?"

"Absolutely. I have to give it to them immediately."

"One of them or all three?"

"I'd prefer all three."

"All right then, I'll go down and get them. But five minutes maximum, okay?"

"That should do it. But please - bring them up as fast as you can."

A few minutes later Oprah reappeared, leading Dawson, Wilson, and Nardella.

"How many times do I have to warn you, Mojo?" Wilson said. "This lying down on the job's gotta cease."

"How are you doing, McCoy?" Eric said.

"Never mind me. What about the bomber? Did we get him?"

"No," Dawson said, looking disgusted. "We lost him. He must've figured out the case had a transmitter. Took out the money and sent the case down the river in a small boat. We retrieved it on the Windsor side, near the Ambassador Bridge."

"Well, here's the up side," I said. "I know who he is now."

All three did double takes. "Holy lizard balls," Wilson said.

"Who?" Dawson asked.

"A guy named J. J. Nails. He was a Blackwater employee in Iraq. I only met him one time."

"Why does he have it in for you?" Nardella asked.

"Because I turned him in to Army CID - their criminal investigation division. An Iraqi contact I had in Fallujah told me there was a Blackwater employee named Nails dealing black market weapons, ammo, and explosives to different factions - some of them pro-government, some insurgents. Said he was the front man for some Russian illegal arms dealer."

"Guy sounds like a real sweetie," Nardella said.

"About as sweet as battery acid," Wilson added.

"Anyways, like I said, I reported him to CID. They must've started an investigation on him, and somehow he got my name as the one who'd filed the complaint on him. One evening Nails came by our barracks and asked for me. He said something threatening about people with big mouths getting what they deserved. I told him to go to hell. That was the only time I ever saw him or talked to him. A couple of weeks later I rotated back home and never heard anything more about either him or the inquiry."

"But you're sure it was him?"

"One hundred percent. His voice and his face came together for me, clear as day, when I was lying there on the bridge. We need to check with CID and find out what happened with that investigation. Maybe Blackwater canned him or something, and that's why he's got it in for me."

"Alright, McCoy. I'll contact DC," Dawson said. "We'll see what we can dig up on him."

"One more thing," I said. "If I remember right, I've got a copy of the original report I wrote up to CID back in my condo. It was in with my discharge papers. It may have mentioned the name of the Russian arms dealer. He could be a player in what's going on here in Detroit as well."

"You mean he may be the explosives supplier?" Dawson asked.

"Exactly," I said. "And might even be his partner."

"Excuse me," Oprah said, interrupting. "The five minutes is up. I need to ask you to leave now."

"Uh-oh," Wilson said. "A party pooper. And just when we were beginning to have fun."

"Or maybe the doctor's a little bit jealous of the time we're taking up with her patient," Nardella said, giving her a sly little smile.

Oprah didn't answer, but I could see the comment made her a bit uncomfortable. Maybe Angie had picked up on a proprietary feeling about me that she wasn't even fully aware of.

When the three FBI agents were gone from the room, Oprah came back over to my hospital bed.

"I'm just going to check you out," she said, plugging her stethoscope into her ears.

She sat down on the edge of the bed, and matter-of-factly pulled my hospital gown forward and down my arms. I watched her face as she began moving the stethoscope's diaphragm around to several places on my bruised torso. She ignored my gaze, her big brown eyes focused on what she was hearing inside my battered body.

Even with that impassive, professional expression on her face, I thought she looked radiantly beautiful, and I bathed in the glow of her as I studied her serious-looking features. I wondered if she had a clue how lovely she was. Probably not, I thought.

"Will I live?" I said when she pulled out the stethoscope's ear tips and put them back behind her neck.

"You'll live long and prosper," she said.

"Maybe so," I said. "With you by my side."

She chuckled. "Don't get ahead of yourself, Agent Johnson," she said. "We haven't even done lunch yet."

"Just a matter of time," I said. "Which reminds me - how soon can I get out of here?"

She shook her head in disbelief.

"Let me explain the term 'recuperation' to you, McCoy," she said.

"Please do."

"The human body is an amazing biological mechanism," she said. "It has the ability to heal itself from a wide range of traumas, ranging from minor lacerations to the loss of limbs, and even some of the internal organs. When the body has been severely traumatized, physical rest and mental relaxation promote and accelerate its self-healing mechanisms. Every day I marvel at the body-"

"I certainly marvel at yours," I interjected.

"-and what it can do," she went on. "But it needs our help. We need to treat it right. Eat well, exercise, and - especially when it's undergone severe trauma and exhaustion - get plenty of bed rest."

"Listen, Oprah," I said. "I know you're right. But there's this problem."

"Which is-?"

"That there's a homicidal maniac out loose somewhere in the Detroit area. An insane, highly-skilled bomb-maker and booby-trapper. He's already killed over two hundred people, and I have not the slightest iota of doubt he's out there right now planning to kill more. Maybe even a hell of lot more."

"But I thought-" she began. "The papers and news channels are all saying that the terrorists were paid off. So the killing would stop now."

I shook my head.

"I don't believe that for a second. I've dealt with too many of these psychopaths. The money won't make him stop. This guy kills for three reasons. One is the pleasurable feeling of power he gets from killing. Another is to fulfill some bottomless craving he has for revenge - for real or imagined wrongs he thinks were done to him. And on top of that, he's got some kind of crazy grudge against Detroit. Getting the money is just going to inflate his psychotic belief that he's the baddest dude on the planet. He won't stop killing till we make him stop. One way or another."

Oprah was chewing on her lush lower lip. I thought about volunteering to do it for her.

"All right," she said. "How can I help?"

"I need to get back to my place to check some papers I've got there. They may contain the name of a guy who could be the bomber's partner. I've got a condo in Southfield. Can you help me check out of here and take me there?"

She looked at me intensely, with a mix of hardness and softness in her big brown eyes. Once again I noticed the same flecks of jade green I'd seen in them the first time we met.

"Alright," she said at last. "I'll take you there."

"How soon can we leave?" I said.

"My shift ends in about two hours. I'll do my other patient visits, input my case notes, and talk to the nursing staff about the ones that'll need some follow-ups. Then I'll come collect you and we'll get out of here. In the meantime, you get some rest."

I reached out and took her hand. "Thank you," I said.

She frowned and twisted her lovely mouth sideways.

"What's the matter?" I asked.

"I must be losing my mind," she said.

Two hours later she came by, helped me get dressed and checked out of the hospital, and then walked me out to the parking structure. When we got to her car, I was a bit surprised to find she drove a sporty new Camaro SS. It was a deep blue metalflake color. I nodded at the other cars nearby.

"How come you don't drive a BMW, Mercedes, or Caddy, like all the other doctors?" I asked.

"My dad put me through med school on his line job at Chevy," she said. "Seemed like a reasonable payback. Besides, I really like it."

I climbed in, wincing as I sat back in the passenger seat.

"Uh-oh," she said. "Looks like those painkillers are wearing off."

"Afraid so," I said.

"We should've stopped at the hospital pharmacy. We could go back in."

"I'd rather you be my painkiller tonight," I said.

She grinned. "You're an idiot," she said.

"Thank you, kindly," I said. "Nicest thing anybody's called me all day. And I mean that literally," I added, recalling all the expletives Nails had used toward me during the money drop-off.

After clearing us out of the parking structure with her ID card, Oprah drove the few blocks from the DMC to I-75.

"I heard that partner of yours, Agent Wilson, call you Mojo," she said as we turned down the freeway entrance ramp. "Is that your nickname?"

"No, it's not," I said firmly. "I've been unable to break him and a few other misguided souls from calling me that. But no, as far as I'm concerned, it's not a name I answer to."

"Where'd it come from, then?" she said.

"There was this big case I worked on a few years back. I came up with some ideas that helped crack it. A few people started calling me Mojo after that - as if I had some kind of special 'juice' or something. I've tried to keep folks from calling me that ever since. With mixed success."

"Well, maybe you do have some kind of special juice. I've never gone out with a patient before, you know."

"Well, I'm glad you made that exception for me. Can I ask why?"

"Because you remind me of someone."

"Uh-oh. Not your father or ex-husband, I hope."

"Lord, no. You remind me of a professor I had when I was in college."

I laughed. "A professor? No one's ever likened me to one before."

"No?" she said. "Well, don't act so surprised. You come across as pretty thoughtful. A little bit deep, even."

"Just a little?"

"About the right amount, I'd say. I'm not looking for too deep. That's what my ex was."

"Can I ask what made him so deep?"

"Has a doctorate in philosophy. Teaches it at U of M."

"Uh-oh. Way too deep for me."

"Yeah, well - he was deep into his students as well. Especially his young female ones."

"Sorry to hear that."

"Well, I suppose I should've known better. He's French - French Canadian, actually. From Montreal."

"Well, I know what it's like to be run around on," I said. "Not that I've always been a saint myself."

"So your ex messed around on you?"

"While I was on that big case I mentioned. Was at least partly my fault, though. I buried myself in that case for months. Ignored her while I drove myself just about batshit-crazy with it. Even jumped all over her when she tried to get me to take breaks from it. I guess it was inevitable she'd turn to someone who'd give her what she wanted."

"Speaking of wanting, McCoy - what is it you want? What are looking for? In your life? And in a relationship?" she asked.

I grinned at her across the console. "Damn, lady - talk about *deep*."

She laughed. "I'm sorry. Too heavy for you?"

I smiled to myself. Then I looked over at as her as she drove.

"I'm just looking for somebody who's got a serious agenda, Oprah," I said. "Somebody who's not just about accumulating lots of stuff or sitting back and sliding through life. Not that I've got anything against people who want to live like that. But I think what I need in mine is someone who's a bit obsessed about accomplishing something. Doesn't much matter what it is. But it's something they've absolutely *got* to do."

"You see," I went on. "I've got an obsession. Call it my goal in life, if you want. It's to stop messed-up people from doing bad things to good people. Simple as that. Probably makes me sound like a cartoon character. But that's what it's been about for me, as long as I can remember. Ever since-"

The words hung up in my mouth.

"Ever since what?" she asked.

"Ever since my sister Ofelia got murdered."

"Murdered?" she said, looking stricken. "That's terrible. When did it happen?"

"Twenty-five years ago. She was seventeen. I was twelve. They never found her killer."

Oprah reached over the car's console and put her hand on mine. Fine-boned and delicate, it looked almost tiny atop my big, powerful paw.

I didn't want to dwell on it. "How about you?" I said. "Are you obsessed with doctoring?"

"Yes, I suppose I am," she said. "And like you, I guess there's a personal reason. My sister died of leukemia when she was ten and I was thirteen. I hated it - watching that little girl fade away and die like she did. That's when I decided I'd go into medicine."

"By the way," she went on. "You were talking to your sister when you were on the operating table, unconscious," she said. "You used her name. I was wondering who Ofelia was."

"Yeah, well I do that sometimes," I said. "Talk to her."

For a moment I hesitated, wondering if I should say more. Would she think I was tetched?

"Actually, she's the one who usually initiates it," I finally said. "And it doesn't just happen when I'm unconscious. She talks to me whenever she feels like it. I think she tries to help me. Sometimes what she says makes sense. Sometimes it doesn't."

"So this is her ghost or spirit, then?" she asked, giving me a quizzical glance.

"I'm not sure I believe in them," I said.

"You don't?" she said.

"No. All I know is my dead sister talks to me and sometimes visits me in my dreams," I said. "And that's all I know. Maybe it's her spirit. Or maybe it's just this messed-up little kink in my brain - a little pocket of craziness. I truly don't know."

"What was she saying to you in the operating room this evening?" she said. "When I was treating your wounds?"

I smiled to myself. "Tell you the truth," I said, "I'd forgotten all about it. But now that you mention it, there's one thing I remember her saying."

"What's that?"

"She said, 'I like her.'"

"Who was she talking about?"

"You," I said.

It was around midnight when we got to my condo building. Since my car was back at the FBI office, I had her park in my reserved slot.

I was aching pretty badly as I got out of the Camaro. But the fact that Oprah was about to come into my home and - if the karma was right - share her body with me did a whole lot to ease the pain. I held out my arm for her to take as we headed toward the entrance.

"I should be offering you mine," she said. "You look like you could use a little help."

"Dr. Cummings," I said. "I may be hurting on the outside, but inside I'm floating on air."

"Why's that?" she said, moving closer to me.

"Because you're here at my side," I said. "And because the two of us are walking together under that big old moon up yonder."

For several moments we stopped and looked up at the pale, eerily-beautiful sphere glowing in the night sky above. Like billions of couples had done before us, and no doubt billions more would do, long after the two of us were gone. But for just those few seconds in time, it was ours and ours alone.

When I unlocked and opened the door to my condo I was expecting to see the Thing, squatting there on the foyer floor in all his hideousness. But he was strangely absent. Hopefully the nasty little sucker had run away - back to whatever planet sent him here.

"Can I get you a drink?" I said. "I've got cognac in the kitchen and I think I've got some wine down in the basement."

"This may appall you," she said. "But would you by chance have any lite beer on hand?"

I chuckled. "Surprises me, but doesn't appall me. And yes, strangely enough, I think I do."

I switched on the light in the living room and had her sit down on the couch while I fetched us a couple of cold brews and glasses from the kitchen. We popped the tops and poured. Then I watched her sit back in her hospital blues and take a long pull.

"Mmm," she said, licking a bit of foam from her exquisite upper lip. "This is one of my rituals when I get home, before I go to bed."

"Knock back a six pack or two?" I said.

She laughed. "No. One bottle."

"Listen," I said. "I need to go downstairs to check on those papers I mentioned. I'll be right back."

"Would you do something before that?" she asked.

"What's that?"

"Kiss me?"

"You're surprising me, Oprah," I said.

"I'm surprising myself," she said.

We shifted closer to one another on the couch. She put her arms around me as I leaned over and pressed my lips to hers.

It started off real gentle, but soon turned hot and hungry. When I found myself on the verge of ripping off her hospital uniform, I figured I'd better take a breather. We were both panting a little as we sat back.

"How was that?" I asked. "All right for you?"

"More than all right," she said, her hand rubbing my thigh.

"What do you think?" I said. "Shall we head on down to the bedroom?"

"Didn't you mention something about looking at papers?" she asked.

"They can wait," I said. "A man's got to have his priorities straight."

"I'd say yours are," she said, glancing down at my middle with a half-smile on her lovely mouth. "Let's go, then."

"If I wasn't in this invalid state, I'd carry you there," I said, wincing a bit as we got up from the couch.

"Would you now?" she said with a soft laugh. "Throw me over your shoulder, cave-man style?"

"I was thinking more of the bridal carry. But I'll carry you there any way you like," I said. "Once I'm up to it."

"I'm going to hold you to that," she said.

When we got to the bedroom, the door was slightly ajar. I pushed it open and in the dim light we both saw something move on my bed.

"Is that you, honey man?" drawled a sleepy but inviting voice, just before the bedside lamp came on.

Lying atop the comforter was Nadine Robinson. She was in her Victoria's Secret finest - an absurdly tiny red string bikini outfit that left very little of her luxurious brown body to the imagination. Several gold rings glittered on her fingers and toes, as did the gold bracelets on both wrists and one shapely ankle.

At the sight of Oprah standing there stunned in the doorway beside me, Nadine's big, brown eyes went a mile wide.

"Oops," she said.

Chapter 36   'Fessing Up

Friday, August 19 - 12:30 a.m.

IGNORING MY spluttering attempts to explain, Oprah rushed out the front door, slamming it behind her. I turned around and stomped back down the hall toward my bedroom. Just before I got there, Nadine came out with the comforter wrapped around herself.

"*Damn*, McCoy," she said. "Is that girl gone already?"

"She's gone, alright," I snarled down at her.

"Hell, I was going to try to explain things to her, but she just lit right out of here."

"Well, golly gee, Nadine - I wonder why?" I said bitterly. "Just because a man invites her home, asks her go to bed with him, and when she walks into the bedroom there's some- some *bimbo* lying there?"

"Now you just hold on a second, McCoy Johnson!" she flared up. "You can call me a slut, whore, harlot, Jezebel, or a floozy all you want. But don't you be calling me no *bimbo*!"

"God damn it, Nadine!" I yelled back at her. "I meet a woman - very likely the woman I've maybe been waiting my whole life to meet - and *you* have to mess it up with your stupid games!"

Her outrage seemed to instantly deflate.

"Really, McCoy?" she said. "It's that serious?"

"It's that serious. I know it's crazy, but the moment I saw that woman, my life changed," I said.

She sighed. "Then I'm sorry, McCoy," she said, sounding genuinely contrite.

"You should be, damn it," I said.

"What's with that uniform she was wearing? She a nurse or something?"

"A doctor. She works ER at the Detroit Medical Center."

"What's her name?"

"Oprah Cummings."

"Oprah?" she said. "You're kidding."

I glared at her. "I am *not* kidding."

228

"Listen, McCoy, I am sorry," she said. "I truly am. If there's anything I can do to make things right between you-"

"I really don't know if that'll be possible, Nadine. But you know what?" I went on. "There *is* something you can do for me."

"What is it, honey man?" she asked.

"Well, for one thing, stop calling me that. But the main thing I want from you is this: tell me why you started coming around again."

"I told you, McCoy. I missed your loving. You-"

"Bullshit. I know you and your reputation, Nadine. You're like a female shark. You only move in one direction and that's forward. There's a reason you decided to take up with me again. And I want to know what the hell it is."

After chewing on her little finger for a few moments, she looked up at me.

"Well, if you really must know, McCoy, one of my current boyfriends made a little bet with me. About you. He knew there was some hanky-panky between you and me a while back, and he bet me I couldn't get you to go back to us being lovers again. I bet him I could. That's all."

"How much was this bet for?" I asked.

"A bottle of Dom Perignon champagne."

"And who made the bet?" I said.

"Come on now, McCoy," she said, frowning. "One of the few rules I enforce about my love life is that I don't tell any of my boyfriends who the other ones are. They may find out, alright - you know how men are. But they don't get it from me."

"Well, I'm not a boyfriend anymore, Nadine. And I'm never going to be again. So you're going to lose that bet, hear?"

She dipped her head and looked up at me with a vampy grin. "Never's a long time, McCoy," she said.

I gripped her shoulder and stared hard into her eyes.

"Listen, Nadine. The man you made that bet with? My gut tells me it wasn't some playful little joke. Not by a long shot. That guy had an agenda that involves harming me in some way. And maybe you, too."

She bit down on her lower lip for several seconds. Then she put her hand on top of mine. The comforter around her fell open and I had to resist the pull of gravity that was trying to drag my eyeballs down onto that voluptuous torso of hers.

"You really mean it, don't you, McCoy?" she said. "That it was some kind of setup?"

"Yes, I do."

"Then I'll tell you," she said

And with a soft, conspiratorial giggle, she leaned up close to me and whispered his name into my ear.

Chapter 37   History Is Bunk

Friday, August 19 - 12:50 a.m.

A COUPLE of minutes after Nadine left, I realized I'd neglected to get my house key back from her. I ran outside and down to the sidewalk to see if I could catch her, but the orangish-red taillights of her Corvette were already half a block away.

I hobbled back inside the condo, wishing I'd gotten that Vicodin prescription filled. When I'd come home with Oprah, the high of being with her had gone a long way toward assuaging the pain of my bomb injuries. But with her gone and the hospital painkillers worn off, I was feeling pretty much the way she'd predicted: as if the Lions' Jason Hanson had kicked me down the length of Ford Field, yard by yard.

Grimacing with each step, I went downstairs to the basement and located the file box that contained my military discharge papers. Under the bare bulb's glow I went through them and found the Army CID report from when I'd fingered J. J. Nails. It basically just reiterated what I'd told them: that he was allegedly selling guns, ammo, and explosives, and that they were supposedly being supplied by a Russian arms dealer. But the report did not, as I'd hoped, contain the dealer's name.

I was walking back through the basement when the Thing came out from behind the furnace. Looking up at me, he gave me a vicious, teeth-baring snarl. Indignant about all the visitors lately, I guessed.

"Thanks, you rancid little mother," I said. "I needed that."

As I achingly climbed back upstairs, I realized I was completely exhausted from the insane day I'd just gone through. Recalling the bottle of cognac I had in the kitchen, I went there and poured myself half a tumbler of the anesthetic. Hadn't even had a sip of it when the Thing showed up, demanding to be fed in that evil voice of his. I put out two cans of Alpo for the corpse-breathed sucker. Then I drained the cognac, rinsed the glass, and headed for my bedroom.

By the time I got there, my head was swimming. I switched off the lamp alongside the bed. After considering the effort it would take to undress, I instead chose to groaningly crawl onto the comforter and collapse there in my clothes, face down.

In just about every way imaginable, I felt like hell. Our mass murderer was running around scot free. Almost twenty-nine million dollars richer and having successfully eluded and humiliated local and Federal law enforcement. And the woman I'd thought would be the love of my life was probably never going to speak to me again.

The last thing I remember being conscious of was the lingering scent of Nadine's musky perfume atop the bed. Taunting me about what I'd lost tonight.

I don't know how long I'd been asleep when I saw Ofelia come through the bedroom wall in her schoolgirl outfit. Not sure how I could see her with my face down in the comforter, but there she was. A pretty brown teenage ghost. Seventeen forever, I supposed.

There you are, she said, setting her books on the dresser.

That's right, sis, I said. *Down for the count. Same as always, seems like.*

You know it's not over, don't you? she said. *The killing?*

I know, I said. *Won't be over till I stop that sucker cold.*

How you going to do it?

No idea. Got any suggestions?

Just one. Take help where you can find it, little man.

Little man. I started to chuckle into the comforter, but it hurt so bad the soft laugh turned into a groan.

What kind of help you talking about, Ofelia? I mumbled when the pain receded.

Where you least expect it, she said, giving me a sly wink.

She was starting to turn transparent now, fading away as she picked her schoolbooks up off the dresser.

What do you mean? I asked.

But she was already gone.

The next thing I knew my cell phone was ringing on the nightstand. The digital alarm clock there showed 4:00 a.m. Thinking it might be Eric Dawson calling with what he'd found out about Nails, I pushed myself up off the comforter, groaning from the pain, and reached for the burbling handset.

"Johnson," I said.

"Hello, asshole," said J. J. Nails.

"Always a pleasure, Mr. Nails," I said. "Not."

An evil cackle came through the phone. "So you finally figured out who I am, eh?" he said. "Or who I was, I should say. Took you long enough, didn't it, shit-for-brains?"

"I can't be expected to remember every insect I've seen crawling into the latrine for his dinner," I said.

He gave a nasty laugh. "Oh, yeah?" he said. "Well, who's got twenty-five million European smackers and a couple of hundred notches on his barrel, asswipe? You or me?"

"You know what, Nails?" I said. "Talking to you is like being in junior high school again. Listening to some sick little creep tell how he likes to stuff cats into mailboxes and throw in a firecracker."

Nails hesitated for a moment before speaking. "How did you know about the cats?" he said.

"I didn't, you pathetic weasel," I said. "You think you're this oh-so-unique evil genius, don't you? But the truth is, mean, overcompensating hunks of rotting garbage like you are a dime a dozen."

"Dime a dozen, eh?" he said, the edge of anger in his voice grown ugly. "I'll show you who's a dime a dozen. Tinhorn FBI agents who'll get to stand there with their thumbs up their behinds while I commit mass murder and fly away free as a bird. How about them apples, buttwipe?"

"You slimy piece of dung," I said. "You'll be a tiny footnote on the back pages of 'Turds Who've Walked the Earth,' Nails."

"I will, eh? Listen, a-hole - you think you're so effing smart? Well, I've got some news for you - in about eight hours from now something really big is going down."

"What do you mean? You've got your money, scumbag. Why don't you just slither back into the hole you came out of and leave decent people alone?"

"Why? Because you smart-ass FBI duds disobeyed my instructions, that's why. Since you dickheads decided to put a transmitter in the money case, I'm going to put one more bomb up Detroit's butt."

"You worthless pile of trash," I said.

"Flattery will get you nowhere, Johnson. But I'll tell you what: since I'm such a nice guy, I'm going to give you a hint about where it's going to be."

"I'm listening, you worthless little puke."

"Here it is, scumbag - 'history is bunk.'"

"That's it?"

"That's it, guano-face. 'History is bunk.' Figure out what it means in the next eight hours and a few hundred people might live. Screw it up and they all die. I'm betting it'll be the latter, butt-brain."

"Fine with me, punk," I said. "Meanwhile, isn't it time for you to go pull the wings off some flies? Or whatever it is putrid geeks like you do for fun?"

"Eat shit, Johnson."

"Screw you, Nails."

On that edifying rhetorical note, we hung up on one another. I was struck by how much the conversation resembled a number of verbal confrontations I'd had with thuggish creeps back in junior high and high school. Some things never change, I guess.

It's been my observation that people often think of criminals who commit horrendous crimes as diabolical, almost larger-than-life geniuses. But the murderers I've dealt with have all been almost childishly neurotic at their core. Self-centered, petty-minded shlubs who get off on having life and death power over people. Which isn't to say they can't be plenty deadly.

I threw my legs over the side of the bed, groaning again as daggers of pain plunged into a dozen places in my body. Then somebody twisted the daggers when I made myself stand up.

I knew Nails wasn't kidding about his threat to kill hundreds of people. I also knew I now had less than eight hours to figure out how he planned to do it and stop him.

Somewhere or another I'd heard the phrase 'history is bunk' before, but wasn't quite sure where. I figured I could find it on the Internet, so I limped like an old man down the hall and into the spare bedroom that serves as my home office.

After booting up my desktop computer, I Googled on the quote and soon found that it was something Henry Ford once said in a newspaper interview. What he'd actually said was "History is more or less bunk," and what he meant was that we can escape our past by creating a new and different present. I sat back in my chair. So there was some kind of connection to Henry Ford. But what did it mean in terms of Nails' threat?

Even though it's spread out all over the world now, the Ford company still has a vast presence in the Detroit area, especially in the adjoining city of Dearborn. There was the Ford Motor Company world headquarters building, visible from the Southfield freeway or Michigan Ave. There was the Rouge Plant, a gigantic, almost century-old industrial complex, which, even though downsized from its heyday, still employed several thousand workers. And there were the Henry Ford Museum and Greenfield Village. The first a huge indoor collection of industrial artifacts, especially automobiles; the second an outdoor museum crowded with historic buildings that old Henry had bought and had transported here.

Wait a minute, I thought. History. The museums?

Just then my cell phone rang again. I wondered if it would be Nails calling back for another session of adolescent put-downs, but it was Eric Dawson.

"Sorry to call so late, McCoy," he said. "I tried the hospital, but they said you'd gone home."

"Yeah," I said. "Wanted to come by here and check my Army papers to see if they mentioned the name of that Russian dude. But I struck out - they don't. By the way," I added. "I got a call from Nails a little while ago."

"You're kidding me."

"Nope. He still has my cell number from the money drop."

"You let him know you knew who he was?"

"Yeah. Didn't faze him, though."

"What did he say?"

"After we exchanged a few pleasantries, he told me there's going to be another bombing in the next eight hours - in other words, right around noon. A big one. Payback for the transmitter we put in the money case."

"Christ," Dawson said. "That's great news. I don't suppose he told you where?"

"Not exactly, but he gave me a hint."

"What was it?"

"It was 'history is bunk.' I checked it out online. It's a Henry Ford quote, so I figure it's got to have something to do with one of the Ford properties. Most likely it's The Henry Ford. Either the museum or Greenfield Village."

"Hmm - makes sense. We'll have to alert their security people and get the Dearborn Police involved."

"Right. The problem is, it's a huge complex and we don't where he figures on planting the bomb. He's talking about killing hundreds, so it would have to be someplace where people congregate."

"Unless he's planning to plant multiple bombs," Dawson said.

"You're right," I said. "Which would just make it that much tougher."

"Nothing's been easy about this case," he said. "Why should this be any different?"

"By the way," I said. "Did you find out anything more from DC about Nails?"

"Some, but not everything we want. I talked to a Major de Coverly in Army CID. Apparently, due to your reporting him, they've got a fairly extensive file on Nails. He was able to give me what they've got on his military record, but the rest is classified. I'm going through channels to get that part released to us, but I can give you what they have on his military service."

"I'm all ears," I said. "Shoot."

"Here's his background. He's from the Toledo, Ohio area. Born Joshua Jefferson Nails in 1980. Known as J. J. since infancy. Grew up in Sylvania, a suburb of Toledo. In high school he was a C student in most areas, but a whiz in shop and auto mechanics. He went into the Army at eighteen. Apparently he got into some kind of trouble with the law, and the judge gave him the option of joining the military or doing time."

"Great call, judge," I said. "Just the kind of recruits we need."

"After his basic training, he trained for infantry. Signed up for airborne school and got through it, despite a few disciplinary issues. Got assigned to the 101st Airborne Division after that. There were some reported behavioral problems involving drinking and fighting, but nothing serious. He then signed up for and completed Army Ranger training. On returning to his unit, however, there were a series of incidents involving insubordination, followed by a physical attack on an officer. During the court martial there were also some allegations of drug use and civil criminal activity, but he was never formally charged with anything else. He ended up serving eleven months for the officer assault and was given a dishonorable discharge."

"So much for his illustrious military career," I said. "What next?"

"Unfortunately, that's where the classified part begins. We won't get it until the clearance goes through. I stressed to this de Coverly that it's critically important, but I'm still waiting to hear back from him."

"Okay," I said. "Then I guess we need to focus on the Ford museums for now. How should we proceed?"

"I'll call Dearborn Police right now and get hold of Chief Mansour," Eric said. "I expect he'll know who to contact at museum security."

"And I'll call Ed Wilkins, the Wayne County Sheriff," I said. "I know they've got bomb-sniffing dogs they use out at the airport. I'm sure they'll be willing to help out."

"We'll shoot for having a task force together at the museum complex by, say, 6 a.m.," he said.

"Sounds like a plan," I said. "I'll take a taxi up to the office and meet you there in, say, forty-five minutes?"

"Fine. By the way," he said. "How are you feeling?"

"Like warmed-over pig slop," I said. "But okay enough to do my job."

"When I called to hospital to talk you, they said that Dr. Cummings took you home. Nardella and Wilson tell me you've got a thing for her. How did that work out for you?"

"Don't ask," I said with a sigh.

Chapter 38   At The Henry Ford

Friday, August 19 - 11:00 a.m.

"NOTHING SO far, eh?" Ellis Sidwell said.

"Afraid not," I replied, scowling as I gazed up at the clock in the tall, cupolaed tower atop the Henry Ford Museum's main entrance.

I'd called the DPD's bomb expert and asked him to help out with the searches. I'd also suggested he bring along a couple of bomb disposal suits, just in case.

Now the five of us - Sidwell, Dawson, Wilson, Nardella, and I - were standing on the sidewalk outside the museum entrance.

"So what was that nifty hint this Nails dude gave you again, Mojo?" Wilson asked.

"'History is bunk,'" I replied. "It's something old Henry once said."

"If he thought it was bunk, why'd he create a two hundred-fifty-some acre place filled to the gills with it?" Wilson said.

I shrugged. "I don't know. Guy was full of contradictions, I guess."

"And the 'history' part is what made you think he was talking about the museum complex?" Nardella asked.

"Yeah," I said. "It seemed to make the most sense."

"It does, damn it. But how come we haven't found anything?" Dawson said, looking around.

"I don't know," I said, glancing at my watch. "Either we haven't looked hard enough, or I just plain got it wrong."

The truth was, I'd spent the past hour second-guessing whether I'd made the right call on Nails' hint.

The task force had all gathered together inside the big entrance gate off Oakwood Boulevard at around 6 a.m. In addition to the complex's security crew, it included the Dearborn Police's sixteen-member SWAT team and another forty of their uniformed and plainclothes cops. Along with Nardella, Wilson, and I, Eric had detailed an additional fifteen FBI agents to the site, and the Wayne County Sheriff's office had supplied around a dozen officers, among them a dog detail with six bomb-sniffing German shepherds.

When I spoke to the assembled group, I told them that we didn't know if there'd be one large bomb or numerous small ones. The one thing we had going for us was that the bomber had threatened to take out hundreds of victims. That meant the explosion or explosions would have to take place somewhere where there'd be one or more large groups of people. Our goal was to scout out every place in the complex where visitors would be concentrated, and then search diligently for any evidence of explosives.

After organizing everyone into teams and issuing instructions, we'd all gone to work exploring the buildings and grounds.

By late morning we'd combed every area of the complex where large congregations of patrons could conceivably occur. This included the several restaurants, the IMAX movie theater, and a few other places where there'd be activities that would draw crowds.

And what had we come up with? Exactly zip.

Shortly after eleven o'clock, a tall, slender, sixtyish guy in a white shirt, tie, and khaki trousers came out of the museum entrance and hurried up to us. He had a bizarre, sweeping pompadour of orange hair that appeared to be modeled on Donald Trump's.

"Special Agent Dawson?" he said to my boss. "You're in charge here?"

"Yes, sir," Eric answered.

"I need to talk to you. I'm Wilfred Canty - director of programs for The Henry Ford," he said.

The two shook hands.

"I'm not sure if you're aware," he went on, "that we normally open our gates at nine, open the museums up at nine-thirty, and have our first show at the IMAX at ten," he said.

"Right," Eric said. "But today isn't a normal day, is it?"

"I understand, sir. I'm perfectly cognizant that there's been a threat," he said. "But my understanding, from talking to the various police officials here, is that nothing has been found."

"That's true, Mr. Canty," Eric said. "Not yet, at least."

"Well, there's a problem, you see," Canty went on. "Today is supposed to be the area grand opening of 'The BloodBot Chronicles' at our IMAX here."

I looked over at the marquee. Sure enough, it was advertising *The BloodBot Chronicles - Part I: Bite Me.*

"And?" Eric said.

"There's been a mountain of expensive publicity for the opening," Canty said, "and my people are telling me that Oakwood Boulevard is backed up for two or three miles in both directions with patrons waiting to get in to buy tickets for the movie. The first show was supposed to be at ten o'clock," he fretted, glancing up nervously at the entrance tower clock, "and now we're getting tons of calls from irate people about the delay."

"Mr. Canty, I'm really sorry that we're disrupting your operation today," Dawson said. "But if you've seen any of the news reports lately about the bombings that have been going on, I'm sure you'll have to agree that a threat like this is not something to be taken lightly."

"Especially when it came directly from the bomber," I added.

"But as I understand it," Canty said, "there really wasn't a direct threat to The Henry Ford. It was more of a riddle. And that we may or may not, in fact, be a target."

"That's true, sir," Eric said. "But it's our best guess."

"I realize public safety is paramount," Canty went on, "but we've had bomb scares in the past and they all proved to be false alarms. Plus, things are complicated. For one thing, the studio flew in three of the stars of the new movie to be here today. They're going to get up on the stage and introduce the film."

"Is that them over there?" Wilson asked, pointing toward the entrance gate.

Just inside the gate was a long, black, custom Hummer limousine. Three movie-star-attractive young actors - two male and one female - along with four older people who looked like they were assistants or makeup people, were leaning against the limousine, smoking.

"Yes," Canty said. "They're asking to get into the dressing room at the IMAX, so they can put on their costumes and makeup and prep for the show."

"They're from Hollywood? What do you think they're smoking?" Wilson said, squinting. "Clove cigarettes? Medical marijuana?"

"The point is, this grand opening's been in the works for months," Canty said. "There's supposed to be local TV and radio coverage, and I understand their crews are also stuck out in that traffic jam on Oakwood."

"Sir, I understand the IMAX holds a bit over four hundred people. You're talking about potentially putting their lives at risk. Is that really something you're prepared to do?" Eric said.

"But the police are telling me you've searched for five hours now, and have found nothing, correct?" Canty said. "And besides, I'm not talking about opening the entire complex - just the IMAX, so we can service our customers and get on with the show."

I spoke up, sensing that Dawson was going to have to accede to Canty.

"Can I suggest we at least make one more walk-through of the IMAX with the bomb-sniffing dogs?" I said. "Before we let anyone in there?"

"Fine," Canty said. "But can you get started on it right away?"

"Alright, sir," Eric said. "We'll do it as promptly as we can."

I located the Wayne County Sheriff Department's dog handling team and had them bring three of their shepherds to the IMAX. They told me they'd already made a pass through the theater with a single dog, but were willing to have another go with the trio.

We followed the dog-handler deputies into the IMAX's lobby. Also with us were some of the theater staff, so they could get us into the locked areas. One dog stayed on the ground floor to sniff out the lobby, concession, ticket, and administrative areas. A second dog was led up the flight of stairs that take you to the auditorium entrances. His handler then began walking the shepherd up and down the rows of folding seats. The third dog was led up to the upper level and into the projection room, a big, high-tech-looking space that houses the elaborate equipment for projecting 3D or 2D movies onto the IMAX's gigantic sixty-foot-high and eighty-foot-wide curved screen.

After twenty minutes of intense searching, all three handlers reported that the dogs had scented nothing at all suspicious. The visual searches Nardella, Wilson, Sidwell, and I had done I had likewise come up with zilch. Nevertheless, I still had a real bad feeling about the theater. Dogs are excellent at finding standard explosives, but plastic explosives like C-4 and Semtex have no scent.

When the search group came back out of the entrance, Canty, Dawson, Mike Mansour, the Dearborn Police chief, and Bob Lustig, the head of The Henry Ford security, were standing there, under the *Bite Me* marquee.

"How about it, McCoy?" Eric asked.

"Came up clean," I reluctantly admitted.

"Then I'd like to start letting people into the grounds and start selling tickets for the twelve o'clock show," Canty said.

"If museum management wants to make that call, then I guess we have to go along," Dawson said. The other officials nodded in agreement.

"Excellent," Canty said. "Mr. Lustig," he said to the security chief. "Go inform the gate guards they can start letting people in. For the movie only, for now. I'll go let the actors know they can come in and started getting costumed up."

"What's this movie about, anyway?" Sidwell asked.

"Robot vampires from outer space versus teenage mutant zombies," Nardella said. "I read about it online."

"Wonder if they based the zombies on my nephew and niece," Wilson said. "My sister named them Brendan and Brittney, but I call them Sid and Nancy."

Soon the complex's big southwest parking lot was filling up and people were hurrying eagerly toward the IMAX. The vast majority were tweenagers, both male and female, and the mothers who'd driven them. Before long the line was backed out the theater entrance. The other agents and I moved away from the throng of kids and moms who were now crowded under the *Bite Me* marquee. I was walking with my head down when I heard my dead sister's voice.

Stop them, Ofelia said. *Or they'll all die.*

I felt the hairs on my neck stand up. I turned away from the other agents, concerned I might say something out loud.

Where is it? I said.

There's an access area under the theater seats, she said.

Under the seating? Damn! How come you didn't tell me earlier, Ofelia? I said, annoyed with her. *When we were inside?*

You didn't ask, she said. *And by the way - you'd better be careful*, she added.

Why? I asked.

It's booby-trapped, she said.

"Got a problem over there, Mojo?" Wilson said. "Your face is twitching like a mouse sniffing cheese."

I turned around to them, my expression grim.

"Yeah, I've got a problem," I said. "I just figured out where the damn bomb is in the IMAX."

"But we just checked out the whole place, McCoy," Nardella said.

"No we didn't. Remember how steep the seats are sloped inside? Underneath them is an access area that nobody showed us. That's where the bomb is."

"How do you know that?" Dawson asked.

"Never mind how," I said. "I just know, that's all. We need to find someone from the IMAX group who can show us how to get in there. We also need to get ahold of Canty, have them stop selling tickets, and get those people out of the theater, ASAP."

"He's going to love hearing that," Nardella said.

"Yeah," Wilson said. "Guy looks pretty constipated. Bet this'll do wonders for it."

I turned to Sidwell then.

"Ellis," I said. "Where are those bomb suits?"

Chapter 39   Time Running Out

Friday, August 19 - 11:40 a.m.

AS THE extremely disgruntled crowd were being evacuated from the theater, Sidwell and I began suiting up in the lobby. Fortunately, he'd included the extra pair of groin protectors I'd asked him to bring along.

"Do we really need to double up on these?" he asked as he watched me strap on my second protective cup over the Kevlar-lined suit.

"This guy likes to go for crotch-shots, Ellis," I told him. "I'd strongly recommend you wear that second groin protector. We did it at the house on Elmore Street and it saved Wilson's balls. Several of the other SWAT team cops who went in there weren't so lucky."

A shudder went through me as I remembered Pitts, the young officer who'd blown his brains out in front of me after his genitals were shredded by one of the booby traps.

"Whatever you say, McCoy," he said.

"Believe me," I said. "You'll thank me later. Your wife will, too."

When we were completely suited up and had our helmets latched into place, Sidwell and I headed down the hallway that ran behind the stairwell leading up to the auditorium.

The entrance to the under-seat access area was in a closet midway down the hall. There was no handle to the closet, just a keylock. The entrance door blended into the wall in such a way you'd never see it unless you were looking for it. Which, the theater staff having forgotten all about it, was how it got bypassed on our earlier searches.

Cautiously, with the key the maintenance crew had finally dug up for us, I unlocked the closet door and we stepped inside. Sidwell found a light switch and, when he flipped it on, we saw a metal ladder built into the wall, leading up to an overhead door.

"Must be the entrance up there," I said. "I'll go up first."

"Alright," he said. "But take care. That door might be wired to trip something."

The ninety-pound weight of the bomb suit was all too evident as I climbed the ladder. When I was about eight feet up, I reached for the knob on the overhead door.

"Easy now," Sidwell said.

Positioning myself as far away as I could, I yanked the door open and ducked.

Nothing happened. No booby trap on the door, at least.

It swung fully open, banged against the wall, and began swinging closed again. I stopped it with my gloved hand. Then I climbed up a couple of steps and peered inside the access area. Except for the light shining in from the closet, it was pitch black. Taking the Maglite from my utility belt, I switched it on and swept it around. Amid the struts and girders holding up the slanted flooring above, I spotted a whole host of suspicious-looking devices.

"Holy crap," I said.

"What do you see?" Sidwell called up to me.

"Bombs," I said. "In aluminum casings. And black metal boxes - some of them with barrels sticking out them. Booby traps, for sure."

"How many?" he said.

"A lot," I said. "I'm counting them now. What time is it, by the way?"

"Just a sec," he said while he took off his glove to check his watch. "Eleven forty-five," he reported.

"Okay," I said after a few more seconds. "I count ten bombs and ten booby traps."

"Now do me a favor," I went on. "Turn off the light down there."

He switched off the closet light and I turned off my Maglite. After a few seconds of adjusting to the darkness, I began to see them: what looked like fifty to a hundred tiny red LEDs, at every possible height and orientation.

"Ellis," I said. "We are in deep shit."

A minute or so later the two of us were up inside the dark underfloor space, huddled close to the entrance door as I pointed out the host of LEDs to Sidwell.

"Nails uses LED sensors for his booby traps," I explained. "At Al-Rafi's house, he had them set up so that you could go past them without triggering them, but when you returned you'd set them off. These could be set up the same way, or they could be set up to go off the first time the beam is broken."

"Got you," he said.

"But the really bad news," I said. "Is that he's got ten bombs up here. Presumably all set to go off at the same time - namely noon. I don't know how the hell we'll be able to defuse all of them in under fifteen minutes."

"Let me take a look around," he said, switching on his own flashlight.

I followed the beam as he swung it around, picking out the aluminum casings.

"Look," he said. "He's got them all wired together."

He moved the beam of light back and forth, and that's when I saw the slim filaments of wire connecting them.

After tracing the path between the bombs for a few seconds, his Maglite picked out a black box on the back wall that had several of the wire filaments running to it. It was about fifty feet away from where we were crouched.

"That's his detonator," he said. "He's got a hub and spoke configuration. If we can disable that detonator box, we're home free."

"Good call, Ellis," I said. "That'll reduce the disable time, for sure. The only question is, are these bomb suits going to protect us enough to get to that box and then get back out of here?"

"Only one way to find out, buckaroo," he said.

He started to rise, but I put my arm out to hold him back.

"Hang on," I said. "I'm not sure we want to take any direct hits from his booby traps. They knocked out both of the first two guys who went in in bomb suits back at Elmore Street. The sensors there were mostly waist-high, so Wilson and I were able to crawl under them. The others we triggered with a curtain rod, so we wouldn't take any direct hits from the booby traps."

"So we need something to trigger them with," Sidwell said and began swinging his Maglite's beam around the space.

"Over there," he said. "I think I see a metal rod."

He was shining his flashlight on a spot about twenty-five feet from us. Sure enough, there was a metal rod on the floor of the access area. It was about eight feet long and looked to be a stray strut left over from construction of the space.

"Tell you what," I said. "I'll do an alligator crawl to it. That'll give me the lowest possible profile."

He pulled off his glove and checked the time again. "Okay," he said. "But we better get to it. It's eleven forty-eight now."

"Listen, if I set off a trap and don't make it, I recommend you just get the hell out of here," I said. "Which reminds me - while I'm going after that rod, you'd better call the people outside and make sure they've got everyone well clear of the building."

"Will do," he said.

With that, I got down onto by belly and began to crawl over the floor toward the metal rod.

By now the old fear I'd felt when doing a bomb disarm had come back over me - in spades - and I was sweating like a four hundred-pound hog on his way to the slaughterhouse. Some of it was the confined body heat of the bomb suit, but a lot more of it was from sheer, unadulterated terror.

As I moved forward, I kept my eyes out for LEDs aimed in my direction. When I was about mid-way to the rod, I must've triggered one I hadn't seen.

WHAM!

I threw myself down flat as what sounded like a shotgun blast went off about three feet over my head.

"Holy moly!" I heard Sidwell shout behind me as buckshot clanged and spattered off the girders and tubing in the floorspace.

"You okay, McCoy?" he called out to me.

"I'm fine," I said.

"Then you better keep moving," he said. "Time's a-wasting."

"Thanks for reminding me, Ellis," I said as I resumed scrabbling forward in the heavy bomb suit.

I managed to get to the rod without setting off any more of the booby traps, but now had to do a turnaround and go back to the entrance door. Keeping myself as low as possible, I shifted myself around and began crawling back to where Sidwell was waiting. Fortunately, I made it without tripping any more of the traps.

"How much time we have left?" I asked as I crawled up to him.

"Eight minutes," he said.

"Let's move then," I said. "Follow directly behind me. I'm going to swing the rod around as I crawl and try to trigger any traps between us and the detonator box."

"Got it," he said. "Let's roll, dude."

I shined my flashlight on the black detonator box to orient myself, then shut it off so I could spot the telltale LEDs. Using my elbows and knees, I crawled forward, extending the steel rod in front of me and swinging it up, down and around.

I'd gone maybe a dozen feet when I triggered the next booby trap.

BAM!!!

It was another shotgun-like explosion, this time from the floor up, and no doubt aimed at the genitals of a standing six-foot man. The blast knocked the rod out of my gloved hands, but I quickly retrieved it and kept going, mindful that the time we'd need for Ellis to disarm the detonator was quickly running out.

We'd gone another twenty feet when the waving rod set off yet another trap.

BA-WHAM!!!

Another crotch-shot went off, this one apparently coming from a double-barreled shotgun. Again the rod was knocked out of my hands, but I retrieved it once more and we continued forward.

Assuming we got out of this alive, I knew I'd want to come back and inspect the booby traps more closely, to see exactly how Nails had set up the triggering mechanisms. But there certainly wasn't any time to devote to that now.

BAM!!!

Another sudden detonation startled me, spattering buckshot or shrapnel off my fiberglass helmet. The sound made me jerk my head so hard I got a bad neck sprain. But it wasn't disabling and I kept on moving.

Finally we reached the back wall where the black detonator box was mounted, about three feet above us. Sidwell crawled up beside me.

"How much time left?" I said.

"Three minutes," he said.

"Jesus," I said. "Is that enough time to disarm the damn thing?"

"It better be," he said.

Sidwell cautiously got up onto his knees and began visually inspecting the black box. I could see he was being careful not to touch it.

"Trying to see if taking off the cover will set anything off," he said.

"Can't you just cut the wires?" I asked.

"Not without seeing how it's wired inside," he said. "The son of a bitch could be set up so that interrupting the current will trigger them."

"Then you better get in there quick," I said.

"One second," he said. "Can you hold your Maglite on the case while I jimmy the cover off?" he said.

"Sure," I said, pointing the flashlight at the black casing.

He had the tip of a flat-blade screwdriver under the top edge of the box. There was a metallic snapping sound and the edge popped out.

Gingerly, he pulled the covering away and set it down on the floor. The inside was a small labyrinth of wiring and electronic components.

"Ever see one of these before?" I asked nervously. I sure hadn't.

"Not since Kandahar," he said.

Feeling slightly reassured by the fact that Ellis had dealt with similar devices in the past, I then made the dumb mistake of shifting my body a step to the left and turning my helmeted head. For about a second I saw two red, eye-level LEDs staring at me. And then:

BAM!!!

A blast slammed into the face of my helmet. The force knocked my head back, but fortunately the suit's oversized collar kept my neck from being snapped like a Tinker Toy.

"Holy Christ, Johnson! You okay?" I heard Sidwell say.

"I don't know," I said. There were stars in front of my eyes from the impact.

As the smoke from the shot cleared away, I realized that all I could see in front of me now was a mottled gray mass of wetness. I tried to wipe it away with my protective glove. I then began hearing an unsettling combination of hissing and crackling. A nauseating stench began to fill the helmet.

I'd taken a direct hit of sulfuric acid into the helmet's facemask. It was now eating its way through the acrylic laminate, filling up my fiber headgear with poisonous fumes. I hadn't even realized I'd dropped the Maglite until I felt Sidwell pushing it back into my gloved hands.

"Listen to me, man!" Ellis said. "I need you to hold that flashlight on the box for just a few more seconds, got it? Just a few more seconds!"

"Alright," I said. "But you've got to aim me, okay? Because I can't see a damn thing!"

"Here you go!" he said, putting my hands into position.

"How much time do we have left?" I asked. My eyes and the insides of my nose were burning now from the acrid, corrosive gas inside the helmet.

"Less than a minute!" he said. There was an edge of panic in his voice.

The stinging in my eyes and nostrils became almost unbearable, and although I'd been trying to hold my breath, the noxious fumes were getting into my lungs.

I began to cough - hoarse, hacking spasms that threatened to quickly turn into retching. I could feel the Maglite wobbling in my hands.

"DAMN IT, MAN! KEEP THAT THING STEADY!" Sidwell bellowed at me.

I could no longer see a thing. Tears were streaming from my eyes and snot from my nostrils. The stench inside the helmet had become horrific. It was all I could do to keep myself from vomiting as my rasping coughs echoed in my ears.

"ALMOST THERE!" I heard Ellis yell.

Almost? Jesus! I thought, gagging uncontrollably now. I'm going to die! It's all over!

Trick or treat, Johnson! I heard Manny, my dead Iraq buddy, say.

I began frantically reciting mental farewells. Goodbye, world! Goodbye, Oprah! Goodbye-

Hello, McCoy! my dead sister said.

"GOT IT!" Sidwell screamed triumphantly.

As soon as it sank in that Ellis had successfully disarmed the detonator, I dropped the flashlight, tore open the helmet's latches and ripped the suffocating thing off my head.

Gasping, I flattened myself against the wall and filled my lungs with oxygen. After having been forced to breathe the sulfurous fumes inside the helmet, the stagnant air of the underfloor area smelled sweeter and fresher than the breeze off a mountain lake. While my coughing subsided, I pulled off my protective gloves and wiped away the tears and snot. With my vision regained, I saw that the glove I'd tried to wipe my visor with was burned black where it had contacted the acid.

"How you doing, my friend?" Sidwell said. "You're looking a bit stressed out."

I noticed the flushed, grinning face behind his acrylic mask was streaming with sweat.

I chuckled. "Doing a hell of a lot better with that thing off my head," I said. "How about yourself, Ellis?"

He rolled his eyes and gave a little "oh, well" shrug.

"Other than that I'm going to have to hose out the insides of this bomb suit?" he said.

As it turned out, we weren't completely out of the woods yet. We still had to crawl through the booby traps to get out of the underfloor space. Since I had no helmet now, Ellis took the lead this time. When we got near the exit door, however, he stood up a bit too soon.

BOOM!

"AAAHHH!!!" he screamed as something exploded out of the floor and slammed into the crotch of his bomb suit.

I seized hold of him as he fell back, terrified that we would trip another one of the acid-to-the-head booby traps. For several moments he stood there looking down at his groin, horrified. But then I heard a loud sigh of relief from inside his helmet; the second protector I'd urged him to wear had saved his family jewels from ruin.

"Johnson," he said after we'd climbed back down the ladder and he'd removed his fiberglass helmet. "I owe you a beer."

"How about a case?" I said.

"Hell," he said. "I might buy you the whole dang brewery."

Chapter 40   Frustration
Friday, August 19 - 12:30 p.m.

SON OF a rotten bitch!" Nails exclaims, glaring at the big TV screen.

On the carpet nearby, Beelzebub lifts his big yellow head. He echoes the man's ill temper with an extended snarl, his bad eye rotating agitatedly.

The news report is showing images of the Henry Ford IMAX theater's facade. In the background a stream of young adolescents and parents are going in the entrance, some of them turning their heads to stare back at the TV crew. "DEADLY BOMB DISARMED IN DEARBORN!" says a scrolling headline at the bottom of the screen.

The camera then cuts to an attractive black female reporter who's standing in front of the theater, holding a microphone.

"Disaster was narrowly averted today as a pair of bomb experts succeeded in disarming a deadly explosive device here at the Henry Ford IMAX theater in Dearborn," she says. *"Acting on a taunting hint from the bomber himself - whom the FBI has now identified as a lone psychopath named J. J. Nails - police and FBI resources scoured the Henry Ford museum complex for several hours this morning.*

"According to police on the scene, a total of ten bombs and numerous booby traps were found hidden under the seating inside the IMAX. The bombs were set to go off at noon today at the premiere of 'Bite Me' - the first in the 'BloodBot Chronicles' movie series.

"With just seconds to go, the two bomb experts - Sergeant Ellis Sidwell of the Detroit Police Department and FBI Special Agent McCoy Johnson - were able to disarm the deadly devices. Authorities say that if they'd gone off as planned, they could have cost over four hundred lives."

"Shit! - Shit! - Shit!" Nails barks out as he clicks off the TV. Four hundred more bodies that could've been added to his head count!

"That sonofabitch Johnson!" he says, turning to the yellow dog. "He frigging figured out the riddle, Bub! Dammit - how the hell did he do it?"

Lowering his head back onto his paws, the pit bull growls dejectedly.

"I spent *weeks* casing and infiltrating that goddamn IMAX place," the glowering man says. "Even got a job there and worked a couple of weeks as a maintenance man. Swept floors and swabbed out stinking toilets and urinals so I could hide out inside the theater after everyone went home for the night."

"And my bombs, boy - they were absolute beauts," he goes on. "Would've blown all those dumbshit kids and their asshole parents to hamburger. Bloody frigging chili burger!"

Still distraught, he plops himself down on the sofa and sits there fuming.

The truth is, he feels like letting his frustration out in a full-blown tantrum. Like slamming his feet and fists up and down while he screams and howls like an out-of-control two-year-old. If it weren't for Beelzebub lying there watching him, he'd very likely do it. But he isn't about to show such weakness in front of his wall-eyed companion. He can't. It would be too humiliating.

After watching the sulking man on the couch for a time, the pit bull flops onto his side. Poking a leg up into the air, he begins to lick his furry testicles.

Frowning, the man glares at the dog as he laps away. It's a job that seems to go on and on, accompanied by occasional swirls of his tongue over his doggy rectum. After a time the man begins to check his watch, wondering how much time that goddamn frigging pit bull is going to spend swirling his goddamn frigging tongue over those goddamn frigging furry balls of his. As the minutes pass, Nails can feel his face and neck growing hotter and hotter at the sight of the interminable lapping. Despite his efforts to contain his swelling rage, he feels his control slipping away, until finally he can't take it anymore. Springing up off the couch, he howls down at the preoccupied dog:

"HOW LONG YOU GONNA LICK THOSE GODDAMN THINGS???"

The startled pit bull shoots up into the air like something popping out of a jack-in-the-box, his short legs scrabbling wildly. When he lands back down on the carpet, he immediately drops into a defensive crouch. Outsize head lowered, he backs away from the man, ears flattened and growling viciously, his bad eye bouncing back and forth as if it were following a ping-pong match.

The sight of Beelzebub baring his teeth at him enrages Nails further, and for several moments he considers getting his Glock and using it on the goddamn, ball-licking yellow monster. Putting a slug between those big, black, crazy-looking eyes and sending the sonofabitch straight to canine hell.

But after a couple of minutes of mutual glaring, his anger began to dissipate. For the past five years Beelzebub has been his one and only companion and co-conspirator. He's even bought a top-of-the-line pet carrier for him, for the flight down to Mexico.

He finds himself remembering the day he bought the dog. It was shortly after he'd got out of that hospital in Germany and flown back to the States. At the time the Master Plan was little more than an evil gleam in his eye and he wasn't even sure why he'd bought a ticket to Detroit. After he'd landed he'd booked a room in a cheesy motel in Romulus, not far from the airport. After hearing about it from a fellow roomer, he'd gone to a dog fight at a farm outside of Ypsilanti. Won a hundred bucks betting on some black pit bull named Bubba, who tore the shit out of his Rottweiler opponent. After the match he got to talking with Bubba's owner, some weird, countrified black dude named Ornie. He looked down and noticed the man had another dog with him, a yellow pit on a short choke chain. The dog was snarling as he stared into the fighting pit with his good eye, while his other one jerked around like it was having a fit.

"That's Bub," the man said. "Short for Beelzebub."

The guy told him the pit had at one time been his best fighting dog. But then one day he'd gotten into it with some ugly, big-ass mastiff and had taken a bad bite to the skull. The mastiff's teeth had apparently gone into Bub's brain and his left eyeball had been squirrely ever since. Said he'd kept him around for old times' sake, but was thinking about putting him down.

"I'll give you a hundred bucks for him," he found himself telling the man.

It wasn't pity that made him offer to buy the damaged dog. More the sense that he and Beelzebub were somehow kindred spirits. He smiles now as he remembers the bartering.

"Two hundred," the guy said.

"One hundred."

"One seventy-five."

"One hundred."

"One fifty."

"One hundred."

"One twenty-five."

"One hundred."

"Sold. You hard-ass mother," Ornie had said.

Now he looks down at Beelzebub, his anger abated.

254

"Hey, Bub," he says, spreading his hands. "Sorry, man - I shouldn't have yelled at you like that. You were just being a dumbshit dog, weren't you?"

The crouched dog is still staring hard at him, showing his snaggly teeth as he emits a low growl.

"Come on, Bub - chill out, dammit," the man says, trying to make himself look and sound congenial. But it's difficult, given how frustrated he still feels.

Nails' eyes then fall on the duffel bag that's sitting on the La-Z-boy across the room. The sight of the red bag makes him feel better. When he pictures the twenty-five million in Swiss and EU banknotes inside, he starts to feel a *whole* lot better.

"Screw it," he says as he plops back down on his couch. "McCoy Buttwipe Johnson may have won today's round, but tomorrow's gonna be a different story."

Having finally lowered his hackles, the yellow dog gets down on his belly and warily watches the man.

"One thing's for sure, Bub," he says. "I'm not gonna call and give the bastard any hints. He'll have to figure it out on his own - and that ain't gonna happen."

Nails' mood continues to improve as the power feeling comes back over him. The power to dispense death - the best goddamn feeling in the whole wide frigging world - is seeping back into him.

"You just wait, boy," he says, already feeling that sense of excitement he gets when he's on the verge of killing. "When The Big One comes down on that dumbshit Dream Cruise crowd, the whole effing world is gonna sit up and take notice. When those thousands of corpses start piling up on Woodward - miles and miles of them - they'll know who they've been messing with. The meanest, baddest dude on the planet - J. J. Frigging Nails."

"I'll be right up there with the all-stars, boy. Hitler, Stalin, Pol Pot, Himmler, Beria," he says, naming a few of his boyhood heroes.

"And you know what's gonna happen afterward?" he goes on.

"We're gonna effing disappear. Poof - like ghosts. I get some plastic surgery down in Mexico to rearrange my face. Then it'll be off to that nifty clinic in Switzerland. A few weeks there and I'll walk out with a fully-functional foot-long dick slapping my thigh when I walk."

"After that, man, who knows?" he says, now musing happily.

"Maybe I travel around the world a few times, seeing how many whores I can screw each time around. Or maybe I set myself up to do a little contract killing on the side, just for fun. Or maybe I'll just find me some nice little island in the Pacific somewhere. Buy it, rename it Nails Island, and surround myself with a bunch of native girl whores. Then sit back and write a memoir. Call it 'J. J. Nails: The Man Who Single-Handedly Annihilated Detroit.' What do you think, boy? Like that title?" he says with a giddy laugh.

Folding his arms behind him, he leans back on the couch and rests the back of his head in his hands.

"One thing's for sure, Bub," he says. "After tomorrow they won't be calling that big circle jerk for car-loving douchebags the 'Dream Cruise' any more. You know what I bet they'll be calling it?"

"The *Scream* Cruise!" he says, with a happy cackle.

Beelzebub, seeing the man relaxed and happy now, has finally dropped his mean, wary look. Lowering his oversize head, he rests his muzzle on his paws and watches the seated man as he chatters on. The dog's bad eye is flicking around strangely, looking almost as though it's tracing out characters from some ancient, evil alphabet. His good eye, meanwhile, is staring at the man with an intensity that's cold and hard and diabolically knowing.

As if it's foreseeing exactly what's going to happen...

Chapter 41   Filling In The Blanks

Friday, August 19 - 3:00 p.m.

I WAS back at my desk that afternoon when my cell phone rang. I checked the number and saw it was Willie the Pimp again. I was a bit surprised to hear from him after our last call, when it had sounded like he'd finally accepted that we weren't going to accept his aid offer.

"Good afternoon, Mr. La Borgia," I answered.

"Agent Johnson?" he said. "How are you doing?"

"Fine sir," I said. "What can I do for you?"

"I was just wondering - what are your plans for the Dream Cruise tomorrow?"

"Don't really have any, sir. Why do you ask?" I said.

"I'm planning on cruising in one of my cars. Care to come along?" he said.

I considered the offer for a few seconds before replying.

"Sure," I said. "Why don't you pick me up at my place? Say at 11 a.m.?"

"Okay," he said. "Where do you live?"

"I think you already know that, Mr. La Borgia," I said.

He chuckled. "What do you mean?"

"Never mind the games," I said. "Pick me up at eleven. I'll be waiting."

La Borgia paused a couple of beats before answering.

"All right, Agent Johnson," he said. "I'll see you at eleven, then. Your place."

We hung up and I sat back in my chair.

Though I felt certain J. J. Nails was going to attack the Dream Cruise tomorrow, I was totally clueless about when and how he'd do it. Since I was planning to be there to respond to whatever what down, I figured I might as well use the opportunity to ask La Borgia some pointed questions.

The cop whose name Nadine had given me had to be the person who'd tipped the porn king off to the fact I was investigating him. Which meant he was on La Borgia's payroll. But why had he then had the cop manipulate her into trying to seduce me back into our old relationship?

257

What was his game?

Shortly after La Borgia's call, Dawson called his four senior agents - me, Nardella, Wilson, and Norm Rasheed - into his conference room office.

"That Major de Coverly in CID finally got back to me with the classified file on Nails," he said when we'd all sat down.

"What did you find out?" I asked.

"A lot," he said. "As you'll recall, he got dishonorably discharged from the Army."

"Right," I said. "What next?"

"He came back to Ohio for a time. Worked in a small factory in Toledo for a few months, doing machine maintenance and welding. Then left the US and went to Sudan, in North Africa."

"North Africa?" Nardella said. "Wow. That's quite a geographic jump."

"Went to work there as a 'security specialist' for a company called Ardis International," Dawson said. "They're a UK-based firm that supplies private security services. Mostly to wealthy and powerful business and government figures in second and third world countries."

"In other words, you're saying he got a job as a mercenary," I said.

"You've got it," he said. "They probably liked that he had airborne and ranger training in the Army, and didn't care about the type of discharge he'd gotten. There are rumors that, in addition to supplying guard services, Ardis also had personnel who gave special ops training to Sudanese military and intelligence forces during the civil war there."

"Any idea what kind of special ops?" I asked.

"Allegedly, training in bomb, booby trap, and chemical weapon technologies."

"Hmm - why am I not surprised?" I said. "Bet that's where he picked up his expertise."

"At this point, a certain shady character started appearing in the background of Nails' activities," Eric went on. "A Vladimir Pavlovitch Simonenko."

"That's him," I said, sitting forward. "The Russki guy I was trying to remember. What else does CID have on him?"

"Apparently, this Simonenko character was a chemical engineer during Soviet times," Dawson said. "After the collapse of the Soviet Union in the early nineties, he formed a small company that supposedly was exporting industrial chemicals and small machinery parts. But then rumors surfaced that what he was really trafficking in were weapons and munitions from officers in the Soviet army - which at the time was basically collapsing from within. Nobody was getting paid for months and even years at a time, so a lot of officers were selling off any kind of military gear they could get their hands on to the highest bidder. Which in some cases was apparently this Simonenko. Who, by the way, also started using a pseudonym with his foreign customers, namely 'Simon Says.'"

"Cute," Wilson said. "'Simon says: buy these three thousand AK-47s from me.'"

"Anyways," Dawson went on. "There were unconfirmed reports from Sudan that Nails had somehow hooked up with Simonenko and that, in addition to his security duties, he was selling arms, explosives, and even chemical weapons to both sides in the Sudanese civil war."

"Playing both sides against the middle," I said. "Same as in Iraq."

"You've got it. After that, they're not sure if Nails got into some kind of hot water in Sudan with Ardis over his extracurricular activities, or if he just saw opportunity knocking, but in 2004 he turned up in Baghdad as a Blackwater Security employee."

"Our government's favorite private security provider," I said. "Back then, at least."

"Correct. So now Nails is in Iraq, guarding US diplomats and bigwigs in the new Iraqi government. First in Baghdad, then later in Al-Anbar province. But apparently, even though Blackwater was paying him somewhere between five hundred and a thousand bucks per day, he started doing his side business again, as a front man or middleman for Simon Says."

"And that's where I came in," I said.

"Exactly. Your Iraqi contact tells you what he's hearing about Nails selling weapons and explosives to different factions. You report it to CID. CID starts investigating and goes to Blackwater, who basically stonewall them, but say they'll check into it. Nails finds out he's in hot water, but he denies everything."

"And in the course of it," I said, "someone mentions my name to him. So he comes by my unit and tries to intimidate me."

"Right - although that's not in the case file. Apparently, you didn't report it."

"It was just a verbal threat," I said. "My being military and him civilian, I wasn't particularly worried about him doing anything."

"And chances are, nothing would've come of it, because neither Blackwater nor CID were ever able to substantiate the arms and explosives trafficking, so they eventually dropped it. But in the interim, something else happens."

"What's that?" I said.

"Apparently, one of the factions - a Shiite clan - gets wind that Nails sold a rival clan the weapons they used to kill the son of the family patriarch. So they start tailing him. They find out he frequents a certain prostitute in Fallujah. They set up a trap for him the next time he goes to see her. She takes him into this crummy little room. While he's on top of her they come in, grab him, tie him up and torture him for several hours. Cigarettes. Lighters. Electric drill."

"Damn," I said, shuddering. During my Iraq tour I'd seen a dozen or so post-mortem victims of torture. It was almost unimaginable what got done to them before they died.

"Then one of them inflicts what was probably supposed to be the coup de grace," Eric said.

"Which was?" I asked.

"Cut off his genitals," he said. "With a commando knife."

"Holy Minnie Mouse," Wilson said, shifting in his seat. "I hope you're going to spare us the details."

"And left him for dead," I said, frowning. Suddenly the genital-destroying booby traps at Al-Rafi's house and the IMAX made some kind of horrifying, vengeful sense.

"Exactly. Presumably they figured he'd bleed to death from the castration, so they didn't cut his throat. And he almost did. But somehow he managed to get free of his bonds and get out of there. An Army patrol spotted him on the street and rushed him to a hospital. They airlifted him to Germany and he spent two months in the hospital there."

"Did he go back to Iraq?" I asked.

"No," he said. "While he was there in the hospital Blackwater terminated his contract. But they - or their insurers - covered the medical costs. And apparently after a bunch of back and forth threatening, he got some kind of settlement out of them. CID doesn't know exactly how much, but thinks maybe a half million dollars."

"Enough to set up a nice little bomb factory, back in Detroit," I said.

"But why Detroit?" Rasheed asked.

"That's another element in his case file," Dawson added. "For some reason, Nails seems to have a pathological hatred for Detroit. Was constantly putting it down to his co-workers at Ardis and Blackwater. Nobody knows why, exactly."

"Hmm. We know he's from Toledo. Why would somebody from down there loathe Detroit?" I wondered aloud.

"Maybe cars give him gearshift envy," Wilson said. "Since he's lacking one."

"Here's the kicker, though," Dawson said. "Want to know the name of the guy who castrated Nails?"

"Sure," I said.

"Amir Sadiq Al-Rafi," he said.

"Al-Rafi?" I said. "A relative of our guy on Elmore Street?"

"He was his half-brother," he said.

"'Was'?"

"Dead. Assassinated in Fallujah a couple of months later, apparently by one of the other factions."

"How about the hooker?" I asked.

"Disappeared," he said. "Maybe dead. Maybe took the money she got for setting Nails up and ran."

"Did CID provide photos of him?" Nardella asked.

"They did and I've already got Mabel Partridge distributing them to the local media," Eric said. "They'll be in the Most Wanted galleries on all the Bureau sites and out on the national media within the hour. Meantime, check your emails. I sent you all a copy of the case file on Nails. Encrypted, of course. The photos are in with it."

"Well, all this explains a lot about where Nails is coming from," I said. "But unfortunately it doesn't tell us anything about what identity he's living under now, or where his hideout is."

"Wait a minute - you think he's still in the area?" Rasheed asked. "He got his money. Why wouldn't he just run? Get out of the country while the getting's good?"

"I suppose it's possible," I said. "But I don't think so. My gut tells me he's got something else up his sleeve."

"It's not up his trouser leg, that's for sure," Wilson said.

"Tomorrow's Dream Cruise day," Rasheed said. "You think he's going to try something there?"

"Even though he's never actually made any direct threats, I'll be very amazed if he doesn't," I said.

"Why?" said Nardella.

"Because of this weird hatred of Detroit he has. It'll be like striking right into the heart of the area. I think he's made no threats against the Cruise because he wants us to let our guard down."

"I agree, McCoy," Dawson said. "That's the other thing I wanted to go over in this meeting.

"First off," he said, leaning forward. "As soon as we wrap up here, I want you four to get the word out to all the other agents that everyone's on call tomorrow."

"Wait a minute. You mean I've got to work tomorrow?" Wilson said. "Dang. I was planning on doing the Cruise in my Gremlin."

"Go ahead and cruise," Eric said. "Just be sure to be armed and be available by phone if we need you to respond."

"You really have a Gremlin, Wilson?" Nardella asked.

"Sure," he said. "A lime-green '72. Traded my Pinto for it."

"Like McCoy said, even though Nails hasn't made any specific threats," Dawson went on, "I think there's a very high likelihood he'll try a bomb attack somewhere along the Cruise route."

"Any ideas about where?" Rasheed asked.

"Unfortunately not," Eric said. "We know that over the course of the day there'll be hundreds of thousands of people along Woodward, from around 9 Mile in Ferndale to 15 Mile - AKA Maple Road - up in Birmingham."

"Right," I said. "Even though the Cruise ostensibly runs all the way to Pontiac and back, there are generally a lot fewer people once you get past downtown Birmingham, so the chances of him doing something further north are fairly slim."

"That's still six miles or so of potential target area," Rasheed pointed out.

"Correct," Dawson said. "And as you know, there are several municipalities along the route. L. Sparks Cunningham has pushed for all of their police departments to have a more visible presence than normal this year."

"Plus they've got that that one-eight-hundred-I-gotcha number people can call," Nardella said.

"Great call name, by the way," Wilson deadpanned.

"Bottom line is this," Dawson concluded, "I want everyone from the field office either at or in close proximity to the Cruise throughout the day tomorrow. Be armed. Be available by phone or pager. And be ready to follow orders if there's an alert."

"Got you, Eric," I said as we all got up to leave.

"Damn it," Nardella groused out in the hallway. "I've got to go to Dream Cruise? I *hate* Dream Cruise."

"Aw, come on, Peaches," Wilson said. "What's there to hate?"

"The traffic. The noise. The fact that you can't hardly get from one side of town to the other," she said. "Not to mention the stink."

"The stink?" Wilson said. "You don't love the smell of all those pre-catalytic-converter engines, belching out mile after mile of noxious fumes? Heck, everyone along the route gets free tear gas endurance training."

"That reminds me," she said. "Where can I get a gas mask?"

"There's an army surplus store on Woodward south of 14 Mile that sells them," Wilson said. "Same place I get my Big Johnson t-shirts."

"Always wondered where you got those classy tees," I said.

"Hey Peaches," Wilson said. "Since you've got to go to the Cruise anyways, want to do it in my Gremlin? So to speak."

"I think I'll just find myself a nice bar on Woodward. Get drunk, depressed, have a crying jag, and then throw up," she said. "Has a lot more appeal."

"Your loss, Peaches," he said, shaking his head.

"Why don't you ask that Catholic girl your mom fixed you up with to go with you?" she said.

"She got all pissed off when I stood her up after the bus bombing," he said. "She thought taking her out to see 'Sex and the City, Part Deux' should've been a higher priority than those sixty-three dead people."

"How about you, Mojo?" he went on, turning my way. "Want to come along with me?"

"Sorry," I said. "I've already agreed to do the Dream Cruise with somebody."

"Really?" he said. "Got a hot date with that doctor lady?"

"I wish," I said with a sigh, wondering if I'd ever be able to fix things up with Oprah.

"Who is it, then?" he asked. "Anybody I know?"

"You know of him," I said. "Charming guy named William Fiorello La Borgia."

"Willie the Pimp?"

"That's him."

"What's his ride?" he asked.

"I don't know," I said. "I didn't ask."

"Bet it's not a Gremlin," Nardella said.

Chapter 42   Dream Cruise Day

Saturday, August 20 - 11:00 a.m.

LA BORGIA ARRIVED at my place at eleven o'clock sharp. I was standing on my porch when he pulled up in some kind of low-slung, incredibly sleek sedan. The red four-door glided up to the curb in front of my place, giving out a sound that was more like a far-off jet than an automobile.

I chuckled as I walked out to the car. Whatever it was, it was a beauty. He reached over and pushed open the passenger door for me as I came up to it.

"What the heck is this thing?" I asked as I climbed in.

"You've never seen a Fisker Karma before?" he said. He was in some kind of expensive-looking black linen shorts and shirt casual outfit that made Tommy Bahama's stuff look cheap and tawdry.

"Strangely enough, no," I said. "Pretty much everyone I know drives government Fords or Chevys."

"Then you're in for a treat," he said as we pulled away.

During my investigation I'd once driven by the huge, stone-walled mansion La Borgia lives in up in the wealthy Cranbrook area. I wondered what may've been going through his mind as we left behind what, in comparison to his palatial digs, must look like a squalid dump.

"The Karma's a four-hundred-horsepower hybrid," he told me. "Powered by dual electric motors and a supercharged gasoline engine. There's a solar panel in the roof that provides some of the interior cooling energy, and the wood you see there in the dash is reconstituted from trees burnt up in forest fires. It's one of most environmentally conscious cars on the road today."

"And costs more than a few dimes, I imagine," I said, gazing around at the two-tone leather interior, which was as beautifully designed as the car's outside.

"They start around a hundred K," he said. "Pretty soon you'll see all your Hollywood actor types in their Priuses getting one of these babies."

"Bully for them," I said. "Got to do something with those millions, I guess."

It was about five miles from my place to Woodward and traffic was heavy when we turned onto Southfield Road. It was a bright, sunny day and the temperature was already in the high eighties, but it was comfortably cool inside the luxurious Karma. Mixed in with the everyday cars around us were a metallic-orange '64 Pontiac GTO, a cherry-red '32 Ford hot rod with a giant, all-chromed hemi engine, and a sleek yellow Chrysler Prowler pulling a matching trailer. All were certainly striking cars in their own right, but the Fisker was drawing the longest and most open-mouthed stares.

"Right now we're in what they call stealth mode," La Borgia told me. "We're running all electric. The motors are actually so quiet you can't hear the car coming. That jet plane sound you're hearing is artificial. It comes from audio generators built into the front and rear bumpers to warn pedestrians."

I was just starting to get used to the gawking and finger-pointing when La Borgia said something then that threw me for a loop.

"Want to know the real reason I've been volunteering to help find the bombers?" he asked.

I turned to him, my brow furrowing. He had an odd look on his face. "Sure," I said.

"It started the day of the Campus Martius bus bombing," he began. "I was at a fundraising cocktail party up at the Cranbrook schools, in the old Booth family mansion. I was with a lady friend - a gorgeous, old-money debutante named Missy Fairchild.

"Anyways, a bit after 5 p.m. people there started getting word about the bus bombing downtown. Everybody agreed it was awful news, but it was unknown people and miles away, you know?

"Then I got a phone call from my mother. She told me my godfather and godmother, Vinnie and Rosie Bommarito, were in a car near the bus when it blew up. Rosie was dead and Vinnie was hanging on by a thread, with third-degree burns on over ninety percent of his body.

"I left Missy there and shot out of the party. On my way out I called my pilot and had him meet me at the airport in Troy. He flew my private copter down to the Detroit Medical Center. I rushed in and found some of my family there, along with a bunch of Vinnie and Rosie's friends and relatives. They told me what they knew about what had happened.

"Vinnie and Rosie were downtown at one of the casinos that day - the MGM Grand. They were in that red Lincoln Navigator of his, on their way home, when they got a few cars behind that bus on Woodward. The blast blew in the windshield, which pretty much tore off Rosie's head, and set fire to the car. Vinnie was severely injured himself, but then got burnt up even worse when he insisted on trying to pull Rosie's body out of the burning wreckage."

I listened in silence. La Borgia's story was bringing back the whole appalling scene I'd witnessed at Campus Martius just five days before.

"After a few minutes of waiting outside the ER, the doctor came out to us - a lovely black lady," he went on.

"Wait a minute," I said. "Not Dr. Oprah Cummings, was it?"

"Yeah, that was her name. You know her?"

"Sort of. Go on," I said.

"She told us straight out Vinnie wasn't going to make it and let us go in to pay our respects. Vinnie was completely wrapped up bandages, like a mummy. His eyes were gone and his lips were charred black. But when we told him we were there, he asked for me. Had me wave the other people in the room away from the bed and told me to lean close to him, because it was hard to speak.

"Billy, he said, his voice all raspy - like he hardly had any lungs left. All my life, I ever ask you for anything?"

"I'm standing there crying, you understand? Because Vinnie and Rosie, they've been like a second father and mother to me all my life, ever since I was a baby."

"No, Vinnie, I said to him. Not one thing. All you and Rosie ever did was give to me."

"Well, I'm asking you for one thing now, *bambino*. Just one thing, he said."

"You got it, Vinnie, I said. What do you want from me?"

"Kill them, Billy, he whispered. Kill the rotten sonofabitches who did this to me and my Rosie. Swear to me on my grave you'll do it, he said."

"I was shocked, Johnson. Jesus, Vinnie, I said. You know I've never killed anybody."

"Doesn't matter, Billy, he said to me. I ain't no killer, either. Not by nature. But I done what I had to. What certain people asked me to do, I did it. You understand me, Billy?"

"Yeah, Vinnie, I think I do."

"Then swear it to me, *bambino*, he said. Swear you'll kill the sonofabitches."

"I looked at that bandaged-up old man. At the dying request coming out of his burnt-up lips. And what do you think I told him?" La Borgia said.

There was a pause. "I think I can guess," I said.

I'd been listening to his story pretty raptly, but in the meantime my eyes had drifted to the small planes crisscrossing the sky east of us. They were towing hundred yard-long banners advertising local car dealerships. I was idly watching this one plane, which looked as if it could be flying directly over Woodward Avenue, when my stomach did a sudden flip-flop.

"Sweet Jesus in the morning!" I said as I recalled Nails' taunting phone call.

"*...while I commit mass murder and fly away free as a bird.*"

La Borgia turned to me with a frown. "What's the matter?"

"Mr. La Borgia, you just might get a chance to make good on your promise," I said, my voice tight.

"What are you talking about?"

"I think I just realized how Nails is going to attack the Dream Cruise crowd."

"How?"

I pointed at the planes trailing their banners.

"An airplane?" he said. "You think he'll drop bombs on the crowd?"

"Could be," I said, my mind racing. "But more likely he'll use some kind of chemical or biological agent. It'll be lot easier and safer than trying to haul a load of armed bombs. Where's the nearest airport to the Cruise?"

"Oakland-Troy. That's where my private jet and helicopter are."

"We've got to stop him - hopefully before he can get into the air," I said. "We need to get to that airport fast!"

The mafia porn king laughed. "Fast?" he said. "Watch this."

Chapter 43   Wild Ride

Saturday, August 20 - 11:10 a.m.

LA BORGIA TROMPED down on the accelerator pedal and we shot forward. The jet-plane sound got louder, but it was still eerily quiet inside the Karma.

"By the way," he said as we began to weave through the heavy traffic en route to the Cruise. "We're still in all-electric mode. When I kick in the gas engine you'll think you're in a rocket."

"Listen," I said. "You'd better call your copter pilot. Have him meet us there."

"Right," he said. He had an iPhone plugged into the console, in hands-free speaker mode. Steering with one hand now, he punched a couple of icons, slid his fingertip down and punched again. A couple of moments later I could hear a phone ringing.

"This is Jeff," a groggy, hungover voice answered.

"Goolsby? It's Bill La Borgia. I need you to be at the Troy airport in fifteen minutes."

"What do you mean, boss? It's a thirty minute drive from my place."

"I know it's a thirty-minute drive, dickhead," he growled. "That's why you better get your butt moving. By the way, what's that slurping sound?"

"I don't know," Goolsby said. "Can't remember her name. Can barely remember mine."

"Well, tell her to give it a rest and get your lame ass out of bed," La Borgia snarled, now in full Tony Soprano mode. "This is a frigging life or death situation. By which I mean yours, you understand?"

There was a faint popping sound over the phone's speaker.

"Okay, boss!" Goolsby said. "Don't get riled! I'll be there!"

"Good. See you there in fourteen and half minutes."

He reached out and ended the call.

"Your pilot sounds pretty hung over. Not to mention preoccupied," I said.

"No doubt. He was out hunting Dream Cruise babes last night. Sounds like he found one."

We were shooting around a parakeet-yellow Seventies-vintage El Camino on giant chrome wheels. "Do we really want some sleepy, half-sloshed pilot flying us over the Dream Cruise?" I asked.

La Borgia shrugged. "Do we have a choice?"

The Fisker continued to draw plenty of open-mouthed stares while we whooshed through the heavy traffic - especially since La Borgia was now doing twenty-five miles an hour over the limit and sliding in and out between cars like a madman.

It remained uncannily hushed inside the hybrid as we ping-ponged through the exotic mélange of vehicles that were making their way toward Woodward and the Dream Cruise. The muted hum of the speeding Karma seemed to arouse some kind of hormonal reaction from the drivers of the hot rods and muscle cars. After we'd blown past them, several roared off in hot pursuit, fat tires squealing, their chrome headers blasting out waves of ear-splitting noise and clouds of gray-blue exhaust smoke as they pulled up alongside and fingered us.

"You don't seem too popular with these guys," I observed.

"Ignorant troglodytes," La Borgia scoffed as he continued to weave in and out of traffic. "I spit on them and their gas-guzzling dinosaurs."

I checked my watch.

"Christ," I said. "Time's getting short. I hope your pilot's there when we arrive."

"Don't worry about Jeff. He'll be there. I just hope you're right about this being Nails' plan."

"It's got to be. The Dream Cruise runs for miles. There could be a half-million Cruisers and spectators along the route from 9 Mile up to 15 Mile right now. With that huge crowd on and alongside Woodward, it'll be the most effective way to slaughter masses of people. From up in the air, all he'll need is some crop-dusting gear. He'll be able to swoop down and in a few minutes drop gas, chemicals, or biological agents on several miles worth of victims. A potential holocaust if we don't stop the sick bastard."

"What's with this crazy son of a bitch, anyways?" La Borgia asked. "He got his money. Why does he want to attack the Dream Cruise crowd?"

"For some unknown reason, Nails despises Detroit," I said. "The Cruise is a celebration of the city's history and auto culture. My guess is he feels committing mass murder at the Dream Cruise will break the city's heart. Maybe even destroy it, once and for all."

We'd just run the stoplight at Southfield and 14 Mile Road when I heard a siren behind us. I turned around in the luxurious leather seat and saw flashing multicolored lights.

"Crap," I said. "We've got the Birmingham police on our tail."

"Shall we stop and explain to them?" he asked.

"No time," I said.

"Can you call that one-eight-hundred-I-gotcha number?" he said. "Maybe they can get them to escort us."

"I'll try," I said. "In the meantime, do you think you can outrun them?"

"Is the pope Catholic?" he said with a nasty laugh.

I punched in the number. After a few seconds a gravel-voiced woman answered.

"One eight hundred, I gotcha," she said.

"This is Special Agent McCoy Johnson of the FBI," I told her. "I need to speak to the Birmingham Chief of Police immediately. It's a matter of life and death."

"Is this about the Dream Cruise?" she rasped.

"Yes," I said. "Listen, this is no joke. I need to speak to the Birmingham Chief of Police. Chief Bradley, I believe his name his. Immediately."

"All right sir, I'll try to contact him. Can I have your callback number?"

I gave her my cell number and put as much urgency into my voice as possible. "Please understand, ma'am - this is matter of *mass* life or death. I need to speak him ASAP, got it? Thank you," I said and hung up.

"Where's a cop when you need one, eh, Johnson?" La Borgia snickered.

We were on a stretch of Southfield where it becomes a two-lane, with a twenty-five mile-an-hour speed limit. There was a line of cars backed up and La Borgia began whipping in and out of the opposite lane to get past them. When I looked back, I saw the Birmingham patrol car doing the same. We'd just made a screeching right onto Lincoln Street, the police siren howling behind us, when my cell rang.

"Chief Bradley?" I snapped into the phone.

"Johnson? Agent Johnson?" he said.

"Yes, sir. You remember me from the meeting at Beaubien?"

"I remember. What the hell's going on?"

"I'm in a Fisker Karma luxury sedan that's just turned from Southfield onto Lincoln Street in Birmingham. We're violating some speed limits because we're on our way to Oakland-Troy Airport to try to prevent a mass murder. There's a Birmingham police cruiser pursuing us. Can you send a broadcast to all your cruisers to cease pursuit? And if possible, maybe escort us there?"

"Have you gone nuts, Johnson?" he asked.

"No, sir. It's J. J. Nails."

"The dirtbag who's done all the bombings?" Fortunately, the chief knew the name immediately, thanks to Nails' name and photo being all over the media for the past twenty hours.

"Yes sir. I believe he's going to drop some kind of poison gas or chemicals on the Dream Cruise crowd."

"Holy Christ!" he said. "You're not kidding, are you?"

"No sir. So can you get that message out to all your men? And maybe the Troy police also?"

"I'll get on it immediately. What's the vehicle you're in again?"

"A red Fisker Karma. Registered to a William La Borgia."

"Wait a minute - Willie the Pimp? What the hell are you doing with him?"

"I'll explain later, Chief. Can you just get that message out?"

"All right, Johnson. But this whole thing better not be bullshit!"

"Thanks, Chief. Talk to you later," I said and hung up.

"He's agreed," I told La Borgia. "Hopefully he'll get the message out quick. And hopefully they haven't already set up a roadblock to stop us."

"Don't worry. I'll get around them somehow. I've driven formula race cars, you know."

"Really? Ever win one? Or even finish?"

"No," he laughed. "I crashed every time."

"Excellent," I said. "That's great news."

"I have a tendency to be a little too aggressive when I'm cornering."

"This thing have a roll bar?"

"Hmm - good question. I know it has that solar panel integrated into the roof, but I never thought to ask about a roll bar."

By now we were fast approaching the Woodward intersection. La Borgia was continuing to shoot in and out between the traffic, accelerating wildly whenever he could. I saw the speedometer hit seventy a couple of times on the twenty-five mile-an-hour residential street. Behind us the police cruiser's siren was still whooping, and I could hear them commanding us to stop through their built-in bullhorn.

"How are we going to get across Woodward?" I said. "Traffic going directly through the intersection will be blocked. "

"We'll turn right onto Woodward, blow through the Cruisers over to the turnaround, and head north. Then blow through them again so we can turn onto 15 Mile."

Ahead of us I could see eight lanes worth of colorful cars on Woodward, one rank moving north and one south. As we'd gotten nearer the cumulative grumbling of the Cruisers' engines had gotten so loud it was penetrating even the Fisker's excellent soundproofing. Alongside us the sidewalks were crowded with summer-clothed pedestrians and further up you could see that spectators were jammed solid along Woodward itself.

"Hang on!" the porn king said as we barreled up to the intersection.

With La Borgia blasting his horn, we took the turn onto Woodward in a terrifying power slide. A couple of hot babes in skimpy Daisy Duke jean shorts, tank tops, and straw cowboy hats were in the crosswalk just then, swaying their pert bottoms as the Cruisers slowed down to leer at them. They shrieked and flung their Evian water bottles up into the air as we slid between them, tires screeching like banshees.

With a bevy of horns honking at us, the Fisker shot across the four lanes toward the turnaround. I twisted around in my seat. The crosswalk babes were shrieking again, hightailing it to the median in their sexy platform shoes to avoid the Birmingham police cruiser that was squealing around the corner after us.

We then got stuck at the turnaround's stop sign. There was an impenetrable wall of Cruisers going by, dominated by a bunch of those chrome-laden, huge-finned babies from the late Fifties and early Sixties that made you wonder what they were putting in the drinking water back then. Despite the urgency I was feeling, I couldn't help but stare in awe as a monstrous pink-and-white '59 Cadillac Coupe DeVille rumbled by, followed by a dark blue '63 Lincoln Continental with painted flames shooting out of its front wheel wells - both looking as if they could've been designed by Salvador Dali.

La Borgia, meanwhile, had dropped the Fisker's transmission into neutral and was gunning the engine as he waited for an opening in the traffic.

"Come on, you dumbshit boomer swine!" he growled.

"You'll never get through," I yelled. "There's too damn many of them!"

The Birmingham police cruiser had meanwhile screeched to a halt behind us in the turnaround.

"Come out with your hands in the air!" they demanded over the cruiser's bullhorn. The two cops got out but stayed behind their doors, guns drawn. Obviously, Chief Bradley's message hadn't gotten out to them yet.

"Screw this! I'm gonna make an opening! Hang on, Johnson!" La Borgia yelled as he floored the twin electric engines and yanked the transmission into gear.

Clouds of grayish-white smoke billowed out from the Fisker's front wheel wells as we fishtailed into the wall of northbound traffic.

A pandemonium of fifty different horn-blasts erupted all around us. Tires shrieked as cars slammed on the brakes. I heard the sickening, telltale crunch of metal on metal as several Cruise cars got rear-ended.

La Borgia was blasting his horn, whipping the steering wheel back and forth while he ploughed between the outraged and horrified Cruisers. Framed in their windows, red-faced, apoplectic boomers were cursing at us, fear and loathing flashing from their rheumy, bulging eyes. I hoped none of them were armed.

La Borgia, meanwhile, was responding in kind.

"*Stronzi! Vaffanculo, pezzo di merda!*" he yelled, blasting his horn as he forced our way between the raging Cruisers. "*Testa di cazzo!*"

I didn't need an Italian translator to know he wasn't begging their pardon.

We finally managed to get through to the far lane, but now found there was a solid line of cars between us and 15 Mile Road.

I looked back and saw the police cruiser had turned onto northbound Woodward as well, with the Cruisers respectfully stopping for its rainbow of flashing lights. I also saw two more black police cars weaving their way towards us a bit further back.

"The hell with this - I'm taking a side street!" La Borgia said as he abruptly yanked the steering wheel and made a hard right.

Moments later we were whooshing down a residential block. I glanced over at the speedometer and my belly clenched as I saw it approaching seventy. The side street was lined with parked cars. If anyone stepped out between them, God forbid, they were doomed. I saw that the Karma's horn was a button on the steering wheel. La Borgia was mashing it down with his thumb as we streaked down the street, ignoring the intersection stop signs and blowing right through them.

Somehow we got to Adams Road without killing anyone, and I'd just started to breathe again when he slammed the transmission into low gear and power-slid into the two-lane road's northbound lane. Tires shrieked as the red, mint-condition '29 Ford Model A we'd cut off jammed on its brakes and got rear-ended by an aqua-blue '57 Olds station wagon. I could hear their furious curses as we sped away.

"Those people are going to beat us to death with their tire irons," I said, looking back over my shoulder.

"Until they find out we've saved untold thousands of people from an agonizing death. Then they'll love us," he said

I shook my head. "You don't know car lovers."

"What's our time frame look like?" he asked.

I checked my watch. "Bad," I said. "Can you go any faster?"

"You're going to wish you hadn't said that," he snickered, reaching for the console lever and shifting it to one side. The eerie whoosh was immediately replaced by an angry, torquing rumble as the supercharged gasoline engine kicked in.

"This is called turbo mode," he said and stomped on the gas pedal.

With an unseemly roar for such an elegant sedan, the Fisker shot forward, pushing us back into the opulently-padded leather seats with what felt like the g-force of a jet plane.

After a squealing right turn against the light at 15 Mile, we left behind the cacophony of horns blaring at us and barreled down toward Coolidge

Highway. We shot past a baby-blue '55 Ford Crown Victoria, our speed apparently unnerving the driver to the point where he went off the road. I glanced back and saw him bounce up over the curb and hit a fire hydrant, sending a geyser of water fifty feet into the air. At Coolidge we made another two-wheeled right turn and roared our way toward Industrial Drive, where Oakland-Troy airport is located.

It was when we came screaming around a curve that we saw the barricade. A hundred yards ahead, the airport intersection was blocked by a solid wall of police cars parked across the road. At least twenty cops were standing in front of the cars, service weapons at the ready. Several, I noticed, were brandishing Remington 870 12-gauge shotguns.

"We're screwed," I said.

"*Mama-frigging-mia!*" La Borgia said as he stomped on the brakes.

The hybrid's front end dipped down hard and we went into screeching slide that flung me painfully against my seatbelt. The insane speed we'd been traveling at made it highly questionable we'd be able to stop in time.

The shriek of the Fisker's fat tires was ear-splitting as we slid closer and closer to the waiting rank of police. I could see the whites of their adrenaline-widened eyes as, in unison, almost two dozen terrified cops raised their gun barrels and aimed them straight at our horrorstruck faces.

Chapter 44   Goolsby

Saturday, August 20 - 11:30 a.m.

"*DAMN*, THAT was close," I said as La Borgia whipped the Fisker into his reserved airport parking slot.

"I'll say," he said, gazing up in the rearview mirror at the two departing Troy Police cruisers that had escorted us in. "Good thing that Chief Bradley got through to them."

After pulling the key out of the ignition, he leaned over in front of me and popped open the glovebox. Then he reached inside and yanked out a fancy designer-looking leather holster with a handgun in it.

"What the hell is that, Mr. La Borgia?"

"It's a Model Thirty-Eight Glock - forty-five caliber. Want to see my CCW permit, Agent?"

"You know how to use it?"

He gave a snarky chuckle as he reached over to the glovebox again and pulled out a couple of loaded ammunition clips. "I've had lessons."

We got out of the Fisker and began looking around for his pilot.

"Where the hell is that a-hole?" he fumed.

"What's this guy's name again?"

"Goolsby. Jeff Goolsby. He's been my pilot for the past four years. Wait a minute - I think I see him coming now."

Escorted front and rear by a pair of police cruisers, a brand new but badly scraped and crumpled gray Mercedes-Benz sedan came roaring through the gates and into the parking lot. It sounded as if it had lost its muffler system. The driver brought the car to a screeching halt in the parking slot behind us.

"Hey, bossh," he called to La Borgia in a slurred voice as he clambered out. "How the hell are you, buddy?"

He lurched toward us, clutching a plastic bottle of spring water.

"What happened to your car?" La Borgia asked.

"A buncha slow fugs got in my way," he said, blinking. "Lost the mufflers when I did some off-roading."

He leaned closer to La Borgia.

"Who's the narc?" he added under his breath, eyeing me suspiciously. Up close the fumes he was giving off smelled about 90 proof.

"Jeff, this is Agent Johnson. He's with the FBI. McCoy - my pilot, Jeff Goolsby."

We nodded warily at each other.

He was a big guy. Fortyish, with thinning, sandy-brown hair. He looked badly hung over and was smacking his lips as if to get the sourness out. There was a hint of derangement in his drooping eyes that made we wonder if he'd not only been drinking but maybe smoking crack as well.

But I didn't have time to worry about Goolsby's fitness for flying. I looked up at the sky to the west of us and could see a number of small planes flying in long, lazy ovals, up and down the length of the Dream Cruise. Behind them trailed their huge Ford, GM, and Chrysler dealership banners.

"How're we going to know which plane is our guy's?" La Borgia asked.

"I don't know, damn it," I admitted.

Just then we heard the buzzy roar of an airplane engine. We turned toward the runway and saw that another small prop plane was taking off. It had a yellow and white fuselage and the number 47 on its tail. There was a big aluminum tank under its belly and what looked like a set of chrome pipes stretching along its wings - crop-dusting gear.

As it sped down the runway, I saw that the plane was trailing one of the long advertising banners. When the tail came up off the concrete, the banner began to unfurl behind it. A few moments later the wheels left the ground. By the time the plane arced up over the trees at the end of the runway you could read the text on the rippling banner.

GOODBYE DETROIT! it said.

La Borgia and I looked at each other and nodded in unison. Dimes to donuts that was Nails, alright.

"Let's go!" La Borgia said, and the three of us began jogging toward a row of hangars.

"How fast can we get off the ground?" I asked Goolsby as we ran.

"Under five minutes if we move like hell," he said.

I checked my watch. It was 11:45 a.m.

Glancing back over my shoulder, I saw that the plane with the *Goodbye Detroit!* banner wafting out behind it had turned north. Was he going to fly north to south?

"Which way is the prevailing wind today?" I called over to Goolsby.

"Northwest to southeast," he said. "I checked the weather app on my Android on the way here."

"He'll have checked too," I said. "I wonder why he's heading north. He'll get better dispersal if he goes south to north."

"Dispersal of what?" Goolsby asked, weaving a bit as he ran.

"Poison gas or a biological weapon. We think this freak's going to attack the Dream Cruise," La Borgia said.

"Really? Holy shit," Goolsby said. "Well, my guess is the control tower must've told him to head north on takeoff due to the other air traffic today. Chances are he'll make a U and head back south to 8 or 9 Mile. Then U again and come up Woodward."

"Will you have to do the same thing in the copter?"

"No. We fly in completely different air corridors from the planes. We can go due south on takeoff."

"Good. That may buy us a couple of minutes to help catch up with him," I said.

After passing four big open hangar doors, we cut into the fifth.

La Borgia's helicopter was a metallic black Hughes MD 500. I was familiar with the model from earlier Bureau jobs. Classified as a light utility copter, it was small, fast, and highly maneuverable - in the hands of an alert, sober pilot, at least.

"We'll need to pull it outside," La Borgia said. "Jeff, you get in and get started on your takeoff routine. Johnson and I will haul it out of here."

"Check," Goolsby said.

Looking as if the run had made him dizzy, the pilot clambered up into the copter. La Borgia and I grabbed the handle of a big pneumatic device used for lifting and towing the chopper, which had skids instead of wheels. The two of us dragged the black helicopter out of the hangar and onto the concrete apron in front of it. When it was clear, La Borgia twisted a valve on the lift and the chopper's landing skids dropped down onto the pavement.

We pulled the lift free, dragged it back inside the hangar's entrance, and then ran back to the helicopter.

The copter's rotor blades were just beginning to give out a squealy metallic whine as we climbed into one of the passenger doors, sat down in the compartment, and buckled ourselves in. There was an open passageway between the passenger and cockpit areas. Goolsby had put on a radio headset and was muttering gruffly into its mike while he flipped a series of toggle switches on the control panel. Soon the rotor blades were a blur and the engine roar was deafening.

"Let's hit it, Jeff!" La Borgia said, smacking the wall of the passageway.

Goolsby, who just then was pressing his bottle of spring water to his forehead, turned and gave us a bleary look. Placing the water in a cup holder, he gripped the copter's joystick.

"Hang on to your stomachs, gents," he said, looking rather queasy himself.

He pushed the joystick forward and we lurched up into the air, thirty feet over the concrete apron. The movement made my breakfast climb halfway back up my gullet. Then we shot up and away at a forty-five-degree angle. Fortunately, my stomach seemed to settle as we gained altitude and I watched the row of hangars shrink away below us.

La Borgia reached over and poked me.

"What's our plan for stopping this guy, by the way?" he said over the choppy roar of the helicopter blades.

In answer, I opened the windbreaker I was wearing, slid the Springfield out of my underarm holster and checked its load.

With a grim smile on his face, La Borgia pulled his Glock out of its fancy holster and jammed a clip of ammo into it.

"Here's to you, Vinnie," he said, staring at the loaded pistol in his hand.

Chapter 45   A Slight Problem

Saturday, August 20 - 11:49 a.m.

WE HEADED south and west from the Troy airport. As we got closer to Woodward, I could see the vast lines of multicolored Dream Cruise cars moving up and down several miles of its eight median-separated lanes. Alongside the broad boulevard stretched a massive horde of spectators. It was estimated that a million people would show up over the course of the day, and it looked as if at least half that many were down there right then. In addition to the several thousand cars that were actively cruising, there were thousands more parked in the innumerable strip mall lots along the roadway. The majority, I knew, would have their hoods open, proudly displaying the chrome-plated components of their oversized engines to the crowd of admirers wandering along the sidelines.

What I couldn't see, however, was Nails' plane. In the course of our take-off, I'd completely lost track of it and hadn't yet been able to spot it again.

"Where is he?" I yelled, twisting around in my seat to scan as much of the sky as I could see through the passenger window.

"Who?" Goolsby called back from the cockpit.

"Nails - the guy with the *Goodbye Detroit!* banner," La Borgia told him.

"Over there," the pilot said. "At about two o'clock."

Leaning forward and sticking our heads into the passageway, La Borgia and I looked up to where Goolsby was pointing.

The yellow and white plane was above and to the west of us, trailing its sarcastic message. I wondered what the people in the crowd below were making of the sign. Probably figured it was somebody who was leaving town and bidding a last fond farewell. Little did they know what the psychotic dirtbag actually had in store for them.

We weren't far from the intersection of 12 Mile and Woodward now. Below us I could see the Shrine of the Little Flower's steeple pointing skyward, looking even more phallic from the air than it did from ground level. To the south of us, the jutting shapes of the Ren Cen, Penobscot Building, and Detroit's other downtown skyscrapers shone bright under the hot midday sun.

Goolsby turned his head to call back to us.

"What're you going to do when we catch up to this guy?" he asked.

"Shoot him down," La Borgia said.

For the first time since he'd shown up, I saw Goolsby crack a smile.

"Awesome," he said.

I leaned forward and spoke to both of them.

"What he'll likely do is make a turnaround, once he gets below 9 Mile Road. He'll come down low, to where he's just a couple of hundred feet over Woodward. Then he'll start releasing whatever chemical or poison he's carrying over the crowd. We'll need to get close enough to where we can get a clear shot at him in his cockpit. Will you be able to get a little bit ahead of him and stay there, Jeff?"

"Assuming he doesn't take some kind of evasive action, sure," Goolsby said.

"Good. Then just keep tracking him. When he makes his turnaround, move in close and try to stay parallel with him."

"Gotcha," he said.

"Meanwhile," I said to La Borgia. "I'm going to call the police again and see if they can't get people to evacuate away from Woodward."

I leaned toward the passenger window and watched Nails' yellow and white plane while I dialed one eight hundred I gotcha again.

"This is Agent McCoy Johnson of the FBI," I said when the operator answered. "I need to speak to the Ferndale police chief immediately. It's life-or-death urgent."

"Yes, sir," the operator said. "I think I can get him for you pretty quickly. Can you hold while I try?"

"I'll hold," I said.

As I was waiting for chief to come on, I noticed an unsettling change in the tone of the helicopter's rotors and engine.

"Aw, shit!" I heard Goolsby say.

I put my hand over the cell phone mouthpiece. "What's the problem?" I said.

"In all the damn rush, I forgot to fuel up before we took off," he said.

"We're running out of gas."

"WHAT?" La Borgia bellowed. "You FORGOT TO GAS UP? Do I pay you to be a frigging numbskull!"

La Borgia began waving his Glock around in a way that made me extremely nervous. When he undid his seatbelt and looked as if he was going to climb into the cockpit to either blow or beat Goolsby's brains out, I grabbed his arm and pulled him back.

"Chill out, boss," the pilot said. "I just need to cut over to the emergency supply."

I wasn't sure if I found the lackadaisical way he said it reassuring or terrifying. But what I was sure about was that I could now hear the engine sputtering. The rapid *whump-whump-whump* of the copters' rotor blades had become an erratic *whump-budda-whump-budda-whump* and the fuselage was starting to shudder ominously.

"Now don't freak out or anything," Goolsby called back to us. "I'm going to cut power for a second while I switch over to the backup fuel tank. We'll lose a little altitude."

All at once the engine sound cut out completely. The propeller blades continued to chop away above us, but the copter began dropping like a stone. The breakfast that had come halfway up my gullet on takeoff made it all the way up to my throat this time.

But it was worse for La Borgia. Having undone his seatbelt, he flew up out of his chair and cracked his head hard against the copter's ceiling. "*FOTTI TUA MADRE!*" he yelled. Unfortunately, he also accidentally hit the door latch on his way down and the door next to him flew wide open.

"*FIGLIO DI PUTTANA!*" he screamed as the helicopter rolled a bit and he started to tumble out. I reached for the nearest part of him I could grab, which just happened to be his face. He screamed into my clasping hand, still waving his Glock around dangerously as I yanked him back into his seat.

"BUCKLE UP!" I screamed at him, releasing his face. The chopper was still dropping like a lead balloon.

"DAMN YOU, JOHNSON!" he screamed back at me, tucking his Glock into an armpit as he frantically latched himself into his seat.

"Excuse me, sir?" I heard on my cell phone. It was the operator.

"Yes?" I said.

"Is anything wrong?" she asked.

I glanced out the window. We were plummeting toward a residential area of Royal Oak, the copter's fuselage spinning and lurching as we went down.

"No!" I said. "Things are wonderful! Couldn't possibly be any better! Is the chief there yet?"

"I'm afraid not, sir. But I'm expecting him any moment now. Can you continue to hold?"

Apparently the cutover to the emergency fuel tank was successful, because at just that instant the engine roared back to life and almost immediately we stopped dropping.

I gave a deep sight of relief. "I'll hold," I said.

I looked over at La Borgia and saw his expression was now an unholy mix of rage, terror, and severe gastric distress. I put my hand over the receiver.

"By the way, Mr. La Borgia?" I said.

"What?" he snarled.

"I just wanted to tell you how glad I am I took you up on your offer to help. The resources you've provided today have been truly invaluable."

He glared at me. "Screw you, Johnson!" he said.

But after a few moments of watching me smirk back at him, the anger on La Borgia's face dissolved into a broad grin of the shit-eating variety. He began to laugh - a deep infectious braying that soon had me laughing as well.

I saw Goolsby turn his head and look back at us as if we'd gone crazy. "Care to let me in on the joke?" he said.

For some reason that caused both La Borgia and me to completely lose it. We sat there, collapsed in our seats, cackling helplessly. Laughing so hard we were crying.

"Sir?" I heard on the cell phone. It was the operator again.

"Yes?" I managed to squeak into the phone between guffaws.

"Are you sure nothing's wrong?"

That set me off on another laughing jag, which La Borgia echoed.

Finally, the Ferndale police chief came on. Though still short of breath, I managed to get out my suggestion about evacuating along Woodward. He said he'd see what he could do.

When I finished the call, La Borgia was just about done wiping the tears from his eyes. He looked at me.

"Okay, *paisano* - countryman," he said. "Enough fun and games. Let's go stop this crazy, rotten son of a bitch."

"Amen," I said.

La Borgia then slapped the wall of the cockpit passageway.

"Hit it, Jeff," he said. "Catch up to that worthless piece of dog crap!"

"Gotcha, boss," the pilot replied.

I'm not sure what Goolsby did then, but it was as if he'd turned on some kind of afterburner. Suddenly the copter was screaming over the giant crowd of people and grumbling mass of cars below. Up ahead, near 8 Mile and Woodward, I could see the yellow and white plane trailing the *Goodbye Detroit!* banner making its turn.

Glancing down at the loaded Springfield in my hand, I felt a stab of doubt go through me. Would we really be able to stop Nails' deadly plane with just a pair of handguns?

The truth was, I had no idea.

Chapter 46   Hydrogen Cyanide

Saturday, August 20 - 11:55 a.m.

HE'S APPROACHING 8 Mile now, the plane's wings angling about thirty-five degrees as he makes his turn. He continues through his U until the Cessna is headed north. Then he adjusts his flight path a bit so that he's centered directly over the broad boulevard below.

He glances at the red duffel bag strapped into the co-pilot seat beside him. He could have left it back at the compound, since he's planning to return there later - after he's turned the Dream Cruise into a frigging holocaust - but it feels good having the money with him. The visible proof of the Master Plan's success, right here alongside him.

He notices there's a small black helicopter heading his way from the northeast, but it doesn't concern him. Probably just a news crew or some rich businessman, taking his drunken pals up for a sky-high spin over the Douche Cruise.

A smile crosses his face as his icy blue eyes take in the kaleidoscopically-colored stream of cars stretching out for miles below him. Even up here at two thousand feet the sound of their massed engines is a steady, grumbling roar. His plan is to begin dumping the hydrogen cyanide cocktail over downtown Ferndale, at Woodward and 9 Mile. That's when he'll get the first big crowd of Cruise bystanders.

They'll be gathered all along the downtown sidewalks, sitting in the lawn chairs they've brought along or standing there talking. Pointing out all the passing cars that catch their fancy as they sip at their soft drinks, beer, or spring water under the hot August sun. There may even be a bunch of them out on the grassy median that separates the north and southbound lanes, if the Ferndale cops don't chase them away.

Ever since completing the turnaround, he's been gradually dropping lower. His target altitude is to be a mere hundred feet over the road when he releases the spray. The nozzles sending out a shower of blue liquid which, on contact with the air, will immediately disperse into a cloud of bluish-white droplets as it descends on the onlookers.

At that height the Cessna's engine noise will have them all looking upward. Mouths gaping in astonishment, they'll see the plane shoot overhead, some of them holding their hands over their ears to lessen the powerful engine roar. As it thunders past trailing its long banner, they'll notice the cloud descending on them, no doubt thinking at first that it's simply exhaust fumes.

When the acrid mist reaches street level, their eyes will begin to burn. A metallic taste and smell will invade their throats and nostrils. Almost immediately they'll lapse into uncontrollable coughing fits, tears flowing down out of their eyes as the acidic-tasting poison works its way through the membranes in their mouth and nose and into their systems. The flesh on their face will turn white, highlighted by purplish flushes as they begin to collapse, hacking out horrendous, gasping, dry coughs.

Some will go into spasms of vomiting, spewing out stinking streams of half-digested food, drink, and stomach bile. Others will drop down backwards and crack their heads against the sidewalk, blood spattering when they're overcome by epileptic-like fits, swallowing or chewing up their tongues as they helplessly loose their bowels and thrash around like dying fish.

In a matter of three to seven minutes after the hydrogen cyanide cloud descends, it'll all be over for them. One by one they'll die as their organs shut down and their nerve systems go into life-ending shock. All along Woodward the corpses will pile up, their dying lips wheezing out a final whimper, moan, prayer, or curse.

He shudders with pleasure as the images shimmer through his mind. He can't even begin to imagine what the energy release from all those deaths is going to be like. But he's dead certain the killgasm will be frigging incredible.

He's down to a hundred feet now. At this height he can see his victims clearly. They look like a horde of insects, waiting to be DDT'd. The huge crowd that's lining the sidewalks are looking up and staring at the plane. Some are pointing at him as he reaches for the lever that controls the crop-dusting spray.

A trigger-like thumb button is built into the lever. With a demonic grin on his face, his thumb presses it down.

There's a thunking pneumatic sound as the '80s-era dusting system is activated. He can hear the breathy whoosh of the poison leaving the nozzles and a quick glance in the cockpit's rearview mirror confirms that the bluish-white spray is shooting downward from the Cessna's wings.

Pock!

His muscular body jerks, startled by the loud, metallic sound.

"What in frigging hell-?" he grumbles, releasing the dusting button.

Moments later there's another *pock!* and this time he quickly spots the ragged hole that's appeared in the engine compartment cover.

He leans forward. To his right and above him, about fifty yards ahead, is the black helicopter he'd spotted while making his turnaround. The passenger doorway on the copter is open and a big, dark-faced man is sitting in it, pointing a pistol directly at him. A man he recognizes all too well.

Special Agent McCoy Motherdumping Sonofabitch Asshole Bastard Johnson!

Chapter 47   A Cloud Of Deadly Gas

Saturday, August 20 - 11:56 a.m.

I'D TAKEN three shots at the windshield of Nails' plane. The sunlight reflecting on the glass was so bright I couldn't even make out which side of the cockpit he was on. But I figured if I hit the windshield there was a reasonable chance I'd wound or at least disrupt him.

I obviously hadn't hit him, since he continued flying steadily over the crowd. But I must've blown his concentration, because the cloud of gas the plane had begun trailing had stopped.

The main problem as I tried to aim back at him was the wind. Between the downward slipstream from the chopper's propeller blades and our hundred-plus mile-an-hour airspeed, it was just about impossible to keep my shooting arm and hand steady.

"Cut over to his other side!" La Borgia yelled to Goolsby. "Let me get a couple of shots at the bastard!"

The pilot promptly obeyed, swinging the helicopter over to the west side of the plane and out of my view. I turned around and watched La Borgia take aim from the opposite doorway.

"That glare on the windshield's a bitch," he complained after squeezing off three shots. Apparently they'd had as little effect as mine.

"Goolsby!" I called out. "Cut back over to his other side!"

"Jesus," I heard him grumble. "Make up your effing minds, will you?"

As he maneuvered us back across the front of the plane, I noticed the sound of Nails' engine get dramatically louder. When we finished our swing to his right, the plane suddenly went shooting by, coming so close it was almost as if he'd been trying to ram us.

"Holy crap!" Goolsby said. "That sonofabitch is crazy!"

Instead of being fifty yards ahead of Nails, we were now the same distance behind him.

Initially, I figured he was trying to get out of the range of our pistols. But then the Cessna abruptly angled up into the air in front of us and a thick blue-white cloud began spewing out from under its wings.

A cloud of deadly gas we were now flying directly into.

"Holy shit!" Goolsby said. "This doesn't look good!"

"Get out of it!" La Borgia yelled at him. "Cut away from it!"

Goolsby yanked his control lever. The copter tipped left and shot westward, but not before the murky cloud had enveloped us.

"Close your eyes and don't breathe!" I screamed as the misty fumes whirled through the cabin.

Even shut, my eyes began to burn and a foul metallic taste spread through my nostrils and throat. Almost instantly, the three of us began coughing violently.

"Damn!" Goolsby croaked out from the cockpit, between hacks. "That crap got in my eyes! I can't see an effing thing!"

I opened my own tear-filled eyes. We were out of the gas cloud now, but were weaving wildly in the air, rocking back and forth in a way that was adding to our gas-induced nausea. I recalled the plastic bottle of spring water I'd seen in the cockpit's cup holder.

"Your water bottle!" I gasped out to Goolsby. "Dump some into your eyes!"

"Then pass it back here!" La Borgia said.

The rocking became even worse for a few seconds while Goolsby tipped the bottle and dumped a splash into each of his inflamed eyes.

"Hey, it worked!" he said, blinking the water out of them as he turned around to pass the bottle back to us. "I can see again!"

"Now if I can just keep from puking," he said, returning his attention to the controls so he could stabilize the erratically-rocking helicopter.

La Borgia and I did the same eye-flush, hacking the gas out of our lungs while we wiped away the excess water with our fingers.

I realized then that I'd lost track of where the plane was.

"Where's Nails?" I said to Goolsby.

"He's down below us," he said. "Over the crowd near 10 Mile."

"Catch up to him!" La Borgia said.

"Shit - he's letting out that gas again!" Goolsby said.

"Hurry!" I said. "Get down over him!"

"Five seconds," he said. "We'll be right on top of him!"

As we rocketed down toward Nails' plane, a thought occurred to me.

"Jeff," I called out. "Any idea where the fuel tanks are on his plane?"

"That Cessna? Top of the wings," he said. "On either side of the fuselage."

I looked at La Borgia.

"Let's give the dirtbag's gas tanks a two-gun salute," I said.

La Borgia's reddened eyes lit up. "Right on, *paisano,*" he said.

We undid our seatbelts and squeezed together into the open doorway on the left side of the copter.

"Keep it steady so we don't frigging fall out, Jeff!" La Borgia called out.

"Gotcha!" Goolsby yelled back.

We dropped down to where we were over the Cessna and matching its speed. As soon as we were in shooting distance, La Borgia and I let loose with a barrage of bullets at the plane's wing-tops. I could see holes appearing in the sheeting over the tanks.

"Closer, Jeff!" La Borgia yelled.

Nails must've heard the shots hitting the plane. The gas ceased emerging from under its wings and it began arcing upward again.

"He's going to try to get in front of us and gas us again!" I called out to Goolsby. "Stay above him!"

"But keep it level so we don't go out the damn door!" La Borgia added.

"You got it!" the pilot said.

As the Cessna zoomed up from the crowd-jammed boulevard to pursue us, Goolsby managed to keep us about fifty yards or so above him. La Borgia and I continued to pump volleys of bullets at Nails, but the angle of the climbing plane was giving us less of a target.

Then the plane began to gain on us.

"Climb faster, Jeff!" La Borgia yelled. "He's catching up to us!"

"Going as fast as I can, boss!" Goolsby yelled back. "This sucker's only got so many horses!"

The plane was coming uncomfortably nearer as La Borgia and I continued firing. We were getting higher and higher over Woodward, with the Cessna right behind us. Directly below us were hundreds upon hundreds of Dream

Cruise cars and untold thousands of spectators. I wondered if the people below were thinking this was some kind of crazy stunt show.

"How come that damn thing won't blow?" La Borgia called to me as we sat in the open doorway, reloading.

"I don't know!" I said. "Must need to be a direct hit!"

We finished reloading at the same time. We looked to be about a mile high over Woodward now and were still climbing. The Cessna was continuing to gain on us, its roaring engine pulling it to within less than fifty yards of us. For a second or two, I thought I could make out Nails' face behind the windshield. He looked totally bonkers.

Then La Borgia and I simultaneously aimed and fired...

Chapter 48   Beelzebub's Face

Saturday, August 20 - 11:59 a.m.

"SON OF A STINKING BITCH!" Nails yells as he once again hears the metallic, hammering *pock!* of bullets striking the Cessna.

Leaning forward in the cockpit, he glowers upward, his thumb distractedly slipping off the gas release button. The shiny black helicopter is about fifty yards above him and just a bit to his right now. Johnson and some other craphead are scrunched together in the copter's doorway, aiming and firing pistols at him.

He weaves left, but the chopper follows. He weaves right, but again it tracks him and there are a couple more *pocks* as their bullets slam into the aluminum wing overhead.

"Okay, butt-brains," he snarls up at them. "One whiff of that cyanide wasn't enough for you, eh? Fine. I'll give you another. Shove it right up your goddamn noses!"

He pulls back sharply on the control wheel and the plane arcs up toward the copter. But instead of remaining at its altitude, the damned helicopter zooms skyward at the same airspeed, so the two douchebags in the doorway can keep shooting at him. Although the plane's engine and prop noise prevent him from hearing their shots, he can see the muzzle flashes as they aim and fire at him in tandem.

Pock! Ka-pock!

"Crap-eating bastards!" he yells up at them at the sound of their bullets pounding into the plane.

Leaning forward, he seizes the throttle lever at the center of the instrument panel and yanks it all the way out. "Alright, scum-suckers!" he growls. "See if you can keep up with me now!"

The roar of the engine becomes deafening inside the cockpit as he rockets upward, the burst of speed pushing him back hard against the pilot's seat. The helicopter, too, is moving fast, but he's gaining on the bastards now.

He glances over at the bulging red duffel bag strapped into the co-pilot's seat and pictures the twenty-five million euro-bucks inside - courtesy of the Master Plan. Then his eyes flick back to the fleeing helicopter.

Those suckers up there think they're going to stop him with their little pop-guns? No way! No frigging way!

Ka-pock!

What's really getting his goat, though, is the sight of that bigmouth scumbag Johnson shooting at him. Seeing him up there taking aim seems to pour even more fuel on the adrenaline-charged rage that's already blazing inside his body and soul. He's glaring so hard at the big, black sonofabitch he can feel his eyes beginning to bulge from their sockets.

"JOHNSON, YOU MOTHERDUMPER!" he bellows up at the agent. "YOU THINK YOU'RE GONNA STOP ME? STOP J. J. NAILS? AIN'T GONNA HAPPEN, YOU STUPID COP SCUM!"

Pock!

He's drawing closer to the two shooters, is less than fifty yards behind them now, the engine and prop-noise roaring hurricane-loud inside the tiny cockpit as he ascends higher and higher over the Dream Cruise below. As soon as he passes those pissbrains, he'll blast a huge, deadly fart of hydrogen cyanide right into their frigging faces and knock them out of the sky!

"NO ONE!" he howls. "NO ONE'S GONNA TAKE OUT J. J. FRIGGING NAILS!"

He's a scant thirty yards behind chopper, closing in for the kill, when his bulging eyes go saucer-wide and his chin drops onto his chest.

Filling the windshield before him is Beelzebub's huge, leering face. His ten-foot-wide muzzle is curved into a hideous grimace, the red pupils of his huge, black, googly eyes gleaming evilly as he gapes into the cockpit through the whirring prop.

"WHAT THE-? GO AWAY, BUB!" he yells. "GET OUTTA HERE!"

He knows damn well the monstrous dog's face looking in at him has *got* to be some kind of awful hallucination! Some weird brain-glitch caused by the too-rapid change in air pressure as the plane climbs. The same pressure that's making his ears feel like someone's stuffing wads of cotton into them.

But it sure as frigging hell *looks* real!

Pock!

"GET OUTTA MY WAY, DAMMIT!" he bellows into the insane roar from the engine. He can barely see the goddamn helicopter with that frigging yellow dog's face in the way!

Ka-pock!

"DAMN YOU, BUB - MOVE!"

But the grotesque apparition remains there, ignoring his outraged howls. Instead the diabolical dog's face looms even larger and looks as if he's about to come busting right through the goddamn windshield! He knows the plane and helicopter are streaking ever-higher over Woodward, but the fact is almost forgotten as the pit bull's enormous jaws drop open.

Horrified, he watches the huge snaggly teeth move toward him, foamy slaver dripping from his snarling, lifted dog-lips. One huge, demonic, red-centered eye seeming to bore right into his damned soul, while the other one whirls around in demented circles beside it!

Pock! Pock!

"OUTTA MY WAY, YOU GODDAMN DUMBSHIT DOG!" he shrieks, as what feels like an icy finger suddenly runs up his spine. "OUTTA MY FRIGGING WA-"

KA-POCK!

Chapter 49   Aw, Crap

Saturday, August 20 - 11:59 a.m.

BLAAAMMM!!!!!!!

FOR a moment La Borgia and I sat together in the windswept doorway, staring dumbstruck at the huge orange fireball below us.

Then - yelling "DOWN!" - I grabbed his head in the crook of my arm and scrabbled backwards across the passenger area floor, yanking him along.

A flurry of machine gun-like *pocks* hammered and thwanged against the fuselage. An instant later, the shock wave from the explosion slammed into us and threw us into a partial rollover.

"Holy crap!" Goolsby called out from the cockpit as he fought to regain control.

Hearing the muffled screaming in my armpit, I released La Borgia's purple-faced head.

"You trying to frigging kill me, Johnson???" he rasped, bug-eyed with fury.

"No!" I snarled back at him. "Trying to save your worthless life! If I'd left you in that doorway, you'd be hamburger now!"

I pointed at the passenger cabin above us. A look at how the shrapnel from the plane blast had come through the open door and chewed up the interior above us quickly convinced him I was in earnest.

"*Mama-frigging-mia*," he said, twisting his head back and forth while we climbed back into our seats and buckled ourselves back in. "You just about broke my damn neck!"

"Better than having your head ripped off by debris," I told him.

Just then an ominous shudder went through the chopper as the engine began to cough and sputter.

"Aw, crap," we heard Goolsby say.

La Borgia leaned toward the cockpit opening.

"What's going on, Jeff?" he said. "Did the explosion damage something?"

Goolsby turned his head.

"Nah," he replied as the engine abruptly cut out and died completely. "The emergency tank's all used up."

"We're out of gas."

Chapter 50   The Madness Of Crowds

Saturday, August 20 - 12:00 Noon

DOWN ON Woodward, over a hundred thousand wide-eyed spectators let out a collective scream of shock and horror as the plane they'd been watching exploded in a massive orange fireball.

Young males and small children stood there enthralled by the awesome fireworks display, while young females squealed, babbled to the friend next to them, or frantically texted "OMG!!!" into their cell phones.

Moving faster than at any time in the past thirty or forty years, a horde of overweight boomers tossed their cold drinks into the air and scrambled for cover as the smoking debris plunged down at them. Visor-capped women screeched and threw their arms around children and grandchildren, while balding, sunburnt men cursed and hovered protectively over their open-hooded cars.

Here and there hysterical shrieks went up as smoking chunks of metal came crashing down, slamming into the pavement or slicing into the grassy boulevard median.

Amazingly, the only person killed by the falling plane wreckage was Father Thaddeus Corcoran, a Roman Catholic priest. He was standing on a strip of grass, praying for the crowd's deliverance from this evil, when a long aluminum strut struck him. Passing through his body at the throat, the strut sank into the earth and left his corpse in a standing position, mouth and eyes wide in Os of astonishment. Nearby, an old Polish lady with vague memories of seeing "The Omen" on TV dropped to her knees and crossed herself. "Mother Mary help us!" she whispered at the sight of the grotesquely-impaled priest. "The Antichrist is near!"

After the debris finished crashing down, the crowd noticed that - along with the ashes from the burnt-up *Goodbye Detroit!* banner - a wispy rain of colorful paper was now fluttering earthward. It wasn't until the first of the crisp rectangles landed on the pavement and people began picking them up that they realized they were some kind of foreign currency.

"Holy shit!" somebody shouted at the sight of the denominations. "Moolah!"

As word quickly swept through the crowd, a rabid scramble to retrieve the errant money ensued. Soon a vast mob of Cruise fans were snatching bills up off the concrete, sweeping them off the tops of parked cars, or chasing after them, arms outstretched, to pluck the billowing banknotes out of the air as they came wafting down. With a hundred thousand people now running around in wild disarray, many grew oblivious to the fact that they were knocking down small children and feeble old ladies in their eagerness to seize the cash from heaven.

With no section of the legal code to guide them, the throngs of police officers who were on hand were compelled to watch the greedy free-for-all, completely at a loss as to who, if anyone, they should bust. After a time some of them, it was later reported, joined right in.

Mrs. Marisa Pellman, meanwhile, was in the kitchen of her Berkley home, listening to a local talk radio show while she made lunch for the children. Their home being just four blocks off of Woodward, the volume was up fairly loud, in order for her to hear it over the steady rumble of car noise from the Dream Cruise.

A couple of minutes ago she'd heard a loud bang. It had sounded like some kind of big fireworks going off. She didn't even bother to go outside and look, though. She assumed it was probably just another left-over 4th of July M-80 those idiot teens over on the next block had set off.

Then the host of the radio show broke in.

"Excuse me, folks. They want me to read this bulletin. Hmm. There's been some kind of big explosion over Woodward, right above the Dream Cruise. It appears there've been some fatalities, but no one knows how many. Stay tuned for more information."

Explosion? Fatalities? she thought.

A tingle of fear went through her. Her husband Stan was riding in the Cruise with his pal Marty, in Marty's '39 Plymouth. Moreover, Kyle and Sean, her four- and six-year-olds, were outside playing in the back yard. She hurried out of the kitchen. On the landing she met Sean as he came bursting through the back door.

"Come on, mom!" he said, his face glowing. "You've gotta see this!"

"See what?" she said nervously.

She followed the excited boy out of the landing and across the patio. Kyle, her four-year-old, was standing in the middle of the yard, staring down open-mouthed at some blackened thing on the grass. The object, which was partly embedded in the lawn's turf, was giving off a little cloud of grayish smoke. Only when she got up close enough to make out the grinning teeth did Marisa realize what the three of them were looking at.

A charred human head.

When he glanced up at his mom, Sean's eyes shone with boyish delight.

"*Sick*, eh?" he said.

Chapter 51   Touchdown
Saturday, August 20 - 12:01 p.m.

When the chopper's engine died, it was as if a trap door had suddenly dropped open beneath us. We began plunging earthward, with Goolsby frantically throwing switches on the copter's dashboard while La Borgia cursed and waved his Glock around.

Horror filled me when I glanced out the window and saw that we were going to crash down into the huge crowd of cars and people along Woodward. For an instant I considered putting the .45 to my temple. But then a series of wild flashbacks to the events of the past twelve days flooded through my brain, faster than the jump-cuts in a music video. I was back at the beginning, with the explosive killing of the two Eastpointe hot-rodders, when La Borgia's hoarse bellow snapped me out of it.

"I'M GOING TO KILL YOU, JEFF!" he screamed.

"Chill out, boss," the pilot said. "It's no big deal."

"NO BIG DEAL?"

"That's right," he said. "We'll just autorotate down."

"WHAT THE HELL DOES THAT MEAN?" La Borgia demanded.

"I disengage the engine from the rotors like so," he said, throwing a couple more switches on the control panel. "And instead of the blades pushing air pressure downward, we freewheel down on the air pressing up from below."

I had to admit Goolsby seemed supremely calm and self-confident, even though a part of me wondered if he wasn't simply deranged.

We were now descending rapidly but not precipitously, in a kind of controlled fall, the copter angled backwards as Goolsby feathered the controls.

I poked my head out the side door. The Dream Cruise had become a gigantic traffic jam, stretching as far as the eye could see.

This is fun! my dead sister said.

"No it's not, Ofelia," I said edgily.

La Borgia turned his head and frowned at me. "Who you talking to, Johnson?" he asked.

"Never mind," I said.

As we dropped toward the car-jammed avenue below, the sounds of horns blaring, brakes shrieking, and the whooping of police, fire, and ambulance sirens became audible over the massive rumbling of thousands of car engines. I saw that a half-dozen police cruisers had inserted themselves into the traffic and were clearing several car-lengths worth of landing space on the northbound side of the boulevard.

Goolsby was leaning to his left, watching them from his side window as we sailed downward.

"Jeez-is! Give me a few more yards, will you?" he complained.

"By the way," he called back to us. "Make sure you're strapped in tight when we land. Touchdown might be a tad rough."

"Thanks for the warning," I said.

We were plummeting faster now - not quite a free fall, but a lot more rapidly than I'd have preferred. The horde of colorful custom and vintage cars down on Woodward looked as if they were rushing up at us through a zooming-in camera lens. As we drew nearer and nearer to the unyielding concrete, I felt my stomach clench up tight. Other parts of me did, too.

Two hundred yards.

One hundred.

Fifty

Thirty.

Ten.

And then we hit-

Chapter 52   Heroes' Welcome

Saturday, August 20 - 12:02 p.m.

WE BANGED down hard onto the Woodward pavement, the impact jarring enough to bruise our behinds and rattle our teeth, but not enough to actually injure us.

For several moments La Borgia and I sat there looking around ourselves, in stunned disbelief that we were once more safely back on solid ground. Above us the whiny *chop-chop-chop* of the helicopters' rotors got lower in tone as they slowed. At rest, the copter was sitting somewhat lopsided and I figured the bumpy touchdown must have bent the landing skids' struts a bit.

Up in the cockpit, Goolsby was flipping off an array of toggle switches on the instrument panel.

"One good thing about running out of fuel," he said brightly. "You don't have to worry too much about an explosion or fire."

He seemed pretty pleased with himself, and I suppose he had a right to be. I found out later that most experienced helicopter pilots take training to do autorotation landings, but I'm not going to carp about the job he did that day.

Still feeling shaky, we unlatched our seatbelts and opened the door. Given that at this point we were feeling like a trio of superheroes, it was pretty disconcerting to climb out of the chopper and find ourselves confronted by at least a dozen gun barrels leveled at our heads and chests. Several voices at once began bellowing hoarse commands at us:

"Hands up!" "Drop your weapons!" "Freeze!" "On the ground!"

No doubt the pistols La Borgia and I were still carrying were an unsettling sight for the assembled cops, but it was still with more than a little chagrin that I dropped my safetied Springfield out in front of me. La Borgia did the same with his Glock and moments later the three of us were prostrate, face down, on the hot, gritty, oil-stained pavement.

"I'm FBI!" I yelled up at the cops as they warily closed in on us.

"And I'm mafia!" La Borgia shouted before lapsing into a wheezy laugh.

"Shut up, you idiot!" I told him, but he just kept laughing.

"Hands behind yours backs!" "Don't move!" "Keep your hands where we can see them!" the multiple cop voices kept shouting at us.

While I kind of hated to bring them down from the testosterone high they were obviously on, I was getting a bit tired of this.

"Take out my wallet!" I yelled. "Right rear pocket. You'll see my FBI shield!"

La Borgia was still chortling. "We just shot down a crazy, mass-murdering terrorist, you assholes!" he less than diplomatically called out to them.

"Officers! Hold on! I can vouch for this man!" I heard a familiar male voice call out.

I lifted my chin off the concrete.

Climbing out of a pink Corvette behind the police-cruiser barricade were Harlan and Nadine Robinson. Harlan the Three was in his white-shirted DPD Deputy Chief uniform, with its gold badge. Nadine was in tall white platform sandals and what looked like a cheerleader's outfit: a sleeveless white top with a pink Detroit Tigers-style "D" on it and a flouncy, crotch-length hot pink skirt.

"That's Special Agent McCoy Johnson!" Harlan told the assembly of gun-toting cops.

"Hello, Agent Johnson!" Nadine said, giving me a little wave as she minced toward us. "Remember me?"

The surrounding policemen allowed the Robinsons to come up close and stand over where the three of us lay, eyes agape, our jaws on the Woodward pavement.

Ever the gentlemen, none of us pointed out to the Deputy Chief's wife that she'd neglected to put on her panties today.

Chapter 53   A Shadowy Shape

Saturday, August 20 - 8:55 p.m.

HOURS LATER, on my way home to my condo that evening, I managed to get to Have A Cow before they closed for the day.

For all my exhaustion and aches, I felt pretty good as I got out of my government Chevy. Amazingly, the only death from the plane debris had been a poor Catholic priest who got impaled by a piece of wreckage. A couple of hundred people who'd inhaled the gas Nails managed to drop were in the hospital, but all were expected to survive. The mile-high explosion over Woodward had safely incinerated the rest of the deadly cyanide.

"Mr. Johnson!" Rachel cried out when I walked in the deli's door. "There you are!"

"The Dream Cruise hero himself!" Sol added, coming out from behind the deli counter. "So you got him - this *meshuggeneh* who killed all those people!" he said as he shook my hand.

"With a lot of help," I said. "Some of it from people you'd least expect."

"Like that Willie the Pimp man?" Rachel said. "That what's-his-name, La Borgia?"

"Boy, you folks know everything," I said, shaking my head.

"It's all over the news," Sol said. "'FBI Agent Teams Up with Mafia Kingpin to Stop Terrorist Madman' they're saying."

"How did you happen to hook up with that La Borgia guy?" Rachel asked.

"Gave him my phone number a while back when I was investigating him. He kept calling me, offering to help. I finally took him up on it."

"So is he a really scary guy, this gangster?" she said.

"Not particularly. Fact is, when I was checking him out, I couldn't find any instances of violence or coercion in any of his operations. He just seems to be kind of - I don't know - sleazy, I guess."

"His father and grandfather were both gangsters," Sol said. "I remember my father, may he rest in peace, talking about the La Borgias back when I was a kid. The grandfather, he was in cahoots with the Purple Gang - those Yid gangsters from the Thirties."

"So I've heard," I said. "But whatever his family was or is, he was a big help today."

"So what can we get you this evening, Mr. Johnson?" Sol asked.

"How's the pastrami today?" I said.

"First rate - nice and fresh, not too fatty," he said. "You want the usual two pounds?"

"Uh-huh," I said. "And a half-pound of Drunken Goat cheese to go along with it. I'm celebrating tonight."

"Good," Rachel said. "You deserve to."

When he was done slicing and wrapping the meat and cheese, Sol handed me my order.

"Can we give it to you on the house?" he asked.

"That's right, Mr. Johnson," Rachel said. "We want you to have it."

I wagged my finger at them.

"You folks better stop trying to corrupt me," I said, reaching for my wallet.

"You know, Mr. Johnson, you're not like some of the other police who come in here," Sol said.

"Don't tell me," I said, holding up a hand. "I don't want to know."

Night was falling as I walked up to my condo, looking forward to enjoying a huge sandwich, a long, hot soak in my bathtub, and my first decent night's sleep in week.

Then I noticed my front door was ajar.

"Damn it, Nadine!" I muttered.

I looked around for her pink Corvette. I didn't spot it, but figured she may have parked around the corner, out of view, just to surprise me.

With a weary sigh, I opened the screen door and went inside. In the dark foyer I stopped, frowning. A deep, growly noise was coming from the living room. It rose and fell, sounding like a far-off band saw cutting slowly through a long piece of timber.

The noise grew louder when I came around the corner and into the dark living room. I could see a shadowy shape stretched out on my couch. I leaned over and, as my eyes adjusted to the darkness, I saw that it was Oprah Cummings. She was in some kind of scanty lingerie outfit and there were a pair of sexy bedroom slippers on the carpet alongside the couch.

A mighty big smile broke out across my face as I listened to her rumble.

Quietly then, I went to the kitchen and switched on the light. I took the egg bread out of the refrigerator and made two oversized sandwiches with the pastrami and goat cheese. I warmed them up in the microwave, put them on a big plate, and brought them back out to the living room. I set the plate down on the coffee table in front of the couch, where the scent would reach her. Then I sat back and started in on my sandwich while I watched her sleep and listened to the steady, nasal growl of her snoring.

I'd left the lights off, but as my eyes adjusted again to the dark I could see her pretty clearly. She looked way beyond adorable. Especially when her nose began twitching. The snoring ceased then, and her beautiful eyes blinked open.

"Oh no," she said in a drowsy voice.

"Oh yes," I said.

Groggily, she sat upright.

"What smells so good?" she asked.

"That sandwich there," I said. "It's for you."

"Really? I'm starving. What is it?" she said.

"Kosher pastrami and Drunken Goat cheese."

"Sounds dreamy," she said, reaching for the sandwich.

"Mmm-" she said, after she'd taken a bite. "Scrumptious."

"Not as scrumptious as you," I said.

She grinned at me as she chewed.

"So how come you came by?" I asked. "And how'd you get in?"

"I got an envelope at the hospital. It had your condo key and a note inside, on pink stationery. The note said 'Sometimes things aren't always what they seem. If I were you, I'd give him another chance.' There was no signature."

"So you decided you'd do it. Give me another chance."

"Uh-huh," she said around the bite of sandwich in her mouth.

"I was going to be all sexy and shamelessly seduce you," she went on, looking down at her skimpy outfit. "But then I got sleepy waiting for you."

I shook my head and smiled.

"Doesn't matter," I said. "You seduced me in your sleep."

I realized then that I hadn't seen the Thing since I'd come in.

"By the way, did you see that worthless cat of mine?" I asked.

"Cat? I thought it was some kind of weird breed of terrier. It never made a sound, though. Just took one look at me when I came in and ran down to the basement."

"He's shy around strangers. I better check on him and feed him. Be right back."

I didn't tell her my real concern: that if she stayed the night and that sucker downstairs got hungry, there was a chance she'd wake up in the morning to the scent of rotting garbage wafting into her face.

I went to the kitchen, where I quickly opened three cans of dog food, dumped them into the oversize metal pet bowl, and hurried down to the basement.

The Thing was hiding behind the furnace. Despite the sulky, miserable expression he wore, he looked almost cute - if you can apply the word to any creature that closely resembles a giant, furry, ill-tempered insect.

"Here you go, you plague from hell," I said, placing the bowl nearby him. "Now please do me the kindness of staying down here while I romance that beauty upstairs, hear?"

Giving out one of his creepy, hissing grumbles in reply, he came out from behind the furnace and headed for his food bowl.

When I turned to leave, though, I felt something rub against my trouser leg. I looked down and saw that the Thing had scuttled over, brushed against me, and was looking up at me expectantly. I frowned. "What in tarnation do you want?" I said. Then I realized that, for the first time in all the years since he'd shown up at my door, the abominable critter wanted me to pet him.

"Dang," I muttered in amazement. "Will wonders never cease?"

I bent over, thumbed his lumpy forehead, scrabbled under his crooked jaw, and then ran my hand down his spiky-furred spine, from his knobby head to his bushy, twisted tail. He didn't meow with pleasure or anything. Just let me do it. Then he turned away and went back to his food bowl.

I shook my head, wondering if there was maybe a full moon out tonight.

Mindful of Oprah waiting, I hurried back upstairs, while behind me the wood-chipper sound of the Thing's eating started up.

When I got back to the living room, Oprah patted the couch alongside herself. "Why don't you come over her and join me?"

"Gladly," I said and sat down next to her.

Then we leaned into one another and our lips met for the second time.

Hard to believe, but the kiss was even better than the first. It went on and on, deliciously, and then our hands got into the act, stroking, squeezing, and caressing. Pretty soon we were both plenty hot and bothered. To put it mildly.

Abruptly, Oprah broke off the kiss. "Let's go to the bedroom," she said, her voice husky.

"Let's," I said.

When we got up off the couch, I leaned over to take her up in my arms.

"You sure you're feeling up to this?" she asked, noticing the way I'd winced.

"I'm sure," I said as I picked her up under her back and knees and held her body close to mine. It hurt alright, but the combination of lust and love I was feeling at that moment was strong enough to make me oblivious to just about any kind of pain.

With her arms around my neck, I carried her down the hall. I was pushing the bedroom door open with my shoe when she murmured softly in my ear. "By the way," she said, "there's something I need to warn you about."

"What's that?" I said as I carried her over to the bed and gently laid her down.

"I've been told I snore like a band saw when I sleep."

I stretched out beside her, took her into my arms, and leaned in for another taste of her delectable mouth.

"Do tell," I said.

Chapter 54   Loose Ends

Monday, August 22 - 9:30 a.m.

IT WAS the Monday morning after Dream Cruise weekend. I and a bunch of agents had spent Sunday infiltrating and exploring Nails' bomb factory, while Nardella had gone down to Toledo to interview members of his family. Now Dawson, Wilson, Nardella, Norm Rasheed, and I were getting together for a wrap-up meeting on the J. J. Nails case.

We met in the small conference room that was still serving as Eric's office. Through the closed door we could hear the sounds of the construction workers' drills, saws, and hammers as they rebuilt the bombed-out agent-in-charge's office.

"How did your interviews with Nails' family go?" Dawson asked Nardella, by way of opening the meeting.

"It was pretty interesting. They're a weird bunch. But compared to J. J., maybe not so much," she said. "He was estranged from them. Hadn't had any contact with the father, mother, or siblings for years. I did manage to find out why Nails hated Detroit so much, though."

That got our attention, to say the least. "Really?" I said. "Why?"

"Turns out the Nails family *all* despise Detroit. His father referred to Detroit as 'Pig-Thief City,'" she said.

"Pig-Thief City?" I said.

"It goes back several generations, all the way to the Toledo War."

"Toledo War?" Wilson said.

"I know," Nardella said. "I had to look it up myself after old man Nails mentioned it."

"Back in the 1830s," she went on, "there was this border dispute between Ohio and Michigan over the strip of land that includes Toledo. Both sides raised militias, and they were close to outright war. Well, apparently the Nails' ancestors were farmers down in that area at the time. One day they had some hogs stolen by some Michigan militia members who were foraging for food along the border strip. Family legend is that the militiamen were all Detroiters."

"Wait a minute," Wilson said. "Somebody stole some pigs from them a hundred-eighty years ago? And the family still hates Detroit?"

"With a passion. It seems the Nails family passed their resentment toward Detroiters down through the generations. Only got heightened when the auto industry turned Detroit into a big, prosperous boomtown that dwarfed poor little Toledo."

"So you're saying from the time he was a kid, J. J. was taught to loathe Detroit?" Dawson said

"You've got it. While I was interviewing him, the father told me some people still drive over the border and dump their trash in Monroe County. Which is on the Michigan side, of course. I think he wanted to brag that it was something he did, but without actually admitting it. Then the wife sneered at the Dream Cruise. Called it the Creep Cruise."

"Holy pork rinds. Are these people wacko or what?" Wilson said.

"Some people live to hate, I guess," I said. It was depressing to think how people passed their irrational hatreds on to their kids.

"How did that Toledo War turn out, by the way?" Rasheed asked.

"At the time Ohio was a state, which meant they had congressmen. Michigan was a territory, with just a single, non-voting delegate. Andrew Jackson was president and he wanted Ohio's votes, so he engineered things so they got the land strip that included Toledo. As compensation, Michigan got most of the Upper Peninsula, which up till then had been part of Wisconsin. At the time everyone thought the U.P. was worthless, so the Michiganders were pretty angry about it. They initially rejected the deal, but in the end accepted it so they could get statehood, which was granted in 1837."

"Well, at least we know now why Nails had it in for Detroit," Dawson said. "Let's go over what we found out about his compound."

"It's almost too ironic for me to believe," I said, shaking my head. "All that time Nails and his bomb factory were less than five miles from where I live."

"How'd you find out about this big place he had in Southfield, by the way?" Nardella asked.

"He used his actual address when he rented the hangar at Oakland-Troy Airport," I said. "Guess he figured that even if the security people there checked him out, his fake ID would be adequate cover. And it was, up until Saturday."

"What ID was he using?" Rasheed said.

"Along with a bunch of disguises, we found several fake IDs in the house. But the main name he was living under was Robert Van Buskirk," I said. "The real one died of MS in his early twenties. He managed to get all the ID for that name - license, auto registration, social security card, passport, you name it - some of it real and some of it forged - and used mostly that identity for the past five years."

"Do we know what his plan was for getting away after he'd attacked the Dream Cruise?" Nardella asked.

"We found luggage and a plane ticket for a tour group going to Mexico. The flight was scheduled for that afternoon. Probably figured mixing in with a tour group would be a better cover than flying out alone."

"And he was probably right," Dawson said. "Pretty smart, actually."

"I understand he had the place booby-trapped," Nardella said.

"Big time," I said. "We went in there real carefully, as you can imagine. But then it turned out he had this complex detonation system that he hadn't armed. Almost certainly he was planning on heading back there and activating it on his way out. But never made it, of course. If he had, the place would've gone up like an ammunition dump. Had enough explosives there to level everything around for about a half-mile radius."

"Speaking of explosives, did you find anything there that showed where he was getting them from?" Nardella asked.

"We found some shipping manifests in his bomb workshop," Dawson said. He was tapping a pencil head on the table as he spoke. "They were sent from some obscure outfit in south Russia. Almost certainly some shell company run by Vladimir Simonenko."

"That 'Simon Says' guy? The arms and chemical dealer?" Nardella asked.

"Right. The same guy he apparently worked with in Sudan and Iraq," I said.

"Any way we can get the Russians to go after Simon Says?" she said.

"Not likely," I said. "Unfortunately, the Russian legal system is one of the most corrupt in the world," I said. "Chances are Simonenko pays off the local police and prosecutors wherever he's operating, and they let him do his thing. As long as he's only arming terrorists who operate outside of Russia, they'll probably leave him alone. If it was jihadists from someplace inside Russia like Chechnya or the Caucasus, it might be a different story."

"What if we told the Russians we had information Simonenko was providing arms and chemicals to jihadists in their territory?" Rasheed said.

"To tell you the truth," Dawson said, "I've been considering it - contacting them through Interpol. Even if it wasn't true, it would at least make trouble for the dirtbag."

"That's the ticket - sic Vladdy Putin's security dogs onto his worthless butt," Wilson said.

"One thing I still don't get is how Nails could afford this big operation he had," I said. "Bomb factory, cars, semi trailer, airplane, chemicals. That half-million settlement he got from Blackwater doesn't seem like it would cover it all."

"Maybe he was a good shopper," Wilson said. "Clipped coupons."

"I asked CID to check into that, McCoy," Dawson said. "They did some further digging and they now think he was able to squeeze more than the original settlement out of Blackwater. Probably by threatening to expose embarrassing details about the company or some of its people. They're pretty sure now he may have gotten up to a million out of them."

"So he invests a million, looking for a twenty-five-to-one return," Wilson said. "A real entrepreneur."

"By the way," I said to Angie. "When we went into his compound with the US marshals, we found this wall-eyed, yellow pit bull there. Homely, vicious thing - looked and acted like he was on some kind of doggy crack. Wouldn't let anyone go near the bomb shop, so we brought in a guy from the Southfield police's animal control unit. Knocked him out with a shot from a tranquilizer gun."

"What'll they end up doing with the dog?" Nardella asked.

"Try to find a home for him," I said. "If they can't, I suppose they'll put him down."

"Maybe I'll take him," Wilson said. "Present for my mom."

"She likes mean, googly-eyed pit bulls?" Nardella asked.

"Probably not," he said. "But it might help lower her cat population."

After the wrap-up meeting broke up, Nardella, Wilson, and I were walking back to our cubicles.

"So did you ever find a babe to go to the Dream Cruise with you?" Angie asked Wilson.

"Actually, I did," he said. "After all the excitement died down, I stopped into a bar in Ferndale. Ran into Candice Cartwright."

"Wait a minute," I said. "Mayor Bling's communication director?"

"That's her. She was a bit tipsy, but we hit it off real well. Took her for a spin up and down Woodward in the Gremlin and ended up back at my place.

"Unfortunately," he went on, "she left first thing in the morning. Woke up real hung over and when she realized where she was, started screaming hysterically, threw on her clothes, and ran out. Called a cab on her cell and wouldn't even let me take her back to the bar to get her car."

"A shame," I said.

"I could go for that woman," he said with a sigh. "Back at that thirteen hundred Beaubien meeting, she seemed like a real tight-bottom, you know? But put about eight shots of Cuervo in that girl and she gets real frisky."

"Oh well. The road to true love never runs smooth," Angie said.

"Ain't that the truth," I said.

"Yeah, but does it always have to be a hundred-mile stretch of potholed highway?" Wilson asked.

An hour or so later I was sitting in my cubicle, grinning like a lovestruck idiot at the framed photo of Oprah I'd asked her to give me, when my desk phone rang. It was Mabel Partridge calling me from the admittance desk.

"You expecting a package, McCoy?" she asked.

"No," I said.

"Well, there's one here at the front desk for you," she said. "Some private courier outfit brought it."

My brows knit. "Who's it from?" I asked.

"Doesn't say," she said. "The girl here says the sender just wrote in 'Private.'"

"Be careful," I said. "Don't handle it. I'll be right up there."

314

I hurried out to the check-in area. The courier was a woman in a dark blue delivery-person's uniform. The package turned out to be a six-inch square cardboard mailer - the kind you'd send a CD or DVD in. Since it looked too small to be seriously dangerous, I signed for it and took it back to my desk.

After cautiously slicing the carton open, I found a plastic case with a read-write DVD inside. There was also a folded note. I opened it up and read.

This is the last remaining copy of these images.

The rest have all been destroyed.

Thanks for giving me a chance to avenge Vinnie and Rosie.

WLB

William La Borgia, I immediately realized. But what were the "images" he was talking about?

I slid the DVD into my laptop drive. It auto-launched a menu program that showed two folder icons, one labeled "Movies" and one "Photos."

I clicked on Movies and a group of video camera icons appeared, with dates from the past week under them. I began double-clicking on them. There were several time-and-date-stamped video clips of Nadine Robinson in a variety of hot outfits, letting herself into my place with the key I'd given her. There were other shots of her leaving. Apparently she'd come by a number of times when I hadn't shown. There was a clip of me on Tuesday afternoon, entering the condo with my gun drawn. Another showed Oprah and me going in together on Thursday night, followed by one of her slamming the door as she left.

I sat back in my chair, my face hot with anger.

It was finally obvious to me now what La Borgia had been up to. He'd had my condo under twenty-four hour video surveillance for the past week. He was trying to compromise me by getting footage of Nadine coming and going from my place. And the man who'd bet her she couldn't get me to go back to being lovers - whose name I now knew - was working for him. He'd made that bet with her to get her to start coming by my place again, so that one of La Borgia's men or maybe some private investigator could get shots of our being together.

I wondered what would've happened if I'd let Nadine seduce me into going to bed with her again. Would the cameraman have shot some *in flagrante* photos through the windows? Or come bursting into my bedroom with the two of us in bed together?

Or even worse, I thought. What if they'd planted little video cams inside my place?

One thing was for sure: even though the DVD was obviously meant as a peace offering, as soon as I got home today I was going to do a damn thorough search of my condo for any hidden cameras and mikes.

La Borgia, you son of a bitch, I thought.

Then a grim smile crossed my face at the irony of it. Having found nothing seriously incriminating on the porn king, I'd pretty much written off investigating him any further. But now I knew he had something to hide. Something serious enough that he was prepared to try to blackmail or publicly embarrass me, if need be.

Which meant that the investigation I'd been very near to closing was going to stay open. We'd meet again, Willie the Pimp and I.

Don't get me wrong. I was grateful to him for his help in stopping Nails' Dream Cruise massacre plan. And I suppose I should've been grateful that he'd owned up to his attempt to compromise me - which he'd presumably called off. But the fact was, I was still plenty pissed about it. Pissed that he'd tried to compromise me at all. And pissed that he'd hired and connived with people to intrude on me and my private life.

The whole thing left me with the same feeling I'd had pretty much all along since meeting La Borgia. I liked the guy. I genuinely did.

But I trusted him about as far as I could throw him.

Epilogue   What My Dead Sister Told Me

Monday, September 6 - 2 p.m.

LABOR Day weekend was sunny and mild that year - perfect weather for an end-of-summer backyard barbecue.

Oprah drove us to the Robinsons' Palmer Woods home in her Camaro SS. We parked up the block, which was lined with cars, including a few white DPD police cruisers. She held my arm, smelling like roses and warm honey, as we ambled up the sidewalk to their house.

"Look at that," she said, pointing to the gleaming pink Corvette parked in front.

"Nadine's," I told her.

"Why am not surprised?" she said.

Going up the driveway, we could hear music from the back yard. I recognized it as an old Motown song - "Heard It Through the Grapevine" - remixed to a throbbing, hip-hop beat.

The yard itself was crowded with men, women, and children, all eating and drinking, laughing and jiving. Most, I was sure, were DPD cops and their families. Among the ones I recognized was Porter, the big downtown precinct captain who'd overseen the Campus Martius bombing aftermath.

I saw Harlan Robinson off to one side of the big yard. He was tending a spread of smoking meats atop a supersized barbecue grill, grinning as he spoke to the small crowd of folks gathered around him. I spotted Nadine on the other side of the yard. She was talking to some hunky young man who I guessed to be a DPD rookie.

Ellis Sidwell came up to us then, along with a nice-looking redhead. We did introductions and found out the lady was his wife, Colleen. She thanked me for having him wear that extra groin protector back at the IMAX. Then I heard my name.

"McCoy Johnson!" Harlan called out and waved. "Come on over here!"

"Excuse us," I said to the Sidwells. "Got to say hi to our host."

We went over and joined Harlan behind the big, sizzling grill.

He switched his meat-flipping spatula to his other hand and reached out to give me a vigorous shake. "How're you doing, my man?" he smiled.

317

"Just fine, Chief," I said. "In fact, mighty fine."

"Bet it has something to do with this lovely lady you've got here, doesn't it?" he said, grinning at Oprah.

"You're a perceptive man, Harlan," I said, with unintended irony. "This is Dr. Oprah Cummings. Works down at the DMC. Oprah, this is Harlan Robinson, Deputy Chief of the DPD."

"A pleasure," he said with a broad grin. "Nothing like a beautiful woman to lift a man's spirits," he said, winking at me.

"Amen," I said as I looked into Oprah's eyes, once again noticing those lovely little flecks of jade in them.

"But if you two lovebird will excuse me," Harlan said. "I've got some *serious* grilling to take care of here."

"There's chicken, steaks, burgers, pork chops, and ribs over there on that table," he added, pointing with the spatula. "You folks go help yourselves."

"And by the way, he said as we moved away. "If you see that wife of mine, send her on over here. Tell her she's missing out on some grilled beefsteaks that are out of this world!"

"We'll do that," I assured him.

The tangy smells of the barbecue had whetted our appetites. We loaded up our paper plates with unseemly amounts of meat and greens. While I fetched a couple of big red plastic cups of lemonade, Oprah found us a pair of seats at a table crowded with pre-adolescent kids.

As we sat there eating amid the giggling children, Oprah nudged me. I followed her gaze to where Nadine was standing with her young cop.

"That's quite the outfit she's got on," she said.

Nadine was in a pair of ridiculously tight and skimpy white jean shorts that showed the bottoms of her butt-cheeks in back and what they call a camel toe in front. Her top was basically a white push-up brassiere with a short fringe on the bottom. On her feet were a pair of five inch-heeled platform sandals.

"Uh-huh," I said. I wasn't about to push my luck by saying more.

"But I have to admit she's got the body for it," she said. "She must work out a lot."

"Yup," I said. "She must."

At that point Nadine turned away from her young man and looked over at our table. She winked at us and I saw Oprah return it over the edge of her lemonade cup.

Nadine's attention went back to the hunky cop. It was pretty obvious the young man was hypnotized by her. Or at least by her décolletage.

Oprah continued to watch her. "That woman knows how to be sexy just *standing* there," she said, admiringly.

It was true. Nadine had this way of gently squirming and undulating even when she was standing in one spot.

"She really is something, isn't she?" Oprah said.

"*You* really are something," I said, putting my arm around her and pulling her close to me.

"Even with my snoring?"

"I bought some earplugs," I told her.

It was just then I spotted Ray Wapshot, the Oakland County Sheriff, walking across the yard. He went up to Nadine and interrupted her confab with the young man. She gave him a sharp glance and said something that didn't look too friendly. Then she took the young cop's arm and led him away.

"Excuse me a second," I said to Oprah. "I'll be right back."

I crossed the yard to where Wapshot was standing. He was scowling as he watched Nadine and the young cop walk away.

"How're you doing, Sheriff?" I said as I came up to him.

He turned. "Oh," he said, his face flushing a little. "Hello, Johnson,"

"Wanted to congratulate you, by the way," I said. "On your early retirement."

He gave me a quizzical look.

"Early retirement?" he said. "Who says I'm retiring?"

I gave him a nasty smile. "I am."

"What the hell do you mean?" he said.

"Talked to an IRS investigator a couple of days ago. Sounds like you've accumulated a number of unexplained assets over the past couple of years,

Ray. Pretty substantial ones. More than you'd likely be able to acquire on your Sheriff's salary."

"Listen, I, um- I don't- don't what you're talking about, Johnson," he stammered.

"No? That luxury beachfront condo up near Traverse City? That spiffy cabin cruiser to go with it? That nice offshore bank account you opened in Belize?"

"Hey, I got lucky," he said, shifting uncomfortably. "With some, um, investments. I mean, the wife did."

"This IRS guy says the money trail leads back - in a roundabout way, of course - to an outfit called Eros Unlimited. Willie the Pimp's company."

"La Borgia? Hey, I never-"

I cut him off. "Understand the IRS folks have already talked to L. Sparks about it, Ray. Heard he was pretty shocked. I expect you'll be hearing from him real soon."

By this point Wapshot was staring at me open-mouthed, with a doomed look in his eyes.

"But don't worry, Sheriff," I said over my shoulder as I sauntered back toward our table. "Could be a couple of weeks yet before the indictments come down."

"What did you say to that man?" Oprah said when I'd sat back down. "He looks like he's about to throw up."

"Just congratulated him on his early retirement. I'll tell you about it later."

She leaned against me. "How about if you tell me about it on our way back to your place?" she said. "I've got to be back to work in-" She checked her watch. "Two and a half hours. I'd like to spend at least one of them *examining* you."

"Uh-oh," I said with a grin. "Going to give me another one of those in-home, bio-energetic CAT scans of yours?"

"With my lips and hands and other body parts?" she said. "I just might."

"Well, in that case, Doctor, let's vamoose."

After a quick thank you and farewell to Harlan Robinson and a goodbye wave to Ellis Sidwell and his wife, we headed for the driveway. As we crossed the yard I saw Ray Wapshot sitting at an empty table. He had his head in his hands and a couple of empty beer bottles before him.

When we were going down the driveway, Oprah again took note of the hot pink Corvette in front of the house.

"That is some car, McCoy," she said. "Want to go take a closer look?"

With its smoked-glass windows, you couldn't see inside the Corvette. But it sure looked to me like it was gently rocking as it sat there at the curb.

"Let's not," I said.

I took her hand and we headed for her Camaro.

A minute later we were on our way. When we rolled past the Corvette, I gave out a soft laugh.

"What's so funny?" Oprah said.

"Nothing in particular," I said, shaking my head. "I'm just happy."

And it was true. As I gazed over at this gorgeous woman beside me, waves of happiness swept over me. I could feel them washing away all the grim darkness that for far too many years had shadowed my mind and soul.

Her hand was resting on the shifter. I reached over and squeezed it. When she glanced back at me the jade gleam in her eyes was like a beacon, guiding me home after what seemed like a lifetime of wandering.

Enjoy her while you can, McCoy, my dead sister said.

My breath stopped and my blood ran cold. We were coming up to a stop sign. I turned my head aside so that Oprah wouldn't see me talking to someone who doesn't, strictly speaking, exist.

Damn it, Ofelia! I said. *What the hell do you mean? Is she in danger? Am I?*

But she clammed up then and wouldn't say another word.

As we pulled away from the stop sign, I looked over again at Oprah. This time seeing with stark clarity how fragile she and I and you and all of us are. And I swore a vow to myself right then. That for however long this woman and I had together, I'd love her the way all of us here on God's green Earth ought to love each other.

Like there's no tomorrow...

About The Author

SCREAM CRUISE is the debut novel of suburban Detroit author Jim DeLorey. For information about his upcoming books (including the next novel in the McCoy Johnson Motor City Thriller series), please visit Jim's website at http://www.jimdelorey.com

Made in the USA
Lexington, KY
01 December 2012